ISLA

———

THE CAÑON SERIES BOOK #4

GIGI MEIER

GiGi Meier

Cover Design by Just write. Creations

Developmental Editing by Jessica Lessor

Editing by Robyne Hunt

Author Photograph by Tara L. Grundemeier

ISBN: 979-8-9877336-6-0 (e)

ISBN: 979-8-9877336–77 (pb)

GiGi Meier Media LLC

DEDICATION

To the brave souls who have endured the harrowing ordeal of domestic violence. Your courage to reclaim your voice, your body, and the very essence of your soul is a testament to your indomitable human spirit.

Your journey, marked by battles fought in the quietest corners of existence, speaks of your profound strength and unbroken will. May it lead you toward healing, transformation, and the triumphant life you richly deserve.

ISLA

1

———

Amid the vibrant pulse of city life, my cozy apartment emanates a sense of familiarity and coziness. The sunlight streams through the windows, casting a golden glow on the walls adorned with my sketches while Anna sleeps on my bed. The distant traffic sounds are white noise to my creative sanctuary, with Lily, my vivacious roommate, bursting through the door. Her eyes sparkle with excitement, clutching a colorful flyer in her hand as if it's a secret waiting to be revealed.

"Isla, you won't believe what I just found out!"

My attention lifts from my sketchbook, curiosity instantly ignited by her exuberance.

"What's up?"

Lily moves with a lively energy. She blames it on her mom's Turkish heritage, something I know nothing about but am slowly learning the longer we live together. As Lily crosses the room in animated steps, the flyer dances in her hand.

"An open audition for Travis Jackson's upcoming off-Broadway production! They're searching for new talent, and honestly, Isla, I can totally envision you shining on that stage."

While I highly regard Travis Jackson's work, stepping onto his stage feels like a distant aspiration—one that directly conflicts with my studies at Parsons.

"Lily, you're the thespian, not me."

Her grin broadens, undaunted by my excuses.

"You exude this old soul aura. Your mere presence could capture anyone's attention. Besides, it's just an open call. A chance to dip your toe in and see how things work."

I shake my head gently, a small smile curving my lips.

"You're the adventurer in this friendship. I'm more of an observer and content being the moral support." I tap my charcoal pencil against my lips. "Old soul aura. I like it."

As she continues prattling on, trying to convince me, my mind drifts back to that enchanting rooftop retreat and the promises we made up there. The rooftop was a tapestry of vibrant blooms and fragrant floral air, with potted plants lining the edges. A rustic wooden bench stood against one wall, where we sat daydreaming about making it big in the city that never sleeps.

Lily as a famous Broadway actress. Me—as a successful fashion designer. One day, collaborating, where I design the pieces for the show she headlines. From our elevated vantage point, the city skyline stretching out before us, we planned where we would live, what type of men we would marry, and how many kids we'd have. She said none, and I said some, undecided on the number. There is a yearning in me to prove to myself that I can be a better mother to my children than my mom was to me. That bar is set incredibly low. Anyone would be better than her.

Lily's touch on my shoulder brings me back to reality.

"Okay, maybe not an audition, but how about working on the sets or costume design? Ya know, get some real-life experience."

Her idea is appealing. Although she's more of a risk-taker

than I am, I need to step outside my comfort zone more often. This seems fairly safe with Lily there. I can sit in the theater and watch how everything is arranged, then decide. Worst case scenario, I bring my sketch pad and do my homework in a place other than my bed.

"All right, I'll go. But no promises on the audition, and I'm bringing my sketchbook, just in case."

I hold up my finger in warning. Triumph shines in her eyes, her infectious enthusiasm unwavering as she does arabesques around the room.

"Yay!" Lily claps with glee. "I just know it'll turn out great for both of us."

As she continues dancing and leaping about the room, apprehension swirls within me. The thought of going piques my curiosity. It is exciting to see how a theater works behind the scenes, but auditioning and being given a part terrifies me. She snatches my sketchbook off the bed, holding it at eye level to study my latest design, due tomorrow.

"The bow is in the wrong place."

I scoot to the edge of the bed, trying to reclaim it from her grasp. This scene is familiar. She often critiques my work, even though most of her advice is misguided. With other pressing assignments demanding my attention, I'm not in the mood to entertain her critiques. Her finger hovers over the illustration of the bow, and she nods with a knowing look.

"Just as I suspected, no bow."

She tosses the sketchbook back onto the bed beside me, sending particles of dust dancing in the sunlight.

"I'm heading out for brunch with my bestie from Connecticut. I'd invite you, but I already know you'll say no, as usual."

"I've got a ton of homework to finish, but if you pass by a salad place, I won't say no."

I glance from my sketch, gauging her reaction to see if she'll bring me back some food, which she typically does. She sighs, and her exasperation is evident in her tone.

"That's the thing, Isla. You're always buried in work. You're never going to meet anyone by holing up in here."

An overly dramatic sigh punctuates her frustration. I can't help but chuckle at her flair for theatrics. If this act keeps up, she'll definitely get a part.

"Love you too," I tease in response, deferring the whole guy discussion as I always do.

Although I'm lonely and the fantasy of my dream guy crosses my mind, given my history, the last thing I want is to get into a relationship and have to explain what I've been through.

With a huff, she flounces out of the room, leaving me alone. Irritation prickles within as the possibility that she might be right about my design lingers. I wait for her to exit the apartment before I mimic her action, placing my finger over the bow.

"Shoot. She's right."

My hand searches for the eraser on the tufted white comforter, finally locating it near Anna, which awakens her. Her sweet eyes fix on me, and her nose dips into the pillow. I crawl up next to her, smothering her in affectionate kisses.

"We don't need anyone else, right, Anna?"

She closes her eyes in contentment as I press my face against her fur. In moments like these, I find solace in her unwavering presence. She's always been there for me. The magnitude of how my life has evolved since the day I got her is nothing short of astonishing. The trial itself was grueling—a painful rehashing of my past, where I had to confront my haunting memories head-on. The courtroom became a battleground of emotions, made even more challenging when my mom made a chaotic appearance, her addiction evident as she pleaded with my parents for money.

Ever my protector, Dani jumped out of her seat, ready to

launch herself at Rick if it weren't for Officer Hamilton holding her back and Uncle Tomlin escorting her from the courtroom. She was almost held in contempt of court that day.

Uncle Tomlin, the pragmatic one, devised a plan that she could put tally marks on a piece of paper every time she wanted to punch someone, then take it out later on the punching bag at her garage. As the days grew and frustrations mounted, her knuckles became redder and redder until one day, she came in with bandages on her hands. He quietly advised me not to inquire about it.

On the other hand, Officer Hamilton was far more subtle, leveraging his size and hard stare to communicate his feelings. Attending all my proceedings in his uniform helped paint the picture of an intimidating law enforcement officer while showing his support. Sometimes, Aunt Molli would attend, only long enough to make an appearance before the testimony made her nauseous, and she would leave. It didn't help that she was pregnant at the time. Another reason Officer Hamilton was so protective was that he was like the uncle I always wanted and never had.

The worst and most heartbreaking part was when my parents were there. They had to hear every detail of the abuse with my mom, her boyfriends, and Rick. Too many times during my testimony, I avoided looking at their faces, choosing to focus on the prosecutor as we practiced behind closed quarters. When the defense's line of questioning began, my eyes flickered between the defense attorney, my crying Papa, and my stoic Dad.

Always the more openly emotional one, Papa wore his feelings on his sleeve, crying into his handkerchief. He'd hug me and apologize for getting upset when we left each day after court, only to repeat it the following days. Meanwhile, Dad would envelop us both in his arms, murmuring encouraging words to calm us both—his quiet way of protecting his family.

The difference in their personalities worked on so many levels. Something I appreciated as time passed, and I realized that both met my needs at various times.

Were it not for their unwavering love, Uncle Alex's quiet yet formidable strength, Dani's audacious defiance of conventional norms, Uncle Tomlin's attorneys' relentless pursuit of justice for me, and even Aunt Molli's involvement in those church pageants, which led to my first costume design gig, I wouldn't be standing where I am today—within the walls of my dream apartment and living my aspirations at fashion school.

"We're doing just fine because we've got each other. Like always."

With one last affectionate peck on her head, I sigh, my thoughts turning resolutely to the homework surrounding me. Clutching the eraser in my fist, I shift back to my sketchbook, making the change that Lily recommends while her audition idea floats around my mind.

2

As the day of the open casting call dawns, Lily's excitement reverberates through our apartment, starting with her running into my room and jumping on me while I slept. Blurry-eyed and confused, I ask what is happening. With infectious enthusiasm, she practically sings the answer into my ear, then dashes out the door to get dressed.

Amidst her energetic chaos, I quietly get ready and stand before the mirror, adjusting my meticulous outfit with a subtle tremor of nervousness. Ensuring I pack my latest memoir, apples, crackers, and water for us in my favorite tote, I check on Lily. She stands in her closet, deliberating between outfits with a furrowed brow and a touch of indecision. Different ensembles emerge from the depths of her wardrobe, each reflecting a different facet of her personality and style. Her gaze shifts toward me, and she raises an outfit in question, seeking my opinion.

"What do you think of this one?"

Uncertainty laces her tone, matching the look on her face.

My gaze roams her room, and from the looks of it, she's gone through several options.

"I like it! It pops against your dark hair."

But her hesitation persists when she tosses it on the bed and moves to the next option, repeating the process a few times. Her bed is a kaleidoscope of patterns and hues, outfits strewn haphazardly, and it looks like an abstract work of art.

"I want to look my best, and I think I look too pale in this."

I chuckle because she's almost as pale as me, which irks her. The truth is, her complexion contrasts against her thick, dark waves, which draws upon her rich Iranian heritage. She's striking, consistently garnering looks and catcalls on the streets of New York.

"Lily, you're going to kill it. Your personality is what they want, not your outfit."

"Ugh! Why is this so hard?"

As another outfit lands on the vibrant palette on the bed, she lets out a resigned sigh and sinks into her vanity chair. While her indecisiveness might have turned her room into an explosion of fashion, I'm reminded that this is just another part of her charm. Delving into the jumbled heap of clothes, I begin to sift through the assortment and gather pieces that I've always liked on her. Then I drape them over her large mirror, waving a hand to the outfit.

"How about something like this? And use this scarf as a headband to show off your long curls while keeping them off your face when reading your lines."

"And this is why you're in fashion school. You're so brilliant."

She springs from her seat, envelops me in a tight hug, and sings my praises. I'm grinning ear to ear.

"Brilliant might be a stretch. But I'm glad you like it."

She releases me, her eyes shining while her fingers trace the outfit.

"You have an eye for this stuff. I'm so lucky to live with a fashion designer. One day, you'll be famous, and people will ask who I'm wearing, and I'll get to say you. Eeks! How cool is that?"

The image she paints feels simultaneously surreal and thrilling.

"Can you imagine?" I playfully exaggerate, walking around the room as she pretends to flash camera bulbs at me. "This is an original Isla Frank creation."

"And everyone will be like, 'Who is Isla Frank?' Then the camera will zoom in on me at my Broadway debut, and I'll say, 'She's my fabulous roommate who just happens to be a fashion genius,' and you'll make even more money."

She mimics my playful tone, adding a touch of theatrical flair. Anna's tiny paws tap across the hardwood floors when she runs into the room to investigate all the fun. I scoop her up and nestle her against me as I walk the imaginary red carpet. She also takes close-up shots of Anna, inquiring about her outfit since she's dressed in a custom piece I designed for her.

Our shared dreams take on a whimsical quality that matches her brightly colored room. I'm so grateful for our friendship, which started with answering an online ad on the school community board for a girl needing a roommate.

"I'm going out to the living room so you can get dressed. We're already running a bit late."

She smiles before catching the door in her hand.

"Sure thing, I'll be out in a second."

As the door clicks shut behind her, I press a kiss into Anna's head and straighten the bow in her fur before lowering her to the ground. I text Papa quickly about Lily's audition and how I'm going as moral support. My fingers hover over the keys, deciding to tell him how Lily also wants me to audition. I'm three-quarters of the way through typing it out when she reappears, looking happy and confident in what I picked out.

Doing a little spin in the doorway, she asks, "How do I look?"

"Radiant, *darling*," I emphasize the word in the same accent her mom uses when she calls, eliciting a knowing chuckle from her. "Now, let's go. Oh, and I packed snacks in case we need them."

Walking toward my tote, I pat the side for effect and swing it onto my shoulder while waiting by the door. She takes a final look in the mirror, pulling a curl away from her face and fixing her scarf before joining me.

"You're such a mom. Are those orange slices like the soccer moms bring?"

"Apples."

With a smugness that has her smiling, I throw open the door and step into the hallway with her right behind me. When we hit the street, the city pulses around us, matching Lily's energy. She chats animatedly about her audition piece the entire way until she asks about my piece. I remind her that I'm merely her moral support unless the notion strikes me to audition. However unlikely that is.

The theater's marquee shines brightly against the sky, a beacon of opportunity for all who pass under it. Lily's eyes sparkle with anticipation, and I can't help but feel a twinge of excitement. As we step into the lobby, the energy of the crowd envelops us—nerves, aspirations, and uneasiness about the unknown in the expression of most of the people waiting in line. I glance at the sign-up sheet, fingers itching as I debate being brave and taking the pen, but I quell the impulse. This isn't my dream. It's Lily's.

"Isla, are you sure about not auditioning?" Lily asks as if reading my mind. I shake my head.

"No, I'm good. My role is the emotional support animal, like Anna of sorts."

Confusion wrinkles across her face before she glances at the competition ahead of her.

"All right, then, wish me luck!"

As she heads backstage towards the audition room, I find a seat in the theater, content to watch the performances. With each audition, the actor or actress pours their soul into the emotional pieces they are reading, some resonating with the few of us sitting in the audience. Minutes stretch into hours, and I'm absorbed in watching the interactions of fellow auditionees.

My heart quickens when Lily takes the stage. Her presence is magnetic, and her performance is vulnerable yet passionate. I watch in awe as she breathes life into her character, captivating me and the judges.

As the day progresses, I feel connected to the people auditioning. Pursuing their dreams in this off-Broadway theater motivates and invigorates my imagination. I daydream of the costumes, bringing my sketches to life, choosing the fabrics, and overseeing the dyeing of individual pieces. It makes me wanderlust as I envision the costume every person auditioning would wear, how the ballgowns would whisper across the stage, and how the beadwork would glimmer in the lights. I regret not bringing my sketchbook to capture the ideas floating before my eyes.

Lily plops into the seat next to mine, her face aglow with excitement.

"How did I do? Be honest. Did I suck or what?"

"Are you kidding? You're one of the best."

My voice is overly loud as an unexpected silence sweeps throughout the room, broken only by light murmurs. A new presence emerges from the shadows at the back of the theater.

"Who's that?"

Her eyes widen, and she leans over to whisper, "Travis Jackson, the playwright. I never expected him to be here."

He stands near the entrance, his keen eyes scanning the room, assessing the sea of potential talent. My heart beats rapidly, and I am nervous for the people auditioning as a few fidget on stage. I instinctively hold my breath, trepidation for Lily, swirling with hope that she gets the part.

With his sandy blonde hair catching the spotlight's glow and blue eyes reflecting the stage lights' brilliance, he stands as a tall symbol of wealth and refined taste amidst the grandeur of his theater. His muscular frame, accentuated by the tailored fit of his designer clothes, commands the space with effortless grace, indicative of his success and dedication.

Travis's gaze settles on me, and for a moment, our eyes lock. My cheeks flush. He considers me for a lingering moment before returning to the proceedings. My heart races from that brief connection across the theater. The auditions resume, the theater slowly fills up with people watching, and Lily whispers in my ear.

"I think he's been here the whole time, watching every audition. Can you believe it?"

"Don't they do that? Fashion designers are always at their runway shows. In fact, most designers pick the models themselves."

She dismisses the notion with a slight shake of her head, her gaze unwaveringly fixed on the playwright even though his back is to us—the intensity of her stare borders on being a tad excessive.

"Not usually. This adds a whole other layer to this audition. This play must be a big deal, but why open casting then? It doesn't make sense."

"Does that mean we can go home now?"

"No way. Not until I figure out what he's doing here."

I'm reminded that even though our creative worlds might have some parallels, others don't, such as playwrights attending auditions. It temporarily piques my curiosity about how these things work before shrugging it off. She'll explain it to me later. I slip further into my seat and drag my book and apple from my tote. With Lily's audition complete and her unwillingness to leave the theater, I remove my bookmark to start reading and eating.

"Tales from the Back Row? Seriously? Of all the books, it has to be a fashion one?"

I flash her a small smile and return to my book, content to sit in this cozy theater now that I'm sufficiently entertained by my book and sated with my snack.

The more time passes, the more engrossed I get in my book until Lily elbows my side. Assuming she wants my bag of snacks, I pass her the tote, but she points to center stage, where the playwright stands facing us.

"Ladies and gentlemen, thank you for sharing your talents today. But I believe someone else in this room has something special to offer."

His voice booms across the rows of attendees. I lower my book, set it on the seat next to me, and wait for his announcement as surprised gasps ripple through the crowd. All eyes are locked on Travis Jackson, whose gaze is locked on me. I slowly finish my bite, the apple skin scraping down my throat and making me desperate for a drink of water. Something unexpected happens when he points to me.

"Miss, would you consider joining us on stage?"

My heart rate, a low thump in my veins while reading and enjoying my book, has now sprinted into my throat. Shock and reluctance pin me in place. I slowly shake my head, breaking his intense stare to look into Lily's equally shocked face. Her response is a subtle shrug, a nonverbal acknowledgment that mirrors my uncertainty.

I'm a casual observer, an emotional support animal, I joked to Lily, not a person auditioning for the playwright himself. I mildly considered it at the sign-up sheet and quickly decided against it, feeling comfortable watching Lily. My thoughts swirl around my brain, trying to make sense of his request. But the truth is, I'm not eager to unravel the mystery behind it. I'd much prefer to suddenly become invisible, blend into the plush theater seat, slide onto the floor, and crawl out of here. Anything that causes his attention to go anywhere else but me.

"Miss?"

I hand off my mostly-eaten apple to Lily, who's reluctant to take it, and I can't blame her. Who wants to hold an apple core? I grip the back of the chair in front of me and hesitantly rise to my feet, ducking my head in a bow of respect to him and his theater.

"Sir? Uh, Mr. Jackson?" My voice trembles from the sheer panic surging through me. My fingertips crush the velvet cushion under them. "With all due respect, I sincerely appreciate your invitation, but . . . respectfully, I must decline."

He runs a hand through his wavy hair, which shows brown strands when it falls back into place. I might be inclined to appease him if it weren't for his commanding presence and obvious good looks. However, something tells me that this man is used to getting his way, and my past experiences with men like him have made me wary of such charm. My mom, charmed by one too many handsome men, failed to convince me that intentions are always pure beneath such exteriors.

"Who is this woman?"

He impatiently snaps his fingers as if that will get me to answer. His assistant, clad in all-black clothing and a bulky headset, hurriedly removes them from her ears, rifling through a stack of papers before showing him something. She then shakes her head, and his attention returns to me.

"You're not on the list?"

His question comes across more as a statement, and the certainty in his voice is hard to ignore.

"No."

I turn and gesture to Lily, still puzzled by the situation, as am I.

"I'm moral support."

My hands wave in front of me as physical confirmation of my words. My gaze wanders the room, and a myriad of expressions bore into me. Disgust, shock, confusion, and amusement —all entertained by this exchange that has me convinced my racing heart will explode in my chest at any moment.

"You're not on the list," he repeats, the certainty in his statement now tinged with a hint of surprise.

It's almost as though he's grappling with the fact that I've thrown a wrench into his carefully organized proceedings while he's thrown that same wrench into my cozy spot, minding my own business.

"And yet, you're in my theater."

"Um, yes, sir."

Lily smacks her hand against my thigh, and I shrug at both of them. What else should I say when he's stating the obvious?

"I can leave. Well, I . . . we can leave. We'll leave."

My words carry a sense of confidence even as panic twists my insides. I can't help but feel responsible for disrupting any chance Lily has of getting a part. Something I'll rack my brain to resolve and make up to her later when I'm not being interrogated.

My actions mirror my words as I swiftly retrieve my book from the empty seat. I whisper to Lily to pass me the tote resting in her lap. However, she seems to be in shock and not moving. Her eyes are transfixed on something behind me.

"Lily, get up. We've got to go!"

"You there."

My attempt at a swift exit is abruptly halted by a sharp snap of fingers and an authoritative demand. My book slips from my grasp, clattering to the floor as the blood drains from my body in fright. Whirling around, I'm met with seeing him, positioned just two chairs away. He effectively blocks the row, squashing any hope of our impending departure.

"What's her name?"

His inquiry pierces through the charged atmosphere. Still clutching my apple core, Lily turns her surprised eyes towards me, the unanswered question lingering between us. He directs it at her but insinuates I should answer. I'm frozen in place—a fish out of water, trying to leave and not being allowed. Do I ask him to move? Do I jump over the seats or climb over Lily?

"Isla Frank."

She answers him, but her tone says sorry to me.

"Well, Isla Frank," he addresses me, his words ringing with authority. "Everyone who steps foot into my theater is required to audition. Hence the term, *open* auditions."

He makes a sweeping gesture around the room, and my gaze follows it, only to realize more people have joined to watch this spectacle we're creating. My body trembles and I feel uncomfortable being the center of this much attention. I clear my throat, attempting to dislodge the sudden lump that seems to have taken residence there. I'm pretty sure his definition of open auditions is wrong and definitely different from Lily's.

"If you please?"

His voice is expectant, an invitation laced with an unspoken challenge. Obligation weighs me down as I glance at Lily, regretful that I ruined her chances. For her, I will do this. I will be brave and read whatever he wants, so she's still a contender. With a sidestep down the row, I navigate past the two seats, conscious of his towering presence as he shifts to the side, allowing me clearance to pass.

"Um, what do . . . what do I do?" I stammer, my voice betraying my nervousness. I didn't bring a piece or practice like I assume everyone here did. Do I recite my favorite poem or maybe some song lyrics? Will they give me something to read? A script, perhaps?

His expression softens, taking my anxiety down a fraction before he shouts, "Lines," to that same assistant, causing me to jump. She darts over, a crumpled script in her hand that she passes to him before hurrying back to her spot at the front.

"Read from here to here."

He moves in closer, his cologne lingering in my nose as he points at the passages. My hands tremble as I accept his script, our fingers brushing. I open my mouth to say them when he immediately shakes his head.

"Not here, up there."

"Oh, right."

I glance at Lily, who has come out of her shocked fog long enough to give me an encouraging smile. Taking a deep breath, I smooth the fabric of my dress and slowly make my way to the stage. My legs feel like jelly while my heart thunders in my chest.

I climb the stairs to the side, noticing the grooves in the old wood as the whole stage seems to tilt toward the patron's seats. The lights are excessively bright, and I put my hand up to block them long enough to find him again.

"Take a moment to read it over. We'll see what you can bring to this character whenever you're ready."

His instructions do little to damper the sudden sick feeling in the pit of my stomach. I drop my hand and glance down at the lines on the page, the words blurring together. Lily's audition echoes in my mind as I inhale deeply, trying to steady my shaking body. I am thankful this is a different part than hers. With trembling hands, I hold the script in front of me and clear my throat, attempting to sound confident as I begin to recite the lines. But my voice falters, barely above a whisper.

"Louder, Isla Frank. We need to hear you project." Travis's tone turns authoritative again. "And think of this as a real-life scene, a conversation you'd have with, say, your friend here."

I swallow hard, my cheeks burning with embarrassment.

The lines are not a conversation, more a monologue, but I'm not about to split hairs with him. Summoning all my courage, I take a deep breath and raise my voice, my words becoming more audible. Travis walks closer to the stage, waving his index finger in circles and urging me to continue.

As I delve into the lines, something strange happens. The nervousness I felt earlier begins to fade, replaced by a growing confidence. Travis's presence, though intimidating, becomes strangely reassuring. With each word, I immerse myself in the character, letting go of my fears and relating to the material I'm reading.

He watches intently, his eyes locked on me when I glance up. Surprisingly, his intensity spurs me on. My voice gains strength, and I lose myself in the moment, forgetting the room full of spectators since I can't see them against the blinding stage lights.

The monologue is about love and loss, abandonment and longing. It is about wanting to be seen, heard, and appreciated for the core of who this woman is and not the mask she presents to the world to feel accepted. It resonates so deeply that a tear drips down my cheek as I come to the final words before quickly wiping it away. When I finish, there's a moment of silence before a smattering of applause breaks out.

"Thank you, Isla Frank. That's exactly what we're looking for."

Travis's tone softens, and when I put my hand back up to block the light, a warm smile appears on his handsome face. I clutch the script, the tremor gone from my hands as I hurry off the stage. My legs are still wobbly as I race to Lily, who's moved up to the front of the theater with our stuff in tow.

She embraces me and loudly whispers, "See, I knew you should have auditioned! You were amazing up there!"

I can hardly believe what just transpired. Travis Jackson, the playwright, noticed me and forced me on stage. Even though I was terrified and trembling, I somehow found my footing. The words swirled around me until I started comprehending the message, the meaning resonating deeply.

Maybe this is the magic that draws people into the theater to audition. The feeling of doing something so outside my comfort zone that I want to vomit until it turns out good, excellent even. Having overcome this personal obstacle of not wanting to stand out or be noticed by others makes me feel empowered, slightly invincible, as if I can do anything I set my mind to.

Blending in and being a wallflower is how I survived most of my life. It's my default behavior. How I assimilated to make it in this world before being adopted allowed me to come out of my shell around trusted friends and family. But this experience, this feeling, being seen and appreciated by a handsome and successful stranger who is not my parents or Uncle Alex or Uncle Tomlin, well, it's something I could get used to. Addictive, almost, if it can transform the quietest observers, such as myself, into an aspiring actress.

"I can't believe I did that."

She releases me, and I hand her the curled-up script, which she shoves into my tote. I shake my hands, trying to expel the nervous energy coursing through my body.

"What happens next?"

"We leave and hope they call us back from another audition."

"Oh, okay, then."

As she transfers my belongings back to me, I begin stowing everything into my tote. Just as I'm about to complete the task, a tap on my shoulder sends a jolt of surprise through me. I pivot around, my eyes meeting those of Travis Jackson—catching me off guard again.

"Isla Frank. Leave your information with my assistant before you leave."

It's another directive, delivered with authority, that has me wondering if I even want a part in his new play or if I'm just proud of myself for being brave and auditioning.

He senses my hesitation and adds, "Please," with a touch of humility.

The juxtaposition of his commanding presence and this subtle plea elicits a smile from me. I can leave my information. It doesn't necessarily commit me to returning to his theater for another audition. After all, is he genuinely open to hiring someone like me with no prior experience, or is this just a fleeting whim of his?

"Of course I will."

I swing my tote onto my shoulder in a bold move of confidence. He acquiesces to that tough playwright's demeanor and lets a little smile slip onto his lips.

"Only if you can guarantee my friend here gets a callback."

The smile falls from his face, and a glint appears in his eye. He wants something from me. I want nothing from him, but Lily does.

"No, Isla!" Her hand is on my arm in a flash. "That's not how this works."

Little does Lily know, this is precisely how it works. I've seen it far too many times with men to know any difference. Everything is a negotiation. Give a little to gain a lot. It's how life works. Nothing is free, and everyone has an angle.

My smile brightens when I gaze up at him, tilting my head toward Lily without her noticing. His jaw clenches, my eyebrows lower, and the trepidation I feel is completely gone. I recall having to negotiate to eat lunch in the library instead of the cafeteria at school when the bullying got too bad. I promised to stay after school to help various teachers grade papers in exchange for peace and quiet to eat my humble lunch.

I realized most life situations are similar to that negotiation.

I casually brush my hair over my shoulder, and the long stare he's giving me now reminds me of my principal when I begged for library time. His attempt to intimidate me into surrendering my contact information is laughable compared to other negotiations I've had, especially with my time with Rick.

Those were some of the worst in my life. I got pretty creative in negotiating my way out of having sex with him, but toward the end, he was catching on. As the tension between us lingers, my confidence continues when I break the silence.

"Nice to meet you, Mr. Jackson," I utter with a final nod. I pivot on my heels and begin to stride towards the exit, Lily's jogging to catch up with me.

"Are you crazy? You can't do that to a guy like him. He's famo—"

"You've got yourself a deal, Isla Frank."

Before she can finish, his voice reverberates through the rows of seats, carrying an unexpected declaration that freezes Lily and me in our tracks. His words catch me off guard for the umpteenth time, and we turn in unison to look at him.

He bows with a gracious flare, the gesture laced with a hint of humor that seems at odds with the stern playwright I had initially perceived him to be. Bemused, I chuckle. Lily gasps at his gesture. It's as if fate orchestrated a scene right here in his theater—one that I never anticipated being a part of.

With another harsh snap of his fingers, the assistant runs up the aisle, clutching the clipboard to her chest before shoving it toward mine. She mutters instructions on what they need, not realizing I already saw the sign-up sheet before. I quickly scribble my information and glance up when done to find his eyebrow cocked when looking at me. I mirror his expression.

Challenge accepted.

The assistant relays a bunch of stuff about callbacks and scheduling, the time commitment for this play, and other stuff that conflicts with my school schedule and makes it nearly impossible for me to be in his play. These are all the things Lily needs to know, and she nods her head as she takes it all in. When the assistant scurries away again, my gaze lingers on his for a few seconds before he turns away, barking orders to a crew member at the back of the stage about lighting.

Lily loops her arm in mine, drawing me close as we turn to exit and waiting until we are out the door and back on the street to explode.

"NO ONE, and I mean no one, is ever going to believe me when I tell them you got THE TRAVIS JACKSON to acquiesce to you! Like no one!"

Her exclamation sails over the loudness of the traffic on the street before us. She walks sideways, excitedly bouncing on her feet to look at me while she talks. I'm busy making sure she doesn't get hit by a car rounding the corner at an obscene speed and turning against the light.

"Guys like that are used to getting their way."

I shrug, appearing calm when I feel as capable as a super-hero saving the city. Not wanting to waste this boldness, I want to try something new and continue the streak of operating outside my comfort zone.

"Let's go to City Climb. Like right now. Wouldn't that be fun, Lily?"

"What?"

Confusion is written all over her face as the smell of waffles floats by us from a nearby street vendor. The aroma causes my stomach to growl as lunchtime was hours ago, and the apple no longer sustains me.

"You heard me. I think they put you in a jumpsuit anyway, so me wearing a dress isn't a problem. Then we can grab dinner at that new place you want to try. Pho something?"

Her hand lands on my arm, pulling me to a stop with an incredulous look on her face.

"You want us to scale the side of a building with a few

cords preventing us from plummeting to our death and then eat pho afterward. Who are you? Are you out of your mind? No way!"

When she says it like that, I guess I did jump ahead three spaces without letting her know what's going on in my mind.

"I feel . . . I don't know, empowered . . ." My hands roll in a circle, causing hers to fall from my arm as I try to harness the profound feeling swirling in my body. "Like I can do anything, you know? Like Superman or something."

"Endorphin rush, that's what's going on, Isla. It's why theater is so addicting and jam-packed with actors auditioning. It's the rush you're feeling, the words coming to life within you in a way that resonates. Don't think I didn't see that happen when you were on stage. It was magical."

The hustle and bustle of the New York streets feels electric, matching the adrenaline still coursing through my veins. As the daylight begins to fade, the city lights start their nightly dance, flickering on one by one, reminding me of a scene from Singin' in the Rain, sans the rain and dancing man. But the joyful feeling on his face as he splashed through that choreography matches my feelings.

"Honestly, I surprised myself."

Lily's imploring eyes expect more of why it resonated. But some things are meant to stay inside, or at least shared between me, my court-assigned therapist, and my family. Although they don't know it all either. Sometimes, there is just too much tragedy to keep piling on people, especially Papa, who cries easily and wants to cloak me in bubble wrap to save me from the world.

"Anyway, if climbing the side of a building like Spiderman is out, what else can we do? I feel like I'm walking on air, and that's too amazing just to go home and watch old movies."

Her laughter rings out loud against two cars, honking at each other over a stolen parking space as we walk by.

"With all these superhero references, I feel as if I should suggest a Marvel movie."

I wrinkle my nose at her idea and shake my head.

"Good, ditch that idea and the Pho place. I know of a cozy jazz club nearby. Live music, dim lights, and some of the best bar food I've ever had."

The idea instantly captivates me. The thought of immersing myself in another form of the arts, the soulful music blending with my new emotion, just feels right.

"Perfect."

She winds her arm through mine, drawing me close as she guides us down the street. Having been in the city two years longer than me, Lily always knows the best little places tucked into the various burrows around town. Her adventurous side takes her places that I could only dream about and, other times, scares me.

Money is also no object to her, as she comes from a wealthy family that runs a thriving import and export business. I asked about it once, and she waved a dismissive hand, unwilling to get too in-depth other than saying it's spices or wine and that she couldn't care less.

I found that odd, as I spent most afternoons after school at Papa's pet shop, which expanded when the landlord remodeled the exterior façade and drew in more business. Dad's work was a little more complicated and, frankly, boring—something about trading commodities, which meant wearing suits and studying the markets all the time.

He loved it and thought it entertaining enough to bore us with all the details over dinner on some nights. The almost three years I spent with them were the most wonderfully normal and quintessentially Norman Rockwell it could get. Those memories are the most cherished and provide the most comfort to me on my lonely nights here.

"You didn't have to make him take me," Lily says out of the

blue, a flicker of uncertainty passing across her face. I feel guilty for hijacking her audition.

"I'm sorry if that made you uncomfortable. I'd been sitting in that theater all day, and when he asked, I was so caught off guard. Then, it seemed like I had to do it, and I ended up loving it. I don't know what came over me, but you're the amazing one. You should be the star of the show."

A radiant smile graces her face as she suddenly squeezes me even closer.

"Thanks, but I want to be the villain, not the star. The villain has more complexity."

With a chuckle, I pat her arm, which is still looped with mine.

"You'd make an incredible villain."

"I know. Now let's go decompress with smooth jazz."

3

_____

"Isla! You won't believe it. I got a call back!" Lily yells, sailing into the living room, her dark hair in waves down her back as she shoves her phone screen into my face. "And when I called his assistant to confirm the time, I asked her if it was because of you."

My heart, swelling with joy for her, is shrinking just as fast as I realize two things. The first is guilt all over again at sabotaging her ability to stand on her own and audition rather than forcing Travis Jackson's hand. The second is disappointment that I didn't get a callback, even when he seemed interested in me.

"Lily, that's incredible! I'm so happy for you."

She snatches her phone away, collapses onto the couch, and wraps me in a tight hug, much to Anna's dismay at being disturbed on my lap. When she pulls back, her face inches from mine, she asks, "What about you? Did you get a call?"

As close as we've grown as roommates, she's a little too close right now, invading my personal space. That is something that always makes me uneasy. I tuck Anna in my arms and stand, collecting my empty glass to retrieve more water while adding the necessary space to make me feel comfortable again.

I'm about to holler my answer, except she's hot on my heels and following me into the kitchen. I use the refrigerator door to hold her at bay, a physical barrier to maintain my safe zone, even though I understand she's overly excited and does not mean any harm.

"I guess not." She immediately lunges for me as my grip on the door tightens. "I'm so sorry! I don't know what happened. I thought for sure you would."

She sees my uneasiness and stops her advancement on me, which has me dragging in a relieved breath.

"It's fine, Lily. I wasn't expecting one anyway."

"Although, the lady did say she didn't know who was with you that day when she looked at the list. I just now realize you never told him my name. So maybe I did get the part on my own merit."

I hate the doubt that lingers, and I immediately close the fridge to reassure her while still holding Anna.

"Of course, you got it on your own merit. You're good, Lily. Like, really good, and that guy would be a fool to pass on you. You didn't need me at all, and I apologize—"

"Don't you dare apologize to me again! You've done it umpteen million times already, and it's water under the bridge. It was the day it happened and every day since." She holds up both hands with emphasis. "You need to let it go."

I open my mouth to object, and she waves her hands in a big X across her body.

"No, I won't hear of it any more. Now, what are you doing the rest of the day? I have a date with this new guy, and I can see about him bringing a friend. Wouldn't it be fun to double date?"

Fun? Or complete misery that has instant dread crawling

through my veins? I don't like surprises, and I certainly don't like them when men are involved.

"Um, I'm behind on my homework." I gesture to the pile of books sprawled open on the coffee table. "Plus, it's Tuesday night, and you know I always call my parents on Tuesdays."

She nibbles on her lip as if trying to think of new ways to rope me into going.

"I know that look, and there is nothing you can say to convince me otherwise." I shake my head at her. "I'm perfectly content staying in with Anna, making dinner, and finishing my assignments."

"Ugh, I love you, but you are such a fun killer." Her smile betrays her words, and when she suddenly spins on her heels to exit the kitchen, I'm a little bewildered. "Give the fathers my love."

Her voice carries through the small apartment, where I hear her rummaging around in her room, probably trying to pick an outfit for tonight. I fill my glass, put Anna on the floor since I no longer need to use her as a barrier and resume my perch on the couch, eager to enjoy a quiet night by myself.

"Shoot, where is it?"

Mumbling to myself, Anna trails behind me as I round the couch for a second time, looking for the book required for one of my classes. I'm sure I bought it at the start of the semester, which wasn't that long ago when my parents were in town to help me move. With my hands on my hips surveying the room, Anna's tiny nails stop clicking on the floor. I'm stumped, trying to recall if I've seen it here or if I just assumed I picked it up when Papa accompanied me to the bookstore while Dad worked at the hotel. If it were here, I'd spot it immediately with its distinctive orange, black, and white cover.

"Crap, I'll be back, Anna."

Glancing at my watch, I'm losing precious time before my planned call. If I leave now, I can make it to the bookstore and back in time to have dinner with them over the phone, something I like to do to feel reminiscent of home. Grabbing my keys and coat, I check my purse to ensure my phone is there before dashing out the door to get what I need.

Twenty minutes later, I'm entering the bookstore, ready to hunt down the book and leave, when I see a new display dedicated to New York fashion. Like a moth to a flame, I'm drawn to the books they selected, glancing at the staff picks and reading their comment cards draped from the bottom of each shelf.

My eyes greedily take in each book, picking them up, reading the back cover, and flipping through the pages. It's a small indulgence, spending a few minutes in the world I aim to be a part of. After rifling through several books I'd love to own for my private collection, I feel a presence beside me that has me cautiously moving away.

"I highly recommend the book you are holding."

A crisp and elegant British accent with a warm undertone grabs my attention. My gaze is drawn upward to a handsome individual with an air of refined elegance, his posture confident yet approachable. His skin is rich mahogany, and his short, curly black hair hints at his racial heritage.

Dressed impeccably, his tailored suit fits him flawlessly in classic colors that enhance his complexion—his attire speaks of wealth. Yet, his taste for subtle yet luxurious details, like the silk pocket square, the expensive gold watch, and finely crafted leather shoes, display his sophistication.

"Excuse me?"

My lowered voice lures him nearer, forcing me to instinctively step back. He briefly glances down at my black ballet shoes, acknowledging my discomfort before mirroring my actions and stepping back.

"That book."

He points to my hands, still clutching the hardbound book and wondering why he's talking to me about fashion. Unless he's either gay or in the industry, both of which would explain it.

"I've read it and found it quite enlightening. It offers a unique perspective on fashion houses. One that's both engaging and thought-provoking. I believe you'll find it interesting."

The book suddenly feels more significant as I glance down at it and back up to his warm chocolate eyes.

"Um, thank you?" I reply, a bit surprised. He's definitely got to be in the industry. Maybe a designer for a fashion house, although I know most of the lead designers as I follow them on social media. "Are you in the fashion industry? Do you work for a fashion house?"

I tilt my head when gazing up at him, trying to connect the dots between this older man and the fashion world. If he's from England, could there be men's fashion houses I'm unaware of? Not likely. Even though fashion is global, it's still a small world.

"Not exactly." His answer is brief before he selects another book and hands it to me. "If you're looking to learn more about the history of fashion, then I'd recommend this book."

I don't even look at the cover as I take it and add it to the arm already holding the other. Despite his recommendation that it would be good, I'm still trying to figure him out.

"I'm sorry, I'm not used to getting book recommendations from strangers, especially about fashion."

I brush my hair away from my face, waiting for him to catch my drift and explain himself. When he remains silent, not contributing anything more, I look around and then lean forward.

Lowering my voice, I ask, "If you're 'not exactly' in the fashion world, then are you by chance . . . gay?"

There's a very uncomfortable pause while his eyes narrow. I'm left scrambling to cover my inappropriate question.

"It's okay, my fathers are gay. I mean, my parents. I have two dads and no mom, well, sort of no mom, not anymore, but I'm rambling. I'm sorry for asking. That was rude and over the line."

I'm so embarrassed that I start shelving the books, ready to run out of the store without the book I need tonight. Suddenly, a delightful chuckle erupts from his deep baritone voice, stopping my actions. As his laughter grows, so does my discomfort to the point where I take a few more steps back.

"Do you always ask strangers that you're not used to getting book recommendations from their sexual orientation?"

Even though the amusement in his tone is still there, my cheeks feel hot, and my embarrassment overrides any possibility of additional conversation. I assume his hand coming toward me is meant to be reassuring. I lean away from his touch, glancing at the front door to figure out how fast I can dash out of here.

"I'm Gabriel Gannon. Most everyone calls me Gabe."

His ringless, manicured hand stills in the air between us, and a sliver of relief runs through me. A handshake I can do, especially if he's gay and not hitting on me. Hesitantly, my gaze moves from his hand to his face, noticing his bright white teeth and how his smile adds age lines around his rich-colored eyes. He looks less intimidating and more like a model found in GQ magazine. I slip my hand into his, the warmth of his fingers curling around mine and sinking into my skin, matching the warmth of his expression.

"I'm Isla Frank."

His grip is firm but not overly aggressive like some men. He releases it with two definite shakes, and I swallow some of my worry.

"I didn't mean to ask. I overshare when I'm nervous."

"I think that happens to the best of us."

He's generous in letting me off the hook, especially since I called out his orientation so bluntly in public.

"Have you read this one?"

He points to a new memoir by a former Vogue executive that I heard about but haven't had a chance to read, given my course load.

"I haven't. Have you?"

That bright smile never fades when his fingertips tap various covers, giving a brief review and his rating system. His voracious reading is impressive, and his ability to recall intricate details from each book is beyond anything I can do. When he finally hits the last book in the display, I'm spellbound by his knowledge. He gushes out a big breath as if all that took it out of him, and I am left shaking my head.

"How do you do that? How do you remember all that, and you don't work in the industry?"

My embarrassment and initial worries are long gone after the dissertation he just gave while looking marvelous and smelling great, with his musky cologne filling my senses. He taps his temple lightly with a finger.

"I have a photographic memory. It was quite an asset during medical school."

"Wait, you're a doctor?" I blurt out, his refined appearance —the Hermes scarf around his neck, the sleek blue DE Bethune silver wheel watch, and the elegant Stefano Ricci overcoat making sense now.

He nods with a humble smile.

"Yes, I am. Reading helps me unwind, and I have a penchant for quality clothing. It's a different world from medicine, but equally fascinating."

His revelation is another fascinating layer to the intriguing man standing before me. Then, a thought. What kind of doctor has the leisure time to immerse himself in fashion books? Surely, a successful medical professional wouldn't have the time to delve into the history of polka dots and Vogue memoirs.

"What kind of doctor?"

I don't dislike the suspicion in my voice when I ask. Men lie to get what they want. He's no different. He picks up on my tone and retrieves his wallet, the same luxury brand Uncle Tomlin carries, to pull out a business card. When he hands it to me, I read it aloud.

"Pediatric cranial neurosurgeon . . . wow."

I know my mouth is open, staring at the card and into his face. His smile is not as bright and slightly smug, probably getting this reaction all the time. The brain surgeon part is sad, but the pediatric part is even sadder.

"Pediatric? That breaks my heart. What type of surgeries do kids need?"

He pauses momentarily, tucking his hands behind his back as if in doctor mode, ready to give the results to an anxious family.

"Isla, would you mind if we grabbed a cup of coffee? They have a café on the second floor, and I could better explain what I do in a quieter setting."

My instincts are instantly heightened. Initially, I worry this is an impromptu date. Then relief washes over me when I remember he's gay.

"Um, sure." I adjust the strap of my bag on my shoulder. "But not too long. I need to study and get a book. It's why I'm here in the first place, but I got sidetracked with this display. It's actually upstairs, the book I need."

He gives an understanding smile, acknowledging my demands.

"Wonderful, let's pick up your book and find a spot to talk about medicine and what you're studying."

We make our way upstairs, the noise of the bookstore below fading into a calmer, less crowded ambiance. The shelves aren't quite as full up here. Academic books tend to be less popular. He trails behind me, scanning the books we pass as I hunt for the one I need for school. His interest in my choice is evident but unobtrusive as he offers to pay, which has me tilting my head in silent inquiry. I respectfully decline and hand over my credit card. He apologizes for overstepping and sounding very formal and very British.

Shortly after, we're drawn to the café by the strong aroma of coffee and the soft murmur of conversations, creating a welcoming atmosphere. I select a small table by the window, the city lights twinkling outside. He orders cappuccinos and a plate of biscotti for us to share. I don't mind him paying for it, as I plan to get the next round if we stay that long.

The conversation flows effortlessly as we sip our drinks. We discuss everything from medicine and my studies to literature and life in New York. He shares amusing anecdotes from his hometown of London, voicing different accents from the various parts of England. I find myself laughing more than I have in a long time. His stories are captivating and filled with a blend of humor and wisdom.

When the conversation turns to his practice and what brought him to the States, his expression changes, morphing into an intensity that shows his passion and dedication to helping children. It all sounds important compared to my world, which he seems genuinely intrigued by while I dismiss my life as unimportant.

The conversation slips into fashion, our shared passion, and one that brings out the best in us. It's so easy with him. It's as if I'm gabbing with my best friend. Time slips away while I pay for more sugary treats and two refills, decaffeinated for him as he has an early surgery tomorrow and needs to sleep.

Caffeinated for me as I still have a pile of homework waiting for me at home.

The café around us gradually empties, and before I know it, an announcement comes over the intercom that the bookstore is closing. We're both surprised to realize we've been chatting for nearly three hours.

"I'm sorry to have kept you, Isla."

He apologizes quickly as he stands to clear away the plate of crumbs and empty coffee cups. I cast him a bright smile, so happy to have made a new and interesting friend.

"Not at all. This has been the most interesting thing that has happened to me this week," I say, gathering my things into my bag before swinging it onto my shoulder and then frowning. "Second thing, actually."

The café staff wishes us a good night before cleaning the table as we walk toward the escalators.

"Second, I'm wounded. What was the first, if I may be so bold to inquire?"

The humor in his voice is unmistakable, and I glance at his face to ensure he's not offended before gripping the handrail to step on it.

"It was earlier this week when Lily, the roommate I told you about, had a casting call and dragged me along. The director, I mean, the playwright, forced me to audition. She got a callback, but I didn't. Not that I was expecting one, though."

As we ride the escalator together, I can't help but notice his proximity. Closer than before when we were downstairs, his arm clasping the rail behind me. Usually, I wouldn't like it, especially considering he's a large man, noticing his muscular frame when he removed his coat upstairs. However, something in the soft depth of his eyes, the way he spoke so highly of his mom back home, and that he saves children for a living makes me feel safe around him.

"An actress too? Did I miss that part of the conversation upstairs?"

His eyebrows wrinkle together, confusion ringing in his tone.

"No, I'm not an actress, and I'm not aspiring to be one either, which I learned is very common here."

My mind wanders back to the script. The character I read about suffered so much loss that it still bothers me.

"I don't know, Gabe. Maybe a small part of me hoped I'd get a callback."

We proceed out the door, the night air cool and crisp compared to the cozy warmth of the café while the city buzzes around us.

"Validation is always appreciated even if we're not obviously seeking it." His eloquence in capturing exactly what I'm feeling in the most concise manner possible is refreshing. "Can I give you a lift? My car is parked right over there."

My gaze follows his finger to a dark, expensive luxury vehicle parked under the streetlamp. Even though I feel comfortable with him in public, in a confined space, it's another thing entirely, and that's the reason I never take a car ride service. Bad things happen in locked cars. I learned that long ago.

"Thank you, but no, I'll take the subway."

It's not ideal to be out this late and alone, but Uncle Tomlin taught me a fair number of moves to protect myself. I always carry pepper spray, so I'm well-equipped. Gabe's face is aghast, the thought foreign to him that I'd turn him down for the subway.

"Uh, I'm fairly certain I'm not comfortable with that. It's late, and the subway at this hour? Are you certain I can't drive you? It's really no bother."

"I'm certain."

The finality in my voice has him frowning, looking from me

to his car as if to invisibly will me into going. He releases a long sigh, obviously conflicted, when I decide for him by backing away toward the direction of the subway entrance.

"If you insist, please let me at least wait until you get on the train," he insists, concern etching his features.

His offer stems from genuine worry rather than any desire to overstep boundaries. I consider it, weighing the comfort of his company against my ingrained caution.

"Okay, that's a compromise I can accept," I relent, offering a small smile to ease the sudden tension. "But only to the station entrance."

As we walk down to the subway, the night's unsavory characters seem less daunting, with his large presence looming beside me. He keeps the conversation light and engaging, skillfully navigating away from any discomfort my initial refusal might have caused. By the time we reach the subway entrance, he's pushing through the turn-style, walking me to the train as he said and ignoring my subway entrance comment. I don't mind. It's nicer to wait with him rather than alone and looking over my shoulder the whole time. His thoughtful actions have further cemented my respect for him.

"Thanks for understanding," I say when the light on the subway barrels toward us. He nods, his expression softening.

"Safety first, always. Can I give you my number so you can text me that you made it home? I'd never forgive myself if . . ."

His voice trails off, but the remainder of his message is implied. It's valid. I'm not yet comfortable being out this late, either. I feel more protected with Lily, which is probably a misnomer as she's not much bigger than I am.

"Sure."

I quickly reach for my phone as the breeze from the subway blows my hair away from my face, distracting Gabe for a few seconds as he stares. The warmth in his eyes and the smile playing on his lips have me questioning if he's gay or possibly bisexual. Snapping out of his expression as the doors slide open, with people pushing past us, he relays his number, barely getting it out before I need to step inside. Without a hug or even a goodbye, I wave to him through the glass pane, our eyes locked until the subway pushes on, and he falls from sight.

Then, a fleeting thought as the train rattles on—I forgot to call my parents.

4

Surrounded by dress forms draped in half-completed garments and sketches that litter every surface, my phone's insistent buzz breaks the concentration of the classroom. I dive to silence my phone as a hush falls over the room, and angry eyes turn to me. The instructor's sharp hand clap, followed by an overly exaggerated point toward the door, has me hustling across the room to dash into the hallway when I see Lily's name on the screen.

"This better be important because my teacher is going to take points off for—"

"Isla! You need to hear this!"

Lily's usually excited voice is panicked with an urgency that cuts through the background chaos of her environment. Over the sound of shouting and what seems like the clatter of equipment being knocked over, I'm confused as to why she's calling me while worried about my teacher's reaction to this unallowed interruption.

"What's going on?"

My voice echoes slightly in the empty hall, the stark white

walls and fluorescent lights contrasting with the vibrant, cluttered studio I just left.

"It's Travis! He's furious you're not here!"

Her words send a shockwave through me. The mention of Travis Jackson wanting me is more than surprising, rooting me to the spot on the floor.

"He was screaming at his assistant for not sending you the callback. He didn't know you were left out. It's total mayhem here."

"Left out? I don't understand. I didn't get anything," I stammer, disbelief clouding my thoughts.

What does this mean exactly? I thought a callback was a second audition—another chance to be chosen for a part. I dismissed it as better off anyway after Lily received hers and a momentary flash of disappointment. My coursework is heavy enough, considering it's my first year at Parsons. Not to mention my first time living away from my parents and all the complex emotions that brought us for all of us, including Dani, who threatened to have Uncle Tomlin buy the apartment building I'm in to beef up security.

She nearly died when I told her where I was going to school. No, actually, she didn't talk to me for a week, then practically kicked down the front door with other design schools in "cities that weren't nasty shitholes." When I declined, she stormed out. Uncle Tomlin had to get involved, and the compromise was a refresher of my self-defense classes and not forcing him to buy the building.

"I know! They are trying to figure out what happened. But he's demanding to know why you aren't there. He specifically asked for you, and he won't proceed with the callbacks until you're here."

The tenseness in her voice is moving through the phone and into my body, causing nervousness in the pit of my stomach.

"You've got to come."

Leave my class, abandon my design, and anger my teacher, who I'm sure doesn't like me with all the harsh criticism she doles out. That's a hard pill to swallow.

"I can't. I'm here, buried in fabric swatches and design drafts. Not to mention, it's the teacher that hates me. I can't leave her class."

"I know, but Isla. You must get here somehow. This could be huge for you! It's Travis Jackson! His demand for you is like . . . like . . ."

"Anna Wintour is sitting in the front row at my show."

I finish her sentence, walking toward the big window at the end of the hallway where the sunshine streams across the white floor. The chaos on Lily's end crescendos—a voice, unmistakably Travis's, bellows for accountability.

"How could she not know? This is unacceptable!"

His anger, even secondhand, sends a shiver down my spine. Lily's breath is hurried as she whispers, "I have to go. He'll see me on the phone, and they aren't allowed. Please, try to make it."

"You there. You came with her."

There's a sharp snap of fingers and a shuffling of the phone, followed by a sudden silence. I move the phone away from my ear to see if the call failed, but we're still connected.

"Who is this? Is this Isla Frank?"

There's no mistaking that voice. Travis Jackson, clear as a bell coming through the phone, causing my heart to race in my chest.

"Um, yeah."

"Why aren't you here?"

The accusation holds a hint of disbelief, something relaying this as my fault when I press the palm of my hand against the warm glass in a moment of bravery.

"You didn't send me a callback. Simple as that."

Even though my remark is witty back to him, my mind is reeling. It's not my fault, nor will I take the blame. Even though I dislike conflict, having had enough to last me a lifetime, I'm not about to let him walk all over me for a dream that isn't mine. If he were the head of Gucci or Tom Ford, I'd apologize and beg forgiveness for his error. Since he's neither, and not in person, only a voice over the phone, I decide to push him further.

"Now, Travis, I can call you that, correct?" I don't bother waiting for his response. His heavy breathing is angry enough. "You've interrupted me in class, so I must go."

My sneaky smile reflects in the window as I remove my palm, enjoying the last moments of warmth before returning to class. A reminder flashes through my mind to snap a picture of my classmate's menswear piece to get Gabe's reaction. I listen to the angry breathing a second longer, about to end the call, when a much calmer pronunciation of my name comes through.

This time, it's my first name. Intrigued, I hesitate, waiting to see if he'll say it again and possibly entertain this call a bit longer before I reach my classroom.

"Isla?" he repeats, and my smile grows wider.

"Yes."

His pause makes me think he was expecting me to say more when I didn't have anything to say. The audition was terrifying but good enough to force me outside my comfort zone. The piece I read was relatable and intriguing, but not something I need in my life. He's going to have to sweeten the pot to get my ass down there, and I certainly won't skip class for it.

"I apologize for the mix-up. However, I'd like you to come read for the role of Marcella."

I stop halfway down the hall, racking my brain as I stare at the ceiling, trying to remember who Marcella is in his play. Lily told me all the parts and her desire to be Rowena, the antagonist, when I made stir fry the other night. For the life of me, I can't remember her talking about that part.

"I appreciate that, but I can't—"

"Marcella is the lead. You would headline the show," he interrupts, and I hear a distinct gasp from Lily, who must be standing by him.

I'm stunned. My breath locks in my chest as I rub my forehead, trying to understand what on earth would possess him to cast me, a total amateur without any experience.

"The lead? Me?"

It's a question I voice aloud as it echoes through my head. I'm not qualified. I have no resume or professional training. Nothing about this makes any sense.

"Yes, I'm quite adept at spotting raw talent. Discovering the undiscovered and turning them into stars."

He rattles off a bunch of names I've never heard of. Maybe Lily has. Regardless, it means nothing to me. Given my already rigorous course load, I'm not even sure I can handle the extra work. The heat from the vent blows down on me, and I move closer to my classroom door, my hand resting on the handle.

"I still don't think it's going to work. I'm at school, and it's a cutthroat program. I can't manage to do both—your play and keeping up with my studies."

Just voicing my worries makes them even scarier when I think about balancing two full-time commitments. I don't know how Lily will do it if she gets the part of Rowena. She's in her third year at NYU. Perhaps it's different there.

"What school?" he barks, his patience seemly running thin. "Tell me."

"Parsons School—"

"Say no more. I have connections over there. Now, when can you be here?"

His interrupting me at every turn is annoying. The fact that he thinks he can boss me around is equally annoying. What makes me mad is his thinking that I will bend to his will and that I even want to lead his play. Sure, it would be a one-in-a-lifetime opportunity, even if I can remember the lines and perform well enough to make it to the opening curtain. If I called my parents and told them I was staring in a play, Papa would surely die of happiness. He loved New York when they moved me up here. Dad said he was like a kid in a candy store when they returned to the hotel the first night.

"Isla?"

His voice softens again when I fail to respond. Glancing at the clock at the end of the hallway, I see that I'm not even halfway through my first class. With two more classes to go and then a voluntary workshop I signed up for, it will be hours before I can leave. Perhaps that will discourage him.

"I have school until 5 pm. And don't think about asking me to skip. I won't. I worked too hard to get in here for a fleeting chance at some off-Broadway play that may or may not succeed."

There's a viciousness in my tone that even surprises me. I'd like to blame it on being hungry and skipping breakfast when Anna didn't want to go potty this morning, and I was running late. More than likely, it's from his presumptive tone that everyone wants what he's offering, whereas I'm perfectly content not doing the play. He clears his throat. My insult hitting the intended target gives me a smidge of satisfaction.

"Oh, and send a car. The subway is a nightmare at that time of day, and walking would take almost an hour."

I exaggerate the time and up the ante with the whole car thing. If I were a gambler, I'd bet no one has ever stood up to him like this, and since he wants something I don't care about, why not make the most of it? Turn the tables on him to see how far I can go. I am not one for usually playing with people like this, but for some reason, I think he can hold his own just fine against me.

44

"Fine. 5:15 pm. Corner of Fifth and 13th. Not a minute later."

My grip on the door tightens as the call ends. When I throw it open, a few puzzled faces turn to see the biggest smile I've had in a long time on my face. I got a call back for a lead in a play in New York with a famous playwright, and he's sending a car for me. Well done, Isla. I couldn't be prouder of my negotiation skills, something I learned from Dani every time she wanted something from someone without giving up anything herself.

Despite the disapproving look on my teacher's face, I return to my station and work on my latest design, my hands trembling from nerves. Standing up to him over the phone or with Lily standing next to me is one thing. It's going to be another when I have to do it alone. That's when I might need to channel Dani's strength and take a page out of her book. Not that I could be as bold and blunt as her. That's years in the making. However, I can emulate her no-nonsense attitude when dealing with Travis Jackson. If I don't hold my own against him, he'll eat me up and spit me out.

I'm tempted to sneak a text in class to Lily yet refrain for fear that he could still have her phone and see it. That would give him the upper hand, and I don't want that. I channel my nervous energy into my work, buzzing through it at lightning speed to the point that it allows me to finish that section of the assignment before calling the teacher over to make observations and judgments on what I need to change. Once that's done, I approach my classmate, discuss his design, and ask permission for a photo. I snap and send it to Gabe with a little note before closing my phone.

He's another welcome surprise. With his busy schedule and our friendship firmly planted from that night, we've traded texts when each has time. It's so low-pressure and easy. I'm finding more and more things to share with him or things that remind me of him when I see them. It's nice.

One class leads into another, grabbing lunch from the vending machine in between. With the workshop the only thing left between me and that awaiting car, nervousness builds in my stomach. It coils into a tight ring until I'm slightly nauseous when the sleek black car pulls up on the corner.

I expect a driver hired by the production company that puts on his shows. I don't expect Travis himself to emerge from behind the wheel to round the front of the car and open the door for me. It makes the ring in my stomach even tighter to the point I want to vomit right on his designer loafers.

"Isla, you look lovely today."

His smile is genuine, with a hint of humor in his tone. The breeze from the bustling corner lifts the front of his hair. When he removes his sunglasses, his blue eyes are piercing, matching his cobalt blue sweater. His light beige casual pants hug his butt, making his package more pronounced.

I lower my eyes, not wanting to get caught, and give him the satisfaction I'm sure many other women have. I'm not immune to his easy-good looks and oozing charm. It's just that I'm not going to fall for it. I'm not here to get a boyfriend. I'm here to go to school and make a name for myself.

"Thanks. It's an Isla Frank original."

I nervously grip the side of my skirt and do a little twirl, which sparks something in his expression when he gazes at me. Beyond that, neither of us says anything else as I slip onto the cool leather seats of his fancy car. If Dani were here, she'd roll her eyes and say he's overcompensating for something. I don't want to find out whether that's true or not.

The moment he slides behind the wheel and steers into traffic, I realize I broke my cardinal rule of getting into a car with a stranger. With my experience, I find my hand clutching the door handle in case I need to escape. Sensing my discomfort, he drapes his wrist over the steering wheel, leaning toward me as I scoot closer to the window. The seatbelt warning annoyingly starts chiming, outing my intention to dart out the door if he takes a wrong turn or tries anything funny.

"Isla, I feel we may have gotten off on the wrong foot."

He tunes out the chiming, but it's practically all I can focus on, especially since rhythmic sounds bother me. I don't acknowledge his words, staring out the window at the line of cars in front of us. If he considers this an apology, he's terrible at it.

"Please, I'm trying to make things right here," he persists, his tone softening, trying for understanding. The chiming continues, a relentless reminder of the disconnect between us and my desire to stay safe in the cramped space of the car. Despite his effort, my attention remains fixed outside, on the slow crawl of traffic, each vehicle adding more time to this already uncomfortable car ride.

The silence stretches, filled only by the sound that grates on my nerves until I relent and buckle my seatbelt. I can feel his gaze on me, hopeful yet hesitant, waiting for a sign of forgiveness I'm not ready to give.

"Look, I know I might not have chosen the best way to express myself earlier," he adds, the words heavy with a sincerity that breaks through my resolve.

"I don't like to be yelled at," I finally say, my voice light in the quietness of his car. If he put on some music, my anxiety might settle down. "Or bullied."

When I look at him, his face is the sincerest I've ever seen. His softness makes him more attractive, as it eases the stress lines on his skin.

"You might be used to getting your way or having people bow down to you because of who you are, but not me. I won't. I don't acquiesce to strangers, least of all pompous or rude ones."

He said his peace, which is still not an apology, so it's time I said mine. I don't need this job. Flattered as I am, I'm still not sure what I am doing in his car.

His light chuckle breaks the tension, and I study his profile when he looks over his shoulder to check for clearance. He's ruggedly handsome, his blonde hair wavy in all the right places. It seems he gets three-hundred-dollar haircuts because of how perfectly messed up it is. Not to mention a shadow of a beard that defines his sharp jawline.

He's older than me, obviously, by nine years when I looked him up the day we left the open audition. Even with the considerable age difference, Lily calls me an old soul. Little does she know I've lived three lives already, four if I count my one in New York.

"It's what I like about you, Isla. You don't see me as everyone else. Tony award-winning playwright, acclaimed thespian, and writer . . . I suspect you see an ill-tempered, hot-headed casting director that—"

"Yes, all the above."

It's my turn to interrupt him. Seeing the corners of his mouth go down lets me know he hates it as much as I do when he does it to me. Good, I'll have to keep that in mind.

"To be fair, I had no idea who you were. I had to look you up."

There, that should put a soundly dent into his enormous ego. Those corners fall even deeper, and I look away, out the window, feeling slightly victorious. Usually, I don't like confrontation, but I learned from Dani that you must bully a bully to put them in their place—something she does a little too much, which is one of many things I love about her.

The silence resumes as we crawl toward his theater. I'm so glad he picked me up, as he probably wouldn't have believed this delay if he weren't experiencing it for himself. I clutch my bag in my lap, my finger tracing the seam as a distraction for texting Lily to see if she's still there.

"Did my friend, Lily, get a part?"

I turn to face him when I ask. His eyes flicker to mine briefly before returning to traffic.

"The person you are blackmailing me with?"

His tone takes a sharp edge, implying he doesn't like what I did. Nor do I. I shouldn't have done it, yet I wanted leverage over him that day.

"I'm sorry for that. I don't want to steal away her chances to get a part on her own. That was unfair of me."

"Why did you do it?" His sudden curiosity surprises me as if he genuinely wants to know.

"To spite you."

A few long seconds pass, and then another light chuckle emits from him.

"I respect your candor. It's refreshing. You're not from here, are you?"

Usually, my apparent Midwest accent is what gives it away, most people say. It's surprising that he asks, given all the actors and actresses he sees auditioning for his cast.

"I'm from a small town in Colorado."

I wait for the usual slight that comes from people here.

"Colorado, huh? That's a long way from here. Bet it was quite the adjustment moving to the city."

Instead of the expected condescension, his response surprises me. His tone is devoid of mockery, a genuine interest taking place. It's a welcome change from the usual reactions I've encountered since moving here, where my background seems more of a novelty or, worse, a point of ridicule asking what a small-town cowgirl is doing in the big city.

"Yes, it was . . . is," I correct myself, admitting that I'm still navigating the complexities of city life. "Everything moves so fast here. People are very rude, and it's much louder than I'm used to."

He nods, a thoughtful expression crossing his face.

"I can imagine. But it seems like you're making your mark despite the challenges."

The compliment, unexpected as it is, warms me slightly, bridging the gap our earlier altercation had widened. It's a reminder that beneath the hustle of the city, the auditions, and the occasional missteps, there's room for genuine connections, even with those I least expected. Similar to my unexpected meeting with Gabe, who's only been friendly and upstanding.

"And you? Are you from here?"

A strange look wrinkles across his face before disappearing.

"I forget you don't know me nor my family. But yes, my lineage can be found in this city."

I didn't dive deep into his so-called lineage. I briefly looked him up before Anna whimpered to go outside, and I needed to start my night routine.

"Ah, then you can tell me all the great restaurants I need to try and places I need to see."

When we first arrived, I had a long list of touristy things that I crossed off with my parents. It was one of the best times of my life with them.

"There are hidden gems in the city that shouldn't be missed, and they're off the usual tourist track. I could show you them if you're interested."

The offer hangs in the air, both generous and sudden. My initial reaction is immediate hesitation.

"Oh, that sounds intriguing," I respond, keeping a neutral tone.

The idea of discovering secret corners of the city with Lily is appealing. His sudden interest sends a ripple of caution through me. We've just met, and even that's been tumultuous.

He senses my hesitance and adds, "Only if you're comfortable, of course. It's just a thought."

Internally, I'm wrestling with the decision. His offer is generous—a chance to see the city through the eyes of a local, someone who knows it beyond the surface shine. Yet, what are his intentions? Is this just a friendly gesture he offers to everyone? Or something more? The uncertainty of his motives and the vulnerability of being a newcomer coils tightly within me.

"I'll think about it."

I opt for a non-committal response that buys me time to weigh the risks against the potential fun.

"Of course. Let's leave it open then. If you ever feel like exploring, you know who to call."

He backs off, which makes me feel like I can breathe again. The rest of the car ride is quiet, save for the music he finally puts on. I'd expected something like Showtunes or Broadway musical numbers, but I was pleasantly surprised when he puts on a pop station, which is the music I listen to.

It instantly settles my anxiety, and my hand slips from the door handle, which doesn't go unobserved from him. By the time we pull up to the theater, the usual twenty-minute car ride has doubled. He tosses the keys at some valet who is scrambling to catch them.

Travis moves swiftly, reaching out to hold my door open—an action that feels a bit overdone since I'm perfectly capable of managing it myself. Just as I'm about to step out of the car, his hand gently grasps my elbow. The warmth of his palm seeps into my skin and sparks an electric jolt between us. In that fleeting instant, my surprise is mirrored by the sudden widening of his eyes, a silent acknowledgment of the unexpected connection.

I quicken my step to move out of his reach, trying to process what that means. Sure, he's attractive. I'd have to be blind not to see that. I've seen plenty of great-looking guys my age or even a little older than me. Social media is crawling with them. That's all one-dimensional.

Having a hot one in the flesh touching me and sending sensations through my body is another thing. One I like and could have me looking at him in a different light. One where we are going to one of those hidden gems restaurants, sharing dinner and gazing out at the city lights right before he kisses me.

"Everything okay?"

His sudden voice near my ear startles me out of my romantic fantasy, and I speed walk to the theater door to throw it open. I don't care how he interprets my actions as I keep up the pace to the next set of doors, where callbacks are underway by the noise seeping into the lobby. I throw open the doors to the auditorium and stop short, marveling. The stage has been transformed into a stark and deeply evocative apartment.

"This is Marcella's world," Travis murmurs behind me, his shoulder brushing my back as he leans closer to explain the obvious, which needs no explanation. It instantly transports me back to my mom's house. The dark and dank set with low lighting captures the essence of my childhood—a world suspended by my monochromatic past and my vibrant future.

The stage resembles the life of a performer whose days of glory have long since faded. The walls, painted in a peeling, muted gray, suggest the passage of time and the weariness that comes with it. Sparse furnishings—a worn wooden table, a single rickety chair, and an old, freestanding mirror with a slightly tarnished frame—populate the space, each telling stories of happier times.

In the corner is a small bed with a thin mattress on a rusted iron frame, so similar to the one where my mother's boyfriend would find me in the middle of the night that a quiet gasp escapes my lips. The bars would press into my back as his weight took hold, staring up at the ceiling, transporting myself to another place until it was over. My hand covers my mouth, holding back the tears that instantly take me back to the helpless little girl who called out for her mom, only to find her strung out on the couch, sitting across from the flickering TV.

A small, makeshift bar stands center stage under a solitary spotlight that casts an elongated shadow. It's here that the audience finds an actress, who I assumed he cast as Marcella in her poignant solitude. The bar is cluttered with an array of bottles, their labels worn and faded, among them a single, open bottle of wine and a dirty ashtray that cradles an unlit cigar. The bottles are familiar.

The cigar is different from the cigarettes I was used to buying for my mom, but this actress isn't strung out. She isn't slumped over the table, drool hanging from her mouth with her eyes glazed over. No, this actress is playing the part all wrong. Her posture is too straight, and her hands are too graceful, reminiscent of a ballerina. Her legs aren't splayed in an open invitation for sex in exchange for whoever will buy her a hit. This actress has never seen the character she's portraying—lucky her.

A circus poster flutters gently above the set, suspended and slightly off-center, illuminated by a soft, amber light. The vibrant and colorful poster depicts Marcella in her prime, contrasting the figure she cuts on the stage below. Its presence serves as a haunting reminder of her past, a ghostly echo of the applause and adoration that once defined her existence. It's how I felt on the rare occasion of seeing an old photo of my mom when she was young, hopeful, and with her whole life ahead of her.

The ambiance of the set is enriched by a subtle soundscape that plays in the background—a mix of distant laughter, the soft hum of circus life, and the occasional mournful note of a forgotten melody. These sounds weave through the scene, bridging the gap between Marcella's isolated world and the bustling life that continues unabated outside her door.

As the actress recites her lines, drawing in the fellow auditions in the audience into Marcella's reality, there's a richness that's missing—a haunting and longing for what used to be and what could have been. Her delivery is mechanical when she should be immersed in a world where the boundaries between the past and the present blur. Where joy and sorrow entwine, the laughter and adoration from the crowd fade, leaving shadows and echoes in its wake.

My hand falls away, my head shakes, and I slowly proceed down the aisle in disbelief at how wrong she's portraying Marcella. Travis, a shadow behind me, follows closely, and the weight of his stare felt on me as I near the front row.

"What is it, Isla?"

His serious tone suggests that he knows something. He may feel what I'm feeling, but he knows this is not how her story should be told.

"What are you feeling?"

I cast him the briefest glance, unwilling to take my eyes off the actress reciting the lines and adding inflection in all the wrong parts. Even without my formal training, I know this will not work. Surely, he thinks the same thing, feels it in his soul that this isn't the right actress.

"Tell me what you are thinking. I see it on your face, and I must know."

The urgency in his voice is unmistakable. It's as if he's equally mesmerized by me as I am with her, for very different reasons, I assume.

"You know something, Isla. Please share it with me."

She finishes the part when the house lights rise and blind everything in the room. The assistant I saw scurrying around the other day is directing people around the stage, starting to change the set when I raise my hand, reaching for the stage, not wanting to move on from the scene as quickly as they are.

"It's not right."

I shake my head, looking up into his intense blue eyes. Lines crease his forehead, and the muscle in his jaw twitches. The urgency from before hangs from his face.

"Tell me what's not right?" His hand cups my elbow again, and I swallow the spark between us. "Show me."

The sincerity in his words, the faith he's putting in me, in this moment to climb the stairs and do it justice, is overwhelming. The nervousness that plagues me around him is dormant by my desire to portray Marcella as I would my mom—devastated by a lifetime of disappointment. She is heartbroken over being used by everyone who comes into her life—destroyed by endless drug and alcohol abuse.

I look away from him, back to the set transforming into another scene when Travis's long whistle rings across the room. He's barking orders to return to the previous set, to lower the lights to a single spotlight on the chair by the bar and the amber light on the poster. It's only a moment before his staff scrambles to follow his command, to bring it back and make it darker and more vacant than before.

"Show me, please."

His whisper matches the sudden dark ambiance, the intensity unmistakable as he snaps his fingers for a script to appear from a cast member down the row from us. I barely register the feel of the rolled-up paper in my hand as I climb the steps.

His hand is still firmly on my arm as I ascend until I'm out of reach, and he's forced to let go. Walking across the slanted stage toward the bright light, I gaze at the poster. Of Marcella in her heyday, the time when she was most adored and appreciated by friends and strangers alike.

I channel her as I reach the edge of the spotlight, choosing to start the scene there in the darkness. A voice in the void leaves the audience wondering what she looks like now. Does she still look like that radiant woman in the poster? Does she still have her youth and vitality?

The lines flow out of me, black and haunting, like the rest of the stage, until I emerge from the shadows. I pause, the bright lights casting upon me as I sink into my mom's form. Eyes unfocused, shoulders slumped and leading with my hips, or in my mother's case, her beer gut.

I grip my hair, pulling it in a panic away from my face and looking at it as if it's the enemy and not the deprivation of my life. My physical responses match the written words, only to be heightened by the pauses, inflections, and lowering of my voice to a whisper.

When I collapse onto the chair, legs splayed like hers, my blouse hanging carelessly from a shoulder, and my hand still gripping my hair, I stop and look around the room. Everything about this scene matters, from my portrayal of Marcella to the deep-seated emotions that only me and the scriptwriter feel in unison.

I don't worry about getting it right, making an embarrassment of myself, or proving anything to Travis. I've experienced this scene more times than I can count from an outside perspective. It's only fitting that I experience it from her perspective.

With the final word spoken, my hand long since removed from my hair, grinding out the cigar instead, I stare into the dark abyss as my mom did at that damn flickering TV. It's so cathartic, far better than all the years of therapy combined, to finally see and feel what my mom did—I vow then and there never to become her.

A thunderous wave of applause and cheering welcomes me as the lights gradually brighten. Travis's assistant dabs at her cheeks, wiping away tears, while I finally spot Lily in the back of the theater with her mouth hanging open in utter shock.

When Travis joins me on stage, his response is somewhere between smug and stunned. Without warning, he yanks me from my chair and clutches me in his arms to spin me around. My breath catches as my feet are swept off the stage, twirling to where I'm forced to look at him as a focal point to keep from getting sick.

"Put me down."

I clutch at his shoulders, the difference in size apparent with how weightless I feel in his arms. He senses my discomfort and immediately sets me down, the room still spinning as I reach for the back of the chair to steady myself.

"This is our lead," he announces to the room.

Another round of applause goes up while the actress who did the first performance runs up the aisle to disappear out the door. Guilt gnaws at my insides for costing her the part, which I will apologize for later. My cheeks flush with his announcement, and I do a little curtsy before leaving the stage to catch up with Lily, who's waiting at the bottom of the stairs.

"Shut up with that performance."

She grabs me in an overly tight hug before slinging her arm around my shoulders as we walk away.

"Are you lying to me? You said you never wanted to be an actress, but what was that?"

"I don't know, Lil. I just walked in, and everything felt off. I just saw it differently, and when he asked, I told him that."

My shoulder raises in doubt as I relay how everything happened.

"I didn't expect to take over. It just sort of came out of me. Like I could relate to this character and saw her in a different light."

"It's a sign."

Her expression changes into thoughtful contemplation.

"Like an opportunity from the universe that you're meant to do this instead of fashion school. This seems easy, whereas you seem to struggle at school."

I don't like where this is headed. I'm not even sure I can take the lead role. It's more than flattering to be seen like that, and the applause could feed anyone's ego. Perhaps this is how Travis always feels, why he has such a big head with all his accomplishments. I feel as if I'm floating on air. Is this how it feels to be him all the time? If so, it makes sense why he is the way he is.

"Regarding school being difficult, I think the best things in life take hard work to achieve. I'm not giving up on school for this pipe dream."

Her frown is instant, and a new kind of guilt washes over me when she removes her arm from my shoulders. I reach for her hand, hold it in mine, and give it a playful swing.

"Lil, I'm sorry. That was rude. I just meant my parents paid, *are paying,* a lot of money for that school and for me to be here. I can't walk away from that because I happened to have one good reading. You know that. Look at how many auditions you nailed and didn't get the part. I got this one, but it doesn't mean I'll be any good. I could cause the play to be a total flop. It's a lot of pressure and something I'm not sure I'm cut out for."

Her expression softens as she listens, her initial disappointment giving way to understanding. She squeezes my hand in response, her eyes sparking with the usual energy that is her essence.

"You're right. School is important, and it's a huge investment by your parents. It's just hard not to get excited for you. Seeing you up there, shining, it felt like everything clicked into place. But hey, it's not like you must decide everything right now. This could be a one-time thing, a story to tell. Or, who knows, maybe you'll find a way to balance both. Acting could become a hobby, a passion project alongside your studies."

Her smile encourages me when they call her name for a scene of her own.

"You're right, Lil. Maybe I'm overthinking this. It doesn't have to be all or nothing. And who knows? This experience might even enrich my perspective in ways I haven't imagined."

Lily nods, her arm returning to my shoulders in a quick side hug.

"Exactly! And remember, whatever decision you make, I'm here for you. Now wish me luck so I can kill it like you did."

"Break a leg," I call after her when she releases me in a hurry to run down the aisle toward the steps.

My mind is confused mush, both wanting and not wanting this role as my gaze darts from Lily to Travis and back. Luckily, he's forgotten me for now, so I can return to the emotional support person I am for her and that she is for me. Collapsing into an aisle seat, I mentally rattle through my strenuous school schedule and wonder how in the world I'll add lead in a play to the mix.

To quote one of my favorite movies, "I'll think about it tomorrow."

5

"Can you believe this fabric?" Gabe's voice draws my attention as I approach him. He's standing amid the opulence of the menswear, and he's supposed to be fitted for a new tuxedo rather than the soft woolen suit jacket draped over one arm. The fabric is a deep navy, which would complement his skin tone. It's clear that the piece would need to be tailored to accentuate the broad set of his shoulders and the narrow trim of his waist.

"Feels like it's worth every penny," he says, his fingers appreciating the delicate material.

I can't help but smile at his appreciation for the garments in this expensive establishment. My fingers dance over the material, giving a low hum as the fabric is coarser than I'd prefer, but then again, I'd never wear a cashmere and wool blend suit.

"It's beautiful," I reply, but a tremor in my voice gives away the storm of thoughts swirling in my mind. "You'd look great in it."

He glances over, his gaze softening when he sees the slight crease in my brow.

"I make everything look great, but that's beside the point." His quick wit and easy charm, paired with that accent, make him more attractive. Too bad for me, he's not into women. "What's on your mind, Isla? You seem miles away."

I hesitate for a breath, then spill the news burning a worrisome hole in my stomach.

"I've been offered the lead role in that play," I admit, watching his reaction closely before continuing. "You know, the one I told you about."

If he's not supportive, I wouldn't share anything else. But if he is, I'll share all my thoughts and worries, as I need someone more impartial than Lily. She's insisted I take the part, drop out of school, and not tell my parents. All that gives me major anxiety, especially considering the level of deception I'd have to put everyone through to make that happen. His eyes light up, reflecting the soft glow of the boutique's chandeliers.

"Isla, that's incredible! Congratulations!" His suit, momentarily forgotten, hangs loosely in his grip. "But you look worried. What is it? Talk to me."

I take a deep breath, the scent of new fabric and leather from the surrounding racks filling my senses.

"It's . . . well, it's a huge opportunity, but it's also a huge commitment. And the timing. It couldn't be worse. With school and my coursework, it's already a lot to juggle. And the director, or playwright, he's pretty demanding. He wants only the best for his play, and I get it. But how am I the best when I don't have any experience? I'm a complete amateur. And I'm scared to add anything more to my already overflowing plate, especially something as big as this. Not to mention my schooling and taking care of Anna. Not that she's a lot, she isn't, but I love her so much and feel as if I'm neglecting her with the lack of time I spend with her."

Gabe nods, his understanding clear in the quiet furrow of

his brow. He's a picture of elegance, even in his casual consideration of gala attire—a crisp white shirt open at the collar, sleeves rolled up to the elbow, and dark jeans that speak of sophistication to offset his Hermes belt and loafers.

"It's a tough call and a great honor to be talented enough at both."

He returns the suit to the rack as I glance at a silk tie that would look great with what he just put back.

"You'll have to weigh it out. Can you give the play the energy it deserves without compromising your designs? Before answering that, do you even want both?"

"I don't know."

My gaze drifting to the people milling about, the hushed rustle of garments, and the quiet clink of hangers.

"On the one hand, I want to do the play. I mean, come on, even I know it's a big deal. I'd be a fool to pass up this opportunity. I might never get it again. And after reading the script, I adore the character. I relate to her on so many levels. But on the other, I'm already struggling with school. I want to do my best, but the competition is legit. Some very talented students go to Parsons, making me think I don't stand a chance compared to them. It's far harder than I thought. I just want to make the right choice."

Gabe steps closer, his presence reassuring when he touches my arm to comfort me.

"Isla, I was first in my class all through secondary school and university with barely any effort. Then I got into medical school, and others were smarter than me."

I do little to hide my surprise, as being a brain doctor to kids means he must be hella smart. A smugness overtakes his features, and he releases my arm to straighten one of his rolled cuffs.

"I didn't say there were many, but a few, and suddenly, I had to work harder than I ever had. Math and science were instinctual, gravitas if you will."

His careless shrug speaks to his arrogance and reminds me of Travis's confidence, which both men possess for different reasons.

"However, doctors didn't select me to work alongside them on some of the most difficult cases. I couldn't figure out why, so I started studying, ensuring I knew the answers to everything they asked, and was assuredly the first one to answer, to beat out those I felt were besting me."

"That doesn't make any sense, though. If you surpass them by putting in the hard work, you should get the most challenging cases."

Defending him comes naturally until he leans closer, lowering his voice to where I can smell the mint on his breath when a couple walks by.

"No, I shouldn't have because my bedside manner was deplorable. Sure, I know the best way to peel back a face to preserve as many capillaries as possible."

"Gross."

I wrinkle my nose. The thought of what he does is impressive but makes me queasy.

"But that doesn't matter when you must convince the parents to trust their precious child in my hands to repair or save what I can. And the results don't always turn out positively, which has to be relayed delicately."

I lean against the rack, truly admiring this man's actions.

"I had to work very hard to change that, and slowly, I turned it around to where I'm being referred to as the top surgeon because of my caring disposition."

"Wow, that's amazing, Gabe. What you do is amazing. I could never—"

"You will," he assures me, his confidence enveloping me just as surely as the fine clothes envelop the mannequins. "You're just as determined as I am. The fact that you are worrying about wanting to do them well speaks to that. A lesser person wouldn't care. They would run the risk of doing both and possibly burning out."

I rub my forehead, the persistent headache living there as I've stalled all week in returning to rehearsals with Lily and avoiding the unanswered calls and messages from Travis.

"Come here, love."

Gabe's skilled and highly insured hands wrap around my arms to draw me into an embrace, one I didn't know I needed until the crisp white shirt bathed in his signature cologne envelops me. I close my eyes, wrap my arms around his waist, and thank the universe that we met in the bookcase two Saturdays ago.

"Whatever you choose, it'll be the right path for you. And as for your little dog, get her a pet sitter. My colleague does it for his animals, so I can give you a great recommendation."

His deep voice rumbles against my cheek as I soak in the security I feel in his hug. For the briefest of moments, it reminds me of my parents and not just because they are all stylish gay men. A comment that made Lily laugh when I told her about meeting him at the bookstore. It's his gentle nature, his calm effect on me, and our respect for each other.

"And I expect front-row seats to the opening performance," he says, moving me away from his chest while still cupping my arms. "Now, let's go see about that tuxedo so I can schmooze the donors at the gala into giving my department more money."

His belief in me is a lighthouse in a sea of doubt as I follow him to the back of the boutique in search of evening attire. With careful planning, I can weave both opportunities into the tapestry of my days and get a pet sitter for Anna, but will I fall behind in my coursework?

My text messages and calls to Lily remain unanswered when I leave the apartment, catch the subway, and walk toward the theater, convinced she's at practice. Our schedules have been a blur, with me up and out the door for school early in the morning and her at rehearsals late into the night. We have been missing each other to the point that the only evidence that we live in the same place is her dirty dishes sitting in the kitchen sink that I swiftly rinse and put in the dishwasher.

Bundling up the lapels of my coat against the chilly wind, I yank on the theater door, expecting the loudness of the stage to welcome me. It doesn't. The place is eerily quiet for a Friday afternoon, drawing me deeper into the foyer until the door thuds closed behind me. There is no one in sight. As much as my inner voice sends a caution signal, I ignore it, caving to my curiosity to check the stage to be sure it's vacant before turning around and making the trek back home.

Pushing through the double doors, I step into a world transformed. A theater stage magically reimagined into a vivid circus from a bygone era. The tired and aging apartment is gone, and the stage now bursts with an iridescent glow, strings of golden lights crisscrossing overhead, mimicking a starlit sky. Rich, red velvet drapes cascade from the wings, the lush fabric parting to reveal a scene teeming with bygone glamour.

At center stage, a grand carousel horse, painted in a kaleidoscope of colors, stands frozen mid-gallop. Its poles are fashioned with shimmering beads and sparkling gems that catch and reflect the light. A trapeze hangs above, the bar glistening like a sliver of moon, awaiting the graceful grasp of a performer. To one side, a mock big top tent billows, its stripes of crimson and white stretching upwards, evoking the dizzying height and grandeur of the circus's once pinnacle of success.

The sawdust and earth that once might have blanketed the ground are now represented by a canvas of intricate patterns, meticulously painted to give the illusion of texture and depth. Props are scattered artfully around crystal balls that seem to hold swirling mists of glitter within, feathered headdresses that whisper of dancing girls, and hoops adorned with flowers and ribbons, promising the elegance of acrobatic feats.

Even the air seems charged with an electric buzz, the imagined sounds of calliope music and the roar of an invisible crowd filling the space, transporting me to Marcella's heyday when she was the jewel in the circus crown. The stage is set not just for a play but for a time travel to the golden age of circus, an era of enchantment and wonder. All that is missing is the ringmaster leading the elephants into the ring, where the trunk joins the tail in a trail of gray tonnage.

"Isla?"

The surprised word travels across the silent seats, standing as vessels to carry the audition to another time when magic and showmanship reign supreme. Travis stands, sauntering toward me while worry etches across his face, the lines cutting deep enough to make him look older than his age.

"Hi."

I wave, awkward as I feel, and surprisingly, he waves back. Gone is the smug arrogance from that day he picked me up from school, replaced with an uncertainty that raises my curiosity again.

"Um, why? Why are you here?"

The tenor in his voice is uncharacteristic yet matches how he looks. His hair is disheveled, purplish hues cling to his under eyes, and redness to his cheeks and nose makes me wonder if he's in here drinking alone.

"I don't know exactly."

I mash my lips together, sliding the lip gloss around as a ripple of nervousness overtakes my body. After discussing it with Gabe, who is quickly becoming the voice of reason in my world, he advised me to talk to Travis directly to fully understand the role, schedule, and commitment before deciding. He also didn't like the idea of keeping it from my parents, yet offered advice to tell them only after I decided. His warning was out of concern that I'd let others influence my decision as I seemed to be a people pleaser. Little does he know how true that comment is.

"I tried to reach out. Called and texted. Myself even." He starts walking down a row toward me, motivating me to walk down the aisle to join him. "I usually don't do that."

I ignore his humbling comment, even though it makes me chuckle internally that he would feel it's such a bother to do things like that himself.

"I know." My hands twist together in front of me, the decision I've put off only making it worse the longer I drag this out. "I don't think I want to be in your play."

Saying the words out loud is scary. The instant they are out, I expect to feel relief. But when I glance at the colorful stage, regret takes its place instead.

"I figured when you never came back."

When my gaze returns to his, those deep blue eyes are asking more than what he's saying. A sliver of vulnerability calls to me as he stands a few feet away, with two seats between us.

"It's a disaster anyway."

He runs a shaky hand through his hair, releasing a frustrated sigh at the same time.

"Why is that?"

I tilt my head, wanting more of that vulnerability, craving to see a side of him that no one else gets. It's the same one I saw in the car, but a deeper version of that now.

"With this set, it's stunning. The imagery alone—"

"Isla, don't. I know when it's a crap set and a crap play. I took too many chances with this one. New assistants, inexperienced cast, and even amateur set designers. The costumes are even worse. They came in today. They're in the back and . . ."

He collapses into a seat, dragging a long leg up to plant his polished dress shoe on the back of the chair in front of him.

"Why are you here?"

Seeing him low and dejected calls to me, something I relate to heavily in all the times I've been disappointed by life. Sour lemons don't always make the best lemonade. Sometimes, they are just sour lemons.

"I wanted to tell you my decision in person. For some reason, I felt I owed it to you."

His chuckle is harsh and bitter, echoing across the empty theater like a chorus of cynical audience goers, ready to boo his most recent risk-taking play. I don't like it. I don't like the sound of it. I don't like how he looks doing it.

"You owe me nothing."

His eyes roam the stage before him, from the painted canvas crossing the floor over the columns painted as tent poles to the flashing sign claiming to be the greatest show on earth hanging from the ceiling. I sink into the chair next to him, preferring if there was an empty one between us but he didn't leave me that chance when he collapsed into his.

My fingers curl around my bag, sitting snugly in my lap as I gaze at the elaborate set. I find it marvelous and not crap, as he said.

I lick my lips and clear my throat before saying, "I made costumes for my Aunt Molli's plays. It was only supposed to be for the Christmas pageant, which is a big deal for the Catholic Church back home. You know the deal, Joseph and Mary. . ."

I feel his eyes on me, but I remain looking forward at the set.

"I'm an atheist."

A brief smile draws my lips apart. Of course, he's not religious. Most people aren't these days.

"Well, I'm sure even atheists know the story of Jesus. I designed costumes for the first family, the three kings, and I don't know how many shepherds, angels, and animals I made. The budget was tight. Nothing like this." I wave a hand toward the stage. His eyes follow when I steal a glimpse at him. "It took me months to find decent fabric and sew the costumes with as much cheap glitter and sequin gold I could find."

I expect him to interrupt or rush me along in his usual impatience, but he does neither of those things, choosing to listen, which is surprising.

"High school in the morning, homework at lunch, then nights and weekends spent working on the costumes all for one night. Two services. Everything was perfect. Then a blizzard hit. Half the cast couldn't make it, but I was steaming all the pieces to ensure they would look magnificent. They live-streamed it for those homebound for the first time in the church's history. The pageant got record tithes that year, and every year since, consequently, my budget grew."

I look at him, the proximity of his body to mine, and that spark that lies dormant between us is firing up again. Wanting to finish my story before he rushes me out or gets frustrated and barks at me, I shove the attraction aside.

"I'd like to think my costumes made the difference that year, but they didn't. They were only a piece of the pageant that made it successful. People didn't see one piece over another. They saw the story of Christ's birth told in the most beautiful way possible. That's what you need to do, Travis. Get people to see the beauty in your play being told through the eyes of Marcella."

A cynical snort rises from him. It must have been a very tough week if he's this resounded to it being a complete failure before it's even begun. Regardless, I press on.

"Make them feel her anguish at being forgotten, becoming irrelevant as she ages, mourn for what she's lost, and root for her to find happiness before she dies. If you can do that, then an inexperienced cast, crappy set, and new assistants fade away. You're too focused on the pieces and not the play. Don't do what I did. Do what the parishioners saw. Give them what they are paying for. Marcella's story."

Travis is still, his breath hitched as the vision of what could be forms from the picture I painted. The stage set for Marcella's tale becomes a backdrop to the real drama unfolding within him and his view of the play in its current state. For a moment, we are no longer just a playwright and a denied cast member. We are two people bound by the power of a story waiting to be told. His silence is a canvas stretching across the room, and I fill it with conviction.

"Give them Marcella's heart, her pain, her hope. That's what they're here for. That's what they'll remember," I finish, my voice a gentle yet fervent whisper, willing him to see my vision.

The shimmer in his eyes tells me he truly hears me. Emotion wells up, and for a heartbeat, the barriers to his expectations of the play seem to crumble, speaking to something deeper in him than worries of failure and embarrassment. In his eyes, I see the dreamer, the artist, the man who wants to create something unforgettable in this unique play he wrote that I'm romanticizing now.

"You have a way with words, Isla," he says quietly, his voice deeper with emotion as the shimmer subsides from his eyes. And you're right. It's about the story of Marcella, not me. Thank you for reminding me."

His gaze drops to my lips briefly, then rises to my eyes. The fire on a slow simmer between us grows hotter the longer we sit, sharing the same dream for his play.

"It's why I wanted you in the first place. When you were on stage, reciting my lines, you were her and I was transfixed. I wish you could see what I see. If you could, you'd be as awe-struck as I am now."

I feel my heart skip a beat at his words, my breath catching in my throat. The intensity of his gaze is electrifying and unnerving, as if he is peering into the depths of my soul and looking for Marcella in me. There's a momentary pause between us, the air thick with unspoken desire and unfulfilled dreams.

"I . . . I don't know what to say."

Goosebumps break out over my skin, not from the chilly theater but from him leaning closer to where his hand touches my arm. That undeniable fire is burning out of control within me. I know the look of men when they want me. I have seen it far too many times in my eighteen years. This time, it's fully reciprocated, eagerly waiting for him to dissolve the space between us and kiss me as I dreamed of the night I killed the open audition.

Without breaking eye contact, his hand raises to touch my cheek, the back of his hand caressing my skin and leaving a trail of sensation in its wake. I'm mesmerized by the intimacy of the action, the gentleness in his touch, and the longing in his stare.

"Say you'll do it. Say you'll bring her to life, captivate the audience with her story the way you captivate me now." His knuckles continue stroking my skin while inching closer. "Your skin is so soft. Fragile like a porcelain doll."

Tantalizing. His words, his expression, and his touch. All meant to seduce me into accepting, and I would if it weren't for needing a few concessions before accepting.

"Travis?"

His fingers slide across my skin, capturing my chin as he stares at my mouth as if wanting to see the words he so dearly desires exit my lips.

"Yes, Isla?"

"School first always. Then rehearsals."

My breath mixes with his. The mingling of minds being negotiated as we speak, our bodies awaiting another negotiation—his place or mine. His touch is a whisper against my skin, and we're suspended in a space for a moment. The air is thick with anticipation, the potential of what could be, what we could create together, both on stage and beyond.

"Yes, of course. Rehearsals after class. We'll manage."

His voice is a soft tenor that resonates with the thrum of my pulse. His eyes flicker to mine, then back to my lips as his thumb swipes across the bottom one, pulling them slightly apart in expectation. I force a small smile, pulling my lips out of his touch, and watch the edges of his mouth curl downward.

Control. It's apparent he likes it, demands it from others, and wants everyone to bend to his will. I can't do that. It will sometimes be necessary, but if this turns into something more than just being my playwright, he'll have to see us as equals. It won't work any other way.

"I'll do it but my way. I retain creative control over how I play her."

My demand draws his gaze back to mine, and he struggles with the compromise he must make for this to work. When the silence stretches between us, I encircle his wrist in my hand, drag it off, and lean back in my chair. With the moment's intensity broken, he blinks rapidly, composing himself and dropping that shield over his vulnerability. Once he accepts my terms, my word is a vow to honor the role and trust he's placed in me.

The moment is delicate, a fragile truce between ambition and the undeniable attraction we both try to navigate. It's a dance as intricate as any choreography on stage, each step measured, each breath a beat in our shared rhythm.

"Thank you, Isla," he whispers, with a curt nod and mirroring my action of sitting back in his seat. "For believing in the play, in Marcella, in me. It's going to be an extraordinary journey."

The rehearsal schedule, the late nights, the lines, and the directions will all come soon enough. But in this moment, there's a sense of beginning, a prelude to creation that feels both exhilarating and daunting.

"Let's make something beautiful, Travis."

6

_____

"Ugh, give me a minute."

I rise from the table cluttered with bottles of alcohol and the fake cigar sitting in the ashtray, which will be replaced with a real one on opening night. Walking away from the stage, away from the hot lights and demanding Travis, I yawn, twist my neck from side to side, eliciting unexpected pops, and stretch my back.

The hours have been longer today than usual, as I didn't have class, and Travis insists on doubling up on rehearsals to maximize production time. In my weary state, the lines are coming slower, with less intention, and sometimes without thought—all unacceptable to him. And to me, after being here over twelve hours, I couldn't care less. All I want is food, my bed, and Anna, but not necessarily in that order. His footsteps are heavy as they pound toward me, his hands plant on my shoulders and spin me around to face him.

"Isla, we've been through this repeatedly, and you keep missing your mark."

Rehearsals have been grueling, and it's only been the first week. Lily has been over the moon with me accepting the lead, pretending I'm already a starlet, and snapping fake pictures with her fingers whenever I walk into the apartment. It made me laugh the first few times, but now it's growing annoying, especially since I'm always exhausted.

I've barely stayed awake in class, used the time in the car he sends for me to nap, catch up on a late assignment, or wolf down something from the vending machine to counter the longer hours that go late into the night at his theater.

Exasperated, I glare at him.

"I need a break, Travis. You can't keep pushing me like this. Everyone else has been dismissed, yet you keep me here, knowing I have class in the morning. It's been two very long days back-to-back, and I'm dead tired."

His hand drops from my shoulders, an unhappy expression appearing on his now permanently shadowy bearded face, a sign of the long hours he's also putting in.

"Turn around."

"What?"

"Turn around, please."

Not in the mood for whatever else he will throw at me, I acquiesce and turn around to appease him. Clearly, I don't understand what standing with my back to him has to do with my rant until his hand plants back on my shoulders. This time is different. His fingers gently start to rub at my fatigued muscles, catching on a knot or two and working through it as I close my eyes and moan my appreciation.

"I know you're tired." His voice softens near my ear, the edge of frustration smoothed away by concern. "But Marcella's posture and how she carries herself are crucial to who she is. The weight of her world rests on her shoulders, just as yours does now. Her slouch is causing all these tense muscles, and it's even throwing off your gate when you amble across the stage."

I let out a long breath, feeling the strain in my back unravel.

"I understand that, but I'm only human, Travis. I can't become her if I'm running on empty."

There's a pause, and I sense him considering my words when his hands still. Too tired to care anymore, I lean into him, dispensing some of my weight onto him in a vague attempt to relinquish some of the exhaustion overtaking my body. Without hesitation, a muscular forearm slides across my collarbones, drawing me closer and allowing me to rest my weary head against his chest. I don't read anything into it. Aside from that near kiss last Friday night, he's been a perfect gentleman, even when we have been alone, such as tonight.

"I sometimes forget you're doing more than any of the others, juggling school and this play. I'll ease up a bit so we can find you some balance."

The tension doesn't just leave my shoulders but also the air around us when his arm clenches me closer to him while his fingertips tickle up my arm. My eyes sting, my stomach growls, and every part of my body aches for a hot bath and a good night's sleep. If I weren't so exhausted, I'd make all sorts of assumptions about if he's trying to make a move on me right now.

"Thank you," I whisper, grateful not only for the reprieve but for his acknowledgment of my efforts.

"Of course."

His fingers trace light patterns up my arm, and a soothing sensation washes over my tired body, the kind of attention that blurs the lines between professional boundaries and the personal connection simmering between us. The steady beat of his heart under my ear is a calming rhythm, a reminder of the human connection we share beyond the roles of director and actress.

"There's nothing I wouldn't do for you. Nothing."

His words are tantalizing, soothing the frayed edges of my irritation with him. We stand in silence, bodies melting together in the most innocent and intimate manner possible. His arm around me feels like a weight against the crazy chaos that has been this week, and I relish the feeling. Rarely have I trusted a man beyond my parents and uncles, yet feeling how I do now, I think I can trust him.

"Well, get some rest, and we'll start again tomorrow after your school lets out."

The nearness, the warmth of his body, and the gentle caress of his fingers stir something within me—a longing for something more than stolen moments of comfort in the shadows of the theater. Yet, the memory of our almost-kiss lingers, a tempting what-if that adds an undercurrent of anticipation to his every touch.

As he steps back, his arm slides away from my body, and his hand lingers on my arm for a moment longer than necessary, almost reluctant to break the connection. I don't move, unwilling to let all the good feelings coursing through me fade as they did last time. If he won't follow through on his unspoken promises and hinted attraction, then I will. The worst he can say is no, and then we'll resume being what we are, director and actress. Or, like in true Broadway fashion, we can have a torrid affair that burns the place down.

"Get some rest," he repeats, his dress shoes clicking on the stage as I turn to see him walking away from me.

The warmth of his touch remains, a ghostly imprint on my skin. The complex blend of gratitude, exhaustion, and budding desire leaves me conflicted yet hopeful that he'll reciprocate if I launch myself at him. What lies ahead is uncertain, but the foundation we're building, one of mutual respect and burgeoning affection, feels like the start of something real, something worth exploring beyond the stage lights and script pages. I do something uncharacteristic of me and completely channel the passionate and fiery young Marcella in her heyday.

"Travis?"

"Yes?"

He spins around, fatigue etched into his features. I dart across the stage, closing the distance between us with swift strides, and then, without a second thought, I launch myself at him. Instinctively, he catches me, hoisting me up as I wrap my legs around his waist and my arms tightly around his neck, initiating the kiss.

Caught in the whirlwind of sudden boldness, he deepens it instantaneously, fueled by the pent-up tension and the unspoken desires that have simmered between us. His hands find a secure hold on my back, anchoring me in place as if afraid I might slip away.

His response is fervent, a mirror to my same urgency. The kiss is a language of its own, speaking volumes of the attraction we've danced around, the chemistry building in looks and half-whispers, now unleashed in the press of lips and the tangle of tongues.

The heat between us builds as my fingers thread through his hair, pulling him nearer, as if I could somehow get closer still. His breath, mingling with mine, is a heady mix that sends a shiver down my spine, igniting that dormant fire that's been waiting to burn.

Eventually, the need for air forces us apart, and he breaks the kiss, foreheads resting together, breaths mingling. Our eyes meet, wide and revealing a mutual surprise at the intensity of our chemistry, a silent question about what comes next hanging in the charged space between us.

This moment, unscripted and raw, marks a turning point. It's an acknowledgment of the undeniable pull between us, a leap into the unknown that neither of us can, nor wants to, walk back from. The realization hits that this is just the beginning, the first step into a journey neither planned but both seem eager to explore.

"I'm twenty-seven, Isla."

"Okay."

In the quiet aftermath of our kiss, with the stage around us forgotten, it's clear that I no longer want to be confined to the roles of director and actress. I've stepped into uncharted territory, guided by my lust and the promise of what lies ahead, ready to navigate this new path with him, wherever it may lead.

"And your employer."

The acknowledgment hangs between us as he removes his forehead from mine, lowers me to my feet, and retains his hold on my waist. It's a reminder of the complexities I'm asking him to navigate. Yet, despite the challenges implied by his words, the chemistry we've just shared feels like it transcends the boundaries of our professional roles and the age gap that lies between us.

"I know," I whisper back, my voice steady despite the rapid beating of my heart.

The gravity of his statement does little to dampen the spark that's been ignited. If anything, it adds a layer of reality to the dreamlike quality of the moment, grounding it in the tangible world with all its potential joys and heartbreak.

His gaze searches mine, looking for hesitation and doubt but finding none. The decision to step beyond the constraints of boss and subordinate appears mutual, made in the silent language of carnal desire and his feverous response when kissing me back. The glances, the touches, and that searing kiss speak louder than words ever could.

"At this moment, here with you, I don't want to be anything other than who I am, Isla."

There's an earnestness in his expression that resonates deep within me. He doesn't want to be the famous playwright or the acclaimed former actor. He wants to be with me in this cold, dark theater at this very late hour.

"And who are we?"

My words are a gentle challenge, a prompt for us both to define this new dynamic still taking shape.

"We're two people who found something unexpected."

His grip tightens, maintaining the intimate closeness that's becoming a sudden necessity rather than a mere desire.

"Something worth exploring, regardless of the complications."

His admission, candid and bold, mirrors my feelings. The roles we've played up until now and the labels we've adhered to seem less significant in the wake of what's unfolding between us. It's a risk, stepping into this unknown, but one that feels increasingly right with every shared look and lingering touch.

As we stand on the precipice of something new—the stage, the empty theater—it feels like the start of something extraordinary, both professionally and personally. All that matters is the here and now, the decision to explore whatever this is and wherever it may lead.

Gently, my hands travel up the smooth fabric of his dress shirt, tracing the line of his torso until I pause, feeling the warmth of his skin and the cresting of his hard nipples beneath.

"What do we do now?"

The innocence in my tone conflicts with the lust burning within me, knowing what I'd like to happen next and awaiting confirmation from him, which I hope matches what I'm feeling.

The look in his eyes shifts, a deepening hue of desire that matches my own. His breathing quickens in a silent testament to the emotions at play. In response, he pulls me against his body to feel what he wants.

"I take you home. With me."

His firm voice leaves no room for doubt about his intentions and aligns perfectly with the longing that courses through me.

"Now go collect your things while I turn out the lights."

As I move to gather my belongings, a flurry of emotions

whirls through me. Nervous energy prickles at my skin. His words, "I take you home. With me," echo in my chest like a heartbeat. It's a bold step that sends excitement and a sliver of doubt spiraling through my thoughts. What am I doing? This is so unlike me. Is this too fast? Should I deny myself what I want because of who he is? Who am I to him?

The questions flicker in my mind, but the pull toward him, toward the unexplored, is undeniable. Collecting my things, my hands tremble, physically manifesting my inner turmoil. The theater dims around me, each click of the light switches punctuating the growing anticipation and the reality of my decision. The shadows that creep in seem to exacerbate the flutter of uncertainty in my gut.

As I turn back to him, now just a silhouette framed by the ambient light, the nervousness tightens around me like a cloak. Yet, despite the jitters and doubts, the draw to him, to the adventure he represents, is irresistible. Even in the darkness, his presence is reassuring, that lighthouse in the swirling sea of my apprehensions.

"Ready?"

His voice reaches me, a lifeline thrown across the dark expanse of the choppy water I'm treading. Swallowing the lump of nervous doubt in my throat, I nod.

"Ready."

His hand finds mine in the dark, a reminder that despite the whirlwind of emotions, I can still turn back. I can still say no and insist he drives me home. Yet, my desire for him and desire to experience something new overrides the fear.

His grip is firm, grounding as we step out into the night, leaving behind the familiar confines of the theater. With each step, I'm acutely aware of the chance I took leaping into his arms and the passion he reciprocated. It's simple whereas I'm overly complicating it. He wants me, and I want him. And nothing else matters beyond that. Tonight doesn't mean tomorrow, and it doesn't mean forever. Tonight means tonight, and that's all I must be concerned with.

"You're very quiet."

He walks us to his sleek black car, illegally parked at the corner. When he opens the door, the scent of leather spills into the air, coaxing me into the luxuriousness of the passenger seat.

"If you're having doubts, I'll drive you home."

I pause at the open door, my bags heavy on my shoulder as I consider his offer. The responsible choice would be to go home, continue ignoring our chemistry, and take that hot bath before food and bed.

"You'll drive me home in the morning?"

I choose the irresponsible option by throwing caution to the wind and slipping into his seat without waiting for his answer. With a quiet close of my door, he rounds the front of the car, his fingertips caressing the hood, foreshadowing what's to come for me. Once he's seated, his arm draped casually over the steering wheel and pulling onto the quiet street, he casts me a long look.

"I'll always drive you home in the morning."

The finality in his voice is the same he used inside the theater when he said I was going home with him. It sends a delicious shiver through my body. His word choice only adds to the allure of the night, whereas he doesn't view this as a one-night stand as I do. He's hinting at it being an ongoing thing, a fling, or an affair, and I smile as I gaze at the city outside my window.

The rest of the drive is quiet as we go to his place on Fifth Avenue. The anticipation builds with each passing block, excitement, and apprehension swirling within me. His assurance, "I'll always drive you home in the morning," lingers in the air without me knowing how to respond.

As we pull up to his building, the luxury is immediately apparent. The structure stands grandly among its peers, its facade paying homage to classic architecture and timeless elegance. The doorman greets us with a nod as he opens my door and collects the keys from Travis. It makes sense why Travis uses public streets as his private parking lot if he's used to this kind of service.

"Is this part of that legacy I should already know about?"

We enter the lobby, with marble floors gleaming under soft lighting and walls adorned with art that likely cost more than I could make in several years. With our hands interlaced, he guides me to the elevator, where he punches the button to the top floor.

"I like that you know nothing about me. It makes things easier."

I'm thinking the same thing. I'd never share my past with anyone who's not my husband and most certainly not a romantic fling. It does make things easier, and I'll leave it at that.

The elevator ride is a silent ascent, with more questions than I care to ask. Tonight is about living with wild abandonment, feeling free to make bad choices, and letting the consequences fall where they may. We enter a spacious hallway leading to his place when the doors open. He unlocks the door, and as it swings open, I'm greeted with a view that takes my breath away.

"Welcome to my little corner of the city."

His place reflects what I imagine generational wealth looks like—high ceilings, expansive windows that offer a panoramic view of the city's skyline, and furnishings that blend modern comfort with antique elegance. Original artworks hang on the walls, and the bookshelves are lined with rare collectibles I spot from the foyer. The space is warm and inviting, with a soft glow from strategically placed lighting, highlighting the luxury surrounding us.

"Wow! This is incredible."

Various lights flicker on as we walk deeper into the apartment. "I'm glad you like it. It's not too often I get to share my space with another person."

His reply piques my curiosity as he leads me through the living area, its open floor plan flowing seamlessly into a dining area and kitchen that looks straight out of a high-end design magazine. Every detail, from the polished countertops to the state-of-the-art appliances, speaks of a lavish and curated lifestyle.

As I set my bags on the couch in his bedroom, the reality of where I am and who I'm with hits me anew. This isn't just a step into the unknown. It's a leap into a world far removed from my own. Yet, as he turns to me, the warmth in his eyes and the gentle smile on his lips fade the grandeur around us into the background. It's not the wealth or the luxury that stands out— it's the chemistry between us, promising a night of passion and, hopefully, many orgasms.

He steps closer, the distance between us diminishing with each purposeful stride.

"I know this might seem like a lot." He gestures to the extravagance of his room and the top of the city skyline. "But I want tonight to be about us. Not this."

The sincerity in his voice anchors me, pulling me back from the edge of my insecurities while his warm hands find mine.

"I want that too."

It's been a long time since I was with someone, high school prom, actually, with inexperienced grunts and premature ejaculation. Tonight should be vastly different, and as nervous as I am, I also can't wait.

"Then come, little one. Let me show you what I like."

7

His voice, rich with anticipation, sends a shiver down my spine. I follow him as he leads me to a small library tucked off the corner of his bedroom. The room is filled with shelves of books, their spines worn and weathered from years of love and exploration. It's lovely and not what I expected.

"This is where I find solace."

His eyes linger on the rows of stories that line the walls before settling on me.

"These words have shaped me, guided me through the darkest nights and into the brightest days. And tonight, I want to share them with you."

He sits at an ornate wooden desk, its surface covered in faded ink stains and abandoned scripts. A single desk lamp flickers on the corner, casting a soft glow over the room. He motions for me to join him, to sit on his lap. His eyes gleam with an intensity in the romantic light.

"Sit."

His voice is a gentle command when he pats his leg and extends a welcoming hand toward me.

"Come and close your eyes, Isla. Let my words wash over you."

I oblige, settling on his thigh with my knees tightly closed and facing toward the desk.

"Close them."

I release a long breath, trying to calm myself enough to close my eyes and listen. The room falls into darkness when I oblige, leaving only the sound of my pulse resonating in my ears.

"The life of Marcella, famous starlet under the big top," he begins, his voice smooth and velvety. "Is one of passion and sacrifice, of dreams that bloom and wither, like flowers in the moonlight."

His fingertips caress up my back, tugging at the back of my shirt until I open my eyes and realize he's attempting to undress me.

"Keep them closed, Isla."

I lick my lips, stare into those imploring eyes willing me to trust him, and slowly nod, gently acquiescing to how he wants this to unfold. I straighten my spine, adjust how I'm sitting on his muscular leg, and close my eyes once more. His storytelling continues, slowly and methodically, dispensing my shirt in the same slow and deliberate manner when I move my arms through the openings.

The cold air nips at my skin, sending a shiver through me that he ushers away by rubbing circles across my bra strap-covered back and kissing the top of my shoulder. It's intoxicating and sensual, forcing me to listen to his words as they seduce my ears while seducing my body simultaneously.

"Your skin is so beautiful, pale, and almost translucent in this light. What I wouldn't give to paint you naked in my studio," he murmurs mostly to himself while his lips explore my upper arm, shoulder, and neck, leaving me fidgeting with lust.

Wetness pools in my panties, and as much as I love his calloused palm against my back, I'd much prefer it rubbing my clit or inside me.

"Patience, little one."

Little one.

It's not the first time he said this to me, being small in stature and petite in size. The way he slurs it with desire and a hint of authoritative correction rockets my lust into another world, and I squirm even more.

"Marcella was a woman born out of her time. A woman who defied societal norms and dared to pursue her desires. She loved fiercely, recklessly, unapologetically."

His fingers pause at my bra, and it slides from my shoulders with a slip of the hooks. I resist the temptation to cover myself. Perhaps him insisting my eyes remain closed is a good idea, in case he's disappointed at my tiny breasts. That's a reaction that I have seen before that makes me feel bad about myself. With the straps scraping down my skin, my nipples pebbling when the air hits them, and the bra is completely gone, his lips return to my skin.

"Stunning, Isla. More perfect than I imagined."

His tone's a distinct rasp, and a hint of a smile whispers at my lips. Appreciation is what he feels and what I deeply desire. I breathe out, relaxing further into this erotic game of his. His words paint vivid images in my mind. I can feel myself being drawn into the story, becoming one with Marcella's spirit while he fondles my breasts.

"Keep them closed," he reminds me when his lips lift from the spot he's been sucking on my neck.

It's unnecessary. Behind closed eyes, I'm braver, more willing for him to see me naked first, but the butterflies in my stomach start fluttering again. His fingers toy with the band on my skirt, unfastening the button and zipper before holding me up to tug over my narrow hips. He continues the story once it slips down my legs and pools around my ankles.

"And in the depths of her passion, she found herself torn between love and duty."

Bittersweet longing brings his story to life as if he is her and she is him, both allowing me into their sacred world to share with me.

"For Marcella, love was both her salvation and her downfall.

I can taste the forbidden freedom that Marcella exudes, the allure of her unconventional choices, and what's about to become my unconventional choice. My senses are in overdrive when he parts my legs, pushing against my inner thighs to widen and making his intent clear. A soft brush caresses my skin, causing me to jump, close my legs, and open my eyes.

"Just a quill, little one."

The pupils of his eyes are wide with desire, eclipsing the blue with his mouth slightly parted. The palm of his hand caresses my back, a reminder of his instructions, and I resume my previous position as the soft feather of the quill teases the delicate skin of my thighs, skipping my clit, which is pressed tight against my panties with wetness I'm sure is seeping onto his pant leg.

As his words envelop me, I see Marcella's world unfold before my closed eyes. A world of longing and unfulfilled desires, of choices that yield both ecstasy and heartbreak as the quill travels across my flesh, leaving me squirming and giggling. When he removes the soft feather, his warm hand on the small of my back is the only touch. I whimper with need until the buzz of something is pressed against my clit.

I jolt upright, the intensity and shock almost too much where his hand steadies me on his leg. It's hard to concentrate on his words, her story, or anything that isn't the rhythmic vibrating rings pressed delicately against those bundles of nerves.

"That's it, Isla. Lean into my hand, enjoy what is happening to you."

Unabashed, my hips move in time with his toy, feeling amazing as my head falls back, jutting my breasts out. He shifts underneath me, and my eyes slip open to see I'm angled toward him. His face mirrors the desire flowing through my veins, from the sensations to my clit.

His lips trail down my neck, his breath hot and heavy against my skin. I gasp as his teeth gently nip at my flesh, sending ripples of pleasure coursing through me. I can feel Marcella's wild, untamed nature within me, the fierce passion that drives her to defy the constraints of society and claim what she desires.

"Her heart belonged to the man she could never have. Their lovemaking was a blazing fire that consumed them both, leaving nothing but ashes in its wake."

His whispered words are as sensual as his gaze, greedily absorbing the pleasure he's giving me. I'm a blazing fire. He's making me one, and it's consuming both of us the same as it did her. I can see Marcella standing on a precipice, caught between two loves and two lives. Heat washes over me, my skin feeling hot and clammy as I continue to grind into his toy and thumb, now rubbing my drenched pussy through my thin panties.

"I'm close."

My body is aflame, aching for his touch, begging for release.

"Come, little one."

He knows what I need and desire and gives it to me without hesitation. Upon his command, I feel myself losing control, the orgasm building within me like a tidal wave. I grind harder, he twirls faster, and I grip his shoulder when I cry out in ecstasy. The climax washes over me, my body shaking and trembling with the intensity. It's unlike anything I've ever experienced, as though I'm a part of a story that transcends reality, lost in the embrace of a lover and the power of our chemistry.

"Your face is flush, the same dusty rose as your small nipples."

As I float back down to earth, my body still quivering with the aftermath of my orgasm, I feel a warmth spreading through me. The fire of our affair has been lit within me, burning bright and fierce, consuming every ounce of my desire and leaving only the ashes of satisfaction behind. If this is the prelude to the actual event, I'm ready. Ready to experience all Travis wants to do to me.

"Marcella's story is not one of despair. It is a story of resilience, of finding strength in the face of adversity. She rises from the ashes, a phoenix reborn."

He moves the toy away, a small red rose still vibrating, as a devious smile spreads across his lips.

"A rose for my rose."

For a moment, I'm lost in the aftermath, feeling the remnants of my orgasm melt away as his flowery words sink into my psyche. My throbbing pussy and racing heart slow, as do my shallow breaths. My nails dig into his dress shirt, needing more of what he's offering. He places a gentle finger against my lips as I open my mouth to speak.

"No words are needed, Isla. Let us become Marcella and her lover. Let us explore the depths of their passion and the boundaries of their desires. Let us rewrite their story together, intertwining our hopes and dreams until reality and fiction become indistinguishable."

Silence is what he wants. My silence, specifically, adds to this erotic experience and raises the stakes on where he wants to take this. I'm enthralled, wanting to see this through in whatever way possible. I realize that Marcella's story is not just a figment of his imagination—it reflects his life, battles, and wants. A passionate love affair that could end in ruin or rise from the ashes as a phoenix. I'm willing to undertake either.

Without hesitation, I lean forward, closing the distance between us. Our lips meet in a hungry, fervent kiss that leaves our tongues clashing for dominance. My arms wind around his neck, my nipples dusting against his crisp dress shirt, hardening and heightening my lust for him to continue. Continue the storytelling, lovemaking, and sensory play.

He abruptly ends our kiss and gently places me back on my feet, rising to tower over me. A ripple of caution moves through me at his sudden action until his fingers dip into the waistline of my panties, and he peels them from my body. Surprisingly, he raises them to his nose and breathes deeply while leveling me with his gaze. His eyes slowly close, shutting off the longing and yearning in them as he takes in my scent slowly and methodically. It's intriguing and curious, a tickle to the taboo in my brain, a flutter in my stomach, and a gush to my pussy.

"I love how you smell, little one."

His throat sounds constricted when his eyes open as windows to his blazing lust. His chest rises and falls with each breath he releases into the nude cotton fabric as if wanting to say more and yet not wanting to ruin it with more words than necessary. I stay silent as he prefers, part of his sensory play, which is turning into a delicious mind fuck.

He removes them from his nose, lingering to look at them before stuffing them in his pants pockets, indicating I'm not getting them back. At least not right now. Standing naked and vulnerable before him, I reach for the buttons on his shirt, intending to level the playing field when he catches both hands in mine.

"Not yet. Your body is a work of art. I want to appreciate it."

His legs shove his chair back, and the squeal of the expensive wood of the floor beneath it echoes in the dimly lit room. His hands release mine to move to my shoulders, forcing me to take a step back until the ledge of his desk hits my bare ass. Reaching behind me, he grabs a rubber band from a side desk drawer, gathers my hair off my shoulders, and tucks it into a messy high ponytail.

"Wear it up when we are together. Show the world this delicate bone structure and slender neck."

The faint wisp of his cologne fills my nose when his lips dip to mine, brushing them softly on their journey across my cheek, over my jawline to the neck he compliments. Gentle nips and bites have me squirming, reaching out to hold his arms, anchoring myself to the source of this sensual fantasy.

"This flawless skin, not even a blemish."

His mouth seeks out every place his words are narrating, and I love it. The soft suppleness of his lips, tongue, and teeth familiarizes themselves with my body as he adores it. It is a blissful experience, one I never expected. I thought he would be a fast and impatient lover, getting his and getting off. But this slow and erotic lovemaking is intoxicating and addictive.

His hands roam my body, sending shivers everywhere as they pull, squish, and spread different areas in their exploration.

"These humble breasts are superb, no bras, little one. Not with me. I want to see the outline of them. And the nipples straining against the fabric, taunting me for my lips."

I'm dripping onto my legs, my pussy a sieve to his lustful words. My hands move up his body, feeling the dips and valleys of his muscles and wanting to undress him so I can appreciate his body as much as he's worshipping mine. His tongue slithers across my collarbones, sucking a trail across each one before bathing each nipple in appreciation.

At least with the flower vibrating, I could satisfy myself and get at least one orgasm. This slow torture is getting to be too much, and I need more.

"Please, Travis."

His head juts up, his command to remain silent broken, and with the intensity of his stare, I wonder if I made a mistake. My hands stop roaming, gripping him as hard as I can to convey the seriousness of my request.

"You'll have to learn patience and how to follow instructions. No different than on the stage, Isla. Can you do that for me?"

The forgotten vibrating flower abandoned on his desk is scooped into his hand and immediately pressed against my clit. Without the fabric between, the intensity is heightened, and I try to move away but am blocked by the desk pressing into my ass.

"It's too much," I protest, trying to push it away with no success, his hand not budging. His face comes within inches of mine. His expression is dark and yearning, absorbing my protests and continuing unabashed in torturing the next orgasm out of me.

"Travis."

"Is this what you want? To come again? Will it make you quiet again?"

His touch lightens, the vibrator moving slightly away from my clit. My body betrays me when my hips rock into his hand, bringing a fast relief as a smaller, more urgent orgasm flows out of me with a string of moans.

"Ah, that's exactly what you needed."

"Yes, I need you. You. Please."

I'm so far gone so in need of feeling him inside me, around me, over me, that I beg for more. For whatever he has in mind, but now. No more games or storytelling, just straight fucking until I can't remember if I'm Isla or Marcella. The toy rides out my climax until I'm too sensitive to handle it anymore.

Thankfully, he turns it off when he sets the glistening rose on the edge of the desk. With a hasty kiss of assurance, he sweeps his arm across his large desk, sending papers flying in a cascade around us, all except for the lamp, which he carefully avoids. The sheets flutter to the floor, creating a scattered sea of documents around our feet.

My eyes widen at the mess he's making, but the sudden urgency in his actions makes me excited that he'll finally fuck me. His finger returns to my lips, another request for my silence, and this I can do with what's immediately ahead.

"You're Marcella, laid out for her lover."

His hands cup my waist, lifting me onto the desk and pushing against my collarbone to lay on my back.

"Warm and inviting, her body a beautiful gift for his pleasure, to do as he likes with it. Can you do that for me, little one? Can you embody her as I will embody her lover, master, and owner? The source of her being, joy, pleasure, and eventual downfall."

I lick my lips. His eyebrow raises in authority, indicating I should not break the silence with my words. To confirm all that he wants, all that I want from him, I move my hands behind my hair, cradling my head and giving him an alluring smile.

"Magnificent."

His fingertips travel up my leg, bending my knee and placing the sole of my foot firmly on the desk as they drift to my pussy, stroking through the wetness and over my swollen clit.

"No panties either. This tiny, little bud . . . my own personal flower is always open to me, eager to be pollinated. Look at how swollen she is, how beautifully engorged and inviting. You test my patience, little one. She's testing my patience as well. I want to make her red with pleasure, a red rose against that translucent skin."

Relentlessly, he tortures me with his soft touch, his words spoken in a murmur, painting a beautiful picture that almost has me lifting to see myself. But I don't. I'm Marcella, playing the part he wants me to play to get what I want. His slow, deliberate, perfectionist way is no different here than on stage, yet I'm rewarded here and not at the theater.

With a suddenness I don't expect, he unbuckles his pants, and they slide down his muscular thighs to a giant curved dick staring at his red rose, ready to obliterate it. I squirm on the desk, adjusting slightly to get closer to it, when his hands press into my stomach to keep me in place. They skim over my skin, grasping my hip and dragging them toward the edge of the desk, where he captures my legs to place them on his shoulders.

"Tonight is about exploration and pleasure. It's about losing ourselves in the moment and discovering new depths of intimacy together. About filling up my lover as Marcella takes her lover deeply, quietly, and without hesitation."

His gaze is blistering, boring into me as my hands drift down to the smooth trim of the wood, my fingertips curling over the side in anticipation. I barely register the condom he's rolling on while stroking my clit. His touch is electric, the lamp's glare bright against my skin, illuminating that translucency he loves so much. The world slips away as he lines up at my entrance, the big mushroom head breaching my tight ring that elicits a long groan from him and a surprised gasp from me.

I expect him to take it slow, drawing it out as long as possible, but he does otherwise. Pushing in with one continuous and unrelenting stroke until I'm stretched full beyond expectation. My breath exits in a long exhalation, taking a moment to adjust, gripping his wrist still at my hip.

Communicating I need a moment with my eyes, I gaze down at where we join, trying to see more of his flesh trapped behind mountains of clothes. The contrast of being spread out, his eyes flashing on my flesh, and him fully clothed, denying me sight and access to his body, is a curiosity that is fleeting once he starts to move that glorious dick.

"Feel me inside you, filling you, making you whole as man and woman were intended. To live as one flesh, never to be parted or separated by life and its inconveniences."

Words spoken more to himself than me. As a poet and a renaissance man with ideas from other times, even past Marcella's time, I don't mind it. It won't be a meeting of our minds and views on the outside world. I'm here for this, for his pleasure, my pleasure, and the romanticized version of her life. The experience to portray her better, having experienced what's in his head. How he sees her, this play, and how it all ends in deep despair.

His narrative continues about seeing her through her lover's eyes and his adoration for her and me. Beautifully flowery words, fragranced with meaning and impact that punctate with each hit of his dick against my clit. It's only when he decides enough is enough, and he cannot hold back any longer that he shakes my hand from his wrist to strum my wrist, the other covering my breast in a possessive claim of intertwined hearts and unacquainted love.

I close my eyes, blocking out the fiery desire, darkening his face, the fall of his hair over his forehead, and the perspiration dotting his skin as he pumps hard and steady in and out of me. My free hand holds onto the desk to stay in place, a smile on my lips as my orgasm revs, pushes in, and fades with each exit. I'd grind against him if I could, needing more friction, but with the weight of his hand pushing my chest down, my shoulder blade into the hardwood, I'm locked in place.

Squinting tightly, I concentrate on the emergence of my desire, a powerful orgasm building deep within me. Never one to be a screamer of men's names during sex, but with the limited amount of consensual sex I've had, the quietness he's requesting suits me better. A chorus of moans pour out of me, and a broad smile welcomes me when I open my eyes.

"Perfection," he rasps, his finger soaked when it raises to his mouth for him to suck.

It's hot as hell and races me even faster to the edge of the cliff, where the open abyss awaits me. His warm dick, hard, pummeling, and punishing, is perfect, sending me spiraling into ecstasy when I arch my back and cry out in pleasure.

"I see the pleasure I am giving you in your expression. The juices from your forbidden fruit spilling out of your loins and onto my flesh. Come for me, my darling. Give me everything. Heart, body, and soul. I want to possess you as easily as you have possessed me."

Like the lines from our play I received earlier this evening, they fall from his lips with grace and ease. Sensual and seductive, alluring, and enchanting. A claim of ownership, a shared passion binding them together. This is what he wants now, what he wants on stage, and what he demands when he obliterates my pussy with another equally powerful orgasm.

My legs, filled with pins and needles, slip from his shoulder, draping in the apex of his elbows as my sweat-laden back slides on the desk with the final pumps from him. He switches into another language, decorative words I don't know the meaning of, with the sweat dripping from his face onto my skin. His mouth parts, his eyes close, and with a distinct punch to my pussy and a shout to the ceiling, he's reached his climax as well.

Of all the sexy moments tonight, this is by far the best. The slackness of his jaw, the pinkness of his lips, the dim light drowning half his face in the shadows, and a hint of a genuine pleasure erasing the harshness I usually see. This is his bliss. The one he could only find here with his lover. As Marcella finds with hers. Never did I expect such erotic and intense lovemaking as this. Yet, it's unmistakably him, signature Travis in demanding silence as he speaks, wanting it only his way and painting an illustrious picture of how things should be versus how things usually are. His lovemaking is more intense than his personality, exacting a specular experience from both of us.

When his hips are still, his eyes return to mine for a moment before his palm lifts from my chest. A new expression forms, one of pure pleasure and delight that utterly confuses me. Sensing or seeing my expression, he explains.

"Your skin is marked with love. My handprint is pink against your breast, and your tiny little flower is red and pulsing. If I had my phone, I'd snap a picture and keep it in our private album. For now, it will remain etched in my mind as the first time you were mine."

He wants a picture. I already have one etched in my mind— the first time I fell in love while lovemaking.

8

_____

"Thank God, you're all right. I texted you a million times, and my calls go straight to voicemail."

Lily's exasperated sigh follows her worrisome announcement, piercing the stillness of the dark apartment. I can barely make out her figure in the dim light, but the chaos of her appearance speaks volumes. Her hair, usually tamed into perfect curls, is a wild, frizzy mane that seems to mirror her current state of mind.

She shuffles toward me, the sound of her fuzzy slippers scraping softly against the floor contrasting the urgency in her movements. Clad in sleep shorts and an oversized shirt that's seen better days, she embodies the image of a worried mom scolding her teenage daughter for breaking curfew. It's not unlike what Papa would do if he were here and a reminder that I need to call him later today.

"I'm sorry, Lil."

I half expect Anna to emerge from the shadows of my bedroom, drawn by the commotion, but the following silence lets me know she's snug asleep in bed, leaving Lily to confront me alone.

"Sorry?!?! It's almost three in the morning. Long past closing time at any bar you would go to. Not that you frequent bars, so where the hell have you been?"

Lily's anger cuts through the darkness with a sliver of relief while her hands are planted on her hips. If she only knew how easily the hours slipped by at Travis's place. His offer and agreement to drive me home in the morning didn't include the middle of the night, and as much as he insisted I spend the night, I wanted to get home, shower, and fall into my bed, replaying what had just happened.

Attempting to defuse the situation and desperately needing a moment to collect myself, I quickly sidestep Lily and head down the hall to the bathroom. She's hot on my heels until I turn around, blocking the bathroom door with my body.

"Lily, I promise I'll explain everything. Just give me a minute, okay?"

Her eyes squint when I flip on the hall light, staring into my face as if she is an imploring mother who knows precisely what happened. My clothes, wrinkled and bearing the unmistakable marks of being hastily thrown together in the dark of Travis's apartment, sans my panties, cling to me uncomfortably.

I struggle to contain my emotions, having kept them to myself on the quiet car ride back home. Even though he was a perfect gentleman, kissing me tenderly underneath the moonlight before watching me enter my building, I need time to think about what this means. The repercussions I threw to the wind in my wanton haze are suddenly catching up with me, especially with the fleeting thought that I was falling for him, which shocked me.

"Fine. I'll put on some decaf tea. Then you'll tell me why I spent countless hours worrying about you when I thought you'd be right home after rehearsals, as you said."

I forgot I told her that. Too tired and frustrated by Travis's demanding ways at the theater and his even more demandingly delicious ways at his mansion. She doesn't wait for my answer, turning to walk away.

"And you're welcome that I took Anna outside for you," she tosses at me while I watch her retreat.

The second she rounds the corner, I dart into the bathroom to wash away the physical remnants of my night with Travis. The need to scrub his scent and sex from my skin, to somehow restore a sense of normalcy before facing Lily's interrogation, feels necessary and overwhelming.

With the soft click of the lock, I lean against the door and exhale, staring at myself in the mirror. My face is flush from rushing around, not the pink or red I'm finding Travis likes. My under-eye bags tell the story of burning the candle at both ends this week. When I pull off my shirt and pull down my bra, I see the trails of love marks he left on my breasts.

That was the second round, in his bed, after he carried me fully sated from his library, ignoring the mess we made of his desk. He set aside the storytelling the second time, asking me to use my new rose toy on his new rose toy. It was a clever play on words while he sucked the skin on my "humble breasts."

With both of us so engrossed in the pleasure he was bringing me, he forgot to ask permission to mark me, and I forgot to demand it. The sting of his suction on my delicate skin worked counter to the pleasure his rose was giving me and heightened my orgasm.

After the second hickey, he undressed, content to stroke his giant dick as he lay on his side. His body was better than I imagined. Lines cut across firm abs, a chiseled chest, and muscular arms, trimming down to a lean waist and hips and flaring to muscular thighs and calves.

When he became too worked up, instructing me to alternate using the toy on my clit and nipples, his mouth started nibbling again, adding more hickeys to my breasts and two on each side of my pussy as he sucked my soaked lips. He murmured how much he liked the love marks. Loved that my pussy was tight and sore from the first round as he set me on his lap and told me to make love to him however I wanted. That lasted about a minute of me grinding before he adjusted my stance into a squat and helped lift me up and down until we were both moaning and coming. That round wasn't silent, but he also reminded me not to scream his name, an oddity for sure, and I assured him verbally I would not.

"Isla?"

Lily's worried voice travels through the crack of the door. If I know her, her face is probably pressed into it.

"Sorry, I got sidetracked squeezing a pimple. I'll be out in a sec."

"Okay."

My behavior is very suspicious. I will have to confess to her where I've been and who I was with, although I'll keep the details of what transpired to myself. The soreness of my pussy, now throbbing from such intense activity, and the sweet sting of his love marks are all very private. Known only to him and me as it should be, something that made him smile smugly when he had the heated seat warmed and waiting for me in the car.

I fix my bra, put my shirt back on, and add deodorant to distract from his heavy scent coating me. I take a few more seconds to clean between my legs, still weeping with wetness that transferred onto my skirt from lack of panties.

Tucked deep inside my bag is his white wife pleaser tank that he insisted I try on for him when he sprang from his bed after the second time. It was surprisingly snug, a second skin against my breasts, my nipples evident in the thin cotton and not long enough to cover my privates.

He gushed about seeing my swollen lips peeking out from

underneath and wanted to go another round before I begged off, knowing that would be too much for me. He immediately apologized, his hands clapped in forgiveness, and asked me to keep it for next time, along with the red rose stowed away in its box. I'm still trying to make sense of odd gifts.

With a deep breath to steel myself, I discard the tissues, flush the toilet for appearances, and thoroughly wash my hands, trying to rinse away the residue of guilt and apprehension that clings to me as persistently as the physical reminders of my escapade.

Opening the bathroom door, I meet Lily's concerned gaze. She's stationed herself just outside, clearly showing her impatience and anger.

"Well?"

"You said you made tea?"

I'm stalling, and we both know it. My voice lacks the confidence I need to start unraveling my story. Admitting what I did and who I did it with feels like I'm stepping into the interrogation light, vulnerable and exposed under her attentive scrutiny.

Lily nods, her expression softening as she gestures for us to move to the living room, a more comfortable setting for what promises to be a possibly tricky conversation. Two steaming cups of tea sit on the coffee table, along with a package of cookies, as if she already knows and is trying to soften the blow or absolve me of my guilt in keeping her up late worrying.

It's something Dad would do, being the levelheaded one and always offering a listening ear, especially on the rare occasion that I'm mad at Papa. We settle onto the couch, mug in hand, blowing on the hot tea and enjoying the warmth seeping into my palms.

"So?" Lily prompts, her fingers drumming on the arm of the couch while looking at me expectantly. I lower the mug without taking a drink and decide the best way for me to start this.

Taking a deep breath, I set my tea aside and curl into the side of the chair.

"Well, rehearsals were running long, and Travis was being . . ." I search for the right word when I flashback to sitting naked on his lap while he got me off to the story behind the play.

"A temperamental prick," she supplies the word I've heard floating around rehearsals earlier in the day. "Yeah, I know. I was there. Like what crawled up his ass and died?"

I smile, unsure I want to continue, especially with how mad she is at him.

"Well . . ." I clear my throat. Lily's eyes, wide with shock and maybe a hint of disbelief, bore into mine, seeking confirmation or denial.

"You slept with him."

An accusation—or is it a realization?

"Yes," I confess, the word barely above a whisper.

The simplicity of the acknowledgment doesn't begin to cover the complexity of emotions and events that led to that moment, but it's a start. Lily leans back, releasing her grip on the arm of my chair, her initial shock giving way to a myriad of expressions. There's undoubtedly surprise but also an under-current of concern, curiosity, and, surprisingly, a touch of amusement.

"Isla, of all the guys I can introduce you to . . . Why him?"

I shrug, struggling to articulate the whirlwind of feelings while trying to sort through them myself.

"It wasn't planned," I start, my voice steadying as I speak. "There's just . . . something between us. I don't know. I don't know why I'm drawn to him. It was intense and unexpected. And tonight, I mean last night, it just happened."

Lily sips her tea, her gaze never leaving mine, as if trying to read the subtext of my words to understand the depth of what I'm not saying. After a moment, she sets her mug down with a clink, her demeanor shifting as she grabs a cookie.

"I thought you hated the guy. Hell, we all thought that."

"What? How? Why?"

Now, I'm even more confused. I thought our attraction was obvious anytime we were close to each other. I'm not that good of an actress to hide the spark between us.

"And who's "we all"?"

"The cast, some of the crew, and that assistant he belittles, that he chewed a new one when I called you at school. The day of callbacks."

"Oh, um."

I pick at a hangnail, wondering how everyone thinks.

"Anyway, you obviously don't hate him unless it was rage fucking. Which can be fun in the right—"

"It wasn't that."

I move to assure her, abandoning my overgrown cuticles, desperately needing attention to sip my cooling tea, and snagging a couple of cookies.

"I think what you guys see as hate is me standing up to him, speaking my mind, and not caring what he says. I mean, to a point, it's still his show, so I have to listen somewhat, but I get most of what he says the first time. He repeats himself in numerous ways to drive home his vision."

My commentary is a neutral and safe assessment of him, hopefully enough to garner her forgiveness while protecting my feelings for him.

"You can get away with that because you're the star of the show. And let's be honest, it sucked with that other chick, your now understudy. So, he's desperate to give you anything you want. You can walk out at any time, leaving him screwed. The rest of us can't, knowing we'll be replaced in less than a minute."

Her analysis is sharp, slicing through the fog of my tangled feelings with startling clarity. I hate that she's right, of course. My position in production grants me a certain leverage with

Travis, a dynamic I hadn't fully appreciated until now. The realization that my newfound boldness with him is partly bolstered by my indispensability on stage adds another layer to the complexity of our interactions and the potential budding of this affair.

"God, I hope it's not like that." The cookie in my hand suddenly feels less appealing as she's struck a chord. "I mean, I didn't realize I have some leverage until now. But that's not how I want things to go, especially whatever happens between us."

Lily studies me for a moment, her gaze hardening.

"Of course you did, Isla. You blackmailed him into giving me a callback. And don't apologize another time for that. We both know how terrible you feel. I'd like to think I got the callback because of you, but I got the part because of me."

"You did get the part on your own. I swear, I had nothing to do with that after my initial meddling."

I rush to drop the cookie on the plate to assure her when I lean forward to touch her hand. She moves it away, not a slight but in halting me from tackling her with another apology.

"I get it. Trust me, I do. You've told me a hundred times that you're not meddling, but I am this time."

She leans back, her expression contemplative.

"You like him. And maybe he likes you back for more than just what you can do for his play. Just be careful, Isla. These things can get messy, especially when there's a power dynamic involved. A power dynamic on both sides, I might add, and he doesn't look like one that likes to lose."

Her caution is like that of a big sister to a little one, protective and concerning.

"Is it so bad that I wanted to have a little fun?" My shoulder raises in a haphazard shrug, coming off more insecure than unsure. "He *is* hot, even though he's a temperamental artist."

She rolls her eyes and adjusts the pillow stuffed between her and the arm of the couch.

"Aren't they all? I guess what I'm trying to say is know what you want. If you want casual sex with the guy, fine, be safe and use protection, but just know, he has a reputation for being a lady's man."

"Like a casting couch?"

I wrinkle my nose. The thought of what women used to have to go through to get parts is repugnant.

"I don't think so much of that, but he likes women, especially his leading ladies. According to Page Six, I think he sleeps with them all."

Her dark eyes stare at me in the dim room, with only the lamp near the window in the corner. A queasy feeling settles into my stomach from this conversation, from her staying up worrying about me, and now from wondering if I'm just another notch in his belt. Probably. Isn't that how all famous men are?

"Lovely."

She eases forward to pat my arm as I absentmindedly pluck at the tufted chair I'm sitting in. Her touch is meant to be comforting but only amplifies the unease settling into my bones.

"Look, I'm not saying this to scare you or make you feel bad. I just want you to know what you are getting into. If it's just fun you're after, then fine, enjoy yourself. But if you start developing feelings for the guy, it could lead to trouble for you. Just be careful, okay?"

The thrill of the connection with Travis, the intensity of our night together, suddenly feels overshadowed by the specter of his past encounters. Am I just the latest in a long line? The thought is unsettling, tainting the memories with doubt and insecurity.

"It's not like I'm planning our wedding," I joke, attempting to lighten the mood, but even to my ears, it sounds hollow. Lily smiles, a wry, knowing curve of her lips.

"Good. Just keep your eyes open, alright? And remember, I'm here if you need to talk, vent, or whatever."

"Thanks, Lil."

"Alright, you got the cleanup? I'm going to bed now that I know you're safe."

"I got it. And thanks for everything."

She gives me a reassuring squeeze before picking up her cup and taking it into the kitchen. When she's done rattling around in there, she turns off all the lights, leaving the one glowing in the living room across from me.

Her reassurance, though comforting, doesn't entirely dispel the knot of worry in my stomach. With the soft click of her bedroom door, the apartment settles back into silence, and I'm left alone with my thoughts. The excitement of my attraction to Travis is now tempered with caution, a bitter edge to the sensuality of our chemistry.

The question of what I want from him—and what he wants from me—hangs in the air, unanswered. I'm left grappling with the realization that life will genuinely emulate art in that I will become Marcella.

The lamp's soft glow casts long shadows across the room, drawing me back to the light of his desk lamp across our bodies. As sensual as that experience was, the revelation that I'm falling for him and now Lily's warning stretches through my mind in an endless cycle.

Two realities twist around each other. One is where I quit the play and return to my life, which seems flat and dull given all I've experienced so far. On the other, I continue the play, see Travis, and stop my feelings from growing. A third flashes forward. I continue the play, go to school, and don't have a torrid affair with the playwright.

A light pressure in my head begins to form with all that has happened, the long day and the impending busy week ahead.

As I clear up the dishes and finally head to bed, the uncertainty of navigating the situation weighs on me. Out of all the flowery words that spilled from Travis's perfect lips, his question lingers in my mind.

Is this what you want?

9

The silence of my room is shattered by a piercing shrill that echoes into my ears and slices through my brain, leaving me disoriented as I struggle to wake up. My mind, foggy with exhaustion and the remnants of last night's events, can't immediately place the source of the shrill. It takes a few seconds to clear away my disorientation before realizing it's my phone, its insistent ring cutting through the quiet that even has Anna dancing around my head to silence it.

Groggily, I reach out, fumbling in the light seeping through the sides of my blinds, my hand patting the empty space on my nightstand where my phone usually rests. Confusion mounts when my fingers encounter nothing but air. Realizing that my phone has somehow ended up on the floor sends me crawling across the bed in a clumsy, half-awake scramble. My hand finally closes around the cold device, dragging it up from the floor as I swipe at the screen, accepting the call without checking the caller ID.

"Hello?" My voice is thick with sleep, barely more than a croak.

"Isla, my dear! Did I wake you?" The voice on the other end

is bright and cheerful, the opposite of the grogginess that envelops me.

"Papa?" I manage, but my brain is struggling to shift gears. "What time is it? Why are you calling so early?"

"It's just past eight here, so that's what 10:15 am your time? I'm sorry if that's too early." His apology comes with a chuckle that would have drawn a smile from me under different circumstances. Right now, though, it only reminds me of how I've overslept and missed my first class. Fuck. "Shouldn't you be in class?"

"Uh, yeah, I was just . . . can I call you back in ten minutes?"

Trying to mask the weariness in my voice, I sit up. The phone is now pressed between my ear and shoulder as I fight the urge to dive back under the warm covers and burn down the rest of this day by blowing off my classes and going to the theater to face my moral dilemma.

"I just need a few minutes to finish something, and then I have to tell you something exciting."

"Oh, yes! Sounds intriguing already." I can hear the smile in his always supportive voice. "Call me back. I'm just finishing up with the furry babies before heading into the shop."

"Will do. Thanks!"

Without waiting for his reply, I toss my phone on the bed and race into the bathroom to start the water warming in the shower. Poor Anna gets scooped up right as she's making a nest in my bedding to run downstairs and take her to the bathroom while still dressed in my clothes from last night, still sans underwear, which feels weirdly breezy in the crisp air.

She seems as disoriented by the sudden activity as I feel, her little body shaking with a front paw lifted in hesitation at my command and sharp point by me to the green grass for her to tee-tee. It takes longer than I'd like, but after smelling around and looking up at me with another reminder of what she's supposed to be doing, she finally sinks into the grass to do her business.

Today was supposed to be straightforward. Attend classes, navigate through rehearsals, and somehow find a moment to address the swirling doubts and feelings about Travis. Instead, I'm starting off on the wrong foot, oversleeping and scrambling to catch up.

Returning inside, the hiss of steam spills out of the bathroom as I quickly feed and refresh Anna's water bowl. She sniffs her food and prances away to curl up in her dog bed by the window. The drapes are thrown open, and the sunshine streams across the floor, casting a peaceful moment in my now chaotic day. Lily is long gone, by the looks of the unrinsed, crusted oatmeal bowl languishing in the sink.

A fleeting thought that I will deal with later, I strip off the remnants of last night's clothes. The fabric is embedded with his scent, which I should have scrubbed from my skin last night but was far too tired for such a task. I step into the scalding shower, letting the water cascade over me as new worries push my Travis worries aside. Papa and telling him about the play. The excitement I felt at the beginning of the week is a little diminished with missing this morning's class, something I vowed the play would not get in the way of.

However, it already is, and I'll be damned if Papa and Dad didn't scrap together enough money between their savings and my scholarship to throw it away on a whim adventure of mine. I need to do better in setting boundaries for myself if I'm going to keep this up and try to do both. As daunting as it seems, will my parents be on board? How do I explain this new chapter to them? To Papa when I call him back? Especially one that's so far removed from the expectations we've both had when I first stepped foot in New York City.

The shower does little to wash away the doubts, but it helps to clear my head, offering a semblance of readiness to face the day, however late I may be while facing Papa. Showered, shaved, dressed, and somewhat composed, I grab my phone, shooting off a quick apology to my professor for missing class, a message that feels like a band-aid over a gaping wound in my commitment to my studies when I see a text from Travis.

> Good morning
>
> little one

The endearment from last night looks as if it was sent as an afterthought or to soften the brief morning greeting. I match his energy, keeping my just as curt.

> I overslept
>
> Missed class
>
> Can't stay out that late

I don't bother waiting for a reply, so I pack my purse and rehearsal bag and stuff some snacks in my tote. I approach Anna for a goodbye kiss. She's resettled onto the floor in a streak of sunlight, watching me with sleepy eyes as I rush to the front door and prepare to call Papa back.

I exit the apartment, lock the door, and dial his number, telling him all about the unexpected opportunity of playing Marcella. The worry I felt in the shower dissipates as soon as he screams excitedly and gushes to tell him everything, warning me not to leave a thing out.

"Isla dear, he's quite famous. There are pages and pages about him."

I don't miss the impressed glimmer in his tone and the dreamy sigh at the end of his sentence.

"Yes, Papa. He's that good looking too."

The subway doors closer to my right send the train whirling down the tracks as passengers in various states of dress from all walks of life either listen to music, read a book, or watch each other in the crowded space.

"How did you know? Sweetie, I love your father very much and would never, ever do anything—"

"I know, I know. You don't have to remind me again," I say with exasperation, as I've heard this every time a good-looking actor is on television or the time we thumbed through the Tom Ford coffee table book at the bookstore and he walked away fanning his face. What do you think?"

There is a long exhalation that has me worried. My gaze fixes on the subway map, counting the number of stops until we reach mine as I wait.

"You're an incredible young lady, you know that, but I worry that this is too much," Papa says, with another long sigh into the phone.

I completely understand his concern. I had the same worries and took some time to think about it. I didn't allow him that time as I just sprung this on him and am asking for his approval simultaneously.

"It's a truly remarkable opportunity, an incredible honor even to be asked to audition."

Deciding there is no way I'd tell him of my involvement with the playwright, I acknowledge his feelings.

"Papa, I get that it's a lot. Trust me, I know. I feel it in just the little bit of time I've been doing both. But how do I pass this up? As unexpected as it is, it also feels like a gift from the universe, a clandestine meeting of passionate minds. I relate to Marcella and everything she's been through. I'll scan the script, and you can see it yourself."

"Sweetie, it's not just the play that concerns me."

As the subway rattles on after making another stop, Papa's tone shifts subtly, laced with a worry of a different kind.

"It's this . . . running around New York late at night, going from school to rehearsals and back. That city is dangerous, especially for someone as petite and beautiful as you are."

I can almost see him pacing, the way he does when he's particularly anxious, with the line of his brow furrowed in concern.

"I'm careful. I have the pepper spray, and you made me brush up on those lessons with Uncle Tomlin," I reassure him, although his fears aren't unfounded. If it weren't for Travis driving me home, I'd be more worried about my safety.

For all its vibrancy and opportunity, New York harbors shadows in its corners. My crazy schedule often has me navigating its streets alone, as Lily and the rest of the cast are usually done earlier than I am because they start earlier than I do.

"But are you careful enough?"

His question hangs in my ear as we blow through another stop, just two more before I sprint out of here, up the stairs, and into Parsons.

"You know I trust you, but I also know how absorbed you can get. You might not notice things around you. And with everything you've been through, it just takes one moment, even with mace and your self-defense moves."

Voicing his fear related to my past heightens my trepidation. Papa is always the one who puts a bright spin on everything. It's one of many things I love about him. So, his bringing it up speaks to his greatest fear, one he rarely, if ever, mentions. I wouldn't have known about it unless Dani hadn't accidentally blurted it out one time during training at her upstairs garage apartment.

"Apparently, the lead in an off-Broadway production gets a car service. I'm not always riding the subway like I am now. In fact, I mostly only ride it in broad daylight."

I have to give him a little bit of truth about the car service, even if it's wrapped in a massive lie about how I secured the car rides in the first place. His worry is not just the typical parental concern. It's a fear born of love, of the knowledge of my past and what I've been through, and the guilty confession that he can't always be here to protect me like he and Dad have been the last three years.

"Well, that's something, at least."

Relief, albeit temporary, seems to seep through the phone line at my reassurance.

"A car service is safer, certainly better than the subway late at night. Just ensure you're always with someone until the car arrives, okay?"

His insistence on safety, on never being alone, on having my defense measure with me always, tugs at a deep-seated concern within me and a fear in him—one I've been navigating ever since the incident that thrust me into a world where caution isn't just advised, it's necessary.

"I will, Papa. And I always make sure the driver is legit before I get in. I'm not taking any chances," I add, bolstering my claim with the precautions I've taken, even if the complete truth about Travis's involvement remains unsaid.

"Good. And sweetie, you know you can always talk to me and your dad about anything, right? Whatever it is, we're here for you. Always."

His words, warm and full of unconditional support, wrap around me like a hug I didn't realize I needed.

"I know, and I do. I tell you guys everything," I say, the last word hanging as another heavy lie between us.

"Okay, be sure to send me that script. I want to read it since your dad is working late the next week for some regulatory audit. And give sweet Anna kisses from me. Her brother and sisters miss her."

I chuckle. Anna ruled the roost back home. I'm sure the only ones missing her and her custom outfits are him and, to a lesser extent, Dad.

"I will. I love you."

"I love you too, my dear. Always and always."

As my stop approaches, his voice fades until it's lost in the subway driver's voice announcing the stop over the loud-speakers. I stow my phone, grab my bags, and run out of the subway by the last ding of the bell to make it to my next class.

Today's class is a lecture, and it unexpectedly brings to mind Gabe's remarks about the history of polka dots, sparking a private smile while I absentmindedly doodle on my notes. I haven't seen him since I talked to him about my reservations about doing the play while tuxedo shopping. Given that Gabe's work commitments are just as demanding as the sum of my own between school and the play, our texts have been very infrequent. Since our friendship is still new, I'm cautious about not overstepping by sending too many messages, a sentiment he seems to share.

When this class finishes, I grab a cold sandwich from the vending machine and head into the lab to work on my design from this morning. The teacher's generous open-door policy to work on our designs throughout the school day allows us to maximize the downtime between classes, such as now.

I'm sitting on my design stool, trying to figure out what's wrong with my bunching while eating my lunch, when Lily texts me.

> You broke him
>
> He's nice today
>
> Likely weirdly nice

I keep my laughter to myself so as not to bother the two

other people working diligently in the room, but I set my food down to respond to her.

> You're giving me far too much credit
>
> Travis is his own man

The three dots circle long enough for me to guzzle down some water and take another large bite.

He's literally whistling

WHISTLING?!?!

either you have a golden pussy

or he won the lottery

> IDK
>
> Gross
>
> Maybe he did win the lottery
>
> You never know

I can't believe what I'm seeing

even his assistant is worried

> It'll pass
>
> He'll be his usual temperamental self
>
> Yelling at everyone

Then don't come lol

got to go food is here

I continue smiling at the screen, knowing she won't be back. As much as I'd like to have that much influence over his moods, something she said outright last night, I seriously doubt I do.

It's a theory I want to put to the test tonight. With my pussy still sore from last night, I vacate the hard stool to stand while I finish eating.

Staring at my design on the dress form, I take a slow turn around it, trying to decide if it's the bunching or the fabric choice. Either way, it has a puff on the side that is unmatched on the other and looks very odd. Even though Papa is not a seamstress, I snap a picture to send to him, asking what he thinks is wrong with it since the teacher is not in the lab right now.

Stuffing the last two bites in my mouth, I set my phone down and walk out of the room to wash my hands in the bathroom. With the bright white fabric, it's been nearly impossible to keep clean, and I'd hate for any residue on my hand to stain the delicate dress. I take a minute longer to go to the bathroom, smooth down my make-up, and press the bags under my eyes to make them less puffy. It doesn't work, and I finally give up when another student walks in.

Back at my station, I ignore Travis's texts asking what time to send the car as I'm still putting off how I feel about the situation. The universe keeps sending me signs to be cautious, but I'm still intrigued by last night and the chance to experience more. I'm surprised to see a text from Gabe and immediately click on it.

Cool design. Is that your wedding dress?

Wedding dress? That's the oddest thing to say. And mine? He knows how old I am, we talked about it at the bookstore.

What???

No!

It would look good on you though.

Wait, I meant to send this to Papa. I look at my text message sand realize I sent it to Gabe by accident.

> What's wrong with the middle?

He sees it, too. That's not good.

> IDK

> That's what I'm trying to figure out

> Hmm. What's the fabric?

> Poly crepe de chine

I chuckled to myself in answering his question, knowing he has no idea what that is or what occasion one would wear that fabric.

> Does it really look like a wedding dress?

> Yes. Poly is wrinkle-resistant, so the lining could be a fraction too tight unless you use a silk crepe de chine.

My mouth falls open, stunned that he knows all this despite having a passing interest in fashion. Either he's holding out that he's an underground fashion designer, or he needs to come clean and admit how he knows.

> What?!?!

> How do you know that?

> Long story. One I'll tell you the next time I see you.

Still staring at the screen, I answer his other text.

> There is no lining
>
> Although

See through. Bold choice. Haha.

I place my phone down and carefully maneuver my dress form into the sunlight coming through the large windows. Its base scrapes against the floor with a jarring screech, and I mouth an apology when their heads jerk up to stare at me. Embarrassed by the disruption, I hide behind my project until they resume their work and then take a step back to assess my work. Crap, it's sheer in the sunshine peeking through the bottom of the dress and flowing away from the dress form. I return to my phone to see another text from him.

Is this a school project? I can come by and look at it if you want.

> Really?

Sure. I'm by that place all the time. It would be nice to see what great minds are doing other than making see-through dresses. Haha.

> That would be great!
>
> Could use another set of eyes
>
> And for the record the dress is supposed to be avant-garde not see-through
>
> NOT a wedding dress!

See you in 30 minutes. I'll text when I'm out front.

Gabe's offer to stop by and see my project injects a new wave of energy into my work. It's one thing to create with only my critical eye and quite another to know that someone with Gabe's unexpected insight into fashion will be giving feedback. His casual knowledge and interest, veiled behind his humor about the dress, still floors me. He's a brain surgeon. I still think he missed his calling.

As I refocus on the dress form, adjusting the fabric to minimize the sheerness without compromising the design's bold statement, I look forward to Gabe's visit. Even in the text, his presence makes the daunting creation process feel more like an adventure.

The anticipation of sharing my work with him, of seeing his reaction and hearing his thoughts, adds a new layer of excitement to the project. I dive back into my work, and when my phone pings with his arrival, it seems like mere minutes instead of thirty.

I hurry out of class, racing down the hallway to find him waiting patiently at the locked double doors. As I push against the middle bar to open them, he reaches out, catching the door with his hand. Once he's inside, I give him a tight hug, grateful for his unexpected visit. He's taken aback by my excitement. I don't care. It feels like I'm drowning with this assignment, getting it all wrong, and he's throwing me a life raft with his opinion.

Gabe returns the hug with a surprised chuckle, wrapping his arms around me in a reassuring embrace.

"It's just me."

He pulls back to look at me with a smile that's both amused and touched by my enthusiastic greeting.

"You don't understand. This has been such a challenge getting it right, and now that I'm doing the play too, it's just been a bit of a whirlwind," I explain, stepping back to lead him down the hall to the studio.

The space is cluttered with fabric, sketches, and various tools of the trade. One student leaves when we walk in, and the remaining student briefly looks at us and resumes working.

"You didn't tell me you decided to do the play. Why am I just now hearing about this?"

I stop just inside the room, and he stops with me. I open my mouth to dispute that when I realize I haven't.

"Yeah, that look, love. Last I heard, you were unsure. So back that tiny caboose up and tell me that first."

A quiet laugh escapes as I lead him to my station. His eyes flicker to the dress, and he gives me a thumbs-up before we sit across the drafting table from each other.

"I decided on the play shortly after we went tux shopping," I start, watching his reaction closely.

His interest is immediate, his posture shifting to lean forward on the drafting table, giving me his full attention.

"I thought about what you said and carpe diem."

He rattles off something in another language that has me moving to the edge of my stool. Then he gives me the sweetest, most genuine smile while my fingernail traces a grove in the desk with a bit of shyness to his actions.

"It's the phrase in Latin. I studied it in school. Turned out to help with medical school, lots of terms or rooted in Latin."

"Well, look at you. Brain surgery and bilingual."

He raises a finger, then another, and another until he gets to five.

"What?!?! You know five languages?!?!? That's. . . prove it. Say something in each, and don't you dare say hello. Everyone knows that."

Gabe chuckles at my challenge, the warmth in his eyes suggesting he's pleased by my interest.

"Alright, you asked for it."

He clears his throat and starts, his demeanor shifting with each language as if to embrace the essence of each culture.

"Amor vincit omnia."

The smooth roll of the words sounds almost poetic.

"Latin. Love conquers all," he translates, his gaze holding mine, a soft seriousness underscoring the phrase. Then, he switches gears, moving into another with an easy familiarity.

"La vie est belle." The words are lilting and light. "French. Life is beautiful."

"That sounded sexy," I say, and he instantly repeats it with a much heavier, charming accent. Without missing a beat, he continues into the next language.

"Dove c'è volontà, c'è un modo." His pronunciation is impeccable, and the words flow naturally. "Italian. Where there's a will, there's a way, and I always have the will."

A determined glint in his eyes. To which I respond, "I'm beginning to see that."

He then surprises me by smoothly transitioning into a much harsher language,

"Die Zeit heilt alle Wunden."

His accent is convincing with its throatiness and intentional deepening of his voice, which causes him to cough while I laugh at him.

"That's obviously German."

"Correct. Time heals all wounds."

A hint of melancholy touches his smile. And the last has a pregnant pause before he unveils it.

"La familia lo es todo." He meets my gaze squarely, the phrase resonant and full of conviction. "Spanish. Family is everything."

"Do you believe that to be true? Is family everything?"

"Absolutely. I wish I were already married with a family."

His answer is swift, without hesitation, and said with such strong conviction. The intensity of his stare is unsettling, as if boring into me. I suppose it's similar to my parents wanting a baby but getting me instead. They both said it was the best thing that had happened to them.

On rare occasions, I mention them having a baby, and they both complain about being too old to start over. It's ridiculous, seeing as if they had a baby instead of me, he or she would only be three years old. I don't give up hope on them, but as the years pass, it seems less likely. But with me gone, maybe it will happen.

"Well, there are plenty of fish in the sea in a city this big. But I'm officially impressed."

His sincerity and depth wash away my previous skepticism. I'm impressed not just by the display of linguistic prowess but also by the choice of phrases, each revealing a layer of Gabe's values and outlook on life while avoiding any more talk of starting a family.

"And a little bit envious."

Gabe laughs. The sound is rich and genuine.

"It's just a party trick. But I'm glad you liked it."

His humility in the face of such talent is both endearing and frustrating. What is this guy terrible at? It makes me want to look ever harder to find the chink in his armor, his fatal flaw, or something to make him not so damn perfect.

"So, what do you think of my design? And if you call it a wedding dress again, I'm kicking you out of here."

As we turn our attention back to the project at hand, I can't help but feel grateful for this unexpected friendship. Gabe's presence, support, and newfound insight into his character add a richness to my day that I hadn't realized was missing. The challenges of balancing school, the play, and now navigating my feelings for Travis seem a little less daunting with such a new guy friend by my side, offering his unique blend of wisdom, humor, and artistic flair.

"Now that I see it, it's far too modern to be a wedding dress.

But why white? What's the inspiration behind it? Maybe if I know that, I can help."

I stand, walking toward it with a fondness on my face.

"The color isn't about tradition or bridal themes. It's about the concept of beginnings. White represents a blank canvas, the starting point from which anything can emerge. It's about potential, the raw purity from which creativity springs."

What I don't say is that it's me. My life started over for the fourth time, leaving the past firmly behind for a new beginning as an adult in a new place, going to a new school in a new city, making new friends, and now lovers.

It's the point that I'm the blank canvas, ready for life to paint her colors on me and make me beautiful. His eyes scan the dress again with a newfound understanding before joining me as we stand side by side, staring at it.

"That makes a lot of sense. The white is a symbol of beginnings, not endings. And the design itself?" he probes further, encouraging me to divulge the details of my creative process.

"The silhouette and structure are inspired by the interplay between light and shadow," I continue, feeling my enthusiasm grow as I discuss the intricacies of my design with someone outside this school. Someone who doesn't have such a critical eye as a teacher or cynical viewpoint as a fellow student but an admirer of the process and finished product.

"It's avant-garde because it challenges the conventional, playing with transparency and form to create something that's both revealing and concealing."

"I see it now. The way the material moves is like watching the interplay of dawn and dusk, the constant cycle of beginning and end. It's . . . it's brilliant, Isla."

He leans in, his fascination evident as he examines the fabric's interaction with the light.

"But now that you called it see-through, I'm worried that it's too sheer. I mean, look at it in the sunshine. What undergarments could a model wear with this that wouldn't show through?"

"A model wears this?"

He moves to the back, tracing with his finger around the neckline by the zipper and then down the side of the fabric where the bunching is occurring.

"Yes, our designs compete in a fashion show at the end of the semester. There are four categories, each with five designs. That's twenty spots out of hundreds competing. I doubt my design would win. I'm only a freshman, and I'd be competing with all levels at this school."

"Isla."

He levels me with his gaze over the headless dress form.

"Don't say that. This early in the semester, it's a level playing field. Remember my lesson about medical school? I had the best scores, and I still wasn't picked, so let that assure you, the most talented are not always the most desired."

His words strike a reassuring chord within me. His perspective, shaped by his own experiences in the highly competitive world of medical school, is not too dissimilar to the unpredictable nature of the selection process here.

"You're right, Gabe. I guess I've just been so focused on the technical aspects and the idea that I'm new to this that I don't stand a chance. But you're making me see it's more about standing out, making a statement."

"Exactly. And regarding the sheerness."

He turns back to the issue at hand, his fingers gently pulling at the seam along the hips of the dress draped over the dress form.

"Have you thought about using a bodysuit underneath? Something that complements the design and plays into the theme of reveal and conceal?"

The suggestion sparks a flurry of ideas, the creative block

I'd been experiencing regarding the dress's transparency beginning to lift.

"A bodysuit? Yes, that could work. It could even add another layer to the dress narrative, playing up the avant-garde aspect."

As I scribble down notes, fired up by Gabe's suggestions, I can't help but appreciate how awesome it is to bounce ideas off someone else. I was just looking for a bit of cheerleading and maybe a fresh set of eyes, but Gabe's turned out vital in fine-tuning my concept and giving my design that extra push it needed.

"A nude to match the model's skin tone to keep up the illusion?"

"Well, one category is set to challenge us, to push the boundaries of what's expected," I explain, enthusiasm creeping into my voice as I warm to the possibilities his suggestion has unlocked. "With this dress, I want to do just that—challenge, provoke, and maybe even redefine some of those boundaries."

"Ah, then, no nude. What are you thinking? Spitfire with me," he suggests, his hands leaving the fabric to join me back at the table.

"Graphic print. Um, introduce an additional layer of meaning or contrast to the design. Maybe an abstract art to more thematic prints that aligns with a challenge to the soft lines and delicate fabric?" His warm brown eyes hold an affection for this kind of stuff, showing he's enjoying himself. "Now you!"

"Lace. Red or black, like you said, opposite of the fabric but provocative."

He shimmies his upper body, meant to be suggestive, but it falls grossly short, earning him a laugh from me.

"Fine. Go."

"Metallic. Silver. Bright enough to see every outline under the fabric to amplify the effect, especially if it shimmers under the runway lights. Statement worthy."

I span my hands across the open ceiling like Aunt Molli always does when saying her name.

"I like the hand gesture. Might be able to get the model to do it at the end of the runway before pivoting."

I love that he knows so much about fashion. It makes this a million times more fun.

"Geometric. Not a full bodysuit. The privates are covered by geometrical shapes and a thong for the back. Redefining societal norms. Women are showing more of their bodies on the red carpet. But if I see one more naked dress on a Kardashian sister, I'm never watching the Met Gala again."

I burst out laughing at his reference to celebrities while discussing fashion. These two things don't mix well and get everyone around here rolling their eyes. His observation would be in great company at this school..

"Stripper. Pasties on the tits and ass," I blurt out, and for a second, his eyes widen before he laughs with me. "No, wait, that black electrical tape stuff."

His hands come out, trying to grab me long enough to add his ridiculous design.

"I got one better, painted ladies like at the Playboy mansion. But only after it dries."

Our laughter fills the studio, and when I look around, we're the only ones left. We probably ran off that last girl with our joking.

"Okay, okay, maybe not the Playboy mansion route," I manage between laughs, wiping a tear from my eye.

"And not the strippers, or else you need the pole and the guys shouting at the end of the runway throwing dollar bills at your model. It would be a trashy scene you don't want. And you wouldn't win your category."

"Are you speaking from experience?" I tease, watching his eyes dart away in guilt before returning to mine.

"I'm thirty-two, Isla. I've lived a little."

His laughter subsides into a more serious expression, and something flashes through it that seems haunting—a bad memory, perhaps.

"Anyway, I like the idea of challenging societal norms. To provoke thought, to make a statement that goes beyond the fabric," I say, flipping open my sketchbook and past the original designs I was working on when Lily said to lose the bow. With Gabe's input, it's pivoting in another new direction, and I couldn't be happier.

"Are these your designs?"

Before I can answer, he moves the pad to face him, studying each page with such care and focus that I'm fascinated watching him. He's more careful when turning the page than I ever am, as if not wanting to crease the paper.

"What's the story behind this one?"

I'm particularly proud of his finger resting on a sketch of several pages. I poured my heart into it, inspired by my personal experiences and buried emotions. I hesitate, not used to sharing the deeper inspirations behind my work. Gabe's genuine curiosity and the safe space he's created just by being himself encourage me to open up.

"It's about resilience. Finding my strength in the vulnerability of life, about the beauty that comes from surviving and thriving, despite everything that happens or could happen."

Gabe listens intently, his gaze lifting from the sketch to meet mine. In his eyes, there's understanding, a kinship that goes beyond a mere appreciation for design and clothing. In this moment, sharing the intimate backstories of my design, I feel a connection to Gabe that's deeper than friendship. His support is unwavering, and his interest in my work and me as a person is clear and genuine.

As we talk, I study his features and how the sunshine coming through the windows reflects in his dark eyes. I appreciate the lightness of his fragrance, the expensive brands he wears so flawlessly, and his overall patient way with me. There's an ease between us, a harmony that is nearly instinctual and rare.

For a fleeting moment, I catch myself wishing things were different—that the wonderful, supportive, and deeply understanding man in front of me wasn't gay. I can't help but imagine how easy and right it would feel to be with someone like Gabe, not just creatively but romantically, despite the age difference that would send Papa into cardiac arrest.

He clears his throat, stands straight, and abruptly snaps the sketchbook closed, cutting through our momentary connection. I'm momentarily startled, blinking at the sudden decisiveness of his movements.

"I need to be heading on, love. I'm curious about what you'll decide, but either way you go will be amazing."

"Thanks for stopping by and for all the great ideas. I still think you missed your calling, but I get saving children is far more important than saving fashion."

That doesn't make sense, but he still obliges me with a gracious chuckle. When he opens his arms for a parting hug, I effortlessly embrace him and rest my cheek against his chest while my arm winds around his waist. He's all lean, hard lines, something about running for stress relief and pumping iron for vitality.

Both I understand even if I don't exercise a day in my life. His arms tighten, partly losing me in his larger size, and it's this type of feeling, safe and secure, I'm looking for in someone. Not that I need to commit to a relationship right now, I don't. I'm too young for something serious. It's why Travis will do for now. His arms loosen, and I immediately step back, avoiding hugging him too long and making it weird.

"Call me if you have another fashion emergency."

He stuffs his hands in his front pants pocket, gracefully looking like a Ralph Lauren model.

"And hey, I have another charity gala coming up. It's a fundraiser at the museum, I think. My assistant just told me about it. Apparently, I did so well schmoozing the ladies at the last event, the one with the tux, that they wanted me at this one. You should come. It's in about a month from now."

The invitation is tempting, a chance to step into Gabe's world again, if only for an evening.

"You're becoming quite the social butterfly, rubbing elbows with the elite," I tease, imagining him in another perfectly tailored tuxedo, mingling with the high society of New York.

"Us Oxford men know how to mingle. Believe it or not, I can be charming when I want to be."

His hand comes out of his pocket, signifying I'm keeping him, so I guide us toward the door.

"I didn't mean anything by it. You're very charming, and I'll think about it."

"Alright, let me know. Good luck with the dress."

I watch him walk out, his natural good-looking, impeccable dress and confident stride garnering looks from passing women. Naturally, he doesn't look at them, leaving a trail of broken hearts. As I lean my head against the doorframe, he glances back, sees me watching, and waves.

His sparkling white teeth are a beautiful contrast against his skin tone, catching the attention of a guy walking out of a classroom who stops short to say something to him. Gabe's attention moves to him, and I disappear back into my classroom to finish a few more things before going to my other classes.

10

Munching on an apple and gripping my script tightly, I push through the theater doors, bracing myself for a marathon session of rehearsals, only to bump straight into Lily.

"Hey, bestie!"

Her voice cuts through the chatter of surrounding cast members who make way for our impromptu reunion. She wraps me in a swift embrace.

"So, how was school today? And why do you smell of men's cologne?"

Startled by the sudden collision and Lily's exuberant greeting, I nearly drop my apple, catching it just in time.

"Hey!"

I return her hug while trying to balance the script in my other hand.

"School was . . . school, you know. And the cologne?"

I pause for a moment, the scent of Gabe's embrace lingering on me, a reminder of our earlier interaction.

"Oh, that. Just ran into a friend before coming here. Nothing major."

Lily steps back, raising an eyebrow. Her curiosity is piqued, but she doesn't press further, for which I'm grateful. The last thing I need is to dive into an explanation about Gabe and the expectedly comfortable and yet confusing feelings it stirs within me. Especially when I kept pushing off my thoughts about Travis until now, a little bit of nerves building within me.

"Ready for another fun-filled night of pretending to be someone else?" she asks, changing the subject and nudging me with my elbow. "By the way, his happiness didn't last. He kept checking his phone, mad about something. It only got worse as the day wore on. Beware in there."

Hearing that he's upset stirs my guilt as I think it might have something to do with me. He texted me a few times today, but all went unanswered unless it was about the car service. I didn't want to talk about last night over text, and today was too busy for a phone call. Although I entertained Gabe for a while, that statement doesn't entirely hold true.

"You wouldn't have anything to do with that, would ya?"

Her eyes narrow, and I look away, pretending not to know what she's talking about until she starts laughing again.

"I don't know how you did it, but he's enraptured with you. Got him wrapped around this tiny little finger."

She wraps her pinky finger around mine and swings them together while she talks.

"I can't claim that much power over him, but he might have texted, and they might have gone unanswered since I was busy."

Lily laughs, a sound that's quickly joined by the amusement of our nearby castmates listening in.

"Well, good luck in there. He's all yours."

She releases my finger and begins to walk past me as I turn around and watch them walk toward the door.

"Where are you going? I thought everyone had late rehearsals tonight to work on the last act?"

I was looking forward to working with Lily to see her in action and vice versa, but her heading out the door with the awaiting castmates tells me otherwise. Lily pauses, glancing back over her shoulder with a mischievous grin.

"Oh, director's orders. He wants to focus on specific scenes tonight, and ours aren't on the docket until tomorrow. So, you've got the stage to yourself, superstar. Make sure to dazzle him."

Her eyes sparkle with humor and a hint of camaraderie as she waves goodbye, her laughter fading as she and the others head out the door. I'm disappointed at the news that they won't be there and a little nervous as I was going to use them as my buffer to avoid him.

"Guess it's just me and the spotlight then," I mutter, trying to muster enthusiasm for the unexpected solo rehearsal as more cast and crew stream out of the place.

Taking a deep breath, I turn towards the theater's interior, my heart pounding with each step I take toward the double doors. Once the coast is clear and most are gone, I toss my apple in the trash, stuff my script in my bag, and slip through the doors.

The empty stage looms before me, daunting and quiet as I look around the empty seats for him or, at the very least, his assistant. With neither in sight, I set my bag on the seat closest to the door and walked down the aisle to climb the stairs to the stage. The set is not her usual apartment nor the Big Top.

This is one from her childhood when she dreamed of being a star and was told it would never happen. I make my way across the stage to the twin bed with the head and footboard rusted. I sit on the edge, my feet turned in and replicating a young Marcella—one where hopes and dreams were possible, not the graveyard where they went to die.

Tonight, it's mine to command a space to explore the depths of my character and the breadth of my talent. With Lily's playful words echoing in my mind, I readily embrace the solitude and the spotlight to transform it into a moment of growth and discovery.

I take a moment, letting my eyes fall shut, and mentally transport myself back to an era when women's voices were seldom heard, and the fight for their rights was still a burgeoning battle. With the suffrage movement a distant future, I immerse myself in the mindset of Marcella in her earlier days.

Not the captivating siren entwined with her lover under the cloak of night, but rather the wide-eyed, ambitious schoolgirl who dared to dream beyond the constraints of her humble beginnings. I roll my shoulders back, loosen my neck with gentle rotations, and embrace the essence of a young Marcella, filled with hope and determination to make it big despite the societal limits of her time and coming from the wrong part of town.

Embracing the quiet of the empty theater, I step into the warm pool of light cast by the stage lamps. The air around me feels electric as if the essence of Marcella's spirit lingers in anticipation of the story I'm about to tell.

With an abandoned script clutched in one hand, I recite her lines, my voice gaining strength and confidence as I delve deeper into her character. The words flow freely, echoing through the vast space, painting a vivid picture of a young woman's struggle and resilience in a world that seeks to silence her ambitions.

As I reach the monologue, a pivotal moment that lays bare Marcella's heart and soul, I forget the script, the lines memorized and internalized. I'm no longer myself but fully Marcella, embodying her hopes, fears, and indomitable spirit. The monologue belonging to her is filled with my words, my struggle, and my fears about this play and school, worrying if this will all work out. Like her own, mine is the same worrisome journey from the shadows of societal expectations to the light of my own making.

"I stand before you, not as a symbol of what could be, but as a testament to what is. In the face of adversity, in the shadow of doubt, I choose to rise, speak, and dream. For every door closed, a window opens, a sliver of light promising more. And it is towards that light I walk, not with fear, but with the courage of knowing that even the smallest voice can echo in the halls of change."

My voice rings out, clear and unwavering, the words resonating off the walls and filling the theater with the essence of Marcella's spirit. It's a moment of pure connection, a bridge across time linking her fictional struggles with the actual battles fought by countless women throughout history and battles of my own.

As the last word fades into silence, I'm left breathless, the intensity of the performance lingering like a tangible force. For a moment, I stand there, caught in the afterglow of Marcella's strength and conviction, reminded of the power of storytelling to inspire, challenge, and transform.

Thinking I'm alone in my dedication to the night's rehearsal, I allow myself a small smile of satisfaction, unaware of Travis and another man having witnessed the passion and depth of my performance from the shadows of the theater.

A slow clap arises from the smaller man at his side. His hair whispers of gray weathered lines crisscrossing his face behind his black horn-rimmed glasses, and his cane accentuates a slight limp. His fashion is impeccable. A black and white dotted ascot at his throat, a matching pocket square stuffed into the breast of his three-piece gray and black tailored suit.

"Magnificent, darling."

My hand raises to my chest, trying to calm my racing heart, and my cheeks brighten from the heat of embarrassment. Beside him, Travis beams with pride, and our eyes lock, mine silently asking who this man is, him smugly knowing and not announcing it. Only when he gestures for me to come closer do I snap out of my daze and approach the edge of the stage.

He raises his hand, signaling an intention for me to leap into his arms—a gesture that feels a bit too theatrical, given the company. Opting for a more subdued exit, I crouch at the stage's lip and gingerly swing my legs over the side, allowing him to assist me in stepping down more gracefully.

"Isla, meet Mr. Julian Hawthorne," he introduces, his voice laced with a hint of excitement. He is a legend in the theater world and a dear friend."

Mr. Hawthorne approaches with an ease that belies his limp, extending a hand that's seen its fair share of applause and critique.

"Your performance, my dear, was truly captivating. To evoke such emotion, to breathe life into the character with such authenticity . . . it's a rare gift."

My performance, which moments ago felt like a private triumph, now stands scrutinized by a giant of the theater. My pulse quickens a fluttery sensation that buzzes beneath my skin as if I were a live wire.

"She's a natural."

I don't miss the pride in his words and the sudden hand on my back.

"We're going to dinner, join us."

I haven't even finished shaking his hand when I look over my shoulder at Travis. I'm still unsure if the praise from his friend is warranted when the offer to spend the evening with him is made. Things are moving way too quickly, and I'm left reeling with a racing pulse.

"Thank you, Mr. Hawthorne. It means a lot coming from someone of your stature."

His hand is delicate, if not bony, in my hand, speaking to the frailty of some condition ailing him. He waves away the formality with a dismissive flick of his wrist after releasing my hand.

"Please, call me Julian. And let's dispense with the modesty, shall we? Talent such as yours deserves recognition. Travis here has been singing your praises, trying to get me down here to see you. And he's right for it. What he said on the phone was one thing, but to witness it firsthand . . . well, it's another thing entirely. And once the curtain goes up and you're in full regalia, you'll be the show's star."

My heart, racing just seconds ago, begins to settle, though my cheeks burn with a blush that I can't control. Travis's proud and smug smile sends a ripple of warmth through me, a silent affirmation of my worth in his eyes. Both their eyes.

"Wow, I don't know what to say."

My hands cup my cheek, trying to calm the blush as I peer from one man to another.

"Say you'll join us for dinner," Travis repeats, patting the small of my back before lifting his hand away and taking the warmth with it.

"It would be our pleasure to celebrate your talent tonight. Consider it a prelude to the accolades you'll receive once the play goes live," Julian chimes in, his eyes twinkling with an encouraging light, echoing Travis's invitation.

Both men are dressed exceptionally well, far nicer than my slightly wrinkled school clothes. I press a sweaty palm over my skirt, trying to straighten out some of the creases that don't go unnoticed by both.

"I'm not dressed for the occasion. Perhaps another time."

The prospect of spending more time in their company, especially under such premature celebratory pretenses, excites and intimidates me. Their belief in my potential, mirrored in their eager faces, is a powerful motivator, pushing aside any lingering doubts about my abilities.

"Julian, will you give us a moment?"

Travis's hand moves to my elbow, his fingers digging into my flesh a little too hard for my liking.

"Of course, take all the time you need."

Like the perfect gentleman he is, he bows his head in respect and adjusts his cane before Travis practically halls me away from the stage. His large hand wraps around my bicep as his sports coat swishes with the determined pace of ushering me through a maze of hallways and doors until he releases my arm to push through the final door. Inside is a dizzying amount of clothes, far more than are at my school.

"What is all this?" I ask, my gaze greedily roaming the room until I look up at Travis, watching me with a contemplative look.

"Wardrobe."

His clipped answer doesn't explain the racks upon racks of clothes, headpieces, shoes, handbags, and every accessory under the sun. I never really thought about all the costumes from his previous plays. It simply never dawned on me to wonder what happens to it all after the show closes. Now I know it lies here in wait for unsuspecting women needing a dress for an even more unexpected dinner with her boss and lover and his influential theater friend.

Travis roams the room, past the treasure trove of sparkly and feathered theatrical costumes to the more contemporary outfits, until he pulls a simple silhouette dress from the pressed-together clothes.

"Here."

He offers me the black garment, the sheer fabric reminding me of the dress I was working on today.

"Try this on. It should fit you perfectly and complement your coloring. It's also the right blend of elegance and comfort for tonight's dinner."

The dress is a stunning piece that perfectly balances sophistication and artistic flair, but I turn in circles looking for a changing room.

"Isla, I saw you naked just last night. You can change right here."

I bite my lip. Yes, he did, but that was in the hazy of a sensual and erotic experience. This seems more platonic and director-actress-related.

"Um, but that was different."

I stand holding the dress away from me, unwilling to change in the middle of this room in bright light. The privacy of his library was utterly different. Sensing my hesitation and seeing the tension in my posture, his demeanor immediately shifts.

"Let's find you a more private space," he corrects himself smoothly, recognizing the difference in context and respecting my comfort.

"This way." He leads me toward a small dressing room at the back of the wardrobe area, then pauses before shutting the door. "And remember what I said, no undergarments."

I'm already shaking my head, unwilling to play that game at dinner with his friend. It was one thing to say that in the confines of his home. It's another to expect it out in public.

"No way am I going to dinner with that man without wearing anything underneath. Plus, I'm still sore—"

"Mmm, little one, let me see that bruised flower."

His hands suddenly tug at my clothes, practically ripping them off as if he wants to get a quickie right here in this tiny dressing room while his friend waits on us.

"Did you use the toy I gave you?"

I'm too busy slapping away his hands to answer him immediately. His head dips toward mine, his lips connecting with the sensitive skin on my neck and nibbling up to my ear.

"Did you bring the shirt as I instructed for tonight when you come home with me?" he whispers, his hands unzipping the back of my skirt before it falls to the ground with a distinct swoosh.

My finger, still clutching the hanger with the dress, tightens when his knuckle brushes against my panties, the dampness a dead giveaway to my attraction for him.

"Is this an invitation? My little flower doesn't seem sore. She seems ready."

His lips skim across my flesh as his words implant in my skin, asking for permission to continue. I can't help but moan softly as he strokes me delicately, understanding what I need and want at the same time. I swallow the lump in my throat, finding the courage to speak up.

"Not here. Not like this."

He pulls away, his eyes searching mine for any trace of hesitation or deceit. He finds none and removes his finger from me, which leaves me whimpering in need. He lifts his hand to his face, breathing deeply before lowering it.

"You're a temptress, Isla, and I'm just a man with a weakness for pretty flowers."

There's a certain sadness to what he's saying. I groan when he closes his eyes and straightens his shoulders before flashing those deep baby blues at me again.

"Now, let's get you dressed for dinner."

The energy between us changes. The desire burning brightly a second ago has flamed out, and he's now turned into a dresser at the back of the house at a fashion show. He makes quick work of unbuttoning my blouse while I'm left to unstick my panties from my wet skin. His wicked smile and brush of the lips against my shoulder, a gesture of appreciation for his work as he tugs the dress over my head, making a mess of my hair.

"Remove the undergarments while I find something for your hair."

He turns me to face the mirror, where my breath catches.

The cut of the dress is spectacular, and I'm tempted to ask who designed it or, at the very least, who is the costumier. What he's undoubtedly correct about is the undergarments, with my bra showing with the low dip of the center of the dress and major panty lines outlined on the front of the dress.

"Oh, yeah."

He accepts my agreement with a knowing smile as he's busy piling my hair up on my head to try different styles.

"How do you know so much about this stuff? You're not a designer."

"When you've been in the theater as long as I have, you learn a few things."

With that brief answer, his hands are out of my hair, and he's out the door to rummage around the large room. Dutifully, I remove my bra and slick panties before scooping up the rest of my clothes and shoving them in between my skirt and blouse. I'm barely done when he's back with a beaded head-piece and some sexy black peep-toe heels with an ankle strap.

"Stand still while I fix your hair."

He places the shoes gently on the floor before me and then, with a light touch, guides me by the shoulders to face the mirror again. Travis's fingers work deftly, weaving my hair into an elegant, effortless, intricate updo with a few vintage hair-pins. As he places the beaded headpiece, it feels like the final brushstroke on a masterpiece—the transformation from every day to extraordinary is stunning.

"Like a beautiful doll."

His murmured words of approval echo in the small dressing room. I can't help but marvel at the image reflected in the mirror. The dress falls perfectly, its lines smooth without the interruption of undergarments. It's a daring look, undeniably, but at this moment, under the warm glow of the dressing room lights, it feels just right.

"You have quite the knack for this."

I watch as he secures a last pin into place before gliding his hands down my body to squat in front of me. I toe off ballet shoes, a little self-conscious of a possible foot odor, which doesn't seem to faze him as he puts the heels on me and buckles the strap tightly at my ankle. He quickly does the same with the other shoe, his hand lingering on my calf, the warmth imprinting on my skin. He stands, steps back, and surveys his work with a critical yet satisfied eye.

"Theater is more than just acting. It understands the character from the inside out, including how they present themselves to the world."

I tentatively step into the borrowed shoes, finding my balance as our gaze meets in the mirror. The heels add a new height and a new attitude, elevating me in more ways than one.

"Like a beautiful doll," he repeats, and I can't deny the pride that swells within me at his words.

"Thank you, Travis. For seeing something in me and for all of this."

My hands sweep over his creation, something I couldn't pick out myself in this overwhelming room of costumes.

"It's all you, Isla. You bring the talent. I just help you shine."

He snaps his fingers with the same vigor he does with his assistant, this time directed at himself when he mutters about forgetting something. He searches for a few seconds before holding up a tube of lipstick.

"Classic red lip. Turn around."

I cast him a skeptical look. "I think I can apply it myself."

"Can I please do it?" He hesitates, a flash of vulnerability in his requests.

The request catches me off guard. This transformation means something to him, not just doing it as a favor but as a creative process in which he's deeply invested. As invested as he gets with his play, he's getting invested in dressing me up to feel comfortable for dinner with them. Being on the same level clothing-wise is a sign of respect for my discomfort.

"Okay, go ahead."

Travis breaks with a glimmer of satisfaction, and I turn to face him, my back to the mirror. He carefully twists the tube of classic red lipstick, his focus intense as he approaches the task with the precision of an artist. The brush of the lipstick against my lips is gentle, a stark contrast to his usual brisk efficiency.

His hand is steady, and he takes his time applying the color with an attention to detail that speaks to his respect for art in all things. I remain still, aware of the careful contact as his eyes catch mine several times.

"Perfect."

Once done, he steps back, his eyes searching my face for approval. I turn back to the mirror, and the impact of the red lips against the elegant lines of the dress and the sophistication of the updo is striking. The color adds a final touch of boldness, a punctuation mark on the entire look, and turns me into the very image of a classic starlet, ready for an evening out on the town. I feel so seen by him that my confidence shoots through the roof as I catch myself. How must he see me?

Turning to face him, I reach for the lapels of his coat, pulling him in for a kiss when he makes a disapproving sound and removes my hands.

"You'll mess up my masterpiece."

His objection is playful yet firm, and I can't help but laugh.

"What was I thinking?" I gasp, still riding the high of seeing myself transformed. "I guess I owe it to both of us to keep this look intact for the rest of the night."

"Exactly. There will be plenty of time for appreciation later, little one."

He hints at what we started but didn't finish. I didn't bring my toy or my shirt, but I really don't think either will matter with how he's looking, as if he wants to eat me right up. He didn't say to bring either, and I'm not sure I am staying the night. I still have school in the morning, and I warned him in my text message this morning that I could not be out late tonight.

He offers me his arm, which I quickly tuck my hand into for him to lead us out of the wardrobe room as if I were old Hollywood glamour.

"Time to dazzle him, Isla."

11

Dazzle him? They dazzled me with dinner at a place so exclusive it didn't even have a name on the door or on the outside of the building. The restaurant was dark and intimate, without menus, as food and wine flowed effortlessly to the table.

Snuggled by Travis in the booth, by his insistence, I barely lifted a finger, being waited on hand and foot by the temperamental playwright. Each course was a surprise, a delight to the senses as Travis fed me from his plate and introduced me to flavors and textures I had never imagined while expertly pairing them with the various wines.

With his wealth of experience and sharp wit, Julian added layers to the conversation, making the evening not just a meal but a memorable experience. It was as if they had conspired to wrap the night around me, a cocoon of luxury and laughter, making me forget the world outside.

As the evening unfolded, I saw Travis in a new light. Away from the stress and demands of the theater, he was more than just a talented director. He was someone capable of joy, of sharing moments of genuine connection. His attentiveness, ensuring I was included and engaged, spoke of a consideration beyond his usual demanding personality. It was as if he was seeing me, really seeing me, for the first time.

Julian's presence added a gravitas to the dinner, yet his easy laughter and insightful comments on the theater world bridged any gap between us. His stories of past productions, triumphs, and trials painted a vivid picture of a life richly lived in the pursuit of art. His interest in my budding career, encouragement, and open acknowledgment of my emerging talent felt like an endorsement I'd only dared to dream of. The acceptance I secretly yearn for.

As the night ended and the final glasses of wine were sipped, I felt more attracted to Travis than before. He had not just dazzled me with the dinner's opulence or the setting's exclusivity. He welcomed me into their world with open arms, offering support and recognition that went far beyond the confines of the theater.

Walking back into the cool night air, arm in arm with Travis, the city's lights twinkling like distant stars, I felt a shift within me. The evening had been a revelation, not just of the kind of life possible but of the person I wanted to be and who I wanted to be with. Surrounded by ambition, talent, and genuine warmth, I stepped forward, ready to embrace whatever came next, my heart full and my spirit lifted.

"You're quiet, little one."

His voice cuts through the silence as the driver helps Julian into the building with the doorman by their side.

"I'm in rapture."

Travis shifts in his seat, the leather groaning in response while offering his open palm to slip my hand into. I immediately do it, his thumb stroking across my knuckles.

"Tell me more. Tell me everything that's happening in that gorgeous brain of yours."

The chemistry between us, heightened by the shared experience of the evening, feels tangible in the warmth of his hand.

"It's hard to put into words, but tonight was more than just a dinner. It was . . . life-changing. I felt seen, not just as a new actress but as a person. And you," I pause, searching for the right words. "Showed me a side of yourself that I hadn't known before. It's made me see you in a new light."

Travis listens intently, his gaze fixed on me, inviting me to continue. Encouraged by his attention, I delve deeper.

"Your generosity, the way you made sure I was included, the laughter we shared—it all made me feel a part of something special. It's not just the glitzy restaurant or this glamour outfit that impressed me, but the genuine admiration you have for each other, the sense of belonging to a people that values art in all its forms and does not have to explain its worth to non-patrons."

His thumb continues its gentle caress, a soothing rhythm, while the blueness of his eyes, with the streetlamp pouring in, bores into me. The driver slips behind the wheel, a murmured apology for keeping us waiting before pulling away from the curb.

"And Julian. His stories, his wisdom, his gentleness—it's all so inspiring. But more than anything, it was being there with you, experiencing it all together, that made tonight unforgettable."

Travis smiles, a genuine expression that softens his features when his other hand finds my thigh to rest upon. The familiarity of it is comforting, an added physical connection to what is quickly cementing more than an affair.

"This is my world, Isla. I wanted you to see there's more to it than rehearsals and performances. It's about people, friendships, appreciation, and camaraderie. It's about finding your place among those who understand and appreciate what you bring to the table."

The car slows as we approach his penthouse. The night is still vibrant around us, but the atmosphere inside the car is cozy and intimate. His words resonate, echoing the feelings stirring within me. As we arrive and step out of the vehicle, the cityscape sprawling before us, I realize that this evening has indeed changed something between us. The bond we've forged, nurtured by this shared experience and mutual respect, has deepened, opening the door to possibilities I hadn't considered before.

"Thank you, Travis, for tonight, for everything. I'll return everything to you after it's cleaned."

The driver lingers, waiting for me to climb back inside to my destination when Travis walks over and tips him. Returning to me, he holds out his hand, his expression reflecting some of what I already feel—appreciation and desire.

"You're welcome, Isla. But really, it's just the start. There's so much more I want to show you, so much more for us to discover together. Will you come up?"

And at this moment, with the city stretching out infinitely and the future looking so damn bright, I smile at him and nod. We're on the cusp of a new chapter, one filled with promise, growth, and the exploration of something more.

"Yes."

His hand tightens over mine in a gentle squeeze, a long whistle passing his lips as the doorman scurries to collect my bags from the driver holding them at the curb. Travis pays little attention to the staff facilitating the ease of his life, a sign he's lived this luxurious life a long time as he guides us into the building and up to his floor. The doorman is in and out with stealth and silence, depositing my bags on his foyer table.

As the doorman departs with a discreet nod, the door closing softly behind him, the penthouse's elegant expanse opens before us. Travis leads me through the lavish space, each step echoing softly on the marble flooring, our intertwined hands a tangible symbol of the connection we've begun to explore. The city lights glow softly through the floor-to-ceiling windows, painting the room in a palette of nighttime hues.

He pauses, turning to face me with an inviting and earnest smile.

"Make yourself at home. I want you to feel comfortable here as you did last night in my library."

I chuckle, the sound echoing across his expansive rooms.

"I was pretty comfortable last night."

A hundred images flash through my mind at once, clips of his face, dark and aroused, my body naked and displayed for him. We both played parts of the script teleporting back to when the characters he wrote lived in passionate ecstasy.

"I want you to feel that same sense of comfort and freedom here. This is our haven, our sanctuary, not just my library. I want that same unabashed version of you out here in the open as if you're on stage."

His words send a warmth coursing through me, making me feel safe and cherished. I take a deep breath, feeling the moment's intensity as goosebumps prickle my skin with antici-pation, and nod slowly.

"I want that too."

His eyes dance with dark mischief, his footsteps clicking on the cold marble floor until he towers over me, leaning down to brush his lips against mine in a gentle, fleeting kiss.

"Good. Tonight, I want you to experience a different kind of comfort. One that comes from freedom and exploration, from a deeper connection that transcends boundaries. Are you ready for that?"

My stomach flutters, anticipation and caution fighting for dominance in my mind as my body is on fire with lust and desire for him. Last night was tantalizing to my senses. The closed eyes, the silence, and the commands overlaid by the story were the most erotic and sensual experiences of my life. If he wants to replicate something like that, I'll throw caution to the wind and transcend almost any boundary he wants.

"Yes."

His kiss is ravenous, the desire in me so great that I want to jump onto him, wrap my legs around him, and have him take me against this wall if only this tight dress weren't confining me in place. His lips are demanding, his tongue plunging in and out, exploring and retreating as if he was starved for me at dinner, and now is his time to feast.

His hands pull at my dress, the fabric rising higher and higher until my pussy and butt are exposed to the cold air of the room. He carefully ends the kiss and gently lifts the dress over my head, skillfully avoiding any contact with my makeup or hair.

"You'll remain like this, little one."

With the dress draped in his hand, he places it on the couch on his way over to the wall of modern cabinetry, pressing against the upper corner for the drawer to slide open. Retrieving something long and sparkly from inside, he closes it with the same touch and pushes a button on the wall. The modern fireplace roars to life. The flames encased in sleek glass create an alluring glow from the orange and yellow flames dancing across the broken glass embers.

He sheds his coat next to my dress, his eyes greedily taking me in as I fight the urge to shield myself. The item he retrieves dangles from his large hand while he slowly unbuttons his shirt, leisurely undoing his cufflinks and tossing them on the table near the couch. I can scarcely breathe with how turned on I am, standing naked in this giant room, the tops of the few buildings surrounding us, becoming voyagers to what is happening inside his penthouse. I can feel myself getting wet. It starts to slide out of me in anticipation of whatever comes next.

With his shirt dispelled by our clothes, he stalks toward me, the intensity in his eyes unmatched from last night. Last night was softer and more caring. Tonight seems more animalist, and I'm ready to be torn up. The soreness that lingered with me all day, forgotten if I'm willing to test the boundaries he's setting for us.

"You're very good at taking direction."

A sly smile plays at his lips, encouraging me to sass back, not follow his lead, and perhaps act on my own accord.

"Maybe I listen to you the first time and then rewrite the script as it really should be."

The emphasis is countered with my finger, drawing a line from the bottom of his throat to the top of his pants, his flesh twisting and flinching as I go.

"You're playing a dangerous game. One you can't win."

His words hang in the air like a challenge, and I can feel my independence begin to flare. I'm not one to back down from a challenge, and I certainly won't let him win this one. I meet his gaze, my eyes locked onto him as I take a step closer to him.

"Is that so?" I ask, my voice low and steady. "You think I can't win? Well, maybe you're right."

My fingers tangle in his soft, blonde hair, and I tug gently to guide his head down toward mine. Our mouths collide in a fiery kiss, and I can feel the heat radiating from his body as he pulls me closer by my hips. The intensity of our embrace sends electric sparks coursing through my veins as his hands travel over my butt, separating my cheeks and groaning when he feels how wet I am.

"But I'm not playing your game," I whisper against his lips, my breath hot and heavy. "I'm playing mine."

Without warning, he picks me up and pins me against the wall, his body enveloping mine with a ferocity that takes my breath away. The cool marble presses against my back, the contrast of temperatures sending shivers down my spine as his lips crash against mine.

It's a challenge, scorching my lust into a wildfire, taking

over my flesh as our tongues twist and fight each other. I gasp for air, my hands clutching at his muscular shoulders, trying to push him away as he keeps smashing me to the wall with relentless kisses.

"You want to play this game, Isla?" His voice is a rough whisper against my ear. "You want to push me to my limits and see how far you can go? Well then, let's play."

Suddenly, the wall behind me disappears, leaving me scrambling to clutch him as he takes me into a dimly lit room, darker than the candle-lit restaurant. I don't even get a chance to look around before I'm placed in a contraption hanging from the ceiling as he steps back with a conniving smile. The air is heavy with the earthy scent of leather and the faint smell of incense, adding an air of mystery and intrigue to the room.

"What is this?"

I gaze around the room. My eyesight is challenged when I make out shapes against the wall and oddly arranged furniture scattered without thought around the room.

"My playroom, little one. Now, your playroom."

My mouth is dry, and I can taste the metallic tang of fear on my tongue. A mix of anticipation and nervousness lingers on my lips.

My eyes widen at the sudden realization that he's placed me in a sex swing. My gaze roams the black straps with various silver rings and hooks dangling from the sides, and a large ring above my head is suspended from the ceiling. My fingers curl around the rough leather on the sides, cradling me as the straps bit into my butt cheeks. The creak of the swing's chains and the sound of my breathing are the only noises in the room, creating an eerie contrast to the wild thoughts racing through my mind.

"I-I don't know about this, Travis."

The sexy siren I was a second ago dissipates rapidly, the game we were playing over in my mind as this took a sharp turn in the perversion I used to read about before being overwhelmed with school and this play. Travis's expression doesn't change from the dark smirk showing he loves this unexpected power play when he steps closer to me, his hand caressing up and down my leg.

"The rules of the game may have changed, little one, but the heart of the game remains the same."

His mouth drifts closer to my ear as he whispers the words, sending shivers down my spine.

"I appreciate the flare of defiance. It's endearing. But Isla, in this room, there's only one person in charge."

I can feel his breath against my skin, and I know that I can either fight against my anxiety or let it guide me into this new experience.

"I'm not calling you master."

His breath against my skin, his hand caressing the part of my leg dangling in midair, it's all intoxicating as I negotiate in ways I don't even have the power to negotiate. His tongue trails my pulsing vein, giving away the rapidness at which I'm cautiously aroused.

"You say it with some familiarity. Have you played this game before, little one? Do you have a past that you need to share with me?"

I'm triggered all over the place by his question. My past is . . . traumatic and scarring. No amount of therapy can erase all I should have never experienced. I would never share anything with him or anyone in a position of power over me to give them a chance to take advantage of me in that way. His inquiry hits parts buried so deeply that I can't fathom letting them out, exposing them to the open air for the demons to escape.

"I read. It's in books."

My answer escapes in rasps. The panic he brought to the forefront is setting off alarm bells in my brain, the risk that he would deny me this relationship due to my past heightening it.

It's making me want to jump out of this swing, grab my dress, and run out of here.

Suddenly, he's around me, lifting me from the swing and cradling me against him as he walks out of the room across the penthouse to his bedroom. We sink into the bed, him hovering over me as my heart races. With my back flat on the soft linens, I release him, close my eyes, and take several deep breaths.

"Isla, I made a mistake."

My eyes flip open to see a mask of sincerity mixed with something I can't make out. His fingers trace my hairline, pushing away a strand as a hairpin digs into my scalp. The roughness of his clothes on my delicate skin is forgotten as he continues his exploration of my face.

"I shouldn't have taken you in there. I should have told you about it first. Asked if you wanted to try my proclivities. I got overly excited by the allure of your game. Please forgive me."

My mouth snaps closed, licking my lips under his watchful gaze, earning understanding and forgiveness. Another facet of his vulnerability, showing me his world and my panicked reaction, has him retreating into a version that's not the man I know, or at least know thus far.

"I . . . I don't know."

The words that should flow out of me to console him aren't there. When he slides off me, angling himself to lay with his head against my chest, I'm surprised. My hands float in slow motion toward him, wanting to comfort him while trying to understand what's happening.

"I rushed things, rushed them with you, just as I always seem to do. You're so perfect, exactly what I've been searching for, and yet, I've managed to ruin everything."

A soft sigh escapes me. His voice tinged with regret, echoing like a distant call through the night, emerging from a shadowy realm of guilt born from the desire so intense we compel it into reality. It's a familiar narrative, striking a chord within me, prompting my hands to instinctively reach out, offering solace through touch where words fail to suffice.

My fingers gently brush through his hair, the gesture tender and reassuring, even as I wrestle with a tumult of emotions.

"You haven't ruined anything."

The words finally find their way out, each infused with the effort to heal and mend. In this moment of vulnerability, the barriers between us seem to dissolve, revealing our feelings' raw, unvarnished truth.

"It wasn't the room. Albeit a heads-up would've been helpful."

His head raises, forcing my hand down his back as those beautiful eyes stare at me. His body relaxes slightly against mine, the tension seeping away as if my words and touch are a balm to his self-inflicted wounds.

"I don't want to talk about my past. It wasn't pleasant."

His eyes hold mine, a silent plea for understanding amidst the storm of his own making.

"Then we don't have to," he says, his voice a gentle anchor in the sea of his unrest. "Your past stays where it belongs— behind you. We all have chapters we'd rather not read aloud. What matters is now, this moment, and all the moments we can shape going forward. I'm sorry if my words were a trigger. I didn't intend them to be."

My hands, still tracing patterns of reassurance on his back, affirm a silent vow to allow this place to be my sanctuary when the ghosts of the past are chased away when they loom too close. It's another new role I find myself stepping into—not just a character on a stage, but a partner in this endeavor, ready to share both the spotlight and the shadows as we encounter them.

"I know you didn't, and thank you."

He lowers his head, hugging me tightly as the room falls silent to our thoughts.

In the quiet embrace, the steady rhythm of his breathing against me becomes a grounding force, a reminder that despite the past's shadows, there's a present filled with support and understanding. His solid and secure arms encircle me, not just as a gesture of comfort but as a testament to the partnership we are building—layer by layer, moment by moment.

The thrill of that room and the promise of the experience that lies ahead intrigues me. I've never been so sure of my safety as I am now, especially after this talk. Thinking about that swing and what it's intended for has my core heating up and my pussy tingling.

"What do I call you when we play in that room?"

His head darts up, his face burning with a new intensity that matches the excitement that's causing my breaths to elongate.

"Are you sure? Do you trust me enough to submit? To put your faith in me that I'll take care of you?"

I appreciate the confirmation and seeking my approval before another mishap. Yet a part of me is curious, and a larger part wants to explore the unknown. I bite my lip, release it, and then smile.

"Yes, I do."

He crawls up my body and gives me a gentle kiss.

"Then let's go figure out what you should call me."

12

Wishing to put me even more at ease after our little misunderstanding, he strips himself bare. No clothed vantage point like last night or a moment ago. Just his flawless body, reminiscent of David himself with a much larger dick bobbing as we walk hand in hand back to our playroom.

His offer to raise the lights so I can roam the room and ask questions is swiftly declined as I wander back to the swing. Half the fun is not knowing what comes next or what he intends to do. Anticipation of any event is usually better than the event itself, although with him, so far, it's all been amazing.

"Do I jump, or how do I get up here?"

The swing is set at nose level, too high for his cock, when his foot hits a peddle on the floor that lowers the swing from the ceiling. His hair-covered chest tickles my back as I watch it descend.

"Badass."

He chuckles, his hands circling my waist as the chains rattle until the swing stops to his desired position and then lifts me in it. The trepidation I had the first time is gone, the intensity not nearly as reckless as I've consented to his control. Submit is not the word I'd use, but it's enough to relay the idea of his intentions.

The stiff leather is just as biting my skin as before, the coarseness scraping against my palms as I adjust my legs to move deeper into the chair. The cold steel of the chain hitting my upper back is a shock and has me lifting up.

"Did you ask for the extra uncomfortable one when you ordered this thing?"

My joke is met with a faint smile. His eyes darken with lust as he captures my heel to place in the stirrup thing.

"And who comes to your house to install this? I'm sure it's not Task Rabbit."

Crackling jokes is my way to release some nervousness coursing through me.

"We need to break it in, little one. It's new."

The rasp in his voice flutters into my stomach, and I like the fact that countless girls didn't break this in before me. As much as I don't want to discuss my past with him, I also don't want to know about him. I don't want anything before now to taint where this is headed.

Once both of my feet are in the stirrups, something clicks, and my upper body is lowered while my legs open wider. I bite my lip, trying not to let the unexpected movements startle me, but it's failing in the worst way.

"Relax. It's all meant for our pleasure."

I try to nod, but it's impossible with the angle he placed me in. Then, with a subtle click from the foot controls hidden beneath us, an unexpected transformation occurs—the ceiling above us begins to retreat, revealing the vast, starlit sky. As the expanse of the universe unveils itself, it's as if the very heavens are peering down, adding a celestial touch to the intimacy of the moment.

"Wow."

The stunning view of the constellation on this clear night chases away my insecurities about being splayed like the gynecologist's office. His hands find their way onto my legs, caressing up and down my thighs, his thumbs coming dangerously close to my pussy without touching it. I try to squirm, to inch lower, but with how he has me positioned, I'm helpless and at his pleasurable mercy.

Patience, he said last night. They need to rename these sex swings into patience chairs since all I can do is lie here, waiting and gazing up the stairs, which is a far better experience than the "Hang in there, kitty" poster stuck to my doctor's ceiling.

"You see that star, Isla? That's Cassiopeia, the queen enthroned. She pales compared to you—you are my guiding star, the one who brings direction to my play and brilliance to my work."

His descriptive words whisper to the romanticism confined behind that unbending exterior. He demands the best out of each of us and relays his disappointment when it's not met.

His hands roam my body in appreciation, gently brushing against my drenched clit, dragging the wetness over my stomach as he traverses each hardened peak begging for a hand or mouth to touch them. When I try to look at him, make eye contact to check in, and see his expression, he puts pressure on my chest. Settling into the stiff leather, I take a calming breath, letting all nervousness ebb away to enjoy this experience fully.

"But even in the vast night sky, amidst constellations that have guided sailors and inspired poets, none shine as brightly as you did tonight. You are my muse. My doll, my perfect creation, the light that pierces through the darkness in me. Your presence, little one, is like a beacon that not only illuminates my path but also warms the very soul of me."

Under the celestial canopy, his comparison feels less like flattery and more like a sacred truth, acknowledging the light he's also brought into me. His world is vast, colorful, and artistic, something I didn't know I wanted to be a part of until tonight. What was sparkling in his hand the first time we entered is dangling in front of my eyes, and my heart quickens at the extravagant starry necklace.

"This necklace, my dearest Isla, is my gift to you. At its heart lies a sapphire as unique and captivating as Cassiopeia herself, but it pales in comparison to your radiance. A ring of diamonds surrounds it, each meticulously placed as sentinels to guard the majesty herself. Their brilliance mirrors the majestic night sky."

He lifts the pendant, allowing the ambient light to dance across its surface.

"Crafted from the finest platinum, its luminosity reflects the light you've brought into my world. And see here, these tiny diamonds scattered around as if floating in space? They are like the countless moments you've brightened my days, adding your sparkle to my play, to Marcella, and to me."

He's bathing me in compliments, a gracious adoration that sends a warm flush across my skin, accelerating my heartbeat and bringing tears to the brink of my eyes. I lift a finger to touch the exquisite surface of the pendant, sending it swinging in the space above me. He gently cups the back of my hand to capture the pendant in my palm before closing his hand over both of ours.

"You will always wear it, symbolizing the unbreakable link between us, even when we're apart. Just as the night sky is incomplete without Cassiopeia, so am I without you."

Under my touch, the pendant feels like a physical manifestation of his words and feelings for me, encapsulating this night as precious as the diamonds adorning it. He uncurls his hand, the star-bursting diamonds leaving an imprint on my fingers.

He raises my palm to his lips and kisses each indentation before placing my hand back on the cold chain, holding the swing in place. My breath catches, and an overwhelming sense of being cherished, understood, and most of all, loved by him, washed over me, even if it is quicker than I imagined.

"Head off the swing, little one."

With his standing at my head, I inch toward him, understanding his intention that he wants me to wear it now. My hands tighten over the chains, and I use the heels in the stirrups as leverage to move up the rugged leather and expose my neck so he can clasp it on.

"Let this necklace serve as a constant reminder of our enduring bond, guiding you back to me like the Cassiopeia guided the sailors at sea. In its glow, see my devotion, unwavering and true, like the constellations, it will never fade."

The cold touch of platinum against my warm skin sends those tears spilling down the sides of my face that he quickly dispels with his thumbs.

"This is us, little one. Always."

Smiling through my tears, I look up at him, my eyes reflecting not just the light glinting off the pendant but also the depth of my emotions.

"I don't. . ."

My throat constricts with emotion, unable to communicate the millions of thoughts rushing about my head. I can't believe this is happening. I'm the luckiest girl in the world. I've finally found someone who allows me to be me without probing around into my past and accepting me as I am. It's overwhelmingly wonderful. His hand cups the back of my neck, applying slight pressure for me to let my head fall back until I see the world upside down and aligned with his giant hard dick.

"Take me in, little one. Let me see how beautiful you look with my necklace at your throat and my cock in your mouth."

The dynamic in the playroom switches rapidly from flowing romance to carnal desire when his large hand, with heavy pressure, strokes from my collarbones down to my clit, swirling it several times and dipping into my pussy before dragging his hand back up.

"Always wet and waiting. And very patient tonight. Good girl."

His hand grips his dick, giving it a tight squeeze at the base before tapping it against my lips. Before we begin, knowing the boundaries is crucial—how to stop if something feels off or isn't to my liking. My trust in him is the reason I'm here, after all. However, being suspended mid-air, with my feet locked in place, doesn't empower me much if something goes too far.

"Wait, do I need a safe word or something? Again, not from experience, just what I've read."

My voice is light as air in the dark room, conveying a confidence I certainly don't feel. The hand trailing down my body for another delicious trail down to my pussy stills.

"No, not that formal. If you're not enjoying yourself, we'll adjust."

I'm about to ask how he will know if my mouth is full of dick, and I don't get it out when he taps my lips and slips the salty head inside. His hand moves to my throat, wrapping his fingers around the slim column to feel himself both inside and out.

"Ah, Isla," he slurs as if I'm doing anything at all beyond letting him use my throat as another vessel of pleasure. I've never done this before. I'm unsure what to do and almost panicky when I need to breathe. My hand loosens from the chair to push him back out of my mouth as I turn to the side and cough several times. "You've never done that before. I apologize for rushing it."

He catches my head, helping me up when I shake him away.

"I haven't," I rasp, clearing my throat from the unusual sensation. "But I want to."

Without waiting for his response, I move back into place

and touch his leg to signify I'm ready. When he steps closer, he leans over, gently kisses me, and whispers instructions.

"Breathe through your nose and relax your throat."

My fingertips slide up his leg, curling into his firm ass and pulling it toward me. This time, I'm in control as he guides the tip back in, pausing to let me figure out my breathing and swallow before allowing him back in. A long groan rumbles out of him as he slowly moves inside me. Releasing the chain, and with both hands on his ass, I figure out a rhythm that works for me, one that has him grunting and groaning, which makes me proud.

I close my eyes, shutting off the view to his perfectly trimmed taint, and start to concentrate on how erotic and almost illicit this feels. My body flares with design, growing wetter and wetter as I do this to him. Taking him deep and making him whimper with pleasure. The necklace at my throat, a symbol of how he feels about me, slides off and dangles toward the floor.

Those glorious large hands are everywhere, pushing against my ribcage to thrust faster, separating my pussy, and plunging in and out with a vigor that has me moaning against his dick. The vibrations from my throat heighten his pleasure as he compliments me.

"My stunning star in my dark night. You're the world to me, my everything."

His breath is hot on my skin as he leans over me, his fingers pounding against my public bone, each thrust sending shock-waves of pleasure through my entire body. I moan, the sound muffled by his dick.

"You're mine, little one, and I'll never let you go."

His words ignite a fire, consuming me from the inside out. I don't care about the rawness of my throat, the slight discomfort of his plundering dick in need of a release, only the feeling of being suspended, floating and fucking at the same time. It is a dizzying feeling that has my heartbeat swooshing in my ears, the blood pooling in my head, and my orgasm boiling within me to finally spill over the edge as my body spills over this swing.

My body tightens, and my feet strain against the restraints, raising my lower body off the leather to pump into his fingers as his semen pumps down my throat. Words of praise float around me, like the very stars dangling from my neck and watching us from above.

The entire experience is otherworldly, and when he removes his fingers from my pussy, his dick from my lips, he sends the swing spinning in circles. My body collapses, my legs tremble, and my arms are like pins and needles stretched in the cool air when I open my eyes to see him sprawled in a silhouette of a chair across the room, watching me.

Swinging, with my head thrown back, I plunge into a realm where stars are beneath me, and the floor stretches out above, a reversal of the everyday. The swing's chains squeal above my twirling abandonment. This spinning transforms the room into a dizzying whirl of light and dark, disorienting yet thrilling, as though I'm floating free from the shackles of gravity.

A fleeting thought of being Marcella, watching the trapeze flying through the air and twirling for the cheering crowd below. My arms, stretched out by my ears, move above my chest, twisting together like snakes from the snake charmer in a sensual dance as I spin suspended from the ceiling.

My body is a whirl of dazzling peep toe shoes, stained red lipstick, and a dangling diamond necklace—a show for Travis as he sits recovering from his release. My limbs flutter weightlessly, a sensation of being untethered from the world as if I am nothing more than a wisp of air. The weightlessness permeates my being, infusing me with a giddy euphoria. My laughter rings out, clear and joyful, as the freedom of flying wraps around me. Here, suspended between the floor and the stars, I revel in the exhilarating trust in surrendering to him.

While the spinning begins to slow, I want to hold onto this feeling as long as possible. My arms slither toward my body under his watchful gaze, now stroking his dick and sinking to my smooth skin. Mirroring his hand, I send one upward, stroking the very throat he held and was in. He rises to his feet, his chest raising in shallow pants and spurring me on to continue this arousing private show for him.

My other hand works in slow motion, grazing both nipples and plucking on them until his calculated steps prowl toward me with a dark expression. When my fingertips make contact with my soaking clit, intending to get myself off, he catches my wrist to stop me.

"No one touches my rose."

A growl of possession, a confession that I'm his, beyond being his muse. I stop spinning with an abrupt jerk, his hands plunging under my body to drag me down the leather seat, and my head no longer dangles. The foot peddle engages, slightly raising me to align my pussy with his hard dick, shoving inside me with one fluid movement without time to adjust.

"Travis."

My hand reaches for his body to push him out when he captures it and places it on his heart. His face is smoldering, his eyes burning with an expression I've never seen before. A man obsessed or possessed—neither of which I can decide.

"My Orion. That's what you will call me in our playroom."

His dick moves very slowly, barely moving away from my cervix and angling to go deeper when my palm pushes against him. He kisses my hand, then places my arm at my side in a quiet display that he's in charge. My legs splay, strained beyond what is comfortable, until he undoes one restraint, bending at the knee and placing the heel against his chest.

"Orion is a prominent and universally recognized constellation, sometimes called The Hunter, little one. He's a striking figure in the night sky, known for guiding and protecting."

His slow strokes, delicious, and teasing are in time with the deliberateness of his explanation. Drawing out the experience as he does, allowing me to soak it all in. With the butt of his hand just above my clit, pulling the skin upward while pressing into my stomach, I gush over his dick. The cold air washing over as he pulls back the hood and exposes it is an unusual sensation.

"Under the velvet sky and inside this velvet cunt you humble me. In this vast expanse of my life, where creativity and doubt mingle, you stand firm in your convictions. You embody Marcella, you enchant Julian, you tempt me in your floating wickedness, alluring me to fuck you repeatedly."

The struggle is apparent. His eyes close, his hand presses harder, and his dick pauses. His beautiful face is twisted, almost in pain, as my fingertips graze his skin, watching it flinch in response.

It's several long seconds before he opens them again, the strain in his expression easing as he starts to fuck me properly, pumping in and out. No games, no waiting, just a perfectly rapid pace that I can concentrate on my orgasm too.

"Like Orion's belt, you bring alignment to my chaotic world. Your beauty guides me, your brilliance supports me, and your fragility empowers me. When my confidence wanes in the darkest of nights, you shine the brightest, guiding me back to my path and reminding me of my purpose. You challenge me to reach beyond my limits, to hunt for the beauty in the mundane, to fight for the passion that fuels my art."

He takes a breath, his gaze never leaving mine.

"Orion is your protector, your hunter, your possessor, taking every inch of you with him and owning you like no other. I don't need to know of your past, Isla. You are only my future.

You're part of me as I'm a part of you, woven together under this starry night."

His pumps become fast and erratic, fucking me harder and harder as if embodied by the very Orion he envisions himself to be.

"Shout my name as your owner, master, lover, and protector when you come."

His hand tightens, the sweat dripping from his body mingling with mine as he drives into me with a fierce intensity. The chains above creak and groan in time with our movements, echoing the primitive rhythm of our bodies.

My breath catches with each deep thrust, matching his vigorous pace. The velocity of the swing works in his favor, pushing me away to impale myself repeatedly. With each word, each echo of this night, I'm drawn further into his world—into the genius of his creative mind, how he interprets the world around him, and how he views me as his muse.

His words, gaze, and even the light musk of his cologne clinging to his skin entrances me. Our bodies are one, our creativity ambitions entwined under the watchful gaze of the starry gods above. The constellations of Cassiopeia and Orion align in our favor as witnesses to the beginning of something special.

My breaths grow shallow and sharp, each one forced out in a huff at the brutally delicious pounding he's delivering. I close my eyes and arch my back into his thrusts as they grow jerky and out of sync, sending me into a climax that feels as if I'm spinning once again.

Amid the rapture, my voice catches in my throat, unable to scream the words he demanded.

"My Orion."

Whispered while ecstasy courses through my veins, enough to answer his plea in its purest form of pleasure. His grip on me tightens, and his dick pistoning out of me as I ride out a series of smaller orgasms, my cries matching his when he spills into me. His flesh slapping against mine settles, the clanging of the chains quieting and our panting breaths echoing across the quiet room.

With my shoe still pressed into his chest, using it as leverage, he kisses my ankle, the strap tight against the flesh, before pushing my leg toward my body. Deep indentations mar his muscular chest, red and painful looking, and I gasp at what I did without thought in the heat of the moment.

"Oh no."

My hand reaches out, trembling, to touch his arm. But as my fingers brush against his skin, he smirks down at me.

"I should say the same to you, little one."

His smirk quickly melts into a look of guilt as realization dawns on him. His warm, hard dick is still pulsing inside my pussy without protection, and I gasp in shock.

"Shit."

Panic and regret flooded my mind. He slowly pulls out, his dick glistening with our combined fluids, and I wince at the sight of the raw flesh between my legs. The chains above creak and groan as I thrash about, freaking out and trying to figure out how I get his sperm out of me.

The last thing I need is to be a teenage mom like mine was. How would I tell Papa? He would be devastated. And Dad, he'd be so disappointed and probably pull me out of school. I'd have to leave New York, leave my dream behind, and stay in my hometown forever, going back to designing clothes for Aunt Molli's church pageants.

"Travis! I need down. I need to get out of here!"

Tears flood my eyes as the panic spreads, trying to maintain my balance while reaching for the restraint on my other shoe. The consequences of our actions loom large. The exoticness, the free falling, and the spinning, all elixirs to a carnal round of sex where protection wasn't even thought of. But I couldn't deny the intense chemistry that still lingered between us.

I fight against the swing, the momentum sending me in different directions as I struggle.

"Calm down, little one. Let me help you."

The authority of his offer doesn't ease my panic even as his foot messes with the peddle, and his fingers quickly get me out of the swing. Ready to dash past him, call a car, and figure out this disaster with Lily at home, I take one step and almost collapse to the floor if it wasn't for his quick actions.

"Isla, you can't move so quickly, especially after how you were positioned."

My head lolls against his chest, dizziness causes the room to spin, and my legs feel like jello draped across his arms as he carries me into his bedroom. Once I'm sprawled out in the comfort of his bed again, I clutch for him to lay with me as I wait for my body to recover.

"I've got to go. I can't get pregnant."

Even with him lying beside me, his arm under my head, cradling me to him, I couldn't stop the rebuilding of the panic, erasing all the good feelings that were coursing through my body.

"Isla, darling."

His embrace is warm and comforting, a rock for me to cling to during this horrific storm.

"I'm sterile."

My ears are deceiving themselves, hearing words I've never heard anyone utter so freely and easily. I pull away, staring into the endless ocean of clue eyes, praying it's true, and guilt wrinkles through me at that disgusting thought. I'm hoping he's sterile because of my recklessness.

"It's okay."

The sincerity in his tone and the tenderness in his touch make me want to believe him, but at what cost?

"But . . ."

I fumble for the words, my heart racing as a million thoughts swirl through my mind. I said I trusted him a few different times. Do I trust him about this? Would he lie to me to end my panic and keep me from rushing out of here?

I must know the truth, even if it means risking the end of us by asking him. If I don't, I'll live with doubt and betray myself even more.

"How do I know you're telling the truth?" I whisper, my voice trembling. His eyes soften, a hint of sadness creeping in.

"You can trust me, Isla. I'd never lead you astray. I've been to the doctor and had tests done. It's a fact, and I'm sorry you had to find out this way."

I search his gaze, trying to discern any hint of deception. It's difficult, for my heart is urging me to believe him, but my mind refuses to let go. The consequences of our actions are still looming large. He reaches out, placing a gentle hand on my cheek.

"I promise you. I wouldn't lie about this." I close my eyes, lean into his warm hand, and take a shaky breath. "Come here, little one."

He extends his hand towards me, and I can feel the warmth of his palm inviting me to lean in. I rest my head on his chest, and his steady heartbeat lulls me into a sense of peace and safety. As I sink into his embrace, the storm of my freak-out subsides as his fingers reach for the necklace pressed between our two bodies. I lift slightly as he removes it from his entrapment, laying it on his chest when I lay my head down again.

The truth of his sterility weighs on my mind, but I can't help but feel a strange relief. This revelation erases the panic and fears about babies and moving back home, leaving behind a complicated mix of emotions about my future and whether I ever want to be a mother.

We sit there for a long while, physically together and miles apart. It isn't until I'm dozing off that he stirs underneath me.

"It's getting late."

I've watched enough movies to know this is the universal guy code to get the hell out after having sex. Quickly, I sit up, scanning the room for my things, piecing together where he might have set them.

"I'll go."

I hurry off the bed, forgetting my heels, leading to a clumsy stumble before I manage to steady myself against the long dresser. He's on his feet instantly, catching me before I regain my balance. His arms encircle me from behind, his skin sticky from sweat and our fluids, halting my escape.

"Please, don't." His breath warms the shell of my ear, carrying a sincerity I don't expect. "Stay with me tonight. I can't bear the thought of sharing what we shared and watching you walk out that door. The emptiness in this house . . . it's deafening."

There's a vulnerability in his plea, a raw honesty that makes me pause. The loneliness he speaks of is not just the absence of sound or company. It's a deeper, more pervasive solitude that seems to gnaw at him, seeking solace in the mere presence of another even after two steamy nights.

I'm sterile.

His confession floats through my mind, a decision thrust upon him by genetics that could add to the siren call of his loneliness. Though the notion of children lies in my distant future, I'm allowed to choose their presence in my life, a liberty he doesn't have. This realization brings a pang of sadness for him, shadowing his lack of choices into a grey, colorless world.

Feeling his heartbeat against my back, the earnestness of his request, I'm moved to agree even though I warned him I couldn't stay out late. It's a side of him I've never seen, another facet hidden beneath layers of composure, self-assurance, fame, and wealth.

The thought of leaving him to face that vast emptiness alone tugs at the depths of my past, wishing someone, anyone, would save me from the nightmare I was living. The emptiness I felt at being worth nothing more than an unwilling minor used for sex by whoever was dating my mom at the time for payment of drugs. The unkempt girl with empty eyes who sometimes had dried blood in her panties at school from a quickie on the way when I missed the bus.

"Please."

I close my eyes, my heart aching at the pitch of his plea to fill the void, if only for one night.

"Okay."

13

One night seamlessly flowed into another, and before we knew it, two nights became a week. Three weeks later, Anna and I find ourselves practically living in the penthouse, all in a frenzied lead-up to opening night tomorrow. Amidst this whirlwind, my schoolwork hasn't been neglected.

Textbooks and notes sprawl across the coffee table, and I am determined to juggle it all, including calls home when Travis isn't around, so I don't have to confess what I've been up to. I even lied to them about opening night, hoping to get several performances under my belt before they flew in to see me—a promise both Papa and Dad have made several times.

Evenings are spent crafting my metallic bodysuit, its design evolving under my hands. At the same time, he paces the living room, phone pressed to his ear, securing critics for different nights with a precision that mirrors the meticulous stitches I sew.

Our days are punctuated by my classes, his playwright duties, and rehearsals that grow longer and longer the closer we get to the big night. Our nights are spent in extravagant restaurants with various friends, critics, and other playwrights in the business, where he shows me off in the outfits he selects for me.

One time, when our eyes met in the mirror, he said it was like playing dress up with his own petite doll, asking me if this is how I felt when dressing dress forms in my designs. I smiled, relating to what he was trying to communicate even though I don't consider fashion school the same as "playing dress up."

Each outing feels like a scene from a play, with him playing the perfect host to his muse, enveloping me in a world of luxury and attention I'd only ever dreamed of. These public displays of affection and admiration seamlessly transition into private nights of passion in our playroom, exploring and pleasing one another, our nights stretching long into the early hours of the morning if we lost track of time. I never felt more adored, appreciated, and loved than I do now, having transcended even Marcella's glory days by miles and miles.

This unexpected routine of my academic commitments and preparing for the opening has created a rhythm to our lives together in the penthouse. His dedication to making every detail perfect, from the critics' attendance to ensuring I shine in every way, both publicly and privately, has woven a new layer into our relationship. The penthouse now buzzes with life, laughter, and the warmth of newfound intimacy, dispelling the shadows of loneliness that once clung to the walls.

My phone shrills through the vast penthouse. Anna's ears twitch in response, the only acknowledgment while she lies plastered to Travis's pillow. I joked that she's more attracted to him than I am, which he chuckled at, saying this was the first time he's ever had a dog in his house so that he wouldn't know. I'm skipping through the rooms on my way to get it when it suddenly is silenced too quickly. When I round the corner, Travis has it up to his ear, roughly demanding who Dani is to the caller.

I stumble to a stop, anger flaring in my chest, not just from the surprise of seeing him answer my phone but from the realization that this simple act has shattered an unspoken boundary between us. Travis's posture is tense, and the phone is clutched a little too tightly as he interrogates the caller with a sharpness I only hear at the theater.

"She's not available right now," he lies with his back to me before ending the call.

This intrusion feels like a cold splash of reality on the dream-like existence we've been living in this penthouse bubble. I watch as his jaw clenches, his eyes flicking from the phone to out the window before he spots me and turns around, my phone in his hand.

I expected him to look guilty or at least rush to explain himself, but he does neither. He looks at me as if I have something to explain when his eyebrows raise.

"What are you doing?"

I can't help the anger surging through my words as the accusation stings the air between us.

"It said Dani on your screen." His response is a sturdy calmness, contrasting the firestorm brewing in my gut. "I wanted to know what guy is calling my girl."

He acts as if that justifies his breach of privacy. His tone, while trying to be nonchalant, can't mask the undercurrent of possessiveness that has no place in our relationship. I walk further into the room to snatch my phone out of his hand before looking through it to see if I missed any other calls. Everything appears in order, even if my suspicions aren't completely erased.

"Dani is my aunt. Not a guy."

Although if she knew what he just did, she'd whip his ass like a guy, that's for sure.

"Not that I have to justify that to you either. You can't just answer my phone without permission."

My hands plant on my hips, trying to convey the seriousness of his transgression. The following silence is charged, a
tug-of-war between my shock at his audacity and his expectation that I brush this off. But I can't, not when it's so clear that
this moment represents more than just an answered call. It's
about respect, trust, and the boundaries we hadn't explicitly set
but I thought were understood. He studies me momentarily,
perhaps realizing he's stepped over a line.

"I suppose I overstepped. It won't happen again," he finally
concedes, though his apology feels more strategic than sincere.
"You're welcome to answer my phone. Even go through it if you
want. I have nothing to hide."

My mouth opens, then snaps shut while my fingers curl
around the device at what he's implying.

"I don't want to go through your phone, Travis. That's not
the issue here. I trust you enough not to dig through your
phone, and I expect the same in return."

Not that I'd have the opportunity to do so since he's on it all
the time lately. He shifts uncomfortably, perhaps not expecting
this hard of a stance from me or maybe realizing his mistake.

"I'm sorry," he says again, this time with a hint of genuine
remorse. "You're right. I shouldn't have answered your phone."

Accepting his apology, I nod and turn on my heel to walk
back into the bedroom, collapse on the bed, and return to my
schoolwork. The penthouse is quiet, Travis going back to whatever he was doing while I slide down the pillows to cuddle with
Anna and call Dani back. Barely a ring gets through when her
voice comes barreling through the phone.

"Who's the rude as fuck asshat that answered your phone?"

I chuckle, missing Dani more than I realize when I hear her
voice laced with her usual profanities. Travis sulks into the
room, looking sort of apologetic.

"The *asshat* is this guy I'm seeing."

I stare right into his dark blue eyes as I say it, letting her words hit the target. It works when he frowns and sits on the bed to pet Anna. The light pink bow in her hair is one from the prop room, with a hot pink feather at the center. It matches an old outfit I made for her well before my commitment to the play.

"Dump his ass. We don't put up with shitty men around here," she demands, unwilling to let it go, which is one of the faults I have noticed about her. If you mess up with her, it's your funeral.

I can't help but smile at her fierce loyalty that hasn't changed one bit in the years she's been in my life. It's one of the constants I like.

"I'll get right on that. Anyway, how are you? How's Uncle Tomlin, Lars, and the shop?"

I divert her attention from him and me, an unnecessary complication with the play just a day away. Today is Travis's self-imposed shut-in, where we rest, relax, and prepare for tomorrow. No going out, not even to dinner, insisting everything come to us. He even swore off sex until after the show, which I could use a break from. Going from none to almost every day made me sore in more places than just my privates.

Dani's mood flips seamlessly from fierce protector to lively conversationalist. She dives into updates about the garage and the recent expansion of their secondary location, now under Lars's leadership, thanks to an entire team. The shift frees her up to accompany Uncle Tomlin on his ventures with his inner-city judo schools. While she misses being hands-on in the garage, she finds fulfillment in supporting Uncle Tomlin's ambitions.

She vents about Uncle Alex and Aunt Molli having a baby, questioning who would ever want to deal with that fucking nonsense. Her frustration bubbles over when she mentions how she learned from Papa, not me, about my starring role in a play.

A play, she hastily adds, that she and Uncle Tomlin intend to watch from the fucking front row so she can hoot and holler her support at the end, not realizing this is the very reason I didn't tell her. With Uncle Tomlin's wealth, they have the freedom and financial means to be at my doorstep in a matter of hours. Something I appreciate in the back of my mind but never want to happen.

Her rapid-fire update, filled with the usual blend of complaints, cussing, and excitement, reminds me of the vibrant life I've stepped away from back home. As she talks, Travis inches closer, moving Anna closer toward me in a sort of truce while his hand caresses down my arm.

"I can't wait to see you both in the audience when my play opens in a few weeks."

A silent inquiry appears on his face, his fingers trailing over my skin to the pendent he gave me weeks ago, nestled against my throat. I've yet to take it off, even in the shower, when I was worried about it tarnishing or getting damaged. He assured me it was far more durable than that.

Travis remains silent, perhaps mulling over the conversation he's only partially overhearing. His seemingly small gesture feels like an attempt to bridge the gap his earlier actions created.

Lily about died when she saw it, asking a million and one questions about what it meant, which I didn't answer directly as it's private between Travis and me. What did it cost? To which I replied, no idea. And what I think about wearing it all the time when it sometimes clashes with my outfits. I agreed with her, knowing I could easily slip it off at school or run the few errands I have left that aren't taken care of by Travis's staff, such as walking Anna three times a day.

Every time the subject of my necklace came up, my hand would touch the beautiful stones, remembering that magical night I floated to new heights and spun amongst the stars.

Although our playroom has been much more fun than I could have imagined, nothing will be the enchantment of that night or the intimate role-playing of the first night in his library despite the multiple role-playing we've done in the playroom.

Dani assures me that they are on the first flight to New York the minute it opens and to text her all the details for Uncle Tomlin's assistant to plan it. The call ends with promises of me sending her pictures of my latest design, a request to give Anna a big kiss from her, and a typical "break a leg" at my rehearsals.

Once I hit the button on my phone, Travis moves Anna to the other side and snuggles closer. He does this when feeling particularly lonely or out of sorts, but I'm still slightly miffed at his previous action.

"Please don't be upset with me. I wanted today to be relaxing, no stress between us."

The fingers tracing the design of my necklace now trail up my throat to circle the outline of my lips while we lock eyes. Not wanting to keep this unnecessary resistance between us after I said my peace, I'm inclined to move on, wanting a peaceful day as well. Especially with the sunshine streaming through the floor-to-ceiling windows and the large lunch we had on the terrace overlooking the skyline.

"You're right, as always."

He winks, gathering me in his arms so that I can lie on top of him. His hand guides my head to rest on his chest, and I can hear his steady heartbeat in my ear and breathe in my favorite cologne, which he wears daily.

"I know. Now tell me why you lied to your aunt about opening night."

I sigh, tucking my hands at his side and squeezing my affection for him, knowing it's too early to say the words that have been growing in my mind.

"I'm already nervous enough. That's why I really appreciate staying home and you allowing us to just be together. I don't need the added stress of my family coming into town and making a big deal out of the production."

As I spill my worries onto him, his hand resting on my head gently moves my hair away from my face, something he does often. I joked with him that he must have been a hairstylist in a previous life. He gave me a small smile, but a haunted look followed, speaking volumes to what I said. Agreeing not to delve into our pasts, there have been many small moments that I've been collecting in my mind all the different ways I think his past is haunting him. One of them is the desire to always play with my hair, style it, or brush it. Initially, I thought it was his way of doting on me, and it is to a degree, but I'm realizing it is deeper than that.

Turning to him, I relay my darkest fear, the one that has been waking me up each night as he lies curled around me.

"What if I'm not good enough? What if I cause your play to be a flop, a bomb, and you hate me for it?'

The subtle hardening of his jaw and the intensifying spark in his gaze silently communicates his protectiveness.

"You could never be the cause of failure," he says with such conviction that it's hard not to believe him. "This play is a collaboration of many elements, not just your performance. And you, you're brilliant. Your talent, your dedication—it's what will make it shine."

He pauses, his hand still playing with my hair, a comforting gesture that now feels embedded with deeper significance.

"And even if, in some impossible world, it doesn't meet expectations, my feelings for you won't change. I could never hate you. You're not just part of this production. You're a part of me, little one."

The honesty in his voice and the intensity in his blue eyes cut through my fears, grounding me back to the present, to him. In his words, I find the reassurance I need—not just about the play, but about us, about where this is headed beyond the rehearsals and nights out.

"I'm never letting you go. You're my muse. If this play doesn't work out, there will be another and another, all featuring you."

He moves a strand of hair away from my face to tuck behind my ear. Hearing his future plans sends a thrill through me. What I thought would be a fleeting affair quickly turned into something far more serious. The ease of being with him, the way he takes incredible care of me, and the richness he adds to my life makes it so easy to fall in love with him.

In him, I've found the love and acceptance I have been looking for. He adores my petite size and my lithe frame, something I have been bullied for my whole life. He puts me on this pedestal where all my desires are fulfilled, my worries are heard, and my fears are soothed over. I, too, want to be with him through this play and as many as he wants to produce, regardless of whether I'm the starring role.

I lay my head back on his chest, soaking in the warmth and comfort of his care. My heart is bursting with so much emotion that I must let a little seep out, even if it's too soon to say the big words.

"I feel the same way."

The fear of saying those big words too soon is overshadowed by the truth of my feelings, a truth that, though unspoken, is as real and tangible as the heartbeat I'm listening to. He kisses the crown of my head, embracing me closer as that hard dick of his, which I'm convinced never goes down, grows against my stomach.

Time stretches on. Laying in the soothing comfort of his arms, I'm lulled into a light haze, imagining us in a year. Where we'd be, how we'd look, and how well the play did. It was like taking the vision board posted in my closet, slotting Travis into all the pictures of male models, and making my dreams come true.

We'd continue our extravagant nights out with our theater friends, attend gallery openings, possibly the Met Gala with Travis's fame and connections, and eventually travel the world, exploring new cultures and places. Daydreaming about our new life together fills me with a warm completeness, like the pages of the magazines that inspired me to move to New York in the first place.

14

_____

"**L**et me paint you, little one."

His whisper breaks the comfortable silence, sending a shiver of anticipation through me. It's a request he's made many times, one we've been too busy fulfilling due to our overbooked schedules. Now, with his self-imposed rest day, we have more time than we've had in weeks —something I'm not used to and find slightly boring, if I am being honest with myself.

"Yes."

The idea of being his muse in actions, words, and art thrills me. I imagine myself through his eyes, on canvas, a tribute to our intense feelings for each other, as an extension of what happens in the playroom.

"Really?"

His hands slide down my back, grabbing my ass to reposition me to straddle his cock.

"I detest you wearing these leisure pants. I want to rub my flower."

"You rubbed her plenty last night."

His fingertips tug at the soft fabric, tugging against the drawstring until it gives enough to slip his warm palm inside.

"No panties. I like how easily you follow my instructions."

The usual wickedness in his gaze is back when his hips buck, splaying my legs for his fingers to find the residual wetness that is always remaining for a night of passionate sex. He strokes back and forth, smearing the wetness from my clit to my pussy and back again.

"I love how red my little rosebud gets. It's one of my favorite things. How swollen these lips are. Are you sore from my cock stretching you out?"

I moan at his gentle touch, angling to kiss him when his hand on the top of my thigh keeps me in place. Rarely do I get to control things sexually with him. I can count on one hand and still have fingers left over.

"Of course I am. You made me wear your favorite little shirt with my stuff showing."

"Mmm. That would be the only thing in your closet if I could get away with it."

His fingers continue their exploration, moving from my clit, tracing circles just below my entrance before dipping inside me. His head tilts as he delves into my wetness with a look of appreciation.

"I love how open you are with me. Giving yourself over to me whenever and however I want."

My hand slides out from the side, raising to brace myself as I get more aroused by what he's doing to me. I gasp when they plunge in and out, the angle hitting so perfectly, I grind against his dick, needing more than he's giving.

"Makes me wonder if you'll ever tell me no," he muses to himself.

I groan as his fingers thrust in and out of me, as my hard clit rubs against the rough fabric of his jeans, sending waves of pleasure coursing through my body. I can't help but rock against him, desperate for more.

"I doubt you will. You're too addicted to my touch, to how I make you feel, to what this little body needs from her Orion."

Heat climbs over me, desperate to get off, even though he entirely ruined me last night. Maybe he's right. I'm addicted to him, addicted to his expert sex skills, his beautiful words fucking my ears and making me crave him more and more the longer we're together.

"Are my fingers all you want?"

His voice cuts low with lust. His pupils dilate as he watches my desperate actions of clutching his shoulders to move with him. My eyes are half open, dazed with desire and a need for him to finish what he's started.

"I want more."

My breath is ragged across his chest, blowing the edge of his dress shirt open.

"I want you to take me hard and fast, to make me scream your name."

His fingers never lose their rhythm, working my tight entrance expertly as his thumb grazes my clit, adding to the tension building into a fierce desire. I whimper, arching my back, needing his cock inside me as much as I need my next breath. He smiles wickedly, pulling his fingers out of me with a pop. I whimper at the sudden loss.

"Convince me to break my rule of no sex until the performance."

Without his perfect strokes getting me off, the build-up is fading fast, even as the wetness continues to pour out of me. I want this, need this, and him denying me for the first time is cruel, as cruel as I were to tell him no, which he just said I never would.

"Travis?"

I bat my eyes at him, looking sweet and innocent to try and

convince him. He cocks his eyebrow at my effort. I crawl up his body, giving him sweet kisses which go unreciprocated.

"After everything I've shown you."

I smile, realizing I'm his kryptonite. I'm not using myself properly to get what I want from him. With determined actions, I suddenly sit up, grinding on his dick before sliding from his body and blowing him a goodbye kiss. His eyes lit up as he watches me slowly unbutton my shirt, exposing the endless pale skin he loves so much and then let the rest of the fabric falls to the ground.

My bare breasts are exposed, the pink nipples hardening when I tease them into crested peaks and shiver with desire. I run my hands over my skin, into the waistband of my pants, and touch the very flower he claims possessive ownership of, one that I'm not allowed to pleasure without him. Without another thought, I shoved my comfy sweatpants he hates so much from my body, pooling at my feet to retrieve the vibrating rose from my dresser drawer.

Now standing completely naked in front of him, I turn it on, select the fastest setting, and lick my lips, ready to put it against his rose. His possessive streak has him scooting toward the edge of the bed with a dark stare, prepared to stop me. I dash from the room, giggling as I race toward our playroom. His long feet slap against the hard marble floors, gaining on me as I'm about to run into the room. He catches me around my midsection, sweeping me off my feet in a fierce growl.

"You're in trouble now."

The toy still hums in my hand as I naughtily try to connect with my clit. He slaps it away, sending it flying across the room before giving me a hard spank to my bare ass.

"Ow! That hurt, Travis."

His breathing is far too rapid to be from chasing after me. When I glance over my shoulder, his eyes are intense, a wild spark of dominance reflecting in their dark depths. He carries me over to a piece of furniture tucked into the corner of the room, a torch-like wall sconce above it that he flips on to illuminate the area.

"It's meant to hurt, little one."

He faces me facing the short, massage-looking table, my knees resting on the black pads as his hand pushes against my back to encourage me to lay on my stomach.

"You broke two rules. Do you know what they are?"

As much as I want to say I hate this, I'm crazy turned on by this dark, dominant side, a peek of it revealing every now and again over these past weeks but nothing to this level. Knowing I trust him fully, I decide to play along. If putting on a show is what he wants, then that's exactly what I'll give him to get what I want. Fucked hard and fast until I'm deliciously sated.

"I didn't do anything wrong. You said to put on a show. That's what I was trying to do, Travis."

I throw in his given name for good measure, knowing that's breaking a third rule of his. When I look over my shoulder, he's glaring at me, his mouth set in the same manner as when he yells at the theater. It's thrilling being on the receiving end now, my mind wanting to push him further until his hand sails through the air with a loud and very painful slap to my ass.

"Oh, fuck, that hurts."

My hand swiftly moves to ease the sting when he captures it by the wrist to strap it to some pads at either side of the bench, forcing me forward.

"Keep it up, little one, and that won't be the only thing hurting."

My ass still smarts, the pain radiating from the initial impact to the flesh surrounding it. As I'm positioned on the bench, the constellation necklace digs into my skin, and I'm adjusting to fix that pain.

"Stop squirming, or it will only be worse."

"Your necklace is digging into my throat, and I don't want marks that I can't hide in my costume."

My attitude continues, wondering what he will do about it as he's occupied with buckling the leather restraints around my calves. They are snug, leaving me little room to move around without leaving marks that my hosiery can't cover again.

Another hard spank leaves me howling and cussing. Fortunately, it's on the other side, disbursing the sting in another direction.

"Drop the attitude and change your tone."

His voice is low, with a steely edge that has me twisting my head to find him to ensure we're still playing and this hasn't taken a severe turn. With the last restraint to my arm, he squats to stare into my eyes. The beautiful blue of his is gone, overtaken by blacked-out pupils full of primal hunger.

"But I didn't do anything wrong," I protest while he gathers my hair and fastens it in a clip at the back of my head, somehow tucking my necklace into it.

"Incorrect answer. I gave you the choice to accept the rules, which you did. Wholeheartedly, I might add. You chose to break them all. Now you will learn that there are consequences to your actions."

"I was trying to give you what you wanted. What we wanted."

His nostrils flare as his mind figures out what to do with this information. A wicked smile tugs at the corner of his lips as he leans closer, his mouth brushing against my ear.

"That's exactly what I want to hear. You, little one, will always give me what I want. Now, let's get started, shall we?"

His hand slides out of my hair to my nape, grips it firmly, and pushes my head down into the padded opening, and I can't help but shiver at the intensity of this moment. My once playful words now sound empty and meek compared to his unyielding mood. With my limbs restrained, my face now looking at his feet, I focus on my breathing, unwilling to say anything else.

With a swiftness that surprises me, he stands up and moves away. Having to rely on my other senses, he intentionally moves with stealth, keeping the noise down until soft furriness tickles down my back, leaving me squirming in delight before another hard spanking jolts me forward against the padding. Another long caress down my back has me twisting and turning away from the source until he pauses, and I brace for another spanking that doesn't come. Seconds tick by, and when I relax, then the smack comes.

"You can't outwit me, little one. I'm watching your every move."

He does it twice, and my cries get louder as the hits get harder and the stinging lasts longer.

"Your skin has the most delicious redness to it. Should we continue and make it purple?"

He's muttering to himself while kneading my ass, massaging the muscles when I want a finger or two to find my soaking core and give me the pleasure I desperately need. With a bit of give in the restraints, I move my body, trying to line his fingers where I want them the most. He reigns down another set of spankings, followed by the kneading and then another chased by the ticklish fur.

"You can't leave marks. My costumes."

My mind is a mess, trying to calculate what comes next with him changing the order. Once he passes ten spankings, my throat is getting raw from crying out, and my ass is on fire, well on his journey to achieving a purple one. A shiver of lust runs through me at the thought of it, my body betraying my concern and desire in equal measure.

"Are you ready to apologize? To obey your Orion? Or should I continue?"

His hands leave my body, and I clench my ass together,

protecting myself while trying to figure out of this is a trick or not. If I answer yes, this will end, but what next? Will he get me off? If I push him, will the punishment continue? I don't know what I want. I haven't had to decide anything between us in this room, so asking me if it is unfair on his part.

"Why are you asking me? Aren't you supposed to be in charge?"

My witty remark is out before I realize it, my brain blurting out my inner thoughts in the quiet room, which has him sharply taking in the air around us. My fate is sealed when something clatters to the ground, and I startle, the loudness making my pulse spike and my pussy throb.

"Thank you for correcting my oversight."

His voice is dark and deadly, above a whisper, when he walks away, opening and slamming drawers. My breath shallows, forcing my rib cage to push against the padding, which I know he'll notice and hopefully go easy on me. Intending to use sound to intimidate me is working. The anticipation of the unknown works more in his favor than he realizes.

"Three times you disobeyed me. Three is what you will take."

His mouth hovers above my ear, his breath tickling across my skin.

"Your safe word is master. And I'll leave marks where no one can see them."

A dangerous thrill slides over me, rocketing my horniness to a new level when he says, "safe word," something he previously said was too formal. We're on the precipitous of something new and unexplored, and a deep level of trust is required, especially with the threat of leaving marks in private areas. My brain is concerned, and my body is on fire, wanting to test our boundaries and traverse paths unexplored prior.

"I'd like to see you try," I slur against the face cushion, met with a dark chuckle and a single finger moving softly down my spine until he reaches my pussy.

"Three. No more, no less."

Three what? My brain is racing through scenarios, knowing almost all the items in this room and wondering what he's counting as punishment. I'll gladly take it if it's only three more spankings and three more feather things. When the sounds of his belt swooshing through his belt loops fill my ears, I bare down, bracing for the worst of it.

The shuffling of materials follows, and I realize he's getting naked himself, a measure of comfort soothing over my fraught nerves, overreacting to every sound he makes. His finger slowly stroked my pussy, and I close my eyes as I moan. The pleasure sparks in my veins, and my hips roll in sync with him.

"My little rose is so swollen, aching to be touched. Wanting to please me. Can we agree on this?"

"Yes."

I breathe into the word, loving the gentleness of his touch while his finger strokes a longer expanse from my clit and over my taint to my asshole, which has me jerk forward and clench my cheeks.

"Your body calls to me, little one. It tells me exactly what you need and what I want. You might think this is punishment, and it will be at first, but soon, you will grow as addicted to this as you are to me."

I can't imagine what he has in mind that I would think to be terrible if this is how it starts. His words send a jolt of excitement through me, the thrill of his dominance sending my nerves into overdrive. My whole body tingles at the thought of what's to come, and I can't help but let out a soft moan.

A quick click sounds, then a thick coating of something warm against my asshole has my thighs clenching and my whole body tightening. A surge of panic fills my mind if he's thinking of anal sex with me, especially with that giant dick of his. I lift my head, wanting to look at him, to convey my worry, when his hand splays across my upper back.

"Relax, it's far more pleasurable when you do."

I don't even have a moment to relax before his fingers spread my cheeks and press something huge against my tight ring.

"This is a trainer plug that goes up in size."

I don't know if his narrating is better or worse, but when he pulls it away to rub circles over my hole, I relax again— moaning at the raw sensitivity of it until he breeches me with a finger. He sets a rhythm my brain can keep up with, circling the outside, pushing inside, and gently moving in and out. My heart races, pounding in my ears, as my mind is flooded with a mixture of pain and pleasure.

It's an erotic dance, one I'm getting used to and moving with when he replaces his finger with the toy. I hold my breath when it breeches me, the size difference from his finger to the toy feeling as if I'm split open, and the pain eclipses the pleasure until it's back out again.

"Ah, you're dripping onto the floor, little one. You love this. I knew you would."

I don't love this. My mind hates it. The pain is all I can focus on as my body is a traitor to his punishment. The pattern continues with me moving away when I know what's coming. He doesn't scold or chastise me for bracing myself. He continues the slow and methodical pace until it stops, deeply impaling me. His thumbs pull at my hole, feeling as if he's trying to rip me apart when the toy settles further.

"Perfect, Isla. You look stunning. Crimson ass, jewel plug, and wetness clinging to your legs."

His words are thick. His desire for how he sees me is a turn-on, making me want to please him and always have him see me as beautiful in every way and position he puts me in.

"I'm sorry, Travis. I didn't mean to break your rules."

My words are muffled, his hand on my back instantly massaging my muscles.

"I only wanted to be playful."

"Thank you, little one. There's my good girl. But you're still not getting out of your punishment."

Slowly, he eases the plug out, my muscles clenching around it in protest. As it pops free, a gush of fluid escapes me. I'm so turned on my pussy pulses in need. My body is on fire, sweat forming as I try to anticipate his every move.

His fingers glide over my slick flesh, teasing me with his painful pleasure or pleasurable pain, I don't know which. The toy slowly re-enters me, its thick girth sliding against the sensitive skin of my ass. I gasp, my body trembling as the pain fades into a dull ache, replaced by a wave of pleasure.

"You love this, Isla. I knew you'd obey."

Travis's voice is a sinuous caress, his words a subtle command that sends shivers down my spine. Suddenly, the toy starts vibrating, sending delicious electrical pulses out from my most sensitive area all over my body. I've never felt this before. The intrusion both hated and loved, wanting more and unsure if I can handle it. When he gently pumps the toy in and out, my breath elongates, holding it when it pushes in and gasping when it exits.

With each slow thrust, he sends me closer to an orgasm, building somewhere in my body. The emptiness of my pussy and the fullness of my asshole is a delicate balance of agony and ecstasy. My limbs strain against their restraints, wanting more of him or more of the toy, something to race me off the edge of the cliff that I'm dangling from. The slow pace my brain has adjusted to, my body meeting every one of his thrusts with one of my own until sharp teeth bite into my pussy.

"Fuck . . . that . . that hurts," I cry, the pinching and weight sending me into a tizzy of panic and wiggling my hips to get it off me.

"It's meant to, as part of your punishment."

His calm voice cuts through the storm in my mind as I try to get whatever is digging into my engorged flesh off.

"The more you move, the tighter the labia clamp becomes."

I scream at the sudden revelation, and my body arches forward, the teeth biting into my skin as I struggle against the pain.

"I'm so sorry, please, it's just so tight," I sob, my eyes watering as I try to regain some level of control.

Travis's fingers gently massage my inner thigh, his touch soft against my flushed skin.

"You'll learn to appreciate the sensation, little one. It will make you crave more next time."

The words resonate through me, a shiver running down my spine. For a moment, I can't decide whether to curse or thank him. As if sensing my distress, he quietly places another vibrating toy at my clit. The pleasure erases some of the pain from the biting teeth and mixes with the incredible sensations of the toy buried in my ass.

"That's right," he whispers, "Climb that cliff, little one."

My body responds to his voice, yearning for the release he promises me. I arch my back, feeling the familiar build-up within me. He continues to tease me, his fingers everywhere, using both toys to, for, and against me. It's a cruel reminder of the pleasure I am denied yet crave so desperately. I gasp, my body trembling as the vibrations intensify. He leans in and whispers in my ear, sending shivers down my spine.

"Let it take you closer to the edge, Isla. Surrender to the pleasure in your mind, and you'll find the release you seek."

I close my eyes, trying to follow his instructions, focusing on the tingling build-up of my orgasm. The vibrations, the thrusts, the pain, and the pleasure all merge into one intense feeling. My entire body is alive, desperate to find what he's freely giving. What my body and mind quickly want is eluding me. My breath quickens, and my muscles are taut, straining and contracting into and away from the various instruments meant to shove me over the brink.

"That's it. Let go. Give in to the pleasure."

The vibrations intensify, and I can feel it deep within my core, a wave of warmth that melts away any resistance I have left. I can't hold on any longer. My body convulses, and I let out a primal scream as I'm pushed over it.

With each writhing motion and deep moan, I feel an over-whelming sense of surrender and release. It's as if I've been freed from an invisible shackle, my mind and body in perfect harmony.

The toys pulsate rhythmically, syncing to the pounding of my heart as the orgasmic waves continue to wash over me. I'm lost in a haze of euphoria, my body pulsating with each intensity of pleasure that surges through me. Every gasp, every cry, every shivering spasm is an audible testament to the release I've been yearning for.

"Good girl," Travis whispers in my ear, messing with the clip in my hair. When I think he'll let it out, he's only removing my necklace, laying it flat in the middle of my back as a posses-sive stamp. "You've taken your first punishment very well. I expected you to safe word at one point."

The thought of safe wording didn't even occur to me. Too lost in his experiment of punishment, pain, and pleasure. He removes the clamp and toys, and the absence of their vibrating pressure creates a strange emptiness within me. My veins feel as if they are vibrating now. My body sags with exhaustion, oblivious to the need to clean up, to walk out of here and resume life. All that matters is the deep-seated feeling erasing all stress and worry from my body.

"I don't. . ."

My eyes close again, my face smashed into the pads while he undoes the restraints that I've been in for a long time.

Without any help from me, he removes me from the contraption, laying me on the tantra sofa across the room while he stands like a naked god before me. There's a debate brewing on his face while he watches me. My arm reaches in a lazy attempt to coax him down to me when he shakes his head and steps to the higher curved end of the couch.

"You're my perfect little doll. To do what I want with."

His muses are to himself, something I've grown accustomed to. My body is weightless, without any strength or will to move. My brain is flying free of negative thoughts or emotions as the endorphin surge is mighty. Despite the intensity of the sensations, I'm aware of the void that still lingers between my legs. I want to feel him inside me, to lose myself to his touch, to know that he's in control.

"Fuck me, my Orion."

His eyes glimmer, taking in the sight of me and deciding what to do next. With a smirk and a flash of his eyebrow, his hands catch under my butt, the tender skin smarting as he pulls me across the couch to align my pussy with his angry red dick. How he's held off from coming this long is a feat, superhero-ish restraint.

"This is for me, Isla. Not a punishment, but without the worry of pleasing you."

I never thought of the toll it might take on him to put me first. The planning or decisions he meticulously makes every time we're in this room. It makes sense that he'd need a break from all that pressure to get his.

"Take me, Travis," I whisper, my voice weak and breathy as my arms splay above my head, content to just lay here. "Make me yours."

With my legs tucked over his hips, legs set in a wide stance, the curve of the sofa stretches my back, the opposite of the pressure placed on the front of my body. This is an inversion of that previous contraption, allowing my pussy to be higher than my head and upper body.

His eyes never leave mine as he slowly enters me, the heat and pressure of his shaft easing in, slightly deeper with each thrust. A groan escapes his lips, his teeth clenched as he adjusts to the sensation. Every part of my body opens for him, yearning for his release and mine.

"It's going to be intense."

I whimper, the thought of his raw desire making me tremble. I've never seen him like this before, never been placed behind his pleasure, and it's exhilarating. His hands grip my hips, guiding me onto him, inch by inch. His eyes are glued to the head of his fat cock, opening me up, stretching me wider when he grabs one of my legs and shoves it down toward my chest. With one leg draped toward the floor and the other forced in the opposite direction, my back arches into his cock. I gasp at the angle, the way it hits my G-spot so perfectly that I moan. This is my favorite new position in this room.

A deep growl escapes him as he slowly speeds up, his eyes revealing the raw intensity of his desire. My hands clutch the side of the couch, trying to hold on while my nails dig into the expensive leather, ready to join him in ecstasy again.

"Fucking perfect little toy."

His eyes glaze, a fierce determination burning in them as if he no longer sees me but a fantasy. Each thrust becomes harder and deeper than the last. I can feel my walls tightening around him, yearning for the release that is so close yet still a tantalizing distance away.

His breaths come in short, ragged gasps, the sound filling the room as we move together in a harsh and primal dance. My moans echo in response, matching his in intensity and desperation. Every sensation and every touch becomes heightened, and I can feel the heat building within me, ready to explode at any moment.

He holds up what looks like a silver bobby pin with four round balls, getting progressively larger on each side. I don't know what it is, and before I can ask, he's fastening it over my labia. The biting teeth are back. I cry out in pain, hating that the most of the three things he did to me. My hands release the couch, my arms moving toward it when he shakes his head to stop me.

"Remember, little one. It's not a punishment."

His hands wrapped around my thighs, pulling me further onto him with each crash of his hips. I thought he was just as close as I was in our mutual frenzy, but with the clamp back on, my orgasm is fading fast, taking the good feeling with it.

"Look at how pretty your jeweled pussy is, little one."

His face stares at it in wonder. The sizzling smolder is mesmerizing as my flesh pinches tight and rises to where I can see it prominently separated from my body.

"You deserve more jewelry."

Lost in whatever world this is, he slips from my body, leaving me sprawled out for his pleasure. I don't know what more I can wear besides earrings, his necklace already at my throat. A couple of drawers open and close before he returns, kneeling beside me to make out with me. It's hot and erotic, precisely what I need when I feel another set of teeth on my tiny nipples. They bite with less pain, bearable as his lips leave mine to place the other nipple.

They carry the same four balls with a chain that connects all three. It's erotic and hot, almost sending my pussy into convulsions when he slides back in and everything tights, the sting intensifying while he fucks the shit out of me.

"Yes, this is how you should always look."

His fingers spread my lips wider, the teeth clamping harder and making the blood rush to my labia, turning them purple. He tugs on the chain, the teeth burning intensely at all three points.

A heated frenzy ensued, his relentless thrusts driving me wild. The pain and pleasure are now indistinguishable, melding into an ecstatic symphony. Our bodies moved in perfect harmony, a wild dance of desire and intimacy.

Suddenly, he releases a primal roar, his hips jerking wildly against me as he climaxes within me. He keeps bucking, riding it out, and dragging mine along with him. Pure bliss washes over me at the sight of him, his blazing eyes staring at me with another claim of jewel-encrusted ownership. Somehow, the pain and pleasure entwined, creating an exquisite climax that leaves me breathless and trembling.

He doesn't remove the clamps as quickly as he did last time, and I wish he would, as it's growing more uncomfortable when his dick slips from me. He pads the room, his tight ass on display as the long, lean muscles in his back ripple when he does a few chin-ups on some high bar we have yet to use. I shallow my breaths, trying not to move my breasts to avoid the toys tightening further.

"Master."

He turns with immediate concern, his eyes quickly accessing me up and down to see why I would safe word after everything he's put me through.

"I'm alright," I manage to whisper, my voice ragged with both pain and pleasure. "Please take the clamps off."

He hesitates for a moment, then crosses the room in silence, reaching out to tenderly remove the clamps from my nipples and pussy, leaving the chain to lie in a pool on my body. I let out a shuddering sigh of relief as the pressure eases and the flow of blood returns to my sensitive peaks. He squats to cup my face in his strong hands, his irises a glowing blue with a hint of peace.

"If you're addicted, then I'm addicted too."

15

"Oh my God, who are you? I'm calling the police right now because some stranger is breaking into my house," Lily declares, her voice dripping with mock alarm when I unlock the front door and find her standing in the foyer with her hand over her chest. Her eyes widen in fear while she pretends not to know me.

This act, meant in jest, sends a ripple of annoyance through me. With an eye roll, I try to brush off the fatigue clinging to my body after yesterday's escapades with Travis and his insistence to paint me nude in the playroom into the wee hours of the morning. Today was supposed to be a rest day for me, but I practically had to beg Travis to let me go to retrieve my lucky charm. Something he didn't believe necessary as "theater superstitions are fodder for old thespians."

"Very funny. We were just together less than two days ago for the final rehearsals," I retort, flinging my keys onto the table and making my way to the kitchen.

I'm greeted by a sink brimming with dishes coated in dried food. On the stove, dirty pots and pans are scattered about, accompanied by half-opened drinks strewn across the counters.

"You do know this is New York, right? Roaches don't need an invitation to come in, and you have a buffet set out for them."

She lifts a careless shoulder before squeezing past me to get a canned drink out of the fridge, ignoring her mess in this room.

"And why are you over here? Did that moody playwright of yours finally let you out of the dungeon he keeps you in?" Lily asks, her eyebrows haughty.

I know it's been a long time since we hung out, but she always left with her theater friends to go out while I had late rehearsals. I overheard them talking about it while behind the sets, saying I only got the part because I was sleeping with him. Lily stood up for me once, but her silence was deafening and hurtful the next time.

I never mentioned the whispers to Travis. He would've waved them off, deeming them too minor to fret over. And with her, the words never found their way out, tangled in my uncertainty of how to start that conversation.

Time trickled on, and her friends swiftly whisked her away whenever our paths crossed, sealing my decision to let the matter rest silently. Meanwhile, my escapades with Travis's theater companions whisked me into grander, influential realms that echoed my ambitions, contrasting the stagnant waters where Lily and her group seemed to float.

Lily's question hangs, but her silence two weeks ago stings more than any rumor could. I shrug, trying to match her nonchalance to shield my bruised feelings.

"Just here to pick up my good luck charm."

I sidestep the real issue, the hurt, and the gossip that has wedged a gap between my old life and the new one I'm carving out with Travis. The apartment's disarray mirrors the clutter in my thoughts—dishes piled high like the unsaid things between Lily and me, the half-open drinks as unfinished as our last conversation when I picked up Anna and she asked if she needed to sublet the place despite cashing my rent check. I clear a small spot on the counter and lean against it.

"How have you been, anyway?"

I attempt to steer us back to safer waters, but the chasm isn't easily crossed. Lily's gaze flickers with something—regret, maybe, or a hint of longing for how things used to be before the roles, rumors, and Travis came between us. Her response is a shrug, a mirror of her earlier gesture, but this time, it's laden with more than just indifference.

"Busy but not as busy as you."

I can hear the unspoken words hanging between us, the acknowledgment of our drifted paths, the unsaid apologies, and the shared memories that seem as distant now as the stars.

"How's school?"

"Suffering."

The word slips out more honestly than intended. The thought of retreating to the lab, to immerse myself in the solace of my project—a refuge from the storm of anxieties about tonight's performance—suddenly seems like the best idea I've had all day, aside from retrieving my good luck charm.

"I might head there after this. It's Saturday, so it'll be quiet."

The once-happy apartment where we made cookies, watched old movies, and talked about our dreams now feels awkward and intrusive as we cautiously dance around the elephant in the room. Lily leans against the counter, her figure framed by the morning light that sieves through the grimy window as she pops the top on her soda, the sound echoing between us.

"Are you still working on that metallic bodysuit?"

Her attempt at casual conversation feels like a probe into unfamiliar territory, which is odd and uncomfortable. A smile finds its way through my raised guard, sparked by the genuine curiosity in her tone.

"Yeah, it's practically become a part of me since I drag it everywhere to work on. I hope it gets selected as a finalist in the competition or, at the very least, a good grade with how much work I'm putting into it."

I change my posture, dropping my arms and opening up to her, hoping it might serve as a bridge between us. But in the back of my mind, I know that some conversations, no matter how daunting, will need to be had, and some bridges, no matter how weathered, are worth trying to mend. Eventually, I'll have to ask her why she didn't defend me that day.

"Well, I'd love to see it, you know, when it's done."

The offer, vulnerable and hesitant, is more an olive branch than interest.

"I'd like that."

My phone pings in my bag, and I already know who it is. Lily's eyes shift as well, a look of irritation crossing her face before sipping her drink.

"Seems like the playwright is looking for his star."

Her comment, laced with a hint of sarcasm, cuts through the tentative warmth we're rebuilding. It's an unnecessary dig into our relationship that speaks to a jealousy I didn't realize she felt. I fish my phone out, glancing at the screen to confirm my suspicion—Travis, indeed, asking when I'll be back. I tuck the phone back, a small sigh escaping me.

"He's just checking in," I say, trying to keep the defensiveness out of my voice.

I don't want to give the impression that I'm choosing sides, but it's hard not to feel like I'm being pulled in two directions. She nods, suddenly disinterested, and pushes off the counter.

"Then you should probably get going. I'll see you tonight anyway."

She doesn't bother waiting for my response when she exits the kitchen to disappear into her bedroom, unnecessarily kicking the door closed behind her even though she'll have the whole place to herself.

"Good luck to you too," I mutter into the fragile silence, leaving the mess in the kitchen and the mess in our friendship behind to retrieve my lucky charm.

Surrounded by scattered tools and fabric scraps, I stand frustrated over my nearly completed bodysuit. It's molded around the dress form, one side protruding by a quarter of an inch too much, as though my measurements and cutting were off. That certainly isn't the case, or else I would have noticed it by now. My phone pings with a text, and after messaging Travis the first time that I was out running another errand, I didn't wait for his reply.

It was nice to have some time on my own. Something I didn't know I missed until I was standing back in the bright lab, with the space all to myself to focus on my project. Now, with another annoying ping, I grab my phone and see it's not Travis but Gabe asking about pregame jitters.

Deciding it's easier to call him, I plop down on the stool and hit his number. It rings several times before he picks up, out of breath.

"Hey, Gabe, it's me." My voice echoes in the spacious lab. "Why are you breathing so hard?"

"Jogging, love."

His British accent wraps around the term of endearment and immediately eases some of my tension.

"I just saw your text. Pregame jitters? You could say that. I'm in the lab at school, wrestling with my bodysuit project. It's. . . challenging."

I cradle the phone between my ear and shoulder, tugging on the ill-fitting side of the bodysuit for the hundredth time.

"It sounds like you're having a bit of a tussle there. Do you need a second pair of hands or just a pep talk?"

My hands fall from the half-finished bodysuit, the metallic catching the light as I step back to look at the sheer dress lying forgotten on the drafting table. He chuckles over the city sounds in the background.

"A pep talk might be more practical, unless you've picked up sewing as a side hustle and are willing to jog over here."

"Actually, I'm not far from you. It's just a few blocks if you can let me in. Then I can see what's got you so bothered."

His encouragement flows through the phone, a lifeline to my frustration.

"Really? Of course, I'll let you in. I'm walking to the door right now."

I spin on my heel, leaving that stubborn body suit askew on the form to leave the room. Through the phone, I can hear the rhythmic sound of his jogging, and I immediately feel guilty that he's helping me again when I haven't talked to him much lately.

"Hey, I'm sorry if I ghosted you the last few weeks."

"Ghosted me? Are we dating, and I didn't know about it?" His teasing words are spoken with such affection that I bit my lip. "I'm joshing with you."

As I approach the door, the hallway feels longer, my steps slow and deliberate. The once stark white walls are now alive with vibrant colors, adorned with an art installation by the upper-level students.

"I know, but you've reached out, and I haven't been the best at responding. Now, here you are, coming to my rescue again. I'm not sure that's how friendship is supposed to work."

There's a pause on his end, the subtext I'm trying to convey without coming right out and saying I've been a shitty friend to him as my friendship with Lily is falling apart.

"Isla, we both have a lot on our plates. I do not monitor

every interaction or tally up who lends a hand more often. That's just silly."

There's a soothing certainty in what he says, making me realize he's the only one who doesn't demand something from me. Travis always makes demands, and Lily's demands are silent and wrapped in the hurt I caused her by spending my time with him. But then Gabe comes along and makes every-thing easy and light—as if we can just be, and that's good enough for him.

"And as one of my patients told me the other day before surgery, "You do you boo."

I bust up laughing, catching a glimpse of him running on the street, his broad smile seen from a distance. The phrase is funnier with his proper accent, sounding more like the Queen saying it than a handsome doctor.

"Did you like that? Should I infuse more of the children's phraseology into our conversations? They are quite adept at making up their language."

His breathing becomes lighter and lighter the closer he gets to my building, unaware I'm watching him through the door. He reminds me of Regé-Jean Page, who has a similar bone structure and coloring. Gabe's lips are a little fuller, and his smile is wider. His broad shoulders are pronounced in his tank, and his legs are defined and shapely. His effortless wide strides display his athletic prowess and grace.

"I forgot that you talk to your patients. I figure it was only their parents you dealt with outside of surgery."

A vision of crying parents in the waiting room always comes to mind, and I imagine him pulling the cap from his head as he explains how it went. Maybe I've watched too much Grey's Anatomy.

"I always make it a point to develop a working relationship with the children and their parents. I see it as an endeavor in which we all play a part, none more important than the other.

Plus, studies show that rehabilitation rates are better when they feel supported by their medical team."

He pauses at a stoplight, keeping the rhythm by jogging and earbuds securely in place as he waits for the traffic to clear.

"You should visit the hospital sometime, see it in action. Or better yet, show up in character. They'd absolutely love that."

"I play an aging, clinically depressed former circus performer addicted to cigars and alcohol, trying to relive the glory days of my fame by entertaining men in a rundown apartment," I say with a smirk as our eyes connect when he sees me through the glass doors.

"Not quite the superhero figure my young patients aspire to emulate."

He ends the call as I open the door for him, and he greets me with a hug, damp with sweat, prompting me to angle my face away.

"I don't smell too bad, do I?"

"No, but I'd rather not wear your sweat."

Gabe laughs, releasing me from the hug but keeping an arm casually draped over my shoulder as we step into the cooler air of the building.

"Fair enough. I'll spare you the 'Eau de Jogging' this time."

We navigate the quiet hallways, our footsteps a soft echo in the empty space. The frustration over my project feels less now with reinforcements arriving.

"About the hospital," he nudges gently as we walk. "Do you think you'd be up for it? Maybe not in your circus performer outfit, but as yourself? The kids would love to meet someone as talented and driven as you. Plus, it might be a nice break from the lab, play, and whatever else keeps you busy."

Dani used to do with me when I was in child protective services. I used to live for her and Uncle Alex's visits. This isn't precisely the same situation, but I understand the difficulty of being in a place you didn't choose, having to deal with choices others have made for you, all under the guise of it being for "your own good."

"Yeah, that sounds like something I could do."

"Good, now tell me what's wrong with your piece."

His heavy arm falls from my shoulder as we enter the room, the stubborn body suit displaying the problem as we walk towards it.

"This is it? This is what we talked about that day, Isla."

The adoration in his voice is apparent. He sprints over to it, leaving me to trail behind as his fingertips run across the silver material and hard boning at the ribcage.

"This is phenomenal work. The precision, the creativity . . . it's absolute artistry."

His eyes sparkle with genuine respect, reflecting the lab's fluorescent lights when I join him. He pulls me into a side hug as we stare at the same thing—the source of my frustration and the work of art in his eyes. Feeling a sense of pride and buoyed by his praise, I lean into him, soaking up all the encouragement he's giving.

I think it's suffering with all the late nights, long hours, and intermittent time to work on this project. This is usually my last priority because I need to concentrate on my other classes and spend enough time with Travis and Anna outside the play and rehearsal.

"Thanks, that means a lot, especially coming from you since this was your idea."

"*Our* idea, love."

He continues to marvel at the design, his enthusiasm unabated.

"The way you've integrated these materials, it's innovative. You're pushing boundaries here."

Encouraged by his words, I point out the flaw nagging at me.

"I appreciate that, but there's the snag. See here?"

I gesture to the side of the bodysuit, where the fabric juts out awkwardly by a half-inch, disrupting the otherwise sleek line that must be resolved before the white dress slips over it. He steps closer, his arm falling from around me as he assesses the issue.

"I see what you mean. But, you know, this could be an easy fix. What if you adjusted the seam here?" He points just below the discrepancy, suggesting a subtle alteration.

"Shift the seam?" I repeat, the solution already tried and dismissed as messing up the other seams and how they fall, creating a noticeable imbalance. "Yeah, I already thought about that. A shift might redistribute the tension across the fabric, evening it out, but it compromises the design."

"Hmm."

He stands, takes several steps back, tilts his head, then walks back to the dress form. Several long seconds pass before he faces me with a look of determination.

"May I?"

"Sure."

I shrug and sigh, content to watch him delicately remove the body suit from the form and then turn it inside out to examine the stitching. When he moves to the table to lay it flat, I realize that this must be similar to brain surgery in a way.

"I know you're a pediatric cranial neurosurgeon. Jeez, that's a mouthful, but do you open the skull and stitch them back up?"

The very thought of it makes me squeamish, all that blood and the sound of the bone cracking. Yuck. Gabe pauses in his examination of the bodysuit, his attention shifting to me. An amused smile plays on his lips as he catches my grimace.

"Who else would do it?"

His tone is light yet underscored by the weight of the responsibility he carries in his profession. What makes me marvel is that he always seems calm and laid back, which is the opposite of what I think a person who operates on brains and saves kids would be.

"I guess I thought maybe an assistant surgeon or something would handle that part. You know, McDreamy doesn't always do the stitching. They've got residents and interns for that kind of thing."

His laughter fills the room, light and unburdened, as he stands up straight, looking down at me with an amused glint. His hand remains lightly on the bodysuit as if he hesitates to step away before offering assistance.

"Did you just compare me to a fictional Caucasian surgeon on television?"

I can't help but grin up at him. The comparison now seems absurd when said out loud.

"Well, when you put it like that, it sounds silly. But you've got to admit, there's a certain dramatic flair to how you handle both brain surgery and bodysuit adjustments."

He shakes his head, still chuckling, with amusement in his eyes.

"I'll take the compliment, though I think the drama in the OR is a bit more intense than what we have here."

His gaze softens as he looks back at the bodysuit, his fingers tracing the seam we discussed earlier.

"But in both cases, it's all about making things right, isn't it? Fixing what's broken or improving what can be made better."

I nod, struck by the simplicity and depth of his analogy. Whether it's stitching up a child's skull or correcting a misaligned seam, he moves through both worlds with a grace and confidence that's both reassuring and inspiring.

"Alright, Dr. McDreamy, let's see if we can perform a successful 'operation' on this bodysuit together."

His laughter fills the room again, making the challenges ahead seem even more manageable.

"I've been called many things but never McDreamy."

A smile blankets his face, and his eyes linger on me as the banter fades, leaving me feeling as light and airy as his laugh. He clears his voice and shakes his head, clearing away whatever he wants to say next and stooping over the garment again.

"Have you thought about darting the fabric here?" He points to a spot just above the discrepancy. "It might pull it in enough to correct the misalignment without redoing the whole section."

"Darting?" I consider his suggestion, the simplicity of it, slicing through my overcomplicated worries. "But what about the boning? I'd have to redo that."

My fingertips run over the boning, which is an absolute hassle to hand stitch, leaving me frustrated and my fingers aching.

"Not necessarily."

He lays the garment flat on the drafting table again, then picks up the tape measure to lay it against the spot he is referencing. Giving him a space to work, I move the stool out of his way and plant my butt on it to watch his genius at work. He mirrors my actions by grabbing the stool closest to him and sitting down, hunching over my design while doing measurements in his head.

"Did you hand stitch this?"

He studies the stitching on both sides of the vertical boning to make the silvery ornate design soften the harsh metallic look.

"Yes, it was such a hassle, and there are not enough thimbles in the world to make me want to redo it."

My words are a warning to devise something else when I know what he's thinking. He smiles, knowing exactly why I'm saying it, but that confident look relays that this is my solution.

"Trust me, a small adjustment here could save you hours of frustration. Plus, it'll maintain the integrity of your design."

"Gabe, no."

I groan, my head falling into my hands to convey that I'm just going to give up on this whole damn thing and get a failing grade.

"I can't do it. My fingers will bleed if I have to mess with that again. The boning is so stiff, and the metallic is hard as hell."

His fingers find my shoulder, gently rubbing the tension in my tight neck muscles to comfort me. I groan at how good it feels but still want to give up and throw my project in the trash.

"I could take a stab at it for you if you don't mind."

His offer is generous and completely unexpected, even if it's meant to be reassuring. My head darts up, and I stare at him so long that he continues.

"I'm not going to redo the whole thing. Just tweak it—minimal stitching is required. I've got an idea that might work without dismantling your hard work."

He explains his plan, outlining a method to adjust the boning without extensive alterations to the existing stitches. His hands move with precision as he demonstrates on the fabric, his fingers deftly avoiding the intricate stitching I'd labored over for hours.

"As for the stiffness," he continues, reaching for a small tool from across the table. "I can gently manipulate the boning, soften it just enough to make your adjustment easier. And for the metallic fabric, there are ways to handle it that won't require as much force."

"Um, okay? Knock yourself out, I guess."

My words drip with skepticism while a smile brightens his face. He moves the stool closer to mine, explaining each step with a clarity that demystifies the daunting task ahead. It's not just his confidence that reassures me but the genuine care and effort he's putting into helping me succeed.

As he puts me to work threading the needle, he reminds me of the upcoming gala and asks if I have decided to go with him. How could I not? After all the help, he's been working on my project and redoing it as we speak. Of course, I'll go to it. He provides me with all the details, understanding that I'll have to go after the play lets out that night, which he says will allow for a fashionably late entrance.

The conversation blends into today with Lily and her not defending me against the casting couch rumors. Gabe's raised eyebrow is like a punctuation mark, highlighting the revelation amid our task.

"You're dating the director?" he asks, a note of surprise lacing his voice, casting a new light on the dynamics of my life that I rarely share.

"Playwright."

I put down the needle, taking a moment to compose my response.

"It's . . . complicated," I admit, the word feeling inadequate to describe the tangled web of my personal and professional life. "Travis and I, we're involved, but it's not what everyone thinks."

He nods, a gesture of understanding, but I can see the wheels turning, reassessing what he knows of me with this new information.

"Doesn't make it any easier with the rumors, I'd imagine?"

"No, it doesn't. I thought she'd stand up for me. Not participate." Her betrayal stings anew as I talk about it. "Why wouldn't she do that? I thought we were friends, and jeez, I'm her roommate even."

"You know I care for you, Isla and—"

I grab his arm, assuring him that the feeling is mutual.

"I care about you too! You're such a good friend, Gabe."

The flash of emotion in his eyes is gone as quickly as it appeared, leaving me to wonder what thoughts lie behind his stoic facade.

"You know, sometimes what people do or don't do says more about them than it does about you."

His hands resume their skilled movements over the fabric, and I retract my hand. Actions often reveal true intentions.

"It's just that Lily and I were close, you know? Or at least, I thought we were. It's hard to realize you might not mean as much to someone as they do to you."

He looks up from the bodysuit, locking eyes with me, and it's as if the air has gone out of the room. The intensity of his gaze, staring at me as if he's staring into my soul when I spoke those words, has me wondering once again if he's gay or if there could be more to this than I think.

"Isla, whoever you're important to, whoever truly values you, will show it."

The sudden deepness of his voice, as if he were struggling to tell me something, is interrupted by the ringing of my phone, which I thought was stuck on silent. The unexpected call slices through the thick tension, encroaching on this secluded space where truths are half-spoken and feelings hang by a thread.

I hesitate, torn between the desire to continue our conversation, to delve deeper into something that might actually be there between us, and the obligation to answer the call. Here with Gabe, this moment feels more crucial than a phone call. Gabe's gaze softens, returning his attention to the bodysuit and silently encouraging me to take the call. With a long sigh, I reach for the phone, glancing at the screen to see Travis's name. With a flash of reluctance, I answer it.

"Hi, Travis."

I keep my tone neutral, not wanting to sound too happy in front of Gabe or upset to Travis.

"Where the fuck are you, Isla?"

Travis's voice roars through the phone, to the point that I'm off my stool and dashing toward the door so Gabe won't hear.

My heart thunders in my chest, my breath coming in my pants as I slip into the hallway and sprint away from the lab. Cupping the receiver and my mouth simultaneously, I try to amplify my voice discreetly, hoping to keep the conversation private and prevent Gabe from overhearing.

"I-I just stopped by the school. My project—"

"I expected you to go to your apartment and come right back here, not go gallivanting around town as if this wasn't the most important day of your life."

His yelling is followed by a clanging sound as if he's kicked or struck something in his fury.

"Did I not tell you to come right back home? Didn't I, Isla?"

Today isn't the most important day of my life. That day happened three years ago on a bright day at a truck stop when a woman no taller than me, wearing a tank top, cutoff shorts, and pigtails, didn't mind her own business and saved my life. Second to that day was my formal adoption day, when the court legally recognized the family we had already become. This day, as critical to him, pales drastically in comparison to those two days.

"Travis, please calm down."

My voice is soft and light, opposite of the panic racing through my body about to give myself a heart attack when I notice the time on the hall clock. I'm so late. The time out, away from the penthouse, flew by as I enjoyed myself with Gabe. There's a sharp intake of breath on the other end of the line, heavy breathing.

"Get home now."

There's a dangerous edge underlying his attempt at control in this tone, scaring me more than the yelling. The calm before the storm, the peace before the first hit. I've been down this road before, knowing what to look for, but Travis is different. He's nothing like those men.

He's loving, supportive, and nurturing and treats me like a princess. His perfect little doll. He's angry, I understand that. I'm cutting it close to getting into hair and make-up for the press junket ahead of the play. It's my fault that I know, and I'll explain it when I'm in front of him. I just need to get out of here as fast as possible.

"Everything will be fine," I assure him, though my voice trembles to sound more assured than I feel. "You'll see."

"It better be, Isla. You know what's riding on tonight, and don't think you won't be punished afterward."

The line goes dead. The threat sends a chill over my skin as I'm left staring at the phone in my hand, the silence of the hallway suddenly oppressive. My mind flashes back to the truck stop and the courtroom—moments that shaped me and held real value. I draw in a deep breath, trying to channel the strength from those days. I return to the lab, where Gabe looks up with concern.

"Is everything okay?"

For a moment, I consider telling him everything—the yelling, the pressure, the unrealistic demands. But I push it aside, not wanting my relationship drama to taint his last memory of today.

"I need to go. I'm late for hair and make-up," I lie, hoping he doesn't see through my façade. He seems to accept my answer, but his eyes narrow with a sliver of suspicion.

"If there's something going on, you know you can talk to me, right? Need anything at all, I'm here for you—"

I'm reminded of how I dragged all those people into my life during my trial. My mom resurfaced. I saw the pain and hurt it caused everyone to hear of my traumatic past. I won't do that to Gabe. I've seen how it changes the way people look at me. The avoided eye contact, the pitying looks, and the disingenuous concern, I won't taint our friendship with any whisper of concern I may have for my relationship with Travis, even if completely unfounded and non-existent.

"I know, Gabe. Thanks," I cut him off, afraid that if I let him continue, I might tell him what Travis said and cause him to worry too. "You can just leave that there, and I'll work on it another day."

He stands, tucking the threaded needle into the inner fabric before gathering it in his hands.

"Tell you what, why don't I take it with me and finish it for you? You have enough on your plate today."

He glances at his athletic watch, the time in bold numbers that adds to my anxiety. I need to make a fast exit, which I can't do. I stand here debating my project with him.

"I can't ask you to do that."

"You didn't ask, I offered," he replies with a reassuring smile, placing a comforting hand on my shoulder. "It's no bother at all, love. I'll have it done in no time, and we can meet up when you're free after the play, maybe in a day or so."

His offer, so freely given, is like a life raft in the tumultuous sea of my current state. The gentle pressure of his hand is grounding, a silent message of support that speaks louder than any words could. His willingness to help, to ease my burden without a second thought, is the kind of friend he is—selfless, understanding, and unwavering.

"But Gabe, you've already done so much—" I protest, but he cuts me off with a gentle yet firm resolve.

"Isla, let me do this for you. You focus on tonight. Shine like the star you are. Leave the bodysuit to me. It's in safe hands."

His voice, stance, and demeanor carry a conviction that leaves no room for argument. My gratitude is immense, and as I look into his kind eyes, I realize that this is his way of being there for me, just as Dani and Uncle Alex were in their own ways. It's not just about the bodysuit. It's about him becoming a steadfast presence in my life, someone I can count on always.

"Thank you, Gabe."

I quickly embrace him, then snatch up my purse, ensuring my lucky charm is safely tucked inside, before darting out of the lab.

Stepping outside, a gentle breeze teases my hair, offering a moment of calm, and I can feel the tension in my shoulders begin to ease, all thanks to his kindness. Gabe didn't just devise a solution and relieve me of my problem. He also gave me the space to breathe and focus on tonight without any extra worries. I'll heed his advice.

Shine like the star you are.

16

The penthouse is eerily quiet, the afternoon light innocently streaming through the bank of windows facing the river as Anna is nestled in her bed, peacefully dreaming by the twitching of her paws. My silent footsteps cascade across the marble floor, having expected an entourage of hair and make-up people to be here ready to get us both opening night ready to walk the red carpet before going inside the theater.

Yet, the absence of the expected flurry of activity leaves the place feeling larger and more vacant than usual. I pause, letting the quiet wash over me, a rare moment of stillness in what should have been a day charged with excitement and nerves. The contrast between expectation and reality is stark, disconcerting, and daunting.

Moving through the penthouse, I check my phone for any missed messages or calls, half-expecting to find an explanation for the unexpected solitude. But the screen is blank. Nothing from Travis related to tonight's preparations as I set my bag on the couch and deposit my phone next to it.

"Travis? I'm home."

My words cut through the silence. The absence of a reply makes my stomach knot. The quiet oasis in the sky, which has always felt like an escape from the city below, does not feel like a foreboding whisper. The air feels cooler, charged with an unspoken tension, as if the penthouse is holding its breath, as I am holding my breath—waiting for something or someone to break the silence.

"Travis?" I call out again, my voice stronger this time, but the only answer is Anna's soft moan as she stretches and closes her eyes. I can't shake the feeling that something is amiss.

I make my way to the bedroom, half-expecting, half-dreading to find Travis there, perhaps lost in work or with headphones drowning out the world. But the room is as empty as the rest of the penthouse except for the bed.

Draped across the plush bedding is a stunning gold beaded dress, its front plunging in a daring V, with crisscross straps revealing themselves at the back. A daring slit runs up the side, complemented by strappy stilettos placed neatly beside the bed.

Beside the dress are chandelier earrings that sparkle with a lavish blend of gold and diamonds, their intricate design promising to catch every flashbulb. A matching cuff bracelet sits beside them, and an exquisitely crafted evening bag rests underneath. The outfit was carefully laid out, awaiting me as I tarnished his consideration with my late arrival.

The sight, though breathtaking, does little to ease the growing knot of anxiety spreading from my stomach into my chest. The meticulous arrangement feels like a silent message, a carefully curated prelude to the evening's expectations, and I've already disappointed him on his big night. I wrap my arms around myself, trying to warm the cold embrace of reality as I glance around and finding nothing so carefully curated for himself.

I exhale deeply, quietly, letting the disappointment in

myself for letting him down settle further into my being. Forcing myself away from the stunning dress and beautiful expectation he had for me, I move through the living room and push open the playroom door.

With a solo torch wall sconce illuminating the otherwise dark room, I find him seated in an oversized chair, a silhouette carved out of the shadows, with only the amber glow of bourbon in a highball glass beside him. The sight of him, disheveled—his hair a testament to restless hands and a troubled mind, his shirt wrinkled and partly unbuttoned to reveal the contours of his defined chest—sitting in isolation and deep contemplation cuts through the guilt gnawing at my conscience.

"Travis?"

My voice is barely above a whisper, laden with apologies, ready to tumble out, hoping he'll understand that time got away from me. The need to bridge the gap between us, to somehow make amends for my unintended neglect, fills me with a desperation I hadn't anticipated on what was supposed to be our important night.

He barely acknowledges my presence, the tension between us making my pulse race into my ears.

"I'm sorry I—"

"Sorry?" His voice cuts through the dim room, sharp and cold. "For what, Isla? For undermining the importance of tonight? For questioning your commitment to our work, to us?"

I flinch at the accusation, the air between us charged with a bitterness I hadn't anticipated.

"I didn't mean to compromise anything. My project at school, it just—"

"Your schoolwork, your precious project, and that ridiculous scrap of fabric you drag around everywhere, they take precedence over the play I've invested millions in to get produced, don't they?"

He doesn't wait for my response, his gaze piercing as if trying to unravel my intentions on the spot.

"Do you even understand what's at stake here? What's at stake for my career? My name? Everything is on the line, and like an idiot, I listen to my cock and cast an unprofessional, unknown like you. Or is it all just a game to you?"

The severity of his words slaps me across the face and punches me in the gut, leaving me reeling. His brutal honesty, laying bare his true feelings about me and our relationship, brings tears to my eyes, and I instinctively wrap my arms tighter around myself for comfort.

This is a chasm I don't know how to cross, a rift so wide in our relationship I'm not sure how to bridge.

"I'm so sorry . . . truly I am. I was trying to do everything. To not let anyone down. I thought . . . I thought you, of all people, would understand."

My words are punctuated by tears streaming down my face and sobs I'm desperately trying to suppress while explaining myself.

"Understand?"

The word is laced with scorn. His face is in the shadows, with the light behind him.

"What I understand is that I've poured everything into this play, into us, and I'm not sure you've done the same."

The room where I once floated with abandoned bliss, high on the ecstasy he brought me, feels like a battleground. My hopes and aspirations turned into weapons formed against me.

"Travis, please, let's not do this now. We can work through—"

Drawing nearer to him, my movements are tentative, fueled by the hope that we can move past this. I know there will be consequences for my actions. He's already made that clear, but I'm willing to accept whatever he deems necessary to make amends.

"Can we, Isla?" His interruption is swift, his voice a fiery rage that has me halting several feet away when he suddenly rises. "Because right now, I'm not sure what we have is worth the effort."

The accusation is another assault on my body, causing my shoulders to slump as the gulf widens with each spoken word. I'm gasping for air and fighting with the sobs breaking free in a relentless torrent of tears. My body trembles, overwhelmed by grief and guilt at the thought of our potential end.

Every aspect of my life is crumbling. My friendship with Lily is on the rocks. I'm falling behind in school, and the sole steady pillar — my relationship with him — is now teetering on the brink of collapse. The silence that follows is deafening, filled with the echoes of our unspoken fears and unmet expectations.

"No . . . no, don't. . . Please don't. . ." I move with an aching slowness, trying to hold myself together and not collapse on the floor in front of him. "I . . . I'll do whatever you want . . . be whoever you want."

Travis remains immovable, his figure a statue of cold detachment against the heat and passion we shared in this very room. Once warm with affection, his eyes hold a detachment that chills me to the bone.

"You say that now, Isla, but can you really change? Be what this is, what I want, and what I need?"

His words slice through the heavy air, each landing with an impasse threatening to crush the last vestiges of hope I cling to. I struggle to find the words to articulate the depth of my commitment and my willingness to transform for us, for him. Yet, the space between is scattered with land minds, filled with linchpins to broken promises and shattered expectations.

"I can . . . I want. For you. I'll be Marcella, Isla, or whoever you want me to be," I whisper, swiping a hand over my cheeks and chin to wipe away the fallen tears while imploring a

GIGI MEIER

pleading look on my face. I search his for any sign that there's something left to salvage.

But he turns away, a gesture that feels like the final blow, severing the thin thread of connection that I desperately fought to maintain. His silence is a verdict that speaks louder than any argument we've had. A declaration that there is no bridge strong enough to span the chasm that's opened between us because of me.

My hands instinctively wrap around my stomach, the physical manifestation of the pain too intense to stand. Tears cascade again as I crumble to the floor, my body curling inward, attempting to shield myself from the heartbreak.

His hand grips the bourbon glass, he swiftly tilts his head back, and he downs the contents in one harsh swallow. The sound of the glass thudding back onto the table interrupts my sobs as I crawl the floor toward him. Slowly, he turns, staring down at me, his stance rigid, his face a storm of quiet contemplation.

There's a calculated stillness about him now, cold and distant as if he's weighing his options, deciding the terms of what he'll require from me.

"You'll be whatever I need you to be?" he finally says, his voice devoid of warmth, more a statement than a question. "Your dedication, your whole self—given over to this production and to me?"

He's contemplating not just the continuation of our relationship but the cost it will exact from me, demanding a loyalty so deep it may just consume my very essence. He steps closer, his shadow falling over me, a dark shroud threatening to extinguish my independence.

"I want your undivided attention, Isla. No distractions, no side projects. Your performance tonight and from now on will reflect where your priorities lie."

His words are a cage, each one a bar locking me in,

226

demanding a fidelity that blurs the lines between love and possession. In his eyes, I see the unyielding expectation of an absolute surrender, not just of my time and energy but of my aspirations, my soul to his vision.

"Your focus, every fragment of your passion, must be on what we're creating. If this play fails . . ." His voice trails off, but the threat hangs unspoken. "You know what's at risk. Not just our reputations but the future we've envisioned, the empire we could build. I can't have you half-committed, distracted by . . . by whatever it was that pulled you away today."

The terms are set, the price of our relationship laid bare in the dim light of the playroom. It's a negotiation of the heart, where the stakes are higher than any stage could demand. And as I lie there, shattered and spent, I'm left to wonder at what point the role I'm playing ends and where I begin.

"You need to decide here and now."

I raise my watery eyes to him, pushing myself to sit as my legs stay tucked beneath me, grounding me to the floor. His tone is unyielding, and his gaze looks onto mine, searching, demanding.

"Are you in this with me completely? Can I trust you to give this—give us—your all?"

In his eyes, I see the reflection of a future where every step I take is for the play, for him, where my dreams are secondary to his ambitions. It's a crossroads, and the path he's offering has no room for deviation, no space for the person I once was or wanted to be.

"Travis, I—" My voice cracks, the enormity of his request threatening to overwhelm me.

"I need to know that you can prioritize and sacrifice. That's what this requires, little one," he continues as if he hadn't heard my attempt to speak. "Sacrifice. Without it, we have nothing. Do you understand?"

I draw in a shuddering breath, the air feeling thick, like wading through a fog of impending loss.

"I do understand," I whisper, my throat stinging from crying. "But at what cost?"

He doesn't respond immediately, and in that silence, my heart races with the fear of all I am being asked to forsake. Finally, he speaks, the coldness in his tone resuming as he takes me by the hand and helps me to my feet. I shiver. My body is heavy with guilt, grief, and sorrow.

"The cost of success, Isla. The price of achieving what few dare to dream. It's not meant to be easy, but you can do it. We can do it together."

The finality in his tone is a shackle, a chain that threatens to bind me to a life where I dance to a tune that's no longer mine. My mind races with the memories of my larger-than-life dreams painted in brighter hues with Lily in my apartment when we walked the imaginary red carpet. The very same one, I could be walking less than a month later.

"You must decide, Isla. Are you with me fully, or are you out?"

His ultimatum settles over me like the darkness in this room. The ground beneath me gives way, pulling me down into an abyss where the light of my hopes and dreams dies. A part of me knows this acceptance is a surrender, a step that might swallow the parts of me I've fought to preserve.

"Yes, Travis," I murmur, the words scraping out from a place of desolation even as a part of me recoils at the starkness of the transaction.

"I'm with you."

My faith in myself begins to crumble, falling away with my surrender. A forfeiture of myself to his design. It's a trade, a barter of my inner light for the promise of outer success that suddenly seems as if I just sold my soul.

Travis's eyes, once a source of solace, now fix on me with a calculating glint as I straighten my posture. He moves closer, his hand lifts and the back of his fingers brushes my cheek. It is a touch of feather-light yet laden with a gravity that tugs at the remnants of my resolve.

Then, bending down, his lips find mine in a kiss that is the epitome of contradiction—gentle, tender, a whisper of the affection that was before today, before now. It's a kiss that carries the uncertainty of my future, a bittersweet mingling of what I've agreed to and what it's costing me. The softness of his lips belies the hard lines of the bargain we've struck, and I'm left reeling from the intimacy that now feels like another layer of my surrender.

As he pulls back, the ghost of his kiss lingers, leaving me more disoriented than comforted, a token of love that feels like the final twist of a knife already lodged deep within.

"That's my girl."

His words leave a slimy resolve to the art of negotiation. When I make to leave, his grip on my body tightens.

"Now for your punishment, little one."

His fingers move to the button on my shirt. Realizing his intentions, I cover them with my own to stop him.

"Travis . . . I already made us late. We don't have time for that right now."

His eyes widened momentarily before narrowing, their glint vanishing into a cold, calculating gleam.

"This will not be like before, dear Isla. You will strip, please me, and then we will get you ready."

A suffocating silence stretches between us, speaking volumes as I blink in rapid success, processing his words. His fingers resume, moving with deft determination in pushing mine away while his gaze remains unwavering. I can see the gears turning in his mind, the calculations of power and control as he pushes my blouse from my shoulders, the crisp cotton caressing down my skin.

I shiver, wanting to shield myself from his appreciative eyes, as this is not how we've made love in the past. When his defy fingers move to the hem of my skirt, I hold his wrist again, needing more than this cold, unfeeling man. Needed his assurances that even though it was a punishment last time, it was meant with love, warmth, and mutual passion.

"Not like this, Travis."

I shake my head, imploring him to change, to revert to the man who made me fly, whispering beautiful words over me and encouraging me to get lost in the pleasure. He pushes my hand away a second time, turning this into a transaction I've been through many times before. When he doesn't listen, insisting on continuing down this isolating road without a thread of connection, I close my eyes, letting him remove my skirt and panties.

"On your knees."

His voice is low and dangerous, and he is a breath away from my ear, forcing me to open my eyes. When I move my head toward him, trying to press my cheek to his for some affection, he intentionally moves away, cupping my elbow as I lower to my knees in front of him. His denial is a vacancy, an intentional detachment to make me feel degraded, and it's succeeding.

"You know what to do. You know how I like it."

His hand cups my chin, his thumb stroking across the hollow of my cheek as I press my lips together, suppressing a sob. My hands tremble as I begin to unfasten his belt. This moment no longer belongs solely to us but to the ghosts of my former life. The leather scraping against the buckle as it slides across the metal takes me back to my time with Rick.

Opposite this opulent playroom in a penthouse in the sky, I'm transported to a motel room reeking of decay and neglect, its walls stained with body fluids and residue. The carpet is matted and threadbare with dubious stains that hint at a history of illegal and illicit activities.

My heart racing, my naked body numb and on display for his greedy eyes, I gather the courage to unzip his pants. Not understanding why, I don't let them fall to the ground on their own accord. I gently lower them, taking care when he steps out of the fabric.

"Get me hard."

The words are spoken in Travis's authoritative voice, yet when I gaze up, it's Rick's chubby face and bulbous nose. His ragged breathing, a steady rhythm in the truck beside him as his body struggles under his excessive weight. Tears drip down my face when his large hand threads into my hair, pulling my face into his smelly groin.

I gag, suffocating on the odor that permeates his dick from the long hours on the road and lack of proper bathing facilities. He laughs, his hand tightening as he rubs the malodorous stench against my delicate face, sneering that this is how little girls receive love from their daddies.

I lift my hand, instinctively pressing against his thigh, to distance myself from the haunting memory of that moment, but my effort is swiftly brushed aside.

"Mouth only."

My body recoils, my muscles tensing, and my heart sinks at his request. I've been down this road before, with Rick and my mom's boyfriend—both loving me in their own twisted ways. But before them, there was my real daddy. He would hold my hand tightly as we walked to the ice cream shop. He'd buy me a cone and tell me to be good to Mommy, promising he would return soon.

But he never returned. Instead, he abandoned me with her, with him, and now with Rick—who insists on being called "daddy" both in public and behind closed doors. It makes my stomach churn, and my soul aches, knowing how his promise to help me out, to give me food and shelter when he found me homeless in the park, turned into this perverse relationship.

As I lower my head, I can feel the disgust of the situation drenching me, consuming me, filling my mouth with his cock as I've been trained to do so many times before. It was his schedule and regimen when we came off a long haul.

The furniture in these cheap motels are relics from a bygone era. Their once-vibrant colors faded to murky shades, and the upholstery, torn and sagging, was always the same despite being different motels across the county.

The heavy curtains, meant to block out the probing eyes of the world, hang limply, their fabric infused with the lingering scent of smoke, allowing anyone who walks by the view of a fourteen-year-old girl on her knees, servicing a man more than twice her age before he showered and would agree to feed her.

"Choke on it, bitch."

He chuckles, the sound echoing in the small, cramped room. His breath, a revolting mix of whiskey and cigarettes, fills my nostrils when he pulls his slithering, shriveled dick from my mouth to kiss me, his stench filling my nostrils when I attempt to recoil. A sharp slap to the head from my disobedience and his fingers down my throat to make me gag while crying is his favorite punishment before shoving me back into his groin.

My lips part, his cock forced in, filling my taste buds with the bitter taste of his spittle as he thrusts against my tongue, forcing me to take more than I can handle. The smell and taste of him are overwhelming, and I repeatedly gag, the sound making him harder and more aggressive until I'm swallowing back the vomit and stomach acid he's churning up.

"This is what you're good for."

Blood pumps into my head, pounding harshly from his painful grip, the crown of my hair holding me like a rag doll as he uses me over and over. My body is racked with muffled sobs, my tears mixing with the saliva dripping from my mouth onto the crunchy carpet. His groans indicate he likes this, likes his cock slick with his saliva being forced in and out of my mouth as an unwilling partner to his assault.

I'm lost in a sea of darkness, my mind taking me to other places while my body remains crouched on the floor of this grimy motel. Revisiting old memories of happier times, which were few and far between before they morphed into Dale, my mom's boyfriend, doing the same thing to me. Having to be quiet, his fingers sometimes pinching my nose to block off my breathing, causing me to blackout and wake up alone and covered in cum.

Rick never did that to me. A glimmer of gratitude that he never figured out that trick. Or maybe it was an unfortunate break for me that I never told him so I could faint, and he could finish using my body the way Dale did.

His thrusts become rougher, forcing my head back with each movement. I gag and choke on my vomit as his cock repeatedly hits the back of it. Yet, he seems to enjoy this pain and humiliation, the feral roars of pleasure getting louder.

A memory flashes through my mind, reminding me of what happened last time and how it ended faster when I actively participated. I mimic the motion I used on him before. It works, and he finishes quickly, spilling his disgusting taste down my throat before angrily punching me in the head.

"Don't do that shit again."

I collapse to the floor as he finishes on me, sending cum into my hair and on my face and clothes before walking away, slamming the thin bathroom door hard enough to make the walls rattle. I curl into myself. Soul-racking sobs overtake my body as my face curls into the floor, hiding away from the pain, humiliation, and suffering that is my life.

At least I'll eat tonight.

17

The world spins in and out from then and now. A flickering fluorescent light casts a sallow glow over the filthy room. The buzzing sound emits a grating of metal and plastic into the stillness, filling with the humid steam from Rick's hot shower.

"Isla?" Flashes of Travis hovering over me, brushing back my hair in a state of panic, draw me back to reality before it spins out into the stench of naked Rick standing over me, wanting me to finish the job I shortcutted.

"Don't. . . don't touch me!"

My skin crawls with the ghostly touch of hands that aren't there, feeling like a continuation of that abuse. Panic, raw and unyielding, courses through me, igniting a primal urge to fight, to flee from the perceived threat. Without recognizing my defender, my Orion, I lash out against him, my arms flailing, trying to push away the shadows of my attacker that cling to the edges of my mind.

"It's me! It's Travis!"

His voice, laced with shock and fear, barely registers as he tries to soothe me, to break through the haze of my flashback.

But his words play into my panic, indistinguishable from the echoes of my nightmares.

"Get off. Please get off me! You're hurting me!"

The scream tears from my throat, a desperate plea born from the terror of the past. He's not my safe harbor. He's my abuser, the one I pointed to in court, the only time I had to identify him as the victim. I fight him with a ferocity born of survival. I'm vaguely aware of the struggle, of hands trying to gently restrain me, of Travis's voice rising in alarm and urgency.

"Isla, it's me! It's okay, you're okay. I'm not going to hurt you. It's me. It's me."

But the distinction between friend and foe has been obliterated by the tide wave of traumatic episodes, leaving me floundering in a sea of past pain and present confusion. Travis, the man I love and trust, has been momentarily recast as my abuser, the source of my fear. I react with a primal need to escape, to protect myself at all costs.

"You're home. You're with me, and you're safe."

He repeats it over and over, a mantra against the darkness, his voice steadying. It becomes the lifeline I desperately need to claw my way back to the present, to him, and away from the grip of the terror that had threatened to consume me.

Then I'm floating, the room spinning from dark to light and back to dark as he carries me through his home to the bedroom we share. The bed, once a sanctuary, leaves me gasping for air. My heart is fluttering in my ribcage, trying to escape as I claw against him, trying to get away from the mattress where all bad things happen.

"Isla, look at me! Show me those pretty eyes. Look over here."

His voice, firmer now, pierces the veil of fear that has blinded me to the present. I feel his hands, gentle yet insistent, pulling me toward him until I'm buried underneath him. My face is smothered in soft kisses as I taste the saltiness of tears on my lips.

"Yes, stay with me, little one."

Blurry-eyed, I focus my vision on him. The blueness of his eyes is filled with panic, and a guilt-ridden face sharing in my sorrows. He brushes back my hair, collecting my tears on his thumbs and wiping them away between soft kisses meant to be comforting, not lingering.

"I pushed you too far."

His admission hangs heavy in the air, a raw acknowledgment of the boundary we've inadvertently crossed.

"I pushed you too far," he repeats, full of remorse even though he didn't send me into that horrific flashback, not willingly.

It was brought on by itself, something so powerful and yet launching spontaneously, at the most inopportune times, with no control by me.

"I was so angry. I wanted to punish you. Make you feel what I felt today."

The confession, raw and honest, strikes a chord deep within me, resonating with the fear and isolation propelling my reaction.

"I didn't mean to . . . I would never scare you like that."

His eyes search mine for forgiveness, for some sign of understanding. The tension that had seized my body begins to ebb, slowly unwinding under the gentle ministrations of his kisses, the warmth of his half-clothed body shielding me from the cold shadows of my past. His confession, spoken with such vulnerability, acts as a salve on the raw edges of my terror.

His whispered, worried words slug through my brain, searching for an apology that is never spoken, more implied. Although the urgency, worry, and concern are evident, I need to hear him say he's sorry, even if he's as overzealous in his explanation as he was shoving me into a sexual dark place and keeping me there until his release sent me colliding to the floor.

The truth of the last statement as accurate at the tanginess of his sperm coating my mouth, a taste I'm more than familiar with. How much further would he have gone if I had not freaked out, not lapsed into the past and its demands? If I hadn't detached my mind from my body, my reality, from my past, how much more damage would he have done and still not apologize for?

After each of these episodes, my body is heavy, laden with crashing adrenaline that wants to pull me under into a sleep that lasts for days. However, tonight allows for no such thing, the ringing of his phone shattering the reflective moment as we are lost in thoughts unknown to each other. He barely stirs, embracing me tightly as if the phone interrupting the aftermath of our fallout will cause me to evaporate into thin air.

I move my cheek to touch his, gently whispering, "You should probably get that. It might be important."

His head rises, the deep blue ocean of his eyes going on forever as he stares at me.

"Nothing is more important than you and us. How it will be always now."

The assurance in his voice, meant to soothe, is suddenly confining and marking the boundary of a new world where my choices and desires are filtered through the prism of 'us.'

"I still think you need to get it. And I'll get in the shower, so when your glam team arrives, I'll be ready."

My fingertips press lightly into his ribcage, a gentle reminder to move off me so I can escape to the bathroom to process what happened privately. His head tilts with the oddest expression.

"Little one, there is no glam team. I'm dressing you, but you do need to shower as you have some cum stuck in your hair."

It astonishes me that he said this in such a condescending

tone and confirmed that he did finish in my mouth when I was spiraling down a dark pit in my memories. The intimacy and control he's asserting over such personal aspects of my preparation, once a gesture I found endearing, now underscores the extent of my autonomy that's been relinquished.

The space of 'me' narrows further, compressed by the omnipresent 'us' that Travis orchestrates, until one day it will be completely eclipsed. He rolls off me with a chuckle, his muscles rippling as he stretches in various directions, attempting to dispel the tension in his muscles.

"Also, eat lightly so you have energy but not too much since we have friends to entertain at dinner after the show. I'll give you about twenty minutes before we start, and I'll have the doorman handle the dog."

Without a backward glance, I'm left staring at the space he occupied at the end of the bed, my mind spinning at how fast he's commandeering even the smallest choices in my life. It's both sobering and chilling.

I move with a numbness that envelops my entire being, locking the bathroom door as a temporary barrier between us. My actions are mechanical. The familiar routine of washing and rinsing is now a task I perform without thought. My mind is ensnared by a more pressing, persistent question. What happens now? After the play and the dinner, then what? Do we resume how we were? Do we go about our relationship in a different way?

The fog in my mind is as thick as the fog inside the bathroom, clouding the mirrors as I towel off, counting down the minutes until he's back, beckoning me to get dressed. I plug in the blow dryer, the hum a comforting, if temporary, escape from my spiraling thoughts. Then, a light tap on the door intrudes a gentle but unmistakable reminder of the expectations, his expectations waiting just on the other side.

"I'll be right out."

I put away the dryer, wrap a towel around myself, and brush my teeth before opening the door for the steam to billow past him. He deposits a kiss on each shoulder and another on the top of my head before stripping and stepping into the shower. An action that's both new to me and delivered with a lightness unbecoming what just transpired between us. I shake my head and stare at the sink, trying to make sense of his action until it's time to spit out my toothpaste and rinse.

"I left a snack out for you. Go ahead and eat it while I get ready. Then I can focus on you."

Unsure of how to respond to this dynamic shift, I leave and head to the kitchen, where a small plate of veggies, nuts, and cheese reside. The numbness that enveloped me before dissipates as I sit on the floor next to Anna's dog bed, gazing out at the endless blue sky with the city spread before us. The sound of the water running in the shower in the background is a reminder that time and Travis waits for no one. I share the cheese with my girl.

"We've come a long way since that big rig, haven't we?"

She gobbles up the cheese, nuzzling my hand for more while I eat the vegetables. The simplicity of her affection has always gotten me through, even on the hardest nights of my life. Today doesn't even compare to what I have been through. I've lost my freedom more than once and been in prisons worse than this gilded cage suspended from the sky. My hand grazes his diamond necklace with the stars and constellation, where all of life starts and where my life has ended. My situation isn't as dire as I paint it.

Dressed in custom gowns that cost more than I once dared dream of, adorned with jewels that sparkle like the stars of the very constellation he made for me. Wrapped in furs against the chill of night, I've become a figure in a world I once observed in Lily's theater rags. At the center of this new universe is my relationship with Travis, a famed playwright whose love of ambition and drive have reshaped my existence and pushed me further than I would have pushed myself.

We continue sharing my plate until everything is gone. I dismiss my worries over Travis as ridiculous compared to that dirty shack I grew up in. So what if he wants to play dress up, call me his doll, and praise me for how perfect I am? There are worst things in the world, and I've experienced them.

"I'm ready for you, Isla," Travis calls through the penthouse.

"Be good for the doorman."

I snuggle Anna to my chest and give her several long kisses before placing her back on her dog bed.

"Coming, my Orion."

"Did you just call me by my play name?"

Travis's demeanor noticeably shifts when I enter the bedroom to find him with a towel draped around his narrow hips, displaying his stunning body.

"I did. Do you not like it or—"

Unsure how he'll react, I stop several feet away for good measure and wait. A broad smile creeps across his face, his hand extending outward to guide me into the bathroom.

"I love it."

Seeing his reaction, I confidently step forward and slip my hand into his. He kisses the top, his thumb stroking across my knuckles as we walk into the bathroom, where a chair in the center awaits me.

"Your throne awaits."

The recent turbulence of our confrontation seems to have prompted a different reaction in him, a desire to mend the frayed edges of our conflict with an outpouring of affection and attention. He handles me with magnified tenderness and gentleness in each gesture as if handling the Queen's jewels.

Upon sitting, legs uncrossed, he advises. He steps back and observes, approaching me as he did the canvas, studying where and how to start.

"I'm thinking of pulling your hair up to showcase your slender neck and the cut of the dress."

His hand covers his mouth, voicing his thoughts without asking my opinion.

"Whatever you like," I supplement, knowing it's unnecessary but wanting him to think I'm invested in the process. His smile widens at my acquiescence, his eyes sparkling with gratitude. He leans in, planting a soft peck on my forehead—a silent thank you—before returning to his role as the evening's stylist.

"Sit still for me. This is going to be perfect."

He moves around me intensely, gathering my hair with skilled hands and brushing each section gently before starting. The hairstyle emerges as a sophisticated arrangement of curls and twists at the top of the head, pinned securely to stay in place throughout the red carpet event. Strands are artfully pulled out to frame my face, softening the overall look and adding a touch of grace and femininity. He works silently, save for the occasional hum of his approval.

"Exactly how I envisioned."

He steps back to assess his work. As our gaze connects in the mirror, his expression is pure satisfaction. I cast him a soft smile that shows my appreciation for doing this.

"I'm keeping it light to not conflict with the theater makeup that will go over this."

He muses to himself, selecting brushes and make-up with the precision and artistry of his painter's palette. The bristles are soft across my skin, dusting, blending, and defining with various powders and creams he applies with a deft touch. His movements are a dance of light and shadow, each stroke adding depth and contour, enhancing my features with a natural elegance.

"There, just a bit of highlight here . . . and there."

His voice is a soft murmur as he considers each application. As he evaluates the effect, the slight tilt of his head makes it clear that he's crafting not just a look but an experience, a presentation of beauty that aligns with his artistic vision.

"No falsies tonight. Your natural lashes are perfect as they are, especially with a touch of this mascara."

He holds the wand inches from my face, and I nod, unsure why he's telling me this. I follow his commands to look up and down as he coats my lashes, adding length and volume. Watching him work, I'm struck by the intimacy of the act, the trust it requires to allow someone so close to shape the face I present to the world. His compliments are sparing but genuine, his approval conveyed in the satisfied nods and the occasional murmured, "Perfect."

As he finishes, he steps back, his eyes roaming over his handiwork with a critic's eye.

"You're a vision, Isla. This is how you were meant to be seen. I want a picture of this."

He retreats with a bounce in his step and an almost reverential awe in his voice when he swiftly returns with his phone.

"Lose the towel. It's ruining your natural beauty," he insists, the soft command leaving no room for objection.

Painting me naked on canvas would be very difficult to transport without me seeing it leave the room. Snapping naked photos of me is another thing, especially since they can be sent to anyone, and I won't have control over them.

"Uh, Travis. Don't you think I should have more on?"

Confusion clouds his handsome face until his eyes light up, and he snaps his fingers.

"Yes, excellent idea, little one."

Travis's response to my hesitance is swift, his presence

behind me almost immediately as he unhooks the familiar weight of the constellation necklace from around my neck. The sudden absence of its touch leaves me feeling exposed, my hand rising reflexively to the now vacant space at my throat.

"Just for tonight, it does not go."

He carefully lays the necklace on the vanity before slipping out of the bathroom and returning with the shoes and accessories. His knuckles whisper across my neck while he fastens the chandelier earrings from each ear and swipes a finger through them to careen across my shoulders. The bracelet cuff is next before he squats to fasten the strappy heels around my ankles. His attentiveness is meticulous, bordering on ceremonial, as he ensures that everything is perfect when rising to his feet.

"There."

His head tilts with an expectancy about the towel.

"Um, but you want photos of me nude?"

My slow tone conveys my hesitancy and confusion once more.

"Could they get out or be leaked?"

He smiles, the confusion clearing as his fingers tug at the top of the towel, pulling it apart.

"Little one, I can assure you that will never happen. I pay top dollar for discretion. Now stand."

He angles the towel out of the frame, taking pictures while I'm thinking about what that statement means. The more problematic part is not that the nudes could eventually find their way onto the internet like most do, but the discretion he pays for. What exactly does that mean? And who exactly is he paying, and for what?

With a gentle nudge, he directs me to stand in front of the chair, his other hand pressing lightly against my lower back. He guides me into a pose that feels both vulnerable and deliberate.

"Lean back onto the chair, arch your back."

His voice was calm but authoritative. I comply, the pose accentuating the lines of my body, aware of how this display is for more than just the two of us. His mention of paying for discretion, the hint of a world that operates behind closed curtains, sends a ripple of unease through me.

"What do you mean you pay for discretion? Is there someone else? Another woman?"

The question escapes me, a whisper of insecurity amidst his orchestrated perfection. But he doesn't answer. His focus fixed on capturing the image of his making. His phone camera clicks, a series of snapshots as he moves around me, capturing every angle and contour. The sense of being observed and displayed is potent and inescapable, and I'm left to wonder at the balance between being admired and being a possession.

"Do not worry, my perfect little doll. You own me as I own you."

His soft lips press carefully against mine to save messing up his strategically applied lipstick.

"Let's get you into that dress so I can finish, and we'll be off."

18

The limousine is a cocoon of quiet anticipation. The hum of the city sounds muffled against its plush interior. Travis sits beside me, his gaze intense and contemplative. His finger rests against his lips, a signature gesture when he's deep in thought, studying me or maybe thinking about us.

The air between us is charged with his expectations for tonight—the red carpet is another performance. Be mysterious and alluring. Beyond that is the meeting between the benefactor and financiers. Be charming with a hint of innocence that all men desire. Basically, be a different actress for each facet of this wild night, never letting the façade drop until we return to the penthouse.

My heart is a drum percussion against my ribs as the limousine slows, signaling our arrival. I draw in a breath, trying to calm the fluttering in my stomach, the tendrils of anxiety climbing up my throat. I pat my dress, feeling for my good luck charm draped from a ribbon on the inside of my dress. A platinum and pearl whisper-thin band with fairy dust and fairies floating on the delicate metal, "with love and courage, you shine" engraved inside.

"I'm nervous," I admit, searching out his hand for comfort. He leans over and leaves a lingering kiss on my cheek.

"To be expected. Follow my lead, and everything will be fine."

His hand cradles my chin, gently guiding it so that our gazes lock, conveying profound intimacy and a yearning to shield me, just as Orion watches over Cassiopeia.

I can hear the muffled chaos even before the door opens— shouts, flashing bulbs, and the buzz of the paparazzi. Travis is the first to emerge, his tuxedo silhouette framed against the flashbulb-frenzied darkness. He extends his hand, an unspoken cue for my entrance into the whirlwind of the opening night.

My hand finds his, and as I step out, the world transforms. Flashes burst like fireworks, shouting my name to face different ways is overwhelming, and my hand tightens in Travis, my anchor in this unfamiliar storm. My legs feel both rigid and fluid, an odd sensation as I navigate the fine line between graceful walking and the threat of stumbling. The adrenaline in my body rockets through my veins the same as coming off an ecstasy high in the playroom, except this time, I have a part to play and cannot lay motionless, floating in the heavenly abyss.

Be mysterious and alluring.

Travis's words remind me to play the part, to harness the invigorating feeling of being famous for however long this lasts, and to make the most of it. Suppressing a shudder against the cool night air and the goosebumps rising along my bare shoulder and arms, I release Travis's hand to walk the carpet without him, as I've seen many famous actresses do.

It sends the photographers into a frenzy, shouting my name from both sides of the carpet, demanding a piece of me, a photograph they can sell, a way to make money off my image— the image Travis hand-crafted for this exact reason. Well, I want a piece of them too. I want their adoration, love, and idolization, as shallow and fleeting as it is.

The dress, a cascade of sequins and silk, clings and flows in all the right places, a second skin that shimmers with each flash of light. Practicing what I saw on YouTube, I twist and turn, posing in different ways to accentuate the luxurious back of my dress, the curve of my spine, and the graceful arch of my neck. The flashes of the cameras blend into a continuous stream of light, blinding but exhilarating.

I can hear Travis's voice in the back of my mind, encouraging me to soak in every moment and use this exposure to catapult myself into the limelight. The idea is intoxicating—becoming someone people admire and leaving that desperate orphan behind. Even if they don't truly know me, they love me already. The facade is thrilling, and the anonymity within the fame is paradoxically empowering.

As I reach the end of the carpet, I pause for one final pose, a look over my shoulder with a mysterious smile, the kind that promises more than it reveals. This moment, captured in hundreds of photographs, will be disseminated across countless platforms, each telling a story they've concocted about me. But the real me, the one beneath the surface, remains my own. This duality, the visible and the hidden, is the essence of my allure. Travis joins me. His face is overjoyed with my performance as he guides me back to the center of the carpet, where we are photographed together. A power couple cast in the glow of fame and success. His hand finds the small of my back, a possessive touch that tells the world I am his creation, his discovery, his star.

He leans in his mouth, pressed against my ear, whispering, "You're going to be rewarded when we get home."

When our eyes connect, our intimate moment is captured in hundreds of flashes, and the smolder in his eyes is unmistakable. Feeling exceptionally brave, my ego stoked by the vast attention, I boldly reciprocate his statement.

"Not if I reward you first."

His hand on my back tightens, the only indication he's heard me when I move away, intent on leaving him behind as the dynamic power play shifts in my favor. Determined to have the final word and not be overshadowed, he swiftly grabs my hand, pulling me into a spectacular twirl that culminates in an embrace—a move that sends the photographers into a frenzy of catcalls and eager shouts.

"Give it your best shot," he teases, his eyes alight with mischief and joy. The genuine happiness on his face sends my heart somersaulting, wishing it could stay like this forever with us.

Soon, the rest of the cast joins us, a host of talent and aspiration. My eyes lock with Lily looking stunning in a blood red, complimenting her dark features, and I smile, genuinely happy to share this event with her. My stomach twists when it's not returned, receiving a blistering look at me, then Travis's back, filled with—anger? Resentment? Jealousy?

"Isla."

Travis's quiet command and squeeze to my back has me looking from her to him as the cast crowds around us for pictures. I smile at him, warm and full of love, receiving the same in return as the camera flashes hundreds of times, drawn to the narrative Travis has woven around us.

"Now them."

He looks away, his mouth set into the firm lip of a temperamental playwright I've seen countless times, while I turn from him with a sensational smile, enjoying every second of this experience. As the flurry of photographs and the clamor for just one more pose begins to ebb, the cast starts to disperse, moving like a tide toward the grand entrance of the theater.

"Remember, play the part of charming and innocent."

Travis's instructions are necessary reminders. I have already forgotten the part I played just now, and he guides me into the theater to the private room down the hall where the financiers await. I tuck my hand into the crook of his elbow, drawing closer to him as the crowd falls away.

"I don't need to play that part. I already am those things."

I cast him a sexy side glance, raising my shoulder innocently. Travis's laughter echoes warmly as we approach the secluded meeting room. His amusement at my playful defiance boosts my ego further.

"You're only one of those things, little one, and it's one of the things I love about you."

Love about me.

Did he just say he loves me? In a manner that's quintessentially Travis, not directly but similar. A warm flush washes over me, my hand tightening on his elbow. As Travis leads me through the elegantly lit corridors of the theater, his offhand declaration causes my heart to flutter.

The private room, set up for the financier's cocktail hour, is intimate and sophisticated, fragranced with the scent of gourmet dishes. As we enter, Travis doesn't miss a beat. With the same ease as he navigates our complex interactions, he introduces me to the assembled guests, his arm never leaving my back.

Playing the part of charming and innocent feels almost second nature, a mask that fits seamlessly over the turmoil of my emotions as I've played this role many times when cops did a wellness check at my mom's house when the teachers saw signs of abuse. People suspected we weren't father and daughter when on the road with Rick.

I engage in conversations, my laughter light, my comments infused with just the right touch of naivety and wit. Yet, beneath the surface, Travis's words echo a constant hum that repeatedly draws my focus back to him. His gaze meets mine across the room, a mix of pride and something indefinably deeper, reinforcing the ambiguity of his earlier confession.

As the evening unfolds, meeting Travis's expectations in front of the financiers while dissecting the implications of his words becomes a delicate balancing act. Due to his admission, each compliment I receive, and every laugh I share feels bigger and brighter.

When he comes to collect me, begging our pardon to whisk me away to prepare for the performance head, I'm floating on air until I catch a friendly face I just saw a few hours ago.

Breaking away from Travis, I rush over to Gabe, nursing a drink in the corner of the room and taking in the event. The surprise of finding him here sparks excitement amid this exclusive event. Without hesitation, I throw my arms around him, my embrace conveying the shock and joy of this surprise.

"What are you doing here?"

My excited words are muffled by the fabric of his tuxedo against my face, the very one I helped him shop for.

"This is unbelievable."

As I take a slight step back, his hand remains softly at my waist, the other skillfully avoiding any spills on my dress as he moves his drink aside. My smile lights up as I look into his eyes, warmth spreading through me.

"I came to see you, love. To cheer you on." His voice is filled with a genuine pride that deepens my smile. "You look beautiful."

"You're looking sharp yourself. Like you belong on that red carpet yourself," I tease, playfully patting his chest before stepping back.

He casually slips his hand into his pocket, a single eyebrow arching in a familiar and endearing gesture as his attention shifts to something—or someone—behind me.

Travis's arm slips around my waist, an action that Gabe notices when his eyes flicker down to it and back up to my face.

My heart buoys at the thought of two important people in my life meeting each other on this important night.

"Travis, this is my very good friend, Dr. Gabriel Gannon. And Gabe, this is—"

"This man needs no introduction," Gabe cuts me off, his smile dimming as he extends his hand to Travis. "I've seen your *work*."

The way his accent hits on the last word has me giving him a confusing look. It's not outright rude, but cool and infused with more meaning than it should. Travis nods and accepts Gabe's handshake, his demeanor unchanging, but their grip speaks volumes about a strange bravado brewing.

"Indeed," Travis responds, his voice hitting the same undercurrent as Gabe's tone. "How do you find yourself at this private event?"

Travis's hand suddenly tightens around my waist, a silent assertion of his role in my life. He pinches the beaded fabric uncomfortably against my skin, something Gabe notes with a fleeting, inscrutable look.

A dazzling smile overtakes Gabe's face, an intention delay in responding when he sips his drink. The air thickens into a weird tension, a battle between egos, I suspect. Both are successful in their own right, both handsome and could easily grace the cover of any men's magazine.

"I believe your largest benefactor is my close, personal friend."

He raises his glass, angling it toward the man Travis had me chat with the longest as he worked the room. My gaze returns, moving between them, catching a glimpse of triumph in Gabe's expression, a discernible displeasure on Travis's face, his fingers tightening to downright painful now.

"I've always had a keen interest in the arts," Gabe continues, carefully setting his drink down. "Supporting projects that

involve people important to me is a passion of mine. It's fascinating to see how interconnected our worlds can be."

His words are smooth, and his smile never falters, but the
glance he shoots me is laden with meaning, a silent message
that his presence here is as much for me as it is for supporting
Travis's play.

Travis's demeanor momentarily shifts, a calculative glint
appearing in his eyes before his grip on my waist eases just
enough to be bearable.

"Yes, it's always *enlightening* to see where loyalties lie, especially in a close-knit community like ours."

The dagger in his words evident, the blade angled at Gabe,
waiting to pierce him with the sharp point.

"I trust that our benefactors recognize the distinction
between personal connections and the genuine talent that
drives projects forward. After all, we wouldn't want to blur the
lines of professional integrity with, say, intimate interests,
would we?"

His gaze locks with Gabe's, a clear boundary drawn, not just
around the project but subtly encircling me, a non-verbal
warning that his interest in my welfare goes beyond the professional. As it should be, Gabe's my friend, only here to support
me, as he said in the lab earlier today.

The tension between them is growing palpable as they
trade barbs. It's an invisible line left for me to straddle. Travis's
presence at my side, protective and possessive, contrasts
sharply with Gabe's more laid-back yet distinctly marked
friendship. It's an odd feeling, being the pivot around this odd
confrontation, each man marking his significance in my life in
his own way. I attempt to lighten the mood, laughing softly.

"Well, I'm lucky to have such supportive men in my life."

My gaze flits between them, seeking to bridge the gap with
levity. Yet, the atmosphere remains unchanged at the surprising
dynamics at play.

"I need to get ready. I'll see both of you later."

Travis's hand clenches, the bite painful against my flesh that will probably leave a mark if I stand here any longer. He leans in, intending a kiss, which is entirely unnecessary and not in character with the mystery and innocent character I'm playing. I nod to both, slip from his embrace, and say partying goodbyes to some people who stop me, wishing me luck before the play. Once out of the room, I walk as fast as the uncomfortable heels carry me until I reach my dressing room. I am about to close the door when Travis barrels through it, causing me to stumble backward.

He moves quickly, yanking on my arm to either save me from falling or wanting to confront me. Stormy and searching, his eyes are fixed on mine, demanding an answer without uttering a word. The lightness from our red carpet walk and the admission of love that followed are all but gone in the wake of their competition.

"You're not fooling me, Isla."

The door shuts abruptly with a sharp thud from his shoe, and in a swift motion, he spins me around, my back pressed against the solid barrier. His face, now inches from mine, twisted in anger, makes my skin grow clammy with a sudden sweat.

"Are you fucking him? Is that where you were today?"

The sting of accusation, the potential of my betrayal, sucks the air out of my lungs. My face morphs into disbelief while his hands wrap around my shoulders, rattling me against the door in rage. The crisscrossing beaded straps dig into my shoulder blades against the wood panels, my hands bracing against his chest, trying to push him off me. Our size difference makes it impossible, and panic surges through me.

"No! Of course not!"

My voice cracks as I try to speak, the words rough against the lump in my throat. With a grunt, Travis slams me against

the door once more, my head ricocheting against the unfor-
giving wood, and I groan in pain.

"Ah, fuck. Trav—"

"Don't you fucking lie to me, Isla!" he growls, his eyes
burning into mine, searching for the truth as his demands are
punctuated with slamming me repeatedly against the door.

I am rendered speechless, my breath stolen from me in
sharp gasps as the searing pain ravages my body. It feels like a
hundred knives stabbing into my back, robbing me of precious
oxygen and leaving me gasping for air. I weakly push against
him, trying to break free from his grasp, but my efforts are
feeble against his strength.

"I see the way he looks at you. The familiarity in your touch.
You let him have what's mine. What belongs to me, didn't you?"

His voice trembles with jealousy and rage. The veins bulge
from his neck, his skin grows redder, and sweat appears on his
forehead. He accuses me of cheating on him with Gabe. I choke
on the tears streaming down my face, my fists shaking with
clumps of his coat entangled in my fingers. My heart feels as if
it will burst from my chest, blood rushing to my head as I feel
lightheaded.

"No . . . I lo-love . . . only you."

My eyes plead for him to believe me, for some shred of
understanding, but all I see is shock and devastation against
the painful possessiveness still coursing through his grip,
ramming me against the door. It's a sickening combination of
emotions, my love, his hatred, my compassion, his fury.

He blinks, his wide eyes in shock as if seeing himself in a
new light, an enraged beast terrorizing a petite and defenseless
girl. Utter disgust that slides onto this face. His grip lightens
until his hands fall away, leaving fiery red handprints seared
into my skin when I look down. His gaze follows mine. His
mouth hangs open in disbelief at the destruction he has caused
in a fit of blind rage.

He recoils, moving across the room, distancing himself from me, the situation, and my proclamation of love for him, still suppressing his abhorrent behavior. His hand plunges into his hair, messing up the careful style as his eyes dart around the room, avoiding mine as if searching for a way to escape what happened between us.

Without his weight against me, I gulp for air, filling the edges of my compressed lungs. My hand instinctively reaches towards my chest as I lean away from the door, wincing in pain. The throbbing in my head intensifies, and a sharp ache shoots through my back, causing me to groan.

"I know you didn't mean to do this, Travis."

My voice is hoarse, too raw for the stage ahead for tonight's performance, but with assurance from him, I'll muddle through. Guilt seeps into his features, the angry redness of his skin clearing, his eyes filled with shame while his hands clench into fists at his sides.

The confident and mostly cocky playwright from before is gone, replaced by my lover, trembling with disbelief that he allowed himself to be consumed by his jealousy and rage. I take a tentative step toward him, reenacting all the times he stalked toward me with deliberate slowness.

"I forgive you."

Travis stills at my words. The sorrow that momentarily creases his brow dissipates as he visibly composes himself. He adjusts his posture, broadening his shoulders and relaxing his hands, embodying a renewed sense of control and determination. A sudden coldness swirls about him as his navy eyes deliberately drag from my gold heels, slowly up the body he primmed and prepared until locking on mine, piercing in their intensity.

"Your offer of forgiveness seems misplaced, little one, especially when your actions have brought us here." His voice is strong and steady, with an unmistakable undercurrent of jeal-

GIGI MEIER

ousy. "As for love . . . our situation requires an understanding, not just of our roles but of the boundaries they entail. Your . . . *friendship* has clouded that understanding, Isla."

His eyes, a stormy combination of possessive and accusation, linger on mine. His dominant stance betrays the look of love he wore on his face at the penthouse many times before while subtly shifting the fault to me.

I want to scream, to lash out at him for the pain he's causing, to take back everything I just said, but the words stick in my throat, suffocated by his devastation. Tears blur my vision as I struggle to remain upright, to not curl into myself and slip to the floor, wishing I could die.

He moves toward me, each step deliberate, his glare darkening as he closes the distance between us. The air grows heavy with unspoken tension, weighed down by the burden of his unsaid thoughts. When he finally reaches me, his hand lifts, and I flinch, unsure what to expect from him.

He frowns, continuing to claim my hand, gentle yet possessive, as if it's his right. It's a gesture filled with contradictions—tenderness mingled with control, a light hold against a stormy expression.

Then, almost as if he's giving in to a longing he's trying to suppress, he leans in, his lips grazing my cheek in a lingering kiss that speaks volumes. It's a goodbye, a rebuke, and a reminder of all we've shared, all at once. And just like that, he withdraws, leaving behind a cold emptiness with the click of the door.

I stand frozen and stunned. His touch is warm on my skin even as the reality of what just transpired hits me like a ton of bricks. I stumble to my dressing room chair and crumble into it, my knuckles white from gripping the armrests. The tears come uncontrollably, staining my makeup and turning my vision blurry. I bury my face in my hands, sobbing harder than I have in years as all the spoken promises he uttered when I committed myself to him are breaking.

My chest clenches with pain so sharp it steals my breath, mourning the audacity I had to proclaim my love, only to have it hurled back at me like a weapon. And yet, despite the agony, he still kisses me as if I were nothing more than the beautiful little doll that he's crafted me into, to be toyed with and discarded at his whim.

I lift my head, confronting my reflection in the mirror, seeing the fear and vulnerability in every line of my face.

"If he wants a doll to control his own living, breathing Marcella, then I shall become her," I vow, my voice unwavering despite the tremble in my hands. "I'll embody her with every fiber of my being when I step onto that stage. I'll set the role ablaze, leaving the audience enraptured, the critics singing praises. And when I walk away, I'll leave him in ruins, just as Marcella's lover left her."

19

———

Seizing the moment to introduce my own twist to his meticulously planned production, I switch into a pair of tap shoes I found hidden away in the wardrobe room. I took this chance while he was occupied, schmoozing with the financiers and critics out in the main hall. I managed to catch the attention of the sound technician, feigning trouble with my microphone and requesting two backups, setting the stage for my performance to unfold without a hitch.

My entrance is planned to be as jarring and unsettling as possible, a beautifully horrific contrast to the immaculate presentation he always insists upon. A cryptic smile spreads across my face, fueled by defiant inspiration. Ideas pour into my mind, each one a thread in the intricate tapestry of performance I aim to weave tonight, skyrocketing his production to new heights while simultaneously burning it down with my rebellious imprint.

My makeup is a chaotic masterpiece, heavily exaggerated and far beyond how Travis envisions his precious Marcella. I craft a version of her that's tarnished and distorted—a reflection of the turmoil he's sown within me. It's my silent protest, a way to shatter the illusion he's created, just as my love has been shattered.

Black lines dance across my pale face, curving and arching with theatrical expression. Smokey eyes ringed with charcoal pop against the bright white face paint of a pantomime, which extends like diamonds down to a point on my cheeks. My eyebrows are drawn in exaggerated arches, framing them in a perpetual state of expressive wonder.

My lips, which he loves so much, are outlined in the same stark white paint of a circus clown, which is more sad than alluring, accented by black lines pulling it into a frozen frown. Ridiculous amounts of rouge color my cheeks, harsh and creepy and accenting the light bruising of his fingertips visible on my shoulders. Charcoal shadow colors the color of my collarbones and the contours of my neck and elbows and stains my hands, looking grim and filthy. It's a stunning look that has me cryptically smiling at my reflection in the mirror.

The amber wig he chose for me is now a forgotten relic beside my abandoned gold dress and the heels he so carefully fitted on my feet. Instead, I crown myself with a vivid orange and yellow ombre wig.

The hair teased rebelliously in contrast to Marcella's usual polished look. I finish it with an oversized top hat too large for my body and pin it haphazardly atop the unruly locks. Its burgundy, gold, and yellow hues clash with deliberate chaos, matching the turmoil he's stirred within me.

Embracing an avant-garde rebellion, I destroy the precious costume he held sacred, tearing the sleeves from the dress to bare the marks of his grip. The dress is reduced to its foundational black bustier, meant to be concealed but now a bold centerpiece. I tie the ripped shreds from the ruins of the delicate cream lace as makeshift arm warmers just below my elbows.

The black silk rose ripped from an abandoned prop is

wound around a black leather belt that I fasten around my neck. It serves as a choker and symbol of the constraints I feel from the play and its unrelenting demands.

I adhered to a metallic pink sticker just below the bustier straps to cover my exposed skin, where the fabric proved tear-resistant. Beyond that is a provocatively short black skirt and artfully vandalized matching hosiery with strategically placed holes.

Moving back from the mirror, I absorb the extent of my transformation. The skills honed through years of crafting costumes with Aunt Molli and the fragments of knowledge from my brief stint at fashion school converge in this singular, defiant moment. It's more than a costume—it's a subtlety of madness.

"Hello, Marcella."

A cackling laugh escapes me as I fling open my dressing room door and move like a shadow down the hall. My fellow actors gasp, exchanging whispers at my shocking appearance. They expect his version of Marcella practiced in dress rehearsals, yet I have something to prove to them, to him, and to me—the show isn't over until the fat lady sings. And this fat lady is singing like a canary tonight.

As I approach, it's Lily's friend who first notices, her eyes widening in shock before nudging her to witness my transformation. The moment is pivotal, a silent declaration that the evening's performance will be unlike anything they anticipated.

Her eyes scan the drastic changes, from the unconventional makeup to the rebellious costume, and finally, her gaze locks with mine. There's a moment where everything is still in a silent exchange filled with questions and a hint of admiration for the audacity of my actions.

"I wanted to wish you good luck tonight. I hope you do well," I say with a sincerity that transcends our unresolved issues in previous tensions.

Momentarily caught off guard by my genuine well wishes, she hesitates and angles closer toward me.

"Thank you." Her voice is steadier than her surprised gaze would suggest. "Am I to assume this is your doing?"

Casting her that same cryptic smile I gave myself in the mirror back in my dressing room, I reply with a gentle sweep of my hands along the dramatic lines of my costume.

"An Isla Frank original."

She lets a small smile escape, then seals it up when it feels like she has received too much approval from her peers, who have been gossiping about me.

"Good luck."

I smile at her, knowing I don't need luck for the part I was born to play. My shoes slide on the floor as I move away from her and the long line of production cast members until I reach the front of the stairs leading to the stage.

I whisper to the crew member not to raise the curtain until I am fully seated, a change dictated by Mr. Jackson when he gives me a dubious look but finally agrees. As I silently ascend the stairs, my vision for this performance unfolds. Trepidation coats my insides as adrenaline forces me into character, fully embodying the vision of Travis's first love—himself.

The murmurs of the cast fade into the background as I reach the top, my focus narrowing to the task at hand. With each breath, I center myself, drawing upon the essence of the character I've spent countless hours preparing to portray. At the threshold of the stage, the murmurs of the audience settle by the dimming theater lights in eager anticipation of my first and, unknown to them, last off-Broadway performance.

With a racing heart and sweaty palms, the silence both up and backstage, I let the first click of my mic'ed up tap shoe fall. The sound on the old stage is beautiful, echoing an ominous promise across the theater that far exceeds my expectations.

Each step is meticulously slow, an eager anticipation of

when the next will fall. Delaying the audience's gratification, I scramble the pattern, some falling in quick succession, while others are drawn out as long as thirty seconds, forever in theater time.

My trepidation falls away, replaced with an emblazoned boldness that makes me feel more powerful than Travis's command of his stage. When I get close to the old wooden chair, my fingers curl around the back, holding my balance as I raise a foot, make eye contact with the crew member watching me, and count out another thirty seconds before stomping it with all my might.

The wooden floor groans, the sound gloriously loud, causing surprised shouts from the audience and a maniacal smile from me. I silently drop into my chair, sprawling out with the smoking cigar in my hand as the silhouette of my figure cloaks in darkness. The curtain rises, unveiling the packed house and introducing them to me.

They're in for the best show of their lives.

I stare at the spot on the floor, guarding my eyes against the bright spotlight coming in three seconds, which is the opposite of how Travis wanted me to start the show. He wanted me demure, downtrodden, and rising from the bed, not my hand blocking a dangerous crotch shot while drawing in an extended inhalation from the cigar I am holding.

It's been years since I smoked, something I did on the back porch of my mom's house when avoiding her and her boyfriend getting high and having sex inside.

The spotlight hits, bright and illuminating, my eyes intentionally blocked by the rim of the hat. A startled gasp rises, the shocking figure I cast enough to make my mouth twitch with satisfaction, playing into the part I embody. My chin raises to the ceiling, and I see two crew members above me, unseen by the patrons, as I blow smoke rings into the air above me.

As the smoke dances in the air above me, I relish the

momentary pause, anticipation hanging thickly in the theater. The audience's reaction is a drug, their gasps, whispers, and murmurs, signaling that I've captured their attention. Suddenly, I'm addictive. As addictive as the drugs my mom fed into her system. Purchased by her boyfriends, too many to count over the years, but only one was my abuser. His face appears before my eyes as I recite the opening lines, their meaning so reminiscent of the pain locked away in that part of my soul.

The script remains intact despite the deviation from Travis's visual scenery—my costume, my opening movement, and how I portray her on stage. The words flow effortlessly between cigar puffs, a prop meant to remain untouched. The strong smoky haze of my exhalations floats into the traveling into the crowd as if freeing the ghosts of my past with each puff, intertwining with the lines and emotions flowing out of me and into her, his Marcella.

My performance is raw and untamed, an emotional retelling of my childhood, the days tainted with my dad's absence and the ache of abandonment. Painting a vivid picture of those lonely days, gazing out the window, yearning for the sight of his car on the horizon, hoping he would return.

Moving to the front stoop when her anger for being stuck with me became overwhelming, and hateful words of blame spewed from her mouth at being burdened with childrearing. Having me was his idea, something she warmed up to after she got pregnant and was declined an abortion due to a blood clotting disorder she had.

With each tap of my mic-ed shoes, I accentuate the lonely passages of my monologue, using it as an exclamation point to punctuate the end of each painful revelation. As I draw the audience in deeper, barely any movement stirs in the audience, all eyes transfixed on my performance of her while revisiting the demons of my past.

With a final drag, I extinguish it on the tabletop, the sizzle echoing into the front row, where I see an enthralled Gabe sitting beside his friend in the silent theater. My gesture mirrors Dale's actions, the memory of those hazy, drugged-out eyes leering at me flooding my mind.

At that moment, I am transported away from Gabe, his friend, and the audience, back to when fear and uncertainty hung heavy in the air when I stood face-to-face with the darkness lurking within him.

He was kind initially, lavishing attention and gifts on my mom that made her giggle with a lightness I'd never seen before. Each gesture was more extravagant than the last as if he were determined to sweep my mom off her feet. She basked in the glow of his affections, filling our home with an unknown warmth.

Then, one day, he overreacted to the dinner she made, accusing her of intentionally burning it before hurtling the plate at the wall. The contents slid down the surface, shattering the peace and happiness of our existence as the plate shattered into pieces. It escalated from there, the screaming matches, the slamming doors, and chasing her down the hall until one day, he knocked her out and came looking for me. I barely escaped through my bedroom window, running up to the school and behind the bus barn until it got dark.

Having to step into that quiet home brought a new fear—he killed her and would kill me too. Unfortunately, that wasn't the case. He shot her up all right, not with bullets but with heroin, the same drug that turned him from her savior into her Satan.

I watched helplessly as the man who had once been the source of my mother's joy became the architect of her demise. His temper flared unpredictably, his words cutting like knives as they tore down her self-esteem and shattered her sense of worth. Yet still, she clung to him, desperate to recapture the fleeting moments of happiness they had shared in the beginning.

And I, too, held onto hope, praying that the man I once thought of as a father would find his way back to us to save me from them and her from him, back to the love that had once bound us together.

But as the abuse escalated, it became clear that there was no turning back. The love bombing had been nothing more than a cruel facade, a mask to conceal the darkness beneath.

As the opening act draws to a close, the final tap of my shoe before the other actors overtake the stage to begin the second act, I realize that I am my mother and Travis is my abuser.

The final scene closes in the same fashion that the play starts, with me sprawled across the wooden chair, my hand blocking my crotch, and an empty bottle dangling where the cigar did. The stage falls silent as I lower my chin. The brim of my hat intentionally blocks my face while I stare at a spot on the floor, guarding my eyes against the bright spotlight, shutting off in three seconds. My silhouette cloaks in darkness until the curtain descends. No more taps from my shoes—the story has already been told.

As the finality of the moment washes over me, I collapse forward in a cathartic release, ripping the tap shoes from my feet in a desperate attempt to ensure that the hot mics aren't heard again. With a sense of urgency, I scramble offstage and into the wings, seeking solace backstage.

It's then that I catch sight of Travis across the troupe of actors. Having taken extreme liberties with his play, I'm curious about his reaction. His expression is of sudden awe and admiration. His eyes are wide, his mouth parted in utter shock with a slight tilt to his head.

I realize that my performance has touched something deep within him, stirring emotions that he may have long buried beneath the surface as they were mine. Our eyes meet across the crowded backstage, sharing a connection that transcends words—a connection forged in the crucible of storytelling and the very life he wrote that I brought to life.

Regardless of the other actors and the audience's experience, only two people know the real intimacy of this story. A guy and a girl, broken in different ways, staring at each other from across the room. Having known each other intimately, they inhabited the roles of Marcella and her lover in the quiet sanctuary of his library.

A faint twitch graces my lips, a silent admission of the sorrowful loss overwhelming me. My eyes betray me as they well up with tears, a desperate attempt to hold them back proving futile. A solitary tear breaks free, tracing a path down my cheek and marring my once-perfect makeup. The irony is not lost on either of us.

As swiftly as the moment arises, it dissipates into the ether, swallowed whole by the crowd's thunderous applause echoing through the theater. Each clap and cheer resonate with an intensity transcending mere appreciation, filling the space with electric energy that crackles in the air and lingers long after the final curtain has fallen.

The cast quietly brushes past me toward the curtain for the final bow, their silhouettes moving into the bright stage lights, leaving Travis and I locked in a silent exchange in the shadows. The space between us is heavy with unspoken emotions, the haunting melody of longing and sorrow woven into the play strums in the background.

With each passing moment, Travis inches closer, his movements slow and deliberate, as if drawn towards me by an invisible force. His gaze, still adoring, a bittersweet realization of how easily he ensnared me as my mom was ensnared by hers.

Before he can bridge the chasm separating us, the chant for my name erupts from the audience, an excited chorus that brings a relieved smile to my face, breaking the tension between us.

With a sense of resignation and a slight lift to my shoulder, I step back, his hand grazing my skin in a fleeting clasp when my stocking feet carry me away from him. With a lingering glance into the shadows where he remains, my expression whispers goodbye as my lithe frame springs into the bright spotlight.

The applause swells to a crescendo, forcing me to nod several times before bowing with my castmates. I let their acceptance wash over me, soaking into the cells I blasted open with the traumatic memories of my past, forcing out the badness and sealing in the goodness.

I'm elated. My wide gaze roams the theater from the top of the rafters, where I often looked during my performance when daydreaming about Marcella's glory days, to the front row, where Gabe stops clapping and nods at my performance. I bow again, directed at him, which the benefactor beside him mistakes as his, and claps Gabe on the back, saying something in his ear.

The curtain call stretches on endlessly, with shouts for Travis to join. When he finally steps forward, his hand slides effortlessly around my waist. The same smile brightens his face when we walk the red carpet before he hurt me with his words and actions. He orchestrates the bow this time, leading his troupe of unskilled and raw-talent actors into a raging success, as evidenced by this packed house of cheering fans.

"Well done, little one." Unwilling to risk smudging my meticulously applied makeup, he leans in to air-kiss the side of my face. "You'll be greatly rewarded tonight."

His words send a shiver down my spine, a reminder of the tangled web that binds us together. Despite the distance I've put between us, there's the small, addicted part of me that can't help but be drawn to him, like a moth to a flame.

With a forced smile, I nod in acknowledgment, masking the turmoil brewing beneath the surface. Tonight may bring rewards, but it also carries a resolution that must be acted upon. How do I do it? I have no idea.

"I'll see you after the stage door."

His hand squeezes my waist, unaware or unwilling to acknowledge the shift in my feelings toward him. He steps back to shake hands with someone as I'm swept offstage into the sea of the cast, heading to the designated areas to meet the patrons.

As I navigate through the bustling backstage area, I consciously shove Travis from my mind, determined to focus instead on the love, support, and joy radiating from the audience members. With a genuine smile, I eagerly pose for pictures and sign playbills, relishing in the compliments and appreciation they shower upon me.

Each interaction fills me with a renewed sense of purpose and gratitude, reminding me of the profound impact that story-telling can have on others. As I chat with fans and share in their excitement, a sense of empowerment and liberation overtakes me as I realize I can do anything I want. The time sails by until the last of the audience members depart, leaving Gabe patiently waiting off to the side, leaning against the wall. With a smile, I make my way over to him, feeling a warmth spread through me at the sight of him.

"Gabe. I did it!"

He pulls me into a tight hug without hesitation, rocking us back and forth in his excitement. The warmth in his gestures soaks into my body, leaving me feeling so contented.

"You were absolute magic out there, love," he murmurs into my ear, his voice filled with genuine awe. "Absolutely smashing. You were completely unrecognizable as yourself—I truly believed you were Marcella."

His words wash over me like a soothing balm, meaning more than the hundreds of compliments I received. I feel seen and understood in his embrace, as I did earlier in the day when I struggled with my bodysuit, and he dived in to help.

"Thank you," I whisper, my voice barely above a whisper. "That means more to me than you'll ever know."

With a final squeeze, Gabe releases me from his embrace, his eyes sparkling with admiration. As he steps back, I am filled with a renewed sense of confidence and purpose, ready to tackle my school project and win the competition as I coast off the success of the opening night.

"I mean it, Isla. You were quite brilliant." His accent thickens with excitement in his cadence, leaving me to chuckle. "Haunting, as Max put it, I think you really won him over. I believe he was going to talk to your beau about financing his next project or something."

The reference to him as my boyfriend has me frowning harder than the perpetual frown painted on my face. If my performance garners Travis more work than I am pleased, it will be my parting gift to him after tonight.

"Thank you, Gabe."

I place my hand on his arm, needing to explain what happened in the dressing room and how that could change things for both his friend, Max, and Travis.

"But I need to talk to you about—"

"Isla, that was incredible!"

Lily's overly enthusiastic voice cuts through the air like a sudden gust of wind, interrupting our conversation with her congratulatory tone. Her eyes alight with excitement as she rushes over to us, her flowing dress as Rowena sways with each step.

"I knew you would steal the show, but that performance was beyond anything I could have imagined!"

The friendliness in her approach and the over-the-top gaiety are more of a show for Gabe as we have yet to bridge the chasm of our fractured friendship.

"Thank you, Lily. I appreciate that."

My tone is as hollow and empty as the words when they leave my lips. Her angle has nothing to do with me and everything to do with the handsome man standing beside me.

Her gaze exaggeratedly shifts to Gabe, her curiosity evident as she takes in his tuxedoed figure and modelesque features.

"And who might this be?" she asks, her tone overly cheerful as she thrusts her chest forward in a blatant attempt to grab his attention. "I don't believe we've had the pleasure of meeting."

I feel a pang of discomfort at how she's putting on a show for his benefit, but before I can ask her to give us a moment, irritated at her interruption, Gabe steps forward with a charming smile.

"I'm Gabe." His voice is smooth and warm, and his demeanor is genuine and inviting as he extends his hand towards Lily. "You must be, Lily. Isla has told me so much about you."

His introduction is seamless, his charm effortlessly bridging the gap between our strained friendship.

"Oh, has she now?"

Her response is immediate. A bright smile lights up her face as she takes his hand, momentarily forgetting any pretense of rivalry in the face of his amicable nature. Her words tinge with laughter and a spark of intrigue in her eyes as she glances between Gabe and me. My discomfort at her initial interruption fades, replaced by a cautious curiosity about how this unexpected interaction will unfold.

His insightful comments and inclusive gestures encourage a more open and relaxed exchange, drawing her into a circle of dialogue that feels unexpectedly comfortable. Her questions to Gabe become more thoughtful about his work and where he's from, causing her interest to be more sincere. I watch this transformation with caution, relief, and astonishment, realizing that

Gabe's influence might be the catalyst needed to heal our differences.

His knack for making connections, for finding common ground where there was once discord, hints at the possibility of mending fences, or at least, building bridges over the chasms that had separated us.

"Isla's been keeping you a secret."

She touches his chest with a familiarity that doesn't exist, and I move closer to Gabe, which doesn't go unnoticed when he brushes his fingertips against the small of my back. Gabe chuckles, inching even closer in an unspoken show of solidarity.

"Isla has her reasons, I'm sure. But I'm glad to finally meet her roommate," he says, warm with an underlying firmness that subtly marks his loyalty.

Her eyes narrow at our joined proximity. Her gaze moves from me to him, her curiosity not fully satisfied but tempered by the exchange.

"Well, I hope this means we'll be seeing more of you."

Ever the diplomat, he smoothly replies, "I hope that as well, Lily. It's been a pleasure talking to you."

A couple of our cast mates, Lily's friends, call to her, motioning for her to join them as they turn to go backstage. As she excuses herself from the conversation, her suspicious gaze lingers on me before giving Gabe a once over and retreating in her signature flare. Unwilling to waste precious time analyzing Lily's look and dissecting what it means, I turn back to Gabe.

"Sorry about that."

"So she's the one from earlier?" His head nods in her direction, unfazed by the interruption and apparent interest in him.

"Yeah, but I don't want to talk about her. I need to tell you about—"

"There you are."

I finch at his sudden touch, Gabe's dark eyes drawn to

Travis's possessive hand wrapping around my waist. The sensation sends a shiver down my spine, which is not pleasant and tinged with an uneasiness that has me straightening.

Gabe's eyes, filled with concern, mirror my inner turmoil, while Travis's gaze remains unreadable, his hold on me tightening with each passing moment. I try to push down the rising tide of discomfort, offering a weak smile to Gabe as I attempt to diffuse the tension as he stuffs his hand in his pocket.

"Here I am," I echo with a feigned enthusiasm that doesn't reach Lily's level.

I forget the thick theater makeup is a protective barrier to hide my true emotions, something I wish I could wear for the rest of the night. Travis extends his hand to Gabe, a strange gesture that leaves Gabe looking down at it without acting.

"Thank you for keeping my girl company, but I'll take it from here."

Gabe's gaze flickers between Travis's outstretched hand and me, a silent question lingering in his dark eyes. I can see the conflict playing out behind his calm façade. The desire to respect me, and whatever this is between Travis and me, even though his instinct to protect me surges forward.

But before either of them can make a move, I step forward, gently extricating myself from Travis's grasp. His touch lingers like a brand against my skin, leaving a burning trail of deceit as to how he's treating me compared to the violent confrontation before.

"We have that dinner, Travis, and silly old me, I can't wear this?"

I slip into another dopey and forgetful character, an act neither buys while defusing whatever is going on between them.

"Gabe, thank you and your friend, Max, for coming.'

Turning to Gabe, I lean in to hug him, a subtle gesture of gratitude and reassurance. But as I do, I feel his hand slip something hard down my bustier, the sudden contact sending a jolt of surprise through me. I break away from the embrace, my heart pounding as I look down to ensure whatever he passed me is safely concealed by my costume.

Gabe's dark eyes bore into mine, a silent inquiry of trust before I step back and plant an innocent kiss on Travis's stony cheek to appease him.

"I'll meet you back out here in, say, twenty minutes?"

Without waiting for either man to reply, I turn and frolic away, knowing both are watching me until I round the corner. Once out of sight, I abandon the facade of false cheerfulness, my pulse racing as I sprint through the halls back to my dressing room. With a sense of urgency bordering on desperation, I throw open the door, cursing the broken lock that offers me no protection.

Leaning against the door to ensure Travis doesn't come barreling through it, I fumble through my bustier for the note. It's his business card, the back adorned with hastily scribbled writing that jolts me.

I see the bruises.

The words hit me like a physical blow, ripping through the veil of denial I had to construct before my performance. Always observant, noticing things that others don't, and possibly being a trained doctor, he would see them beyond the stage makeup and gritty performance.

Tears prickle at the corners of my eyes as I clutch the note to my chest. Gabe knew what I was going to tell him in my desperate moment through all the interruptions. I exhale. I'm not alone like my mom was.

20

Having his assistant usher in a new black beaded gown and accompanying shoes for my dinner, I am left to my own devices to get ready. The oddity of preparing myself for such an event felt stranger and out of place. Stranger still is the realization that, after carefully removing all traces of my theater makeup and applying the limited cosmetics I could find, he isn't waiting for me in the lobby as I had thought.

Instead, the limousine driver collects me from the foyer with a clipped, "Mr. Jackson is on the phone," while he guides me past the paparazzi to the awaiting car.

Once I slip onto the firm leather seats, a chill slides over my bare skin, both in temperature and the frosty mood emanating from Travis. His eyes barely register a glance, offering me a glass of bubbling champagne before lifting his own, muttering a vacant "cheers" and clinking the stemware. With that, he resumes his animated conversation about the play's success, his attention elsewhere despite the celebratory atmosphere surrounding us. The abrupt change in his demeanor has me biting my lip with uncertainty, wondering what other surprises await me this evening.

As we arrive, he whisks me through the restaurant door, past curious patrons, and into the private room in the back. Ever the showman, he throws open the doors, and the room erupts in outrageous applause, the sound echoing off the walls as happy faces move around us. They congratulate him, shaking hands and clapping him on the back.

His hand separates from mine as the sea of congratulations separates us and sweeps him to the outside terrace for a round of cigars, much like the one I smoke on stage. But as he leaves, I'm left alone amid the celebration, the warmth of the applause fading into a hollow echo, and a sense of loneliness washes over me like a cold wave when his friends dissipate, as fleeting as they approached.

I wish I had my phone, something I left back at the penthouse at his insistence to enjoy the night. He's soaking up the attention I received in droves back at the play and in the fan line. It's hard to begrudge him the same attention lavished on me, even if my desire to remain here diminishes with every passing minute.

Needing an escape, I seek refuge in the bathroom, locking the floor-to-ceiling stall door and pulling Gabe's card from my undergarment near my good luck charm. My fingers trace his messy doctor's handwriting and then glance at the bruising conspicuously hidden by the gown's cap sleeves.

I'm almost certain his choice was strategic to avoid questioning from his adoring circle of influence while still satisfying his need to play dress up, and I fell for it again.

The fact that Gabe knows brings comfort to my situation, an ally in my corner if I should need one. As I stand there staring at his card, I formulate my plan for tomorrow. I'll rise early, say I'm taking Anna for a walk, and grab coffee from the café on the corner. From there, I'll catch a lift back to my apartment, explain to Lily that I need some time away from Travis to work on my project, and then call Papa to confess I lied about opening night and hope he understands.

When a sharp rap on the door startles me, I stuff the card back where I hid it, flush the toilet with my dress shoe, and casually unlock it to wash my hands and return to his party. Standing at the side of the doorway, I observe the room and its occupants.

Crystal chandeliers hang from the ceiling, casting a soft glow over the opulent private dining room. Each table is adorned with elaborate floral arrangements, set high above the center of the table to avoid blocking the conversations.

The walls are lined with intricate tapestries and gilded mirrors, reflecting the flickering candlelight. Plush velvet curtains frame the windows, their deep burgundy hue adding warmth and intimacy to the room's grandeur.

Travis sits at the center of it all, surrounded by his closest friends and confidants. They are a picture of sophistication and elegance, a modern-day Rat Pack in their tuxedos. Their laughter rings out like music in the air as they raise their glasses in toast after toast.

The aroma of gourmet cuisine wafts past me, tantalizing the senses with its rich and complex flavors. Plates of delicacies are brought out one by one, each dish more exquisite than the last, a testament to the culinary mastery of the chef of this three-star Michelin-rated restaurant.

A passing waiter interrupts my observations, offering me champagne, which I swiftly decline. I request sparkling water while pointing to my table, the empty seat by Travis and my vacancy going unnoticed by him and his troop.

With dread in my stomach and an overwhelming desire for a bubble bath and a good night's rest, I move slowly through the room, keen to the eyes that watch me play my next part. My smile is soft, my gaze loving as I take calculated steps to approach the table head-on, forcing Travis to acknowledge me or risk looking an ass to those he holds dear.

As if coordinated in advance, he stands, moving with chivalry and grace to collect my hand, making a motion to kiss the top and eliciting an echo of ah's from the ladies at the table. My smile is equally coordinated, breaking into a coy smile and shy giggle that sells it even to him. Handling me now as if I were delicate china, instead of slamming me up against doors that leave bruises, I float to my chair that he pulled out for me and ease into it before he sinks into his own.

The delicious dishes streaming past me in the doorway are now past my way. Ever the doting partner, he tends to them, spooning various dishes onto my plate into tiny portions. Something he murmured about watching my weight as the costumes were custom-made. Weight gain during the play's run would be problematic. A quiet thank you, a lean into his arm for him to kiss the side of my head, all a show for the patrons at the table.

Demure and quiet, I let the conversation swirl around me, offering minimal input so as not to be considered rude and using the slow eating of my food to not participate beyond a yes or no here and there. All of which pleases Travis, so long as I don't step into nor steal his spotlight.

As the evening wears on, the atmosphere becomes increasingly lively, filled with the clinking of glasses and the hum of animated conversation. The guests are enveloped in a cocoon of luxury, their cares and worries forgotten in the face of such abundance and splendor.

For Travis and his inner circle, this is more than just a dinner— it's a celebration of their success and proof of their wealth and influence in the glittering high society world. Of the power and privilege that comes with being among New York's elite.

Dinner seamlessly transitions into dessert, which blends into after-dinner drinks and more cigars out on the terrace. Exhaustion creeps over me like a heavy blanket, weighing down my weary limbs. The room gradually empties, leaving me alone in the dwindling crowd at our table. The chill in the overly air-conditioned room seeps into my bones, leaving me shivering despite the warmth of his jacket around my shoulders.

Longing to call it a night, I yearn for the comfort of my bed, forging the bath hours ago. When the clock strikes 2 am, a blessed and beautiful restaurant manager approaches the collection of men on the terrace, advising of their closing. I could kiss him out of gratitude. Rising to my feet, the last of the ladies here, many left an hour or two ago, I move with stiffness toward the terrace where things are wrapping up.

Travis, having had far too many drinks and not enough food, staggers dangerously close toward me when another man, his friend and drinking companion, captures him under the arm, leading him out as I trail behind. If it takes a man the same size as Travis to get him out of the restaurant and into the awaiting limousine, I have no idea how I will get him upstairs by myself unless I enlist the help of the doorman or building security.

With drunken hugs and slurred goodbyes, he's placed in the back seat, where he slumps to one side. The driver avoids my eyes as he holds open the door for me to slip in beside Travis.

As I settle into the seat beside Travis, his gaze glassy and reeking of alcohol, a faint smile tugs at the corners of his lips.

"You . . . little Isla Frank . . ."

His finger wags in my face before pressing the button that triggers the partition to slide up, closing us off from the driver's curious gaze that meets mine before disappearing.

"Isla, Isla, Isla. It's all I heard tonight."

There's a snideness to his tone, an undercurrent of jealousy, and something darker that sends a cold chill over my skin as my finger grips the edges of his coat, drawing it around me like a protective shield.

"You think you're really something special, don't you, Isla? Acting like you're the center of attention . . . like you matter. But let me tell you something, sweetheart."

Travis's words cut through the air like a knife, his tone dripping with acidic contempt as he taunts me.

"You're just a piece of ass like all the rest. My name should be on everyone's lips, not yours."

His words strike a nerve, igniting a surge of anger and defiance within me. I square my shoulders, refusing to let his cruelty break me.

"You're drunk, Travis," I retort, my voice steady despite the tremor in my hands as I remove his jacket from my shoulders, not wanting the smell of cigar smoke on me any longer. "You don't know what you're saying."

But Travis only laughs, a hollow, mocking sound that makes my pulse quicken and a fleeting thought of being trapped in this car as we careen down the street, catching too many green lights to be this lucky.

"Oh, I know exactly what I'm saying, Isla," he sneers, his breath harsh with alcohol while he sways to one side. "You got lucky tonight. It's an opening night fluke, but you'll have to recreate that *character* you took great liberties of destroying with your performance. You ruined Marcella. Tainted her beautiful story with your . . . your depravity."

I shake my head, stunned at the damage he's accusing me of causing.

"If anything, I infused your vapid, one-sided play with real emotions and entanglements. I made her real. Her struggle to hold on to a dream that her lover, a man of higher stature, snuffed out when he used her up and left her behind to rot in that filthy apartment for decades."

Rage overtakes my body as I adjust on the seat next to him, ready to defend my performance after keeping quiet the entire night.

"I won't let your twisted version of reality prevail. I made your play what it is. I am the star. My name should fall from their lips. It will be my face in all the papers tomorrow."

With a dark vengeance marring his features, clearing the haze from his eyes, he balls up his fists and rockets it at my face. The swiftness of his delivery is surprisingly too fast to be avoided, and it collides with the side of my eye, rocketing my head toward the side window. Pain explodes in my face as I scream, and for a moment, everything goes black. As my vision clears, I see Travis's victory smirk until another blow hits my lower lip, busting it open and sending blood droplets into the air.

"No! Travis!" I scream, his face a blind fury launching at me as the blow I expect to my head is delivered to my stomach, and I double over in pain. Tears pour from my eyes, mixing with my blood as I scream for help.

Another blow lands with a sickening thud against my kidney and a second to my spine. Agony washes over me, stifling my scream into low, guttural moans. The pain is overwhelming, consuming every fiber of my being and leaving me gasping for air.

For a moment, everything seems to blur as I collapse to the floor of the limousine, the impact jarring my senses and leaving me reeling. The world spins around me, and I struggle to regain my bearing. Each breath is a struggle, the sheer pain radiating from my back and side with every movement. I clench my teeth to suppress the cries threatening to escape my lips, the taste of blood filling my mouth.

As I lie there, vulnerable and helpless, dread surges over me. Realizing what is happening and who he is sinks in, and fear grips me tightly in its icy embrace.

Dizziness sends the interior of the car spinning as tears pour out of me. His vindictive laughter ricocheting off the plush interior. Through the haze of agony, I catch a glimpse of Travis's face looming over me, his expression twisted with anger and contempt. His movements are wild and savage, a man possessed by the fury of rage, jealousy, and possession as his murmured words of "fucking cunt" chant under his breath.

As I lay there gasping for air, another blow lands on my side, forcing blood and spit from my mouth as I crawl toward the petition for help. His hand claws my dress, ripping the fabric away from my legs in a blind rage while the other fumbles with his unzipping his pants, intending to rape me after beating me unconscious.

Despite the pain and fear, I refuse to let Travis break me as Dale broke my mom. I summon every ounce of strength, clinging to the flickering hope that I will get out of this car and away from him.

Through the twisted fog of my brain coating my slow movements, the long-forgotten self-defense moves that Uncle Tomlin taught me resurface.

Aim for the soft parts.

My fist clenches, bracing myself as I drag my legs up, an action that draws a leer out of him as if I'm suddenly a willing participant. Travis, oblivious to my intent, slips to his knees, dick in hand, ready to ravage me one last time. The floor beneath us shifts, the car jolting to a stop, and with a surge of adrenaline, I launch my stiletto directly at his cock, hitting it with all the strength left in my body.

His eyes widen in shock, his breath leaving his lungs in a guttural roar as he crumples toward me, his hands cupping his dick as I stomp at him repeatedly. My heel sinks into his thigh just above the crunch of his kneecap, grounding the joint under the balls of my feet. His howls overtake my screams as I jab my heel into his stomach, groan, and ribs, anywhere I can fight back.

My fury burns hotter with each stomp, driving me to unleash my pent-up rage upon him. His cries of pain only fuel my determination as I continue to rain down blows upon him, each strike driven by a primal instinct to fight for my life.

His eyes widen in shock, the realization of his vulnerability dawning upon him as I refuse to relent. His breath escapes in guttural roars of agony, drowned out by my screams of fury. I feel a sick satisfaction with each blow, a twisted sense of justice as I deliver retribution for the damage he's done to me.

The sound of the limo's door flinging open pierces the air, the driver yelling into the back of the limo, yelling for Travis to stop or he'll call the cops. With a surge of adrenaline, I seize the opportunity to escape. Ignoring the burning pain coursing through my body, I crawl towards the open door, my sole focus on my imminent escape.

The metallic stench of blood and the acrid scent of alcohol fill my nostrils as I clutch the driver's hand, using his strength to pull myself from the carnage. My legs give out beneath me as I stumble to my feet, lightheaded and disoriented. The driver's firm hand on my shoulder steadies me, providing a lifeline as I cling to him for help.

I'm trying to get my bearings and register where we are when Travis yells in fury, "Don't let her get away!"

The driver's hand tightens in response, sending me into a complete panic.

Fight or flight.

Uncle Tomlin always said to run, that I was small and lithe, easy to hurt but hard to catch. With a clandestine clarity, I cup my hand over his, digging my nails into his doughy flesh and twisting around in with a practiced fluidity to crack his nose.

There's a sickening crunch as bone meets bone, and the driver recoils in pain, his grip on me loosening instantly. A primal satisfaction washes over me as I see the blood spill from his broken nose, staining the pavement beneath us as I shake out the ringing pain radiating from the butt of my hand.

I ditch my heels, feel the icy pavement under my bare feet, and take off down the street. Despite the agony, adrenaline courses through my veins, drowning out the sharp pain stabbing from different parts of my body.

The relentless pounding of my heart echoes in my ears, drowning out the sounds of my ragged breaths. I stumble forward, my pulse racing in double time to the rhythmic throb of my injured eye. Each step is a battle, fought against the pain and exhaustion threatening to drag me down.

My vision begins to wane as my eye swells, but I refuse to succumb to the darkness. I push forward with every ounce of determination, fear fueling my desperate escape. The relentless pounding of my heart echoes in my ears, drowning out the sounds of my ragged breaths. I stumble forward, my pulse racing in double time to the rhythmic throb of my injured eye.

Glancing back over my shoulder, I see Travis's figure growing smaller in the distance, his shouts lost in the vast expanse between us. But he can circle the car around and cut off my escape route. With a surge of panicked adrenaline, I push myself harder, gasping for breath as I sprint.

The street seems endless and strangely vacant for a big city. Shrouded in darkness, only the dim streetlights giving any sense of direction, I see the angelic glow of a twenty-four-hour diner at the end of the street and sprint towards it.

As I draw towards it, renewed tears flow down my bloody face as the relief of knowing I'm about to get help overwhelms me. My sprint slows to a fast walk, wrapping my arms around my body, clutching the sides as pain shouts from various places.

With trembling hands, I push open the diner's door, the simple bell ringing out my arrival and survival. Exhausted and battered, I collapse to my knees on the dirty floor, relief washing over me in waves as I sob uncontrollably.

21

Movement swirls around me. The fall of hurried footsteps slapping against the tile floor causes me to look up. A concerned couple rushes forward, the man helping me to my feet, and the woman warns him to be careful as they guide me to the closest booth.

They want to call 911. I shake my head, my gaze fixed on the torn fabric of my dress as I dig frantically into the slit to retrieve Gabe's business card. With trembling hands, I hold it out to them, my voice barely a whisper as I ask them to call his mobile number, knowing he's the only one I can trust in this vulnerable situation.

The man takes the card and steps away to make the call, worry cutting across his features. The woman's gentle hand rests on my arm, her voice soft with compassion as she asks what I need. Before I can respond, the waitress arrives with a glass of water, a bag of ice, and a stack of napkins. Her actions are swift and practiced, as though she's seen or experienced similar situations.

I attempt a smile of gratitude, but the movement reopens my busted lip, sending a sharp pang of pain shooting through my already throbbing face. The metallic tang of blood fills my mouth, and I wince as I taste its bitterness.

Grimacing, I take a sip of water to wash away the blood, the cool liquid soothing against the rawness of my swollen mouth. Setting the glass back on the table with a distinctive thud, I reach for the bag of ice the women wrapped a few napkins around.

Leaning my head against the booth, I press the icy pack against my bruised face and injured eye, the cold wetness already seeping through the paper napkin. It offers some relief from the throbbing ache, and I let out a soft sigh as the coolness numbs the pain.

Amidst the faint sounds of the man's voice on the phone and the woman's murmurs to the waitress, speculating about what happened to me, I take a moment to assess the damage and mentally catalog all the places that hurt.

How could I have been so naive, blind to what I've already witnessed and experienced firsthand? Every touch and look from Travis seemed to speak of a love as vast as the cosmos. He presented me with the constellation necklace, symbolizing his claim to be my Orion, my protector in the stars. But what celestial protector demands the surrender of one's entire being?

From the start, he showered me with affection and gifts, enveloping me in his adoration. What woman wouldn't want that? Calling me his star, his muse. I basked in the glow of it all, believing myself to be cherished and unique in his eyes.

But beneath the love bombing, his script was being written. Slowly, Travis became the director of our lives, and I was the willing actress. The necklace, a sign of his devotion, also linked me to him and his vision of who I should be.

He orchestrated our days and nights, my interactions, and even my thoughts. I was his little one, his Marcella, his creation, shaped and molded by his will. I wore it proudly, not realizing it was a shackle disguised as a star.

The isolation was subtle, gradually pulling me away from my small world and into his large universe until all that existed was the galaxy he created for us. Friends, family, and my sense of self became distant, like stars fading at dawn, except Gabe. The one who saw what was happening and who Travis was fighting against, the one who would foil his perfect plan.

When I'd question, when I'd doubt, he was always there to realign my thoughts, to pull me back into orbit around him with more praise, adoration, and sex. The sex was amazing, sending me to the moon and back, but now that I look back on the intensity, it was all heightened to make me that much more addicted—a word he often used to reinforce his programming.

But stars are not meant to be owned, and constellations do not dictate destiny as he proclaimed of sailors and poets. The realization dawns on me, harsh and unbidden. I am not his Marcella, not a character in his play, and not his doll to play dress up with. I'm a living breath being with goals and dreams, a life of my own that I desperately want to return to.

I'm breaking free from his narrative, from the illusion that being his muse, his love, was the pinnacle of my existence. I'm more than a figure in his constellation—I'm a galaxy unto myself, and it's time to reclaim it.

The bell on the door rattles violently. The heavy fall of foot-steps and the resounding gasp announce his arrival.

"*Isla.*"

His voice relays everything I'm feeling, pain, worry, relief, and confusion. I open my eye to see his face, a beautiful sight with the diner light glowing around his head like a halo.

"My savior," I murmur, half jest, half earnest truth. He crouches before me, setting aside the bag of ice to replace it with careful dabs of dry napkins. Each wince I can't suppress translates into the tightening of his expression. Next to him sits his doctor's bag, already splayed open, waiting to assist him.

"He did this to you."

He doesn't ask—it's more like he's stating the obvious. His jaw sets hard, his whole face turning into a storm of quiet anger from the truth he already knows.

His hands are soft as they work, accessing the swelling and pushing against different parts of my face, eliciting a hiss or moan. There's a tremor of something fierce in his touch. He's not just here to fix my cuts and bruises. He's here to make things right. His touch is warm and solid, and I can't help but lean into it, soaking up the kind of care that's real and without strings attached. It's clear as day in his eyes—this is what it feels like to be looked after by someone who's got your back, no matter what.

"I need to take you to the hospital, Isla. They'll need to do an exam, take pictures for the police report, and the charges they'll press—"

Gabe's all about action, ready to whisk me off to the ER to document everything and make it all official. But I can't, not yet. I hold onto his wrist, a silent plea.

"No," I insist, my voice a bare whisper but firm.

He pauses, his motions stilling. Confusion creases his brow, and I see the storm of anger and concern raging behind his eyes. He doesn't get it, not entirely—not how I'm not ready to turn this night into a series of cold clinical procedures and reports. I've already been down this road many times before, and I'm not sure I want to do it again. The man from earlier steps closer, exasperated when he points his finger directly at me.

"I told her the same and tried to call 911, but she refused. She only wanted you, doctor."

Gabe's eyes lock with mine, searching for an explanation in the silent communication amidst the onlooking couple. I know he's battling his professional judgment and the oath he took to help others, not wanting to respect my wishes. His lips press into a thin line, a visible sign of his internal struggle.

"Please, Gabe."

He exhales deeply, a sound laden with concern and reluctant agreement. His hand, which I'm still clutching, returns the pressure, a wordless vow of his support. Then his attention shifts to the man at his side, leaning in a little too close, the scent of his curiosity almost as strong as his aftershave.

"You're coming home with me," Gabe declares, a finality in his tone that brooks no argument. "I still need to check you over for a concussion, and I'll need to keep an eye on you. Just in case things . . . worsen."

The man beside him seems about to protest, but one look from Gabe, a mixture of authority and a plea for privacy, has him stepping back. Still captivated by the unfolding drama, his wife bites her lip, sensing the shift in the room's energy.

Gabe's declaration is more than an offer of medical aid. It's a sanctuary—a place where Travis can't find me, opposite my apartment, to which he has the address. Knowing Lily, she'd let him right in.

I won't be a spectacle or a case study in his care. I'll just be Isla, injured and vulnerable but safe in the hands of a friend who's seen me at my worst and still stands steadfast by my side.

"Okay."

As I let go of his hand, I steady myself on the table, feeling the room sway with the movement. Gabe moves efficiently, snapping his bag shut with a decisive click and tossing the strap over his shoulder. He's by my side in an instant, his hands carefully positioned to support me without causing further pain.

I can't suppress a groan as I stand, every bruise and ache protesting the motion. Gabe's grip is firm and gentle. His concern is etched in the lines of his face as he helps me rise. I wince, biting back the sharp stabs of pain that come with moving toward the door.

Together, we navigate the short distance to his luxury car, parked haphazardly on the curb. He helps me into the passenger seat, then tosses his bag in the back before jogging to the other side.

Gabe's voice is earnest, filled with a resolve I don't have.

"Isla, I want you to know I'll help you as much as possible. But this needs to be dealt with—reported at the very least."

I close my eyes, leaning back into the seat, feeling every bruise and every bit of soreness as I try to find a comfortable position.

"Please."

I understand the importance and the necessity of what he's saying. Every fiber of my being knows that standing up and reporting is what should be done. But he doesn't know, can't fully understand what I've been through. The thought of recounting everything, of making it real by speaking it aloud, is overwhelming.

I've already dredged up enough old demons today, from Rick in the playroom to my boyfriend and mom during the performance. It's not just the physical pain that holds me back. I'm mentally exhausted with the flickering thought of quitting and returning home.

"I know I should," I continue, my voice straining as I open my eyes to fresh tears flowing out at my realization. "Every woman should . . . But, Gabe, maybe it's best if I just leave town. Quit school and go back home. It's not just about what happened tonight. There's so much more, and it's not something I can face right now."

The car is filled with my admission, a truth laid bare in the dim light. His eyes bore into me, a pleading in them but for what I don't know. His lips twitch, fighting the frown that rarely appears on his face.

"What? Go ahead and say what you want to say."

His eyes soften, brushing back a stray strand of my hair, the tenderness clenching my heart that one man can be so violent while another can be so gentle.

"I, for one, would be very sad if you did such a thing."

The same tenderness in his touch appears in his tone. He doesn't push further, doesn't demand an explanation for my defeat, and just leaves it as messy as the rest of this night. The drive to his place is quiet. The city sounds occasionally rise around us.

The silence that fills the car as we drive isn't uncomfortable. It's a quiet understanding, a shared space where words aren't necessary. Gabe drives with deliberate care, navigating the late-night streets with an attentiveness that suggests he's trying to make the ride as smooth as possible for me.

As we approach his home, the car slows to a stop before a modern roll-up door. Curious, I watch Gabe press a button, and the door smoothly ascends. Whereas Travis's penthouse is steeped in old-money elegance, Gabe's place, nestled in a newer building, speaks of a different kind of life, perhaps less ostentatious but no less inviting.

The transition from the city's chaotic energy to the quiet, secure entrance of Gabe's building feels like I'm hiding away from reality, from my problems. But I can't handle anything else right now.

"It's quite a ways from the garage to my door, and I don't have a wheelchair. I'd like to carry you if you are okay with that."

His low and considerate voice breaks the comfortable silence, cloaking me in safety as he maneuvers through the garage's levels.

We reach the top level, and he parks in the first spot by the elevators, the engine's hum ceasing with a turn of his wrist. The quiet that follows feels heavy with his awaiting response, a pause filled with the unspoken understanding of my vulnerability and his willingness to ease it.

I nod, my agreement whispered, trusting in his caring nature and livelihood as a doctor to protect me from further injury. His approach is gentle, and his actions are measured as he approaches my side of the car, ready to lift me into his arms. In this gesture, there's an intimacy that our friendship has always hinted at, his sexuality preventing my initial attraction to him from going any further.

As the car door opens, he leans in, throwing his bag over his shoulder again and asking, "Ready?"

"Yeah."

As he carefully lifts me out, ensuring not to jostle any of my injuries, I groan in pain as his hand presses against the kidney that Travis punched.

"Does this hurt too much?" Before giving me a chance to respond, he continues, "I'm going to have to access you. You understand that, right? I need to know what I'm dealing with."

The doctor in him prevailing, surpassing our friendship for a moment as his eyebrows knit together in worry. My pounding head rests against his chest, the pulse still strumming through my injured eye, and I lick my split lip to get some relief from the throbbing there too.

"I know." His light cologne swirls into my nostrils, bringing a sense of serenity as he cradles me against him. "Thank you again, Gabe."

"Anything for you, love."

His movements are fluid, blocking any jostling as he steps toward the elevator. The elevator doors slide open with a hush, and as we step inside, Gabe hits the button for his floor, his other arm securely holding me. In this quiet, suspended moment, between the safety of his arms and the sanctuary of his home, I find a momentary peace, a breath between the beats of a heart still racing from the night's ordeals.

"Tell me about London. Describe it as if I'm blind. How does it smell, feel, taste?"

This was one of Travis's exercises he made me do to get into characters on long nights when I wanted to throw in the towel.

It helped paint a canvas of someone's life in ways that weren't commonly described.

For some reason, I want to revisit that innocent night on the bookstore's second floor where we shared secrets like gossiping girls, well before Travis, the play, and everything else. That and I need something to distract me from the pain that is intensifying as the adrenaline dissipates from my body.

"Odd, but I'll indulge." His voice rumbles against my ear as he begins. "London is not too dissimilar to New York at times. It's crowded and noisy, albeit not as rude as the traffic here. Days on the end where there's no sun, the overcast clouds settle low over the city and dumping copious amount of rain on the city."

The elevator comes to a halt, the doors whispering open, and with effortless grace, as if I weigh nothing, he continues down a long corridor with very few doors.

"How does London smell?" he questions as if never considering it before. "It smells . . . like a rain-soaked pavement and the rich aroma of freshly brewed tea from the corner shops. There's a hint of the Thames, a briny, earthy scent that underlies the city's history. Early mornings are crisp, especially in the fall when the leaves are turning, and the air is cool and damp. You can catch the scent of wood smoke on the breeze, a reminder of cozy firesides. It's my favorite season to walk to work."

His rich baritone voice is soothing as his narration carries me away from the pain, away from my problems in the heart of this city, transporting me across the ocean to the heart of London.

"And feels?" I prompt, eager to immerse further in the distraction when we stop at the door, and he enters a combination into the lock.

He's careful not to lose his grip on me as he moves us through the front door. His place is opposite the maximalist opulence of Travis's penthouse. It's spacious, minimal, and tidy, almost what I expected without thinking about it. The decor is a tasteful myriad of creams and tans, understated with a richness that reflects his personality—functional with an eye for comfort.

"It's a city alive with stories," he continues, easing me onto the plush couch with careful hands. The cushions welcome me into their softness as he adjusts the pillows behind my head. "Lay back and rest while I get a few things."

I stare at the ceiling, trying to breathe calmly against the sharp pierces to my back.

"I hope you're bringing painkillers."

It wouldn't be the first time I was in a painkiller-induced haze. The first was when I tried to escape the abuse of my boyfriend, but he punched me in the stomach, forcing some to come back up with my vomit. He doesn't answer, just scraping things somewhere near me and crinkling hard plastic as if unpacking stuff.

He appears in front of me, having gotten rid of his athletic jacket. His t-shirt is stretched across his chest, showcasing all the hard work he puts into running.

"You wouldn't have your phone by chance, would you? I texted and called you numerous times today, and they weren't unanswered."

"No, that's back ho—his place."

He nods, although his look is not approving, matching mine as a fleeting thought of Travis intercepting them crosses my mind.

"Just say it, I see the wheel turning in that big brain of yours."

"I know you said you don't want to call the authorities, at least not right now, but down the road, you'll need the evidence if there were no witnesses."

He's going into doctor mode, the same inclination as the

waitress bringing me that stuff—this isn't his first time dealing with assault.

"You want to take pictures."

"Yes, exactly."

His tone shifts into that of a clinician, albeit one deeply entrenched in concern for a friend. The room's ambiance fades into the background as he focuses on me, his dedication to his profession evident.

"It's crucial, Isla, not just for legal purposes but also for your healing process. Having tangible evidence can be a powerful step towards reclaiming your story, your truth. Not to mention counseling and support groups for victims of domestic violence. All resources you would have immediately if you let me take you to the hospital."

He tries a third time. His overwhelming desire to do this the right way is impressive. The hospital would lead to a call to my emergency contact, which is not Gabe but my parents, who don't need to see me like this after everything I've already put them through. Gabe seems to sense my reticence, his expression softening.

"Only if you're comfortable." The earlier command resolves into gentle persuasion. "I just want to ensure you have all the options laid out for you."

"Okay."

Gabe nods, pulling his phone out of his pocket.

"But only pictures, not the hospital."

"I strongly advise against all of this, love. I wish you'd tell me why." A frown sets into his expression as he walks closer. "Close your eye and let me move your face, okay?"

"Only pictures," I reiterate, a small measure of control in a situation that feels overwhelmingly out of my hands.

I follow his instructions and then click his phone as he unlocks it. It sounds deafening in the quiet of the room.

"I respect your decision, Isla, but I'm here whenever you're ready to talk about it."

The invitation hovers near my ear. His touch is featherlight. He methodically moves across my face, ensuring the camera captures the extent of the injuries without causing me further pain.

"Are there any more?"

My good eye flips open, and I stare at him even though we both know the answer to his question. Seconds tick by until I attempt to move, and his hands hover to stop me.

"Whoa, take it very slowly."

He flips them over his palm open for mine to join to help me rise from the couch. Once on my feet, I grimace as standing feels worse than lying down.

"Why don't we take this into the bathroom? I can also dress your wounds in the better light."

"Sure."

We move together towards the bathroom, Gabe's pace unhurried, matching my slow shuffle. The care he takes with every step and touch speaks volumes of his dedication to the well-being of others.

The guest bathroom is bathed in a brighter light, the illumination gentle yet sufficient for Gabe to tend to my wounds with the precision his profession demands. He guides me to stand in the center of the room.

"I'm going to retake the pictures. It's much better at capturing the bruising."

His explanation is unnecessary as the pain is mounting a major attack on my body.

"I don't care anymore. Can you finish telling me about London to distract me from the pain?"

My hand cups my head, the pressure building into a migraine as if my eyeball is going to be ejected from the swollen tissue.

"Of course."

He's gone and back in a flash, his bag on his shoulder, a sheathed needle in his gloved hand, and a small glass vial with some clear liquid in his hand.

"Do you have any allergies to medications?"

"No."

He thoroughly explains what he's about to administer, and his professionalism is evident even in this informal setting. The cold swipe of disinfectant on my upper arm precedes the pinch of the needle—a brief intrusion that promises relief.

"That should take effect quickly. I apologize for not administering it sooner."

The effect is immediate, and suddenly, I feel great, better than great, under Gabe's watchful gaze.

"Whoa. I forgot how doctors have the good stuff."

The words slip out with a hint of humor tinged with underlying truth. His frown deepens as he dispenses with the sheath and the needle, placing everything on the bathroom counter.

"Why do I think there's more to that statement?"

"Because there is."

The ease brought on by the medication opens to the past, memories blurred with substance use, escaping reality, and creating a new one became a double-edged sword.

"My offer still stands if you want to talk about things. I've been told I'm an excellent listener."

He returns to his medical bag, pulling out various things without waiting for my response. At this point, I'm buzzing on the stuff he gave me, I couldn't care less about talking. I simply want to be and let my body and mind wander away from this horrific night.

When he picks up his camera, I close my eyes, following the same process as in the living room. His fingertips feather across my shoulders, taking pictures of the bruises from earlier before they float down my bare back, pulling the fabric away from my skin in the low form of the dress. When he speaks again, his voice cuts through the fog of my drugged state.

"Isla?"

My good eye opens, feeling woozy and heavy as I look over my shoulder at him.

"I'm going to need to remove your dress."

His eyes, dark and filled with concern, search mine for consent. This moment, this decision, feels like another layer of exposure, yet in Gabe's presence, I find a measure of safety. His professionalism and his care have already offered me solace in ways I hadn't anticipated. With a nod, I give him the permission he seeks, a silent acknowledgment of my trust in him.

"I'll do my best to preserve your dignity."

His response is immediate and careful as he stands behind me. His actions match his words as she unzips the back of my dress, letting it slip from my shoulder and helping me move my arms out of the holes before using my hands to cover my breasts.

"Stay like that as I take the pictures, and then I'll assess the damage done."

The dress falls with a whoosh to the floor, standing only in my panties as his phone clicks, documenting more photos for the medical or police file. Neither matters to me at this point. He flashes a light over my eye, looking for signs of a concussion.

His fingertips are dipping and pressing into different spots, causing me to flinch or move away as a haunting hint of phantom pain floats through the painkiller. He pauses with soft apologies, acknowledging the discomfort and pain his actions inadvertently caused.

He reiterates his desire to go to the hospital, murmuring about an x-ray and CT scan confirming internal damage as my back is covered with extensive bruising. He follows the injuries to the front of my body, the warmth of his hand pressing against my stomach while cupping my back. He hums to himself or verbally notifies what he feels or sees with a few final pictures.

After the evidence collection, he transitions to tending my wounds, retrieving a bottle of antiseptic from his bag, warning it might sting as the cool liquid cleans each cut. The most painful one being on my lower lip.

His movements are slow and calculating as he opens a small jar of topical ointment, his fingers lightly dabbing the cream on the rawness of my injuries. When he's finished, he steps back, puts the lid on the cream, and rips off his gloves to toss them on the counter next to the needle.

"How does that feel?"

His focused gaze scans my face for any sign of discomfort or pain he might have missed.

"Feel what?"

My limbs are growing heavier the deeper the painkiller sets in, my hands slipping from covering my breasts as I close my eye, ready for sleep to pull me under for the next ten years.

"Uh, Isla . . . I'll get you something to wear."

The discomfort is evident in his tone as his shoes squeak on the bathroom floor when he retreats. I open my eye and step back to lean against the counter, my fingertips curling around the edge to stay upright until he returns. When he returns, he stops short in the doorway, awkwardly clearing his throat as my desire to maintain my modesty isn't a care anymore.

"Here . . . let's uh . . . let's get you covered up."

In his hands, he holds an oversized shirt and a pair of plush joggers. His eyes, however, speak volumes of his discomfort.

"I don't care if you see. My parents are gay," I mumble, my words slurred by the delicious haze of the drug.

My logic, fuzzy at best, fails to connect the dots in a way that makes sense to him by the look on his face. His expression flickers through confusion, understanding, and then amusement as he processes my statement.

"Because you think I'm gay?"

A hint of laughter warms his voice, his previous discomfort melting away in the face of my nonsensical reasoning.

"Yes," I insist, a smile tugging at my lips despite the pain and exhaustion. "You're safe. Gay guys don't like naked girl boobies."

With a gentle chuckle, Gabe helps me into the shirt, the fabric soft and comforting against my skin. It covers me completely, the warmth of his laughter cutting through the haze of my discomfort and bringing a momentary lightness to the room.

"That's not quite how it works, love, but I can assure you that I am not of the homosexual orientation." He's still smiling as he ensures the shirt is settled over my thighs. "Where did you get that idea from?"

I focus intently on his face, searching his expression for any hint of deceit.

"At the bookstore. Duh. You even told me as much. You're trying to find the right guy and have a family or something." My hand cups the side of my head, the pressure and pain gone. "Is it supposed to be hard to think?"

"I'm fairly certain I didn't say that. Regardless, let's get you in bed."

He guides me gently toward the guest bedroom, his hand supportively at the small of my back.

"The pain medicine is making you groggy and affecting your memory. It's normal, just let them do their job and try to relax."

He throws back the linens, helping me settle into bed. The softness of a cozy cocoon around me when I feel a sudden hardness against my panties has me attempting to smile and grimacing.

"Wait."

I shimmy out of my panties and feel for my good luck charm, relieved it's intact after the fight with Travis.

"Here's my good luck charm. Keep it in a safe place."

With the only light from the bathroom streaming into the bedroom, he's backlit, like that glowing angel, the same as the diner when I hand them to him.

"Uh, I'll just leave your underwear—"

I giggle, the sound foreign to my ears, even though I know it's too high to be his.

"No, silly Gabriel. My adoption ring is on the inside. On a ribbon."

He takes the panties with an awkward nod, his fingers deftly finding the ring attached to the ribbon inside.

"Your adoption ring?" he murmurs with recognition, a newfound tenderness in his tone as he holds the small, significant token. "I'll keep it safe for you, love."

With the ring secured, Gabe finishes tucking me into bed, his movements efficient yet full of care. As I nestle into the pillows, the grogginess from the medication deepens, pulling me toward the brink of sleep.

"I've got some work to do, so I'm going to stay in the room observing you."

Gabe remains vigilant, pulling a chair beside the bed where he can monitor me, his laptop open. His attention never fully leaves me when the click-clack of his keyboard starts.

"Gabe?"

"Yes?

"How does it feel? London? You never answered."

He pauses, turning off the bathroom's light and drowning us in complete darkness save the night sky outside his windows and the glow from his laptop screen.

"London feels like home."

The words hit with a nostalgia that is unmistakable in the dark.

"The cobblestone streets underfoot provide an uneven rhythm to your walk, a tactile reminder of the city's age and history. The ever-present rain feels like a constant caress, gentle or insistent, depending on the day. The chill in the air bites at your cheeks, leaving them flush and alive."

I hum with pleasure. The description is so inviting that I want to hear more and eventually experience it myself.

"Taste."

"Ah, that's a bit trickier. Let's see . . . the taste of London is as varied as its people. There's the sharp tang of fish and chips, wrapped in paper and sprinkled with vinegar, eaten with your mates and a pint. The sweetness of a jam-topped scone accompanies the subtle bitterness of tea, a combination that warms you from the inside out every afternoon. And then there's the smoky flavor of the street food in markets like Borough, where each stall offers a bite from a different corner of the world."

His description is a balm, a momentary escape that dulls the ruins of my life. For a brief time, I'm not just lying here, bruised and battered. I'm wandering the streets of London, experiencing its essence through Gabe's words. Long second pass, sleepiness drawing in as the blue glow of his laptop displays his homesick look.

"Gabe?"

"Yes?"

"Will you take me to London?"

As silence falls, sleepiness settles over me. The gentle lull of Gabe's voice and the dim glow of his laptop are the last things I'm aware of as I drift over the edge of consciousness.

"One day, I'll show you the world."

22

Sunlight pours in, a flood of unwelcome brightness that nudges me from the depths of a very deep sleep. Blinking against the glare, my eye opens to an unfamiliar, unadorned ceiling. The confusion in my foggy brain is almost as heavy as the thick comforter I'm buried under. I drag a wet washcloth from the side of my head, confused about what it's doing there.

As consciousness seeps back, so does the pain—fierce and consistent, settling so deep into my body that it even gnaws at my bones. With every shift in the cloudy mattress, the memories of last night's horrors resurface, the assault in the limousine crashing over me. The brutality of his fists and the dark, almost possessed expression marring his face, has my pulse quickens and me clutching the comforter to pull up to my chin.

The room is quiet, except for the city's gentle hum beyond the windows. Not having gotten a good look at his guest bedroom last night, I take in the same monochromatic minimalist decor, the clean lines of the furniture, and the personal touches that are undoubtedly his.

There's a bookshelf filled with medical texts and clusters of photos, each showing either a smiling family, bro pairing, or him traveling to far corners of the world. I never thought of Gabe beyond New York, but something from last night pulls at my memories about London or the world. The memory dances on the edge of my consciousness until it's lost and fleeting away.

I attempt to sit up, but my body protests, each movement igniting fresh pain that lances through me. I wince, sucking in a sharp breath, and lay back down, allowing my body the time it seems to demand. The assault from last night isn't just a series of bruises and cuts—it's a deep-seated trauma that's settled into my very marrow.

"Ah, you're awake."

His tone is as casual as his athletic wear. He's clad in a snug T-shirt that outlines his physique, paired with relaxed joggers and Gucci sneakers. He approaches, holding a tall glass of water that I guess is meant for me.

"Barely. I hurt everywhere."

My throat is raw and sore, probably from all the screaming and sobbing. The pain isn't just physical. It's the mental and emotional trust I placed in someone I cared about violently shattered.

"Let me help you."

Gabe sets the glass on the nightstand, hovering by the bed with his hands extending. I flip back the covers and try to move on my own, but the pain surges forward, causing me to abandon that thought.

"Fuuuck," I groan, my hand moving to my chest as if it can somehow heal all the hurt.

"I can give you more pain medicine, but it's best with something in your stomach first. It can tend to bring about nausea, and the last thing we want is the violence of vomiting added to your suffering."

His face is a mask of worry, eyebrows pulled tight, jaw

clenched, and hands strained on his hips. Suggesting to eat something before taking more pain medication makes sense, yet the mere thought of food already makes me nauseous—or maybe it's the pain that is making my stomach queasy.

"I don't think I can eat."

The thought of sitting up, scrunching up my aching back against the pillows, and grappling with the ache that pulses against the mattress sounds terrible.

"We'll try something light, okay? Maybe some broth and toast," he offers, his voice gentle, coaxing. "Just a little to cushion your stomach and get you feeling good like last night."

I nod reluctantly, understanding the logic behind his words but dreading the effort it requires.

"I can't even remember last night. It's like bits and pieces."

"I can imagine the body keeps score of the trauma it endures, and the mind protects you from reliving it. It's why you would benefit from counseling when this is all over with."

I squint, the words sounding familiar.

"Did you tell me that last night?"

He frowns, his shoulders rolling forward in defeat as his hands move to drape loosely by his side.

"That and wanting to take you to the hospital, which you refused several times."

I smile and immediately stop. The biting sting has my tongue darting out to feel it. The last time I was in the hospital, I had a broken arm from getting jumped at the child protective facility, which accelerated my foster placement. That was a good thing. Being in the hospital now won't be.

"I applied more salve, but lips are tricky with the movement."

The tang of the bitter, sticky substance has me scrunching up my nose.

"I don't like hospitals."

I leave it at that, letting the subject drop as I muster the strength to sit up. Remaining laying isn't going to help me heal. Bracing myself, I press my palms into the mattress, ready to hoist myself upright, but Gabe moves to my side, offering his gentle support to ease me back against the pillows.

My breath catches, pain stabbing from various parts of my body as the movement was just too much. His concerns etch deeper with every rasp until he hands me the glass of water he had set aside earlier.

"While you sip that, I will get lunch and the pain medicine."

Gabe moves to the kitchen, and I hear the quiet sounds of him preparing something simple. The domesticity of the action is oddly comforting compared to Travis, who had a rarely seen chef make the meals and keep them in warming drawers for us.

When he returns, he brings a tray with a small bowl of broth and a piece of lightly buttered toast. The smell, normally appetizing, is now a test of my will, but I do not want to disappoint his patience in taking me in and treating me.

"Let me know if it's too hot."

He sets the tray across my lap and adds another pillow behind me as I smother a hiss. I take a small sip of the broth, its heat spreading through me, contrasting with the cold dread that's taken residence in my heart. The toast follows, a bite so small it's laughable, yet Gabe watches with pride as if it's a monumental achievement.

"Very good. Just one hundred more of those, and you'll be finished."

I smile, the busted lip a reminder not to, until an overwhelming surge of fear overtakes me.

Anna!

I left her behind with that monster. My poor girl, so small and vulnerable, could be dead because of my selfish actions last night. If I had kept my mouth shut, not got into an argument, and gone home with him, she'd be safe, or at least safer with me there than by herself. I'll never forgive myself if something happens to her.

"Oh my God."

My hand cups my mouth, tears surging from nowhere as my heart beats in triple time. Gabe's posture instantly shifts from gentle encouragement to high alert. He reaches out, his hand hovering just above my back, cautious not to cause further discomfort.

"What is it? What's wrong?"

"Anna." The name slips out, a whisper coated with fear and guilt. "My Yorkie. She's with him . . . with Travis at the penthouse."

The thought of my sweet, potentially in the clutches of the same violence that had been directed at me, sends a fresh wave of panic coursing through my veins.

"I've go . . . I-I got go."

My hands shake as I attempt to shove the tray aside, desperate to rise, to flee to her rescue, but Gabe is quicker, steadier. His hands clasp over mine, halting my frantic movements.

"Isla, listen to me. You can't go there, not in this state." His voice is firm, rooted in a resolve to protect me from further harm, yet unaware of the stakes for my sweet Anna, who's seen me through my darkest days. "Certainly not back to him."

"Gabe, please! You don't. . ."

My protest breaks into sobs, my grip slackening as I grasp his hands instead, seeking some form of support, some acknowledgment that what he fears for me is what I fear for her.

"If anything happens to her . . . if he does anything . . ."

The words choke me, too dreadful to fully articulate, each one a potential reality I'm unprepared to face. Gabe's eyes meet mine, and I see the conflict of my plea against his better judgment. But I can't leave her to him. He wasn't keen on her being there in the first place, having never grown up with pets.

It was a compromise that he didn't want to make when I kept saying I couldn't stay the night because of her. Allowing her to move in removed any reason for me to be out of his presence outside school. I attributed it to the heat and passion of a new relationship, not the control and ownership it became.

"I'll go. I'll get your dog and whatever else you need that he has."

I gasp, releasing his hand to cover my mouth as my uninjured eye searches his face. He's already done so much, taking me in, cleaning me up, and is now taking care of me. This is too much to ask of him. I could ask Lily and tell her to get Anna for me. I'd have to tell her what happened last night. She'd demand to know since we hadn't fully bridged the chasm yet. But would he let her? Would he let Gabe in? Certainly not.

"How?"

The logistical hurdles, not to mention the risk of confronting Travis directly, seem impossible. What if he attacks Gabe? They traded intelligent insults already. What's to say it won't escalate?

"What if he goes after you? What if he hurts you? Or your hands, and you can't operate ever again? All those children you help?"

Gabe snorts, not intentionally but at my statement, which seems humorous.

"I'm a third-degree black belt, Isla. I'd relish the opportunity for him to try."

My breath hitches at Gabe's revelation, surprised at this new information. The doctor and caregiver is a fighter?

"You're what?"

Gabe's slight chuckle does little to ease my concern, but it does shift the atmosphere, lightening the heavy air between us.

"Yes, I've trained for years. It's about discipline and control, not just fighting, as some might think. It also means I can handle myself if things get . . . difficult."

The thought of Gabe facing off against Travis is both comforting and terrifying. It's comforting because, for the first time since this nightmare began, I feel like we have a fighting chance. It's terrifying because the stakes are so high, and the thought of either getting hurt is unbearable.

"But still, the risk . . . I should go," I start, the worry threading through my voice again.

Gabe sits on the edge of the bed, his gaze steady and reassuring as he finds my hand again.

"I wouldn't offer if I wasn't sure I could handle it. And I'm not about to let him—or anyone—continue to hurt you. Not if I can do something about it."

An assuring squeeze runs through him into me, bolstering his conviction.

"I need you to trust me. This isn't just about retrieving Anna or getting your things. It's about taking a stand, showing him that this ends today, and he won't ever hurt you again."

The depth of his commitment, the readiness to confront my nightmare head-on for my sake, forges a new layer in our friendship. It's a strange position, Gabe's willingness to dive into danger for me and my instinct to protect him from it.

I squeeze his hand back, gazing into his warm brown eyes that reflect the sun streaming across the bed. For a split second, I sense something more in the gentle way his thumb passes over my knuckles, more romantic than reassuring. Another nagging memory tickles my brain as his expression softens.

"Okay. But please, be careful. I couldn't bear it if anything happened to you because of me."

His gentle smile calms the swirling fear about Anna and now him.

"I'll be alright. Now, please eat so I can give you the pain meds before I retrieve your dog. We're going to get through this together."

He rises, pausing to kiss my hair, the only spot on my body that doesn't seem to hurt. It's sweet and caring, as he's always been with me. As I resume eating, the soup cooling from our conversation, I watch him walk out of the bedroom with a determined gait.

The soup is impeccable, and the crispy sourdough is a perfect pairing, even though the hardness elicits too much pain from my jaw and head. I place the sourdough inside the bowl, letting the soup drench it in flavor. I eat several more bites, savoring the taste, as I didn't realize the nausea was hunger. He returns, texting on his phone while walking into the bathroom.

"I hope you don't mind, but I threw away your underwear."

I choke on my soup. The resulting coughing has him darting into the room with a glove on and the pain meds in his hand, which will be needed with the pain ricocheting off my ribs.

I hadn't paid much attention to my nether regions as the oversized t-shirt still fit over my hips when sitting up. The fact that he mentions them now makes me worried. Did I read Gabe all wrong? Could he have taken advantage of me in my most vulnerable state? Did I somehow jump from the frying pan into the fire?

I collapse into the pillow, gazing at the ceiling to let the pain and aches settle when he comes into my line of vision.

"Whoa, easy now. Are you okay? What happened?"

"Um, why do you have my underwear?"

"You don't remember last night, do you?" A beautiful, brilliant smile slowly spread across his face, bringing my trepidation down a tad. "You handed them to me last night, wanting me to keep your adoption ring safe."

"Where is it?"

A surge of panic flows through me as I sit up, grimacing against the pain and looking around for it.

"It's my good luck charm."

"With love and courage, you shine." He swipes it off the nightstand, reaching for my hand to slide it on my ring finger as if in a marriage ceremony. "It's a lovely sentiment and very fitting."

His gloved finger toys with it before releasing my hand. I gaze at it on my finger, not having worn it in so long. It looks both new and foreign.

"Yeah."

A flashback to the day in the courtroom when it became official, and my parents gave it to me before we all piled out of the courthouse and celebrated at Dani and Uncle Tomlin's cabin.

"If you don't remember that, then I assume you don't remember . . ."

Humor laces his words as I drag the mushy toast from the soup and nibble at it. He's busy preparing my arm for another shot. The smell of the antiseptic temporarily turns my toast unappealing.

"Questioning my sexuality?"

The heat of embarrassment rises in my face as I comb through my memories, the least accessible being after I got here.

I carefully shake my head, watching him draw in the magic liquid that both took away my pain and, apparently, the memories with them.

"I apologize, Gabe, it's not my place to . . .um . . . how did that even come up."

"Slight poke. Breathe in if you can." The poke is nothing compared to everything else in my body that ache. "I had you covering yourself."

"With my hands. I think I remember that part."

I resume eating, knowing this stuff must be pretty fast-acting if I don't remember blurting out that I know he's gay.

"Well, when I returned with that shirt, you were leaning against the counter, topless, telling me your parents were gay, so you didn't care if I saw your 'girl boobies.'"

I chuckle when he does as he shares my ridiculousness, which must have taken place after I was flying on the good stuff.

"I'm fairly certain I saw that exact term in my medical journals. But it's been curious to me all night. Why would you think that? I told you I wanted a family, but that still doesn't add up."

I don't remember that last night, but I remember the night we met. Guzzling down more water, he dispenses with the needle and medicine before examining my swollen eye and face.

"Look at you, Gabe. You're stunning. Only models and gay guys look like you. And then your fashion, the luxury brands. Heck, you were stitching my body suit, fixing my project for me. How could I not think that?"

"Your logic is flawed." His response is tinged with amusement, a hint of chiding in his tone. "Not all guys who care about fashion or can handle a needle and thread are gay. Not all of us who might fit your stereotype are off the market for women. You, of all people, should know that."

He places the glass down carefully, turning back to me with a smile that softens the admonishment.

"I guess we can add 'jumping to conclusions' to the list of your many talents."

There's a warmth in his gaze that speaks of a deep-seated kindness, and I can't help but feel a little sheepish under his scrutiny.

"Sorry."

The flush of embarrassment heats my cheeks.

"Apology accepted. But maybe next time, ask before you

assign me a life story, hmm?" His gentle ribbing is short-lived when he pulls out his phone again. "Now tell me everything I am picking up. I'll also need Travis's number to coordinate my coming."

Worry for Anna surges back, overshadowing the moment of levity.

"Anna, first and foremost. Please, make sure she's okay."

I lick my bottom lip, the scab rough against my tongue as I hold back my tears. The thought of her being with him sickens me to the point that I push away the tray of uneaten food.

"And my school laptop has all my work and my designs. It's vital," I continue, trying to keep my thoughts organized despite the fog of medication and pain.

"My phone, too. Travis didn't want me to bring it so I could focus on the performance. If he is willing to pack any of my clothes or anything he gives you, I guess."

The words taste bitter, a reminder of the desperation that led me here. The idea of Gabe negotiating with Travis, of entering that space that once felt like a shared sanctuary now tainted by violence, worries me, even if he is a three-time black belt. His fingers fly across the surface of his phone, including when I relay Travis's phone number to him. His expression is determination, the earlier warmth replaced by the gravity of the task ahead.

"I'll make sure to get everything. Now don't worry about Anna or your things. Focus on getting some rest."

His frown is brief but telling as he gathers the tray from the bed, pausing momentarily at its foot.

"I don't have any other way for you to get ahold of me, so please try not to move around too much. I worry that you're a fall risk and without being in the hospital with bed alarms. Try not to get up if you can. Just relax and rest, if possible."

His request for me to remain still, as simple as it may seem, underscores the gravity of my injuries and the care he's providing.

"Honestly, I can already feel this stuff working again. Why does it make me so sleepy, though?"

I yawn, my eyes growing heavier, just as they did last night. I groan, moving down the bed to position myself for sleep.

"Because you're a lightweight. That's a good thing."

"Mmhmm."

I adjust the bedding, piling it over my shoulders to block out the bright light as I turn away from the window and give my poor back a break from lying on it. The sound of his shoes walking away has me closing my eyes, relishing the pain-free floating my body is experiencing.

Several quiet minutes pass, with my steady breathing and the low throbbing of my pulse in my ear smashed to my pillow until Gabe's voice rises from the silence. His deep baritone sounds authoritative, but his words are muffled until I hear a distinct "not your concern anymore."

Who is he talking to so harshly?

The thought is fleeting as the medicine tugs me deeper toward sleep, not caring and succumbing.

23

I'm awoken by the sensation of wet kisses streaking across my face and tiny paws dancing across my chest. Anna is a whirlwind of excitement, her tail a furious blur, her tiny body wiggling, barely containing her excitement. The pain that has been resident in my bones is momentarily forgotten, eclipsed by the pure love of my furry girl back with me.

"Easy, Anna."

His voice is a gentle rumble, but his eyes are bright with amusement. Anna doesn't seem to understand, her excitement undimmed. Gabe stands at the side of the bed, a cautious observer, intervening when her enthusiasm becomes too much when she accidentally head-butts my injured eye. He picks her up, his large hand dwarfing her already small body, and holds her against his chest. She's slathering him in kisses, something she never did with Travis as he didn't want to be entangled with her.

"I'm so glad she's alright. It was hard not thinking the worst," I admit again, echoing my initial fears I couldn't quite choke out.

"She's more than alright from the looks of it."

She's still going nuts in his arms, her front paws clawing at his chest as she rubs her face against his shirt, leaving a distinct wetness behind.

"I have to say, she has more energy than I imagined. My mum has corgis. I thought the energy level would be the same."

I prop myself up on one elbow, the painkillers still working wonderfully as I feel very little from all my injuries. Anna yaps at my movement, wanting to be back with me, and he warns her to be good before setting her back on the bed. She barrels toward me, taking the opportunity to climb closer, her tiny paws finding a precarious perch on my stomach.

"Did you see him? Travis, I mean," I ask, the question hanging in the air, heavy with unspoken fears.

The dark and scary chaos of the night compared to the bright and peaceful day hidden in his place brings me an unexpected sense of security. With getting Anna back and in Gabe's care, he seems less daunting, as if the power dynamic has shifted in my favor. Gabe's gaze flickers, a shadow passing over his features.

"Yeah, I saw him."

There's a note of something I can't quite place. Warning? Reluctance or rag?

"He gave me the necessary things without much fuss."

There's so much more to the interaction that he's not telling me. A sudden aloofness that could be protective if I know Gabe and his caring disposition.

"And?" I prod, needing to know more while a bit of dread swims in my stomach.

Gabe sighs, moving to sit at the edge of the bed. Sensing the shift in mood, Anna settles down, her tiny body a warm presence against mine.

"He wasn't happy, but he didn't try anything if that's what you're wondering about. He asked about you, asking how you were doing and if you were with me. I made it clear in no uncertain terms that your whereabouts were no longer his concern."

I widen my good eye, surprised at the strong vein of forwardness in his tone, matching the stiff rigidness in his spine.

"I bet he didn't like being told that," I murmur, petting Anna's soft fur.

Gabe shakes his head, a grim line forming at his mouth.

"No, he didn't. But he doesn't have a choice in the matter. You're safe here. You and Anna are welcome to stay as long as you need to. That's what matters."

I nod, his offer generous but filled with apprehension for imposing. Travis's obsession has always been a tightly wound spring, ready to snap. Gabe standing up to him and drawing boundaries for him is probably new to Travis. As Lily told me all those weeks ago, before all this started, no one stood up to him. I did, and now Gabe did. I'm sure he hates me for it.

"There's another thing." Gabe's voice is hesitant, unsure how I'll take this news. "He said he'd change. He wants to talk to you, explain things, and work this out."

A bitter laugh escapes me.

"Explain? What's there to explain?"

The very thought of Travis trying to justify his actions makes my blood boil. A part of me aches, a remnant of what we had or what I thought we had—grief for all the now broken promises. I watched my mom believe the lies of men for too many years, and the same with Rick. I won't fall into that trap myself.

"How do you work this out?"

I wave a hand over the damage administered by Travis until Gabe's hand finds mine, his touch grounding as tears well once again.

"I know, love. You don't have to see him or talk to him if you don't want to. As someone who cares about you, I'd advise you to focus on your recovery. Just know I'm here, whatever you decide."

He squeezes my hand, Anna's light snores filling the quiet space between us as those dark eyes stare into mine. Gabe watches us, a softness in his expression.

"She loves you. Wouldn't settle when we first got home until she was with you."

The thought warms me. Our unconditional love is the only anchor left in my everchanging world here.

"I love her too."

The tears that had been threatening to fall finally break free as my mind flashes back to the fear of losing her to his violence after all we've been through. Without hesitation, Gabe leans in, gently wiping away the tears with the pad of his thumb. His actions are tender and caring, as is his usual demeanor.

"You're stronger than you know, Isla. And you're not alone. You've got your little dog, and you've got me."

His words are comforting, but his intention seems to mean more, leaving the door open for what may lie ahead.

"Thank you, Gabe," I whisper, my voice steady despite the emotions swirling within me. "For taking care of me, getting her, and just for everything."

He offers me a smile, one that's both encouraging and sad. "Always. We'll get through this."

The promise of "we'll get through this" feels like a lifeline, a possibility of a future where the pain of the past doesn't dictate the course of my life as it mostly has. Gabe's gentle understanding reminds me of Dad's quiet strength. The irony of my parents appearing in my life in the middle of a crisis and Gabe's doing so as well is not lost on me. Maybe it's meant to mean something.

"By the way, he said you didn't keep much there, clothing-wise."

A bewildered look passes through his face as he stands to

walk out of the room and return with my full backpack and a large Bergdorf shopping bag with my belongings. The lack of clothing isn't surprising, with Travis's rules about undergarments and other ways he controlled wardrobe choices. Not that I'd ever tell that to Gabe. I'm already embarrassed that I allowed it to happen at all.

"That's fine. When you take me home later today, I'll be set."

Gabe stops at the end of the bed. The backpack clenches in one hand, straining his forearm muscles under the weight, while the shopping bag dangles in the other.

"I strongly advise against that. Not that I'm trying to tell you what to do, but unless you allow me to take you to the hospital—"

"Which would trigger a police report, pictures, and more. Gabe, I'm not sure that's a road I want to go down. I have my reasons."

Anna shifts in her sleep, a tiny whimper escaping her. Automatically, my other hand goes to soothe her.

"I get it, Isla. I'm not trying to infringe, but it's very difficult for me to see what he's done to you and you not seeking justice on your behalf. That's all."

His admission makes sense. That's why I'm hesitant to call my parents and explain what happened.

"In actuality, I'd love to beat him to a bloody pulp, but out of respect for you, I won't, so you don't have to worry about that."

I open my mouth at his confession, then close it when realizing I feel the same way.

"I think it's best that you stay here a little longer so I can observe you—medically speaking, of course."

The shopping bag crinkles when he lowers it to the bed, the backpack hitting with a deeper thud due to its weight.

"I appreciate the offer, but I can't hide out here forever."

I didn't mean for my statement to come out as a question. Yet it hangs between us, loaded with the unspoken acknowledgment of our growing closeness and the complicated emotions it brings. His gaze never leaves mine when he walks closer.

"You can stay here as long as you need. And when you're ready to return to your place, I'll be there with you. Every step of the way."

The promise, so earnestly given, fills me with warmth. I am slightly overwhelmed by the support and care Gabe has shown me.

"Thank you."

"But." His head tilts, a determined edge creeping into his voice. "If we're not going the hospital route, then we need to ensure you're taking care of yourself properly. I'll help you with that. Let's start with getting you cleaned up and dressed. Then, a proper meal while we talk about the next steps."

His words are assuring, not the possessive commands of Travis, but a supportive action plan to help me move forward. Truth be told, with my body and mind so bruised and battered, I want help so I don't fall into the trap of my past, sucking me back to the darkness of wrong decisions.

"A shower would feel good."

I smile, then gaze down at Anna without a care in the world as we move to a new location. To be a dog without the weight of the world bearing down on her. Her sleep is so innocent and unbothered, unaware of today's threats to her safety as she remains curled in my lap.

"If only life were as easy as this."

I look up at Gabe, whose eyes never seem to leave us.

"Who said it can't be?"

"Why are you so good at everything?" I groan, pushing away my empty plate after scarfing down an obscene volume of food. More than I've eaten at one time in weeks. "I'm going to burst if I move."

His chuckle sounds through the open concept room as I'm perched on the couch, showered in fresh clothes bundled under blankets and pillows behind my back. My pain is still at bay with a lighter dose, and my injured eye is open after an ice treatment. Loyal Anna is buried by my feet, basking in the luxury of being allowed on the couch, unlike at the penthouse. The pots and pans he insisted on washing by hand clink against the sink when our gaze meets.

"I appreciate the compliment, but there are a few things I'm brilliantly lousy at."

"Like what?" I ask, curiosity peeking through my lethargy.

It's hard to imagine Gabe being bad at anything, given how effortlessly he manages everything from crisis situations to culinary exploits. And let's not forget his prowess as a blackbelt and a visionary seamstress.

"Well, for starters, I'm an absolute disaster at singing. Can't carry a tune to save my life."

I laugh, a genuine sound that feels foreign after the last twenty-four hours.

"I find that hard to believe."

"It's true," he insists with a grin. "And I'm also notoriously bad at video games. My hand-eye coordination apparently doesn't extend to virtual worlds."

The revelation brings a smile to my face, the brevity to our conversation.

"You? Bad at something? This I got to see."

"Maybe one day. But for now, I'm just glad to see you smiling." His expression is laden with an emotion I can't quite name before he continues, "Your phone is going nuts over here on the charger. Do you want it?"

A deep sigh rattles through me. The life I've been avoiding dealing with because I enjoyed hiding out with Gabe as he lavished attention on me is haunting me. Its ghosts are demanding my attention, and they threaten to bring more bad news that will ruin the smile he just commented that he likes seeing.

"Time to face the music, I guess."

He dries his hands on a dish towel before joining me on the couch and hands it to me. I glance at the notifications appearing on my locked phone screen and hesitate. The pain meds blocked my thoughts from penetrating anything shallower than the here and now, Gabe effortlessly handling everything for me as I slept. Even confronting Travis to pick up Anna and my electronics, but this is something I must handle myself, and anxiety cloaks me in a dreaded coldness.

"I don't want to deal with this, but I know I must," I voice my worries, trying to channel that strong version of Isla that Gabe claims me to be.

"What can I do to help?"

I am not surprised by his offer. It's all he's been doing since I met him, helping me at the bookstore, at my school, and last night, which has continued into today. My fingers hover over the phone, not knowing exactly how he can help.

"I don't know. Just be here. Is that too silly to ask?"

"Not silly at all."

Understanding flashes in his eyes. He doesn't press further, doesn't ask for details, or try to solve my problems for me. He settles in more comfortably, stretching his legs onto the table and draping his arm over the couch's back, his fingers lightly grazing the edge of my blanket.

I unlock my phone, the screen lighting up with a barrage of missed calls and messages. I start to sift through the messages, mentally preparing myself for the conversations I'll need to have, the apologies I might need to make, and the decisions awaiting me.

"I'm going to take the easiest first," I say mostly to myself as I try to put some semblance of order to my dread.

"Good idea."

Anna decides she's done snuggling with me and heads to Gabe. She walks over to his stomach as if staking her claim and lies back down.

"Anna!" I reach for her, but he gestures for me to stop, gently stroking her fur and coaxing her to stay put. "She's obviously loving you."

"What's not to love."

I laugh, delaying the inevitable, and turn back to my phone, hitting a call from Papa asking when the play starts so they can book their flights and hotel arrangements. Gabe's eyebrows rise in surprise. Otherwise, he remains silent, and I owe him an explanation.

"I didn't want them there opening night, in case I didn't do good."

"Yet, you were phenomenal. Really moving performance that I'd still like to discuss sometime."

His compliment is a double-edged sword. On the one hand, I appreciate his saying so and know I did everything I could to burn the house down. On the other, I would have to disclose where all that pain, hurt, and disappointment came from to play the role of Marcella, something I do not want to discuss right now.

"Okay." My tone is noncommittal, delivered with a frosty coolness, and his eyebrows remain high in his hairline. "I don't mean I won't. It's just a lot to unpack."

"Whenever you are ready."

Turning my attention back to the task at hand, Dani's message is brief. Call her, and then she's yelling at someone in the background at her shop when she forgets to hang up.

"That's my aunt. She's the one . . . she's something else. My uncle, Tomlin Takahashi, is a world-renowned judo champion, having gone to four Olympics. I should hook you two up, and then you can spar with him."

"That's really impressive," he admits, his interest piqued despite the humility in his voice. "I'd love to meet him, though I doubt I'd stand much of a chance. My training's in karate, not judo."

"He's incredible. I'm sure you guys could work something out between the two sports. He even taught me some self-defense."

A bitter snort escapes me as I recall the events of last night, such as how Travis managed to land several punches before any of the techniques my uncle taught me came to mind. I berate myself internally. I should've responded after the first punch, but shock and pain overwhelmed me.

There is a missed call from Uncle Alex and several from Lily when a text comes in from her.

Gabe's hot

He single?

I look from my phone to Gabe stroking Anna, her eyes closed in contentment.

"Lily texted that you're hot and wants to know if you're single. Apparently, she got your sexual orientation right." I chuckle, but the joke falls flat when he merely smiles.

"We see what we want to see." I open my mouth to object when he continues, "Any other messages from her?"

"Yes, a lot."

I begin to recite them in the order they came in.

Want to grab lunch tmrw?

You're mad. I get it

I want to fix it

BTW you did terrific last night

I mean it

Why is Travis calling me?

Are you okay?

Call me

I'm freaking out

You're not performing tonight?

What the hell is going on

CALL ME!!!

Isla

PLEASE

You're sick?

Who gets food poisoning the night after the performance?

Seriously?!?!

With each message, his demeanor remains calm, unwilling to sway me in either direction as I read the flood of texts, each one revealing Lily's growing worry and desperation to understand the situation.

After I finish, Gabe murmurs, "Sounds like she's really worried about you."

His gentle acknowledgment of her concern for me without overwhelming me with advice or suggestions is helpful. He understands the chasm that still exists between us.

"Is she? Or is she being nosy? If I were to call and tell her the truth, would she understand like you? Because honestly, I think she'd just say I told you so?"

He looks perplexed.

"I should hope a female friend wouldn't say such a thing as the threat of domestic violence is all too common for women all over the world."

His reaction speaks to the steady support he's been since we first met, always listening without judgment. I jump when the phone starts ringing in my hand as if I have a guilty conscience about talking about her. I toss the phone on the blanket to avoid answering when her name marques across the screen.

"I don't want to talk to her." I shake my head a little too emphatically, making me suddenly dizzy. "I wouldn't know what to say."

Panic grips my body, even in my words, as I stare at Gabe's sympathetic expression. His long fingers reach for my phone.

"May I?" He questions, answering it, saving me once again from the reality of my life crashing down on me, and I nod. "Lily, hello. This is Gabriel."

He doesn't put it on speaker, and in a way, I'm glad. I don't want to hear her voice, the accusation, or anything else. Focusing on his smooth delivery and drawn-out accent in this one-sided conversation calms me. He listens to her excited tone blaring through the receiver and turns the volume down while keeping it at his ear.

"It's all very concerning. I can assure you that she'll be back to tip, top shape before too long."

Hearing his reply, he's continuing with Travis's food poisoning narrative. If our stories align, it will buy me some time until I can work this all out.

"No, dear, she's quite ill and unable to take calls."

Gabe's handling of the call with Lily is a masterclass in calm and collected diplomacy. His long fingers cradle the phone, his voice soothing and composed as he navigates the conversation.

I can't hear Lily's responses, but I imagine them as demanding and frantic as her text messages.

"It's unfortunate, really. She's in good hands," Gabe continues, his assurance sounding so genuine that, for a moment, I almost believe the fabricated story myself. "We're doing everything we can to ensure she recovers swiftly. When she's on the mend, I'll have her reach out. Thanks for calling, my dear."

I expect the call to end, and when it doesn't, his stony gaze focuses on me, his lower jaw tightening. His side of the conversation stays silent far too long, and my curiosity rises.

"That's very much appreciated, but I can assure you I'm very much smitten by another."

My eyebrows raise in surprise. She's hitting on him while calling about me. Well, damn, that's brave.

The call stretches on, and Gabe's expression shifts as he navigates Lily's unexpected advances. His responses are polite yet firm, but he still must decline her far too many times to be respectful of the boundary he's setting. The room is thick with awkward tension, at least on my part, witnessing this bizarre twist in what was supposed to be a concerned inquiry about my health. Finally, Gabe ends the call, placing the phone down carefully, almost deliberately slowly.

"Well, that was interesting. She's clearly concerned about the both of us, come to think of it."

"Lily never does anything by halves," I reply, trying to shake off the residual shock. "What exactly did she say? I heard you turn her down many times, so why did it go on for so long?"

"Let's just say your friend has quite a vulgar mouth and a petulance for fetishism."

I gasp in renewed shock. "You can deduct all that for that brief call?"

The ghost of a smirk plays at the corners of his mouth as his annoyance fades.

"She's very . . . *descriptive.*"

Torn between feeling insulted for him due to her blatant vulgarity and irritated by her bold flirtation, I find myself at a loss for how to react.

"I'm sorry. I wouldn't have had you take it if I had known, but thank you."

Gabe shrugs, his demeanor relaxed despite the odd turn of events.

"Part of the service," he jokes, then his expression softens, becoming more serious. "Even if it's just to ward off abusive lovers and overly forward friends."

Now, he's the one with the failed joke that leaves us both frowning as he resumes petting Anna. The silence stretches on between us. My mind wanders to the theater and what Travis will do now. My understudy, the one I replaced when I first arrived at the callback that day, is probably overjoyed. Who wouldn't be?

It's a killer part. One, I knew I would burn down to spite Travis, but now I'm really burning it down by leaving. A part of me wonders how he's acting. To be a fly on the wall as he loses his temper, he screams down at his assistant and throws his usual tantrum.

How could I not have known it would all be directed at me? It was only a matter of time. I was too smitten to use Gabe's word. Too enthralled by the glamorous life Travis lives, the wealth, the fame, the gowns, the exclusive restaurants, and the famous friends —all things I still want, but not at the cost of being beaten for it.

I tried to cheat the system and fast-track the result without putting in the hard work and paying my dues, and I got burned for it. I'll still get there but of my own accord this time.

Isla Frank will give Isla Frank that life.

"Are you alright?"

"Tell me more about you. Who are the people in those pictures in the guest bedroom?"

Getting bored with all the attention he's lavishing on her, Anna suddenly moves away, wanting off the couch for some reason.

"Should I put her down?"

I nod, and he sits up, brushing the imaginary shedding from his shirt, not understanding that they don't shed.

"You're in my bedroom, love."

I rise up, surprised that I've displaced him when I thought I was in the guest like he initially said.

"Gabe! Why? I would have easily taken—"

"My mattress is softer, and it was just easier with the bathroom in closer proximity."

He cuts me off with a reassuring smile, appearing completely unbothered.

"It's no trouble at all. You needed the rest and comfort more than I did. Besides," he adds, a playful glint in his eyes. "I've slept on that couch before. It's not as bad as it looks."

I'm momentarily lost for words, touched by his thoughtfulness and the casual sacrifice of his comfort for mine—one of many.

"Gabe!"

"I'm joshing with you. After staying with you for a few hours working last night, I slept in the guest room. I need to advise you that I must go back to work tomorrow. Surgeries I cannot move, and such. I'll leave a key, order whatever food you want, and the building will ring you when it arrives. That reminds me, I need to have you added."

He snaps his fingers and jumps to his feet to look for his phone. When he returns, his thumbs are flying across the screen.

"I can take Anna out in the morning before my morning run, but beyond that, do you think you can manage, slowly, of course?"

The lengths he's going to to take care of me and now Anna is remarkable and endearing him to me more and more.

"Thank you, Gabe. That's very considerate of you."

He plops back down, the movement bouncing down the couch into where I'm sitting.

"Not at all," he quips, setting his phone on the coffee table before getting comfortable again. "To answer your earlier question. I'm from a big family, all Oxford alums except for one sister who went to Cambridge. But don't hold it against her. She couldn't get into Oxford."

He chuckles at his inside joke, not realizing most people would kill to go to either school. As his storytelling takes on an animated, almost reverent tone while explaining his utterly boring childhood, I snuggle into the couch, content to get lost in his world as an escape from my own.

At one point, he pauses after saying I'm going to love a particular family member of his when I go there, the expectancy hanging between us. The way he looks at me then, full of hope and an unspoken invitation, shifts the dynamic away from friendship and adds a layer of intimacy to the conversation I hadn't anticipated.

I wait for him to recover, to back out, and to shy away from his offer, but he doesn't. He continues his story, dropping hints of my coming, and I'm left spiraling. Am I the one he's smitten with, or was that an excuse to deflect Lily?

24

The apartment is quiet. The only sound coming from the city is Anna snoring on the couch in the pile of blankets left from last night. Leftover from when I emailed all the teachers about being out with food poisoning, perpetuating Travis's lie to my benefit. Gabe worked in the chair adjacent to me after he insisted we order groceries for the week since he's rarely home and doesn't stock his kitchen.

A faint lingering of dark roast coffee is the only hint of him being up, aside from the note he left on the counter with various numbers to the building staff, his office's emergency line, and the deli across the street that apparently has "the best Philly cheesesteaks in town."

As I circle the kitchen island, my search for coffee is momentarily paused by seeing a cloth placemat against the wall. Atop it are two white china bowls—one filled with water and the other with dog food for Anna. It's a small gesture, another sweet one in a dozen since being around him.

I want to do something nice for him, as a thank you or to balance the scales slightly, even though I could never fully repay him for all he's done and is still doing for me. Dad used to cook fabulous dinners all the time. A creative outlet opposite of the number crunching all day, and I racked up a lot of favorite ones. After starting my coffee brewing, I lean against the counter to look up the recipes on my notes app when Travis's call comes through.

My hand starts shaking, dropping the phone and watching it ring while I hold my breath as if he can somehow see me. The vibrating phone skitters across the countertop, its insistent ringtone echoing into the pit of my stomach. Gabe told me that Travis wants to work this out. I should have expected this. With the immediate certainty I had yesterday that I never need to see him again, now that I have Anna, I didn't even consider him calling me. I don't ever want to deal with him again. Not if I can help it. The thought of facing Travis, even just hearing his voice, churns my stomach.

I let the call go to voicemail. When it rings again, his name scrolling a second time, I silence it, then put my phone on Do Not Disturb. My fingers ghost across my injured eye, getting better with the salve and cold compress Gabe insists on applying as I stare at my screen. The voicemail notification appears in the bottom right corner, and I can't bring myself to listen to it.

His incoming call has disturbed the peace of this quiet morning without even knowing it. He haunts me even when he doesn't know where I am. With my coffee done brewing, I add creamer from the fridge and sugar, mixing it before moving to the island to sit and stare at my phone.

My stomach is still tight, and my heart is calming as all calls and texts bypass me. I sip my drink, relishing Gabe's flavor choices, which rival Starbucks, and contemplate what to do. To press charges for assault against Travis means embarking on a legal journey fraught with complications compounded by his wealth and connections all over this city. Not to mention the emotional toll, as the process is not just about making a phone call to the police. It's a lengthy and expensive process that can stretch over months if not years.

Recounting the trauma to the police, my attorney, and the court, then being subject to the trial, the defense painting me as a harlot and not the victim, turning the tables where every action and decision of mine are scrutinized, judging me for things I did or did not do.

Should the case proceed, the daunting reality of Travis's wealth and influence looms large, opposite of the public defender Rick had. Travis's resources allow him access to top legal representation, skilled at navigating the penal code and using my failure to go to the hospital immediately against me.

His ties to influential figures, some of whom I recognized from television there last night, and smoking with him on the terrace could potentially sway opinions and outcomes in subtle ways. The fear that these connections might lead to the case being dismissed outright and countersuing me for slander, which he would probably do.

My fingertips gently trace the curve of my eyebrow, a reminder of the tenderness that lingers beneath the surface. As I mull over my options, it becomes clear that there's only one person with whom I can truly dissect this dilemma. I pick up my phone, ignoring the looming red voicemail bubble, and scroll my favorites to find his number.

As it rings, I sip my coffee, savoring the taste when he answers.

"Chief."

The gruff tone in his voice immediately tells me he's on duty, causing a moment of hesitation. My eyes dart to the stove clock, a reminder of the time difference back home, and a wave of regret washes over me for not considering the hour before calling.

"Hey, Uncle Alex."

The simple act of speaking his name brings a flood of

emotions to the surface, tears welling up as I brace for the conversation ahead.

"Hey there, is this Isla Frank? Or do I have the wrong number?"

His tone immediately shifts, affection ringing his words as he jokes.

"Very funny, but it's not been that long." The truth is it has, and I'm immediately swamped with guilt. "Actually, I'm the one who called you."

As his police radio crackles in the background, a lifeline to the chaos of his daily life, it contrasts the quiet apartment. The sound brings back memories of being in the back of squad cars far too many times over my eighteen years. It was a regular occurrence at the time when my mom and her boyfriends would get into fights, and the police would get called.

"Yeah, returning my call. Molli showed me your pictures. Wow, I almost didn't recognize you. You look very grown up, kid."

A brief silence on the line, punctuated by the distant sounds of dispatch calls and radio chatter, heightens my anxiety. It's a sound that's all too familiar. Outside of my experience, it has also been the background noise to many of our conversations. It never ceases to remind me of the risks and responsibilities he shoulders every day, in addition to caring for Aunt Molli and sweet little Ansley.

"Pictures?"

Worry churns in my stomach.

"Yes, from your play. Molli found them online. You stood next to that guy, Travis, was it? On some red-carpet event for the opening. You looked stunning, Isla. Truly. It's just ... It took me a moment to realize that it was my niece. You've stepped into this whole new world, haven't you?"

His voice softens, perhaps sensing my sudden apprehension. The words, intended to be reassuring, only heightened my worry. I should be proud of my accomplishments and the thrill of the play, but the underlying fear of what I need to tell him and what happened after makes me grab my coffee and move to the couch. I need to cuddle with Anna, and I need her to soothe me as I reveal everything.

"Actually, that's why I'm calling. But first, you must promise not to tell my parents, Dani or Uncle Tomlin either."

He becomes silent, and only the background noise comes through.

"I don't like where this is headed, Isla."

His reaction makes my heart sink, complicating my already daunting task.

"I know. It's already hard to make this call, Uncle Alex. Please don't make this harder."

The plea hangs between us as I brace myself to enter a conversation that will change everything. I'll have to tell my parents. This is too big to keep from them, including lying about when the play started and why I didn't want them there.

"I can't make that promise to you," he finally says with a heavy sigh. "Are you in trouble?"

Sensing my distress, Anna nestles closer, her body a small comfort against my fear. I take a deep breath that feels like it's dredging up the silt from the bottom of my soul and begin.

"Yes," I start, my voice barely above a whisper. "It's about Travis—the guy from the play, the one you saw in the pictures with me. Things turned really bad after my performance. Travis and I were . . . involved in a relationship. It started out as everything I ever dreamed of."

I pause, the words catching in my throat as tears flow down my face, and his deep voice rumbles through the phone, taking a professional tone I heard when he testified at my trial.

"I think I know where this is going, but continue."

With my hand on my chest, I recount everything that happened, from the possessiveness between him and Gabe, leading to throwing me against the door in my dressing room, taking liberties with his play, and the jealousy at dinner leading to the assault in the back of the limousine. The words tumble out with a torrent of tears, to the point I'm sobbing on the phone. Uncle Alex's voice is full of concern, wishing he was with me, or at minimum, my friend, Gabe, was there to comfort me.

I explained that I wanted to do this privately, as Gabe doesn't know my past. No one does beyond my uncle and my parents, as that was all sealed in my courtroom records. Not even Dani or Uncle Tomlin knows the full extent, even though the family attorney was his friend.

"I have a buddy from the Academy, a captain with NYPD, that I can call—"

"No . . . I can't. It's . . . It's . . . no."

My sobs interrupt my words until I blurt out all my fears to him. Another trial, dissenting the nature of my relationship with him, sharing the intimate details, details no one beyond him and I should know, on full display to paint him as a controlling monster. My God—my parents would have to hear that, the same as they listened to the horrific details recounted from Rick's trial. I can't go through that again. I can't put them through it again.

Not to mention dragging my large extended family through another trial. Dani nearly broke her hands at the punching bag every night after the court let out—something I overheard Uncle Tomlin telling Papa. And the prosecution would be here, in New York, stretching on for weeks. The exuberant cost and expense of housing them here and then the loss of business to my parent's companies, Dani's garages, and Uncle Tomlin's crucial work with the youth, who rely on him for a reprieve from their troubled environments.

He doesn't interrupt other than a low hum, acknowledging he's listening.

"And he's loaded. Like Uncle Tomlin, he has unbelievable connections in the city. You may know a captain, Uncle Alex, but he's connected to the Chief of Police for the entire NYPD. He was there, sharing cigars with him just the other night. He can afford the best of the best in defense firms. How can I possibly stand a chance?"

His voice, when he finally speaks, is steady, infused with a calm that only facing down by criminals like his own police chief can bring.

"Isla, first, you're not alone in this. You've got me, your parents, and, whether you believe it or not, a whole family who will stand behind you, no matter what. This isn't about fighting alone or fighting fair. It's about fighting smart. We'll navigate this together, step by step."

He pauses, letting his words sink in before continuing.

"As for his connections and wealth, yes, that's intimidating. But remember, the law is about justice, not just who can pay for the better lawyer. I know it doesn't always work that way, but you have the truth on your side. That counts for a lot. And about the chief? That's a concern, sure, but it doesn't mean justice is out of reach. I have friends, too. Not just captains and lawyers but also people with influence across the board. We'll find a way to get you the help you need, the right kind of help."

There's a firm resolve in his voice, unwavering support mixed with the desire to act right now.

"And if it comes to it, we'll bring in external resources. Some organizations and advocates specialize in this—people who won't be swayed by local politics or personal connections. We'll make sure your voice is heard, Isla, and that you're protected throughout this process the same way we did last time."

He lets out a sigh, a mix of determination and concern.

"Don't let his influence scare you into silence. You have a voice, you have rights, and you have people who love you and are ready to fight for you. Let's think this through, get all the advice we can, and make a plan. Together. You're not in this alone, Isla. Never were, never will be."

I stare out the window, the fight rallying in him at my expense, demanding to seek justice. A justice I'm too overwhelmed to fight again.

"I'm not sure I can go through with this again."

My voice trembles as the words escape, and I wrap my arms around myself. Anna is barely budging.

"What if I decide to move forward with it, and it just gets dismissed? Or thrown out?"

I pause, the memory surfacing like a dark wave. I can see the squad car pulling up to the front of the house, his grimy face sneering through the backseat window as I crushed out the cigarette. The smoke still lingers in the air above my head at my last exhalation. He looked victorious when they popped open his door, without handcuffs, and walked him to the door. The cops explained that the charges were dismissed, and they were bringing him home.

"Like what happened with my mom's boyfriend, Dale, when I was fourteen. He was allowed to return home. He's the reason I ran away," I whisper, more to myself than to him.

I tremble in the safety of Gabe's apartment as if I'm still sitting on that front stoop, watching my rapist walk back into my house. The desperation and fear drove me to leave everything behind in hopes of finding a real family and a better life.

"Travis isn't like those nobodies my mom used to date. He's got fame—like you saw in those pictures, and you're miles away, in a whole different state. This whole thing would turn into a media frenzy. My life would become an endless nightmare, not just for the duration of the trial but for months, even years after. My name would be forever linked to his, and that's the last thing I want."

My voice cracks, breaking under the weight of my fears and

the reality of the situation—a situation that I wish had never happened at all. I wish I had never met him or even gone to that audition in the first place.

"Everything from my past, all the stuff from when I was a minor, it's sealed. But this? This would stick with me forever. Imagine, if I ever do make it as a designer, someone Googles my name, and this scandal is the first thing that pops up. I can't have that, Uncle Alex. I just can't."

I move Anna off me, hugging my knees closer to my chest and trying to ward off the chill seeping into my bones. The thought of my future, my dreams, all tainted by this ordeal, is too much to bear. I feel so trapped by circumstances Travis forced upon me that now feel out of my control.

A deep sigh blows into the phone from him, upset by the entirety of the situation.

"Isla, I hear you loud and clear. The fears you're voicing are valid, and I won't lie to you—it's going to be an uphill battle if you decide to pursue this. And yes, you'll always be linked to him if that's how the media portrays it. Naturally, we'd have to hire security, which might make school impossible for now and until this thing is over with."

My head is shaking before he barely finishes.

"No, I refuse. My parents worked too hard, saved too much, and sacrificed too much for me to quit because I didn't see the signs of what my mom went through until it was happening to me."

He pauses as if choosing his words very carefully.

"Okay, let's consider the broader implications, especially concerning your friend, Gabe. He's a medical professional bound by the Hippocratic Oath, which fundamentally commits him to prioritize patient care and do no harm. The fact that he didn't immediately take you to a hospital after the assault raises serious questions. It's not just about the immediate physical care. It's about the documentation of injuries, potential collection of forensic evidence, and the psychological assessment that emergency care providers are trained to offer victims of assault."

His pivoting train of thought unlocks a new fear. I hadn't even considered the ramifications for Gabe. The harsh realization hits me like a tidal wave. Could my decision to stay silent and protect my future inadvertently harm Gabe, who was only trying to help me?

"In a legal context, if this situation were to go to trial, Gabe's decision would be scrutinized closely."

Uncle Alex's voice is steady, but the seriousness of his words makes my stomach churn.

"But it was my choice. I told him not to. He practically begged me to go, and I kept refusing," I defended, trying to keep the nausea from coming up.

"Doesn't matter. Defense attorneys will question why a medical professional, especially someone sworn to uphold patient health and safety at all costs, opted against seeking immediate medical assistance."

The thought of Gabe being dragged into this, his career and reputation at risk because of me, is too much to bear. At my silence, he continues.

"Professionally, Gabe could face inquiries from his medical board or employer. Medical professionals are often required to report certain types of injuries, including assault. Failing to do so, especially when he was directly involved in the care or decision-making process, could be seen as neglecting his professional duties."

I mute the phone, sobbing so hard that I start gagging at the stomach acid coming up. It's several long seconds before I return.

"But he only did what I wanted, Uncle Alex." I drag my arm across my face, cleaning the tears and snot from my nose. "He wasn't failing me. He was helping me, protecting me. It's all my fault, not his."

The guilt is crushing. My chest is so heavy I can barely breathe.

"I know he had good intentions, but the court wouldn't see it like that. The defense could use ethical division against him to get his testimony thrown out, especially if he took pictures but didn't collect anything else, such as skin scraps and finger-nail clipping, to collect DNA evidence."

My head falls against the back of the couch, the tears slipping out of my eyes and down my temples at the realization he did just that. Medical ethics are not just about the actions taken in a clinical setting but also about physicians' moral obligations towards individuals needing care, regardless of the setting. His failure to act according to the expected standards of his profession could tarnish his reputation among peers and patients, potentially impacting his career long-term.

"He's a pediatric cranial neurologist. The best in New York," I whisper with deep sorrow. He'd disgrace his family, all those generations of Oxford men in his pictures. "He's at the start of his career."

"It's a complex situation. I'm not bringing this up to sway your decision. But you must consider all facets, consider both the immediate and long-term implications of how you proceed."

"Okay."

My voice is small as I stare at the ceiling, on the verge of bawling my eyes out when we get off the phone.

"And Isla, you need to tell your parents. They are very understanding men. They won't love you any less because this happened to you."

The floodgates open when he says that last sentence. It was the same thing he said, standing outside the courtroom before I had to go in and testify about the sexual side of my situation with Rick.

"Okay," I repeat as Anna paws at the side of my body.

"I'll check in tomorrow to see what you decide. Otherwise, you can call me if you have any other questions or need to work through this more. I love you, kid. I only want the best for you, as we all do."

His words wrap around me like a cherished hug, even though his honest insights scared me more than the night I got beat, especially the damning repercussions to Gabe.

"Love you too," I say, ending the call.

The phone slips from my hand, landing softly beside me as I curl into the corner of the couch with Anna trying to lick my face, and heartbreaking sobs rack my body once more.

25

Anna's head lifts from her post on the couch as I do my homework on my laptop. Her ears twist when the lock on the door turns, opening up to reveal an exhausted Gage. He suddenly smiles as if forgetting I'm here, softening the tired lines on his face. He adjusts the crossbody bag that's snug against his torso, resting at his hip, before casually tossing his keys onto the table by the door.

Dressed in a white shirt with sleeves rolled up and the top few buttons undone to reveal a hint of skin, his attire—flat-front dress pants—seems more suited for a day on a yacht than the hospital scrubs I had pictured him in.

"Rough day?" I ask, setting my laptop on the coffee table and retrieving Anna as she dances around the couch, still too scared to jump off it by herself.

"You could say that." I walk over to him, holding Anna in my arms as she wriggles excitedly, her little yaps greeting him. "It smells amazing in here."

I can't help but smile, thankful that I chose to prepare one of my dad's favorite and simplest recipes. I found the ingredients for it at the little market shop downstairs at the base of the building.

"I made dinner for you. A small, and I mean super small, token of my appreciation for what you did and continue to do for me."

"You're kidding."

He unloads his bag, sitting on one of the barstools while emptying the pockets of his wallet, badge, and phone.

"Nope. I didn't know how late you'd be, so I made a meal that would keep."

I gently place Anna on the floor to step around him, feeling his gaze follow my every move as I unveil the mix of bell peppers, zucchini, and squash, then give him a glimpse of the lasagna still bubbling away in the oven.

"You have no idea how much this means to me." The tender look in his eyes and the disbelief in his voice at such a small action surprises me. "It's like . . . coming home to a 1950's wife."

The domestic scene he's imagining unfolds like a vignette to the past. Coming home to a cooked meal, his wife waiting with a martini, and their dog waiting for him. The notion is so simple, yet miles away from who I am and who I want to be, that I laugh, the lightness making more lines on his facelift.

"I'm far from that, but I'm sure I could whip up a 50s house-wife costume in my spare time."

He joins me at the stove, his hand grazing my back when I replace the lid on the veggies and cook them.

"Oh, and I have no idea how to make a martini, so there's that."

"I don't fancy olives."

His proximity, the warmth of his hand briefly on my back, ignites a different kind of warmth within me, one that's less about the food and more about the connection between us. It confuses me as I had proclaimed my love to Travis not two days ago. In hindsight and after everything that happened, I think it was more lust, caught up in the whirlwind of his luxurious life.

"Everything will be ready in about ten minutes or so."

I clasp my hands and move toward the cupboard to get the dishes and silverware to set the table.

"Did you want some wine to decompress?"

Here I am, playing house, so far away from being waited on hand and foot at the penthouse and from any reality I've envisioned. Yet, there's an undeniable appeal in the normalcy of this scene, a quiet comfort against the homesickness plaguing me all day after talking to Uncle Alex.

"No, but thank you. If I have ten minutes, I'll grab a quick shower, though." His gaze watches me as I continue pulling out various things I need to put this meal together. "This is . . . nice. More than nice, actually."

"I'll get the table ready then." I force a lightness into my voice that I don't fully feel and playfully push against his arm. "Now, out of my kitchen. Go."

His smile brightens as he acquiesces to my attempts to change our dynamic.

"Now I know where Anna gets it from. You're both small and feisty."

I laugh and wait for him to disappear into his bedroom, the door closing. The complexity of my emotions swirls in me, both wanting and needing to discuss with Gabe what I learned today. Gabe has no idea how much he risked for me, and I need him to know. Like Uncle Alex advised, he's a huge facet of this, and I can't make the final decision alone. He needs to be a part of it.

My hands move almost mechanically, setting plates and forks in their places, a mundane task that grounds me as I prepare the table with drinks and garlic bread. The timer dings, signaling that the lasagna is ready. I take it out of the oven, the heat flushing my cheeks as I set it on the stovetop.

When Gabe returns, the transformation is subtle yet notice-able. The weight of the day seems lifted from his shoulders, and his damp hair adds a boyish charm to his usual composed demeanor. It's a look that suits him, reinforcing the ease and comfort of this casual evening.

"Dinner's served," I announce with a flourish that elicits a chuckle from him.

"I still can't believe you did all this for me."

His accent hit thick for some reason, and I curtsied at him as if he were part of the royal family.

"It's nothing. But Bon appetite," I reply in a terrible British accent.

"What is that all this?"

His shoulders shrug as if trying to figure out who I am mimicking. His confusion suggests that he has no clue.

"The royal family, of course."

He laughs. "I wouldn't have guessed that from your performance."

"Yeah, me either."

I chuckle alongside him while cutting the lasagna into hearty squares, sinking a serving spoon in the middle. The vegetables are then transferred to their serving dish before I carry them to the table. He follows, hands covered in oven mitts, carrying the bubbling lasagna. After setting it down, he retrieves the drinks, and we sit to eat. He moans at how good it tastes, asking about the ingredients.

I share the story behind the recipe—how my dad and I prepared it for a family potluck for my extended family. I tell him numerous stories about Papa and Dani when he says they sound like trouble together. More about my Uncle Tomlin and his success at his last Olympics, earning the gold medal we all watched from home, except Dani, who practically stormed the podium after it was done.

I even delve into Lars's new girlfriend and how that came

about. I carefully dance around one family member. Through these stories, I dance around the branch of my family that I talked to today, saving that for after we eat.

He asks about my well-being, checking on how I'm feeling. He's curious if I ran into any problems getting downstairs for Anna to do her business outside, mentioning that she seemed reluctant to go with him until, after twenty minutes, she finally obliged.

As easy and natural as our conversation flows, I'm delaying what I know I must bring up.

"Gabe."

I reach for his hand, resting on the table, and cover it with my own. He tenses, his eyes moving silently from me to my hand and back, his jaw tightening.

"I need to tell you something."

"This doesn't sound good."

He slides his plate to the center of the table, leaning forward to gently encase my hand with his other one.

"It's not."

I pull my hand away, adjusting in my seat to face him directly as I deliver the bad news. Gabe's gaze locks onto mine, concern deepening his features. He's always been perceptive and able to read the slightest shift in my mood, and tonight is no different. His earlier laughter and easygoing demeanor give way to seriousness as he prepares for what I will say.

"I spoke with my uncle today. He's the chief of police in Cañon City, Colorado."

He nods, encouraging me to continue, but I can see the worry deepening in his eyes.

"I learned some things . . . about me, well, us. About what I'm facing, that could impact you. Far more than I thought."

His hands cup together as he leans closer to me.

"What exactly are we talking about here?"

His voice is calm, but there's an undercurrent of tension

that wasn't there before. I take a breath and recant my conversation with my uncle, excluding the parts about my past. I slow down when it gets to his oath and the trouble he could be in if I pursue a charge against Travis for what he did. When I finally finish, his dark brown eyes don't even flicker in response.

"You have a right to know everything."

Silence envelops us as I finish, thick and charged, and Gabe absorbs the magnitude of everything I share. Then, with a voice that resonates with a quiet strength, he breaks the stillness.

"I was aware of consequences from the start."

Stunned, I fall back in my chair, speechless at his admission. Gabe knew the dangers all along yet chose to stand by me. Instead of telling me the risks to his medical license, reputation, and career, he stood by and silently took care of me. It jolts me from my chair and amplifies the anxiety crawling under my skin to an almost unbearable level.

"Isla."

His chair scraps against the floor as I pace in front of the windows, my mind racing as I try to process the extent of the risks he took for me. When I turn to make another pass, I find him standing in my way. His shoulders sag, and wrinkles set across his forehead, this resignation speaking volumes.

"Why?" The question escapes me, a whisper lost in the space between us. "Why would you risk so much for me?"

"Because it's the right thing to do," he says simply as if the answer is the most natural thing in the world. He moves closer, his hand reaching for mine as if needing my reassurance before he proceeds. "And because I care about you deeply."

As his fingers gently wrap around mine, his thumb softly strokes my knuckles, and I hold my breath, wondering what exactly is happening.

"Isla, when that man called saying you had been in an accident, I was terrified. I dashed out of here with my bag, not knowing what to expect or what condition you'd be in." His inflection is rimmed with panic as he relays what he experienced. "I was worried when you left with Travis. A gut feeling that something wasn't right. I should have acted on my reservations, but I didn't. My failure contributed to that happening to you. I wasn't going to allow that to occur again."

I squeeze his hand, edging closer. "It's not your fault, Gabe. I'm a grown woman responsible for the choices I made. I'm so sorry I dragged you into all this."

He draws a deep breath, steeling himself as if preparing to share more.

"But when I saw you, I knew it was not an accident. I was blind with rage, wanting to kill the bloody bastard myself. And in that soft voice of yours, you asked for my help. How could I deny you, Isla? I knew the risks every second it took to drive here. And I . . ."

His eyes briefly drift upwards as if trying to calm himself, his voice heavy with emotion. Then, his gaze meets mine again, intense and searching, as if willing me to understand the depth of what he's about to say.

"And you?"

"And I felt an overwhelming sadness. How could anyone hate you? Inflict so much pain and destruction on someone as wonderful as you? Someone they claimed to care about. And that performance . . . it haunts me. I saw the real you, beyond the stage makeup, portraying Marcella. It was as if I was seeing you, exposed and defenseless."

The intensity of his confession leaves me breathless, his raw emotions mirroring the turmoil within me. I look down at the floor, feeling seen and vulnerable simultaneously. It's one thing to live through this, quite another to hear them through Gabe's perspective.

I release his hand and move closer, wrapping my arms around him in a hug. He stiffens for a moment, surprised at my sudden gesture. But how could I not embrace him? We both could use the comfort from the confession on both sides tumbling out. His arms wrap around me, tightening as I lay my cheek against his chest.

His heart beats steady against my ear, a reassuring rhythm amid the chaos I've caused in both our lives. I close my eyes, soaking in his strength. His chin rests lightly on the crown of my head, and his hands rest on my back.

I didn't need to hear his confession to know what I would do, the course I already set into motion. Going after Travis would be the right thing to do, touch the untouchable and hold him accountable for his actions. Prove to the world that even the rich and famous who commit crimes are brought to justice.

Uncle Alex described the three-ring circus to me in great detail, and the one I'd be dragging Gabe to with me would have another disgruntled clown in attendance—Travis. As much as I don't think I can handle another courtroom showdown, even with my family of support, an assault trial would be the last thing he would want. The last thing his play could handle, considering all the other gambles he made with inexperienced staff and that laundry list of issues he complained about way too often. It would burn his world down the same way I intentionally burned down the play with my rebellious performance.

"Gabe?"

I stir in his arm, pulling back slightly to meet his gaze. His hands cup my waist, the warmth seeping through my clothes and into my tender kidney, which hasn't bled into my urine like he wanted me to watch out for.

"Thank you for sharing that with me."

"Of course."

His finger brushes back a strand of my hair with a new tenderness, more romantic than clinical, adding another suspicion to what I've wondered all day. Are his feelings for me more than platonic? I'm terrified to ask for fear of losing him—something I couldn't bear if I assumed wrong.

"You shouldn't have to face something like this alone. It's why I'm here. Together, remember?"

"I remember."

Our gaze locks with our agreement, a passing moment of something happening before we slowly separate, and he clears his throat while I look away.

"Since you cooked, I'll clean up."

He breaks the tension with his offer, something I can't let him do.

"No, you worked all day. I laid around. Let me."

I move the same way he does, an awkward little dance to get around each other as the big feelings of whatever is happening between us remain unspoken. He chuckles, a nervous tinge to it, gesturing for me to lead the way. His footsteps barely touch the floor behind me as I walk to the table and collect my dishes and his. He grabs the hefty lasagna dish, which we barely put a dent in, and reassures me with a smile that it'll be finished off within the next couple of days, given how delicious it was.

While he's breaking down the remains into meal prep containers, I rinse and load the dishwasher. It is quick work with both of us doing it. With the awkwardness cleared away and the clock crawling toward bedtime, I pause to check my phone, having put it on do not disturb as calls kept coming in from Lily and Travis. None, thankfully, from my parents, meaning my uncle hadn't told them.

"Everything okay?"

Gabe stands behind the couch at the opposite end while I stand in front of the coffee table. My lips twist with indecision, not at his question but at whether I'm up for listening to them. Today has already been hard with recovering. The pain medicine was replaced with over-the-counter medicine this evening, which is not the same, and I'm feeling more of it. It was made harder with everything Uncle Alex shared, and I relayed it to Gabe.

"Do you ever just want to put your brain on a shelf and not think?"

I turn toward him, lowering my phone, and see a bewildered look.

"Of course not. You're literally a brain doctor."

"Surgeon," he murmurs, sounding awfully egotistical. I laugh when he shrugs, knowing it's true. "Let's get out of here. Go for a drive and give your brain a break."

He moves with determination to the pile of stuff he tossed on the table when he first came home, shoving it in various pockets. I remain rooted where I am, watching him.

"But you just got home. Don't you want to relax, or I don't know, go to sleep?"

I'm stunned that he has so much energy from working long hours and doing what he does all day. It can't be easy. He turns to face me, a soft smile on his lips, signaling he's ready.

"Relaxing can take many forms. Right now, I think a change of scenery might do us both some good. Trust me, I've got the perfect spot in mind."

The idea of stepping out into the cool evening, leaving behind the confines of the apartment and today's revelations, suddenly feels enticing. There's something about Gabe's energy, his unwavering determination to lift the heaviness from my shoulders, that's irresistible and hard to say no to.

"Okay," I say, a tentative smile breaking through my reservations. "Let me go get my things, and I'll be right back."

"Tell you what, I'll take Anna down to the bathroom for the night and be back up. Will that give you enough time?"

Once again, I'm surprised at how easy he's making this one for me. I couldn't even get Lily to take her down once in the months we lived together. Gabe has taken her down twice in one day. He's amazing.

"That would be great! Are you sure you don't mind?"

I shove my phone in the back pocket of my shorts, needing to change out of those, too, if we are going on at this late hour, which tends to get breezy.

"Not at all, I'll be back."

The way he says reminds me of the Terminator, and I chuckle, even though the accents are different. He stops advancing on an unsuspecting Anna, a question in his expression, and I wave my hand as if it's nothing.

"I'll be ready."

26

We drive aimlessly at first, the car's seat heat wrapping me in a cozy blanket. I'm wearing a pair of his sweatpants, the waistband rolled a few times for a better fit, and one of his Oxford sweatshirts. I had apologized for borrowing his clothes, but Gabe just smiled softly as he handed them to me, assuring me that it was no trouble. I need to get clothes from my apartment or go back to living at my apartment, for that matter.

It's one of many pieces I dread, knowing Lily wouldn't buy the food poisoning the moment she sees my face. It's one thing to have a secret that only three people know—Travis, Gabe, and myself—and now Uncle Alex. It's quite another when it's Lily who could whisper it to her cast friends, and the truth would be out, no longer a secret that will remain in the vault of us initial three.

"I'm sorry I can't find an open ice cream shop."

His soft voice cuts through my worries, so much for putting my brain on a shelf.

"It's fine. Really."

I touch his arm, resting closer to me on the console than

himself, making me curious why that is. Damn, brain. If I'm not commenting on every little thing related to this assault, I'm read into every action of his.

"Are you warm enough?"

His eyes flicker to mine, the instrumental panel bathing his face in a cool bluish-white hue.

"I'm good."

"And how's the brain? Is this shelf worthy enough, or must we pull out all the stops?"

I chuckle at the over-the-top manner in which he's trying to distract me from myself. It's considerate and sweet.

"I don't know what all the stops are on a weekday night when you have work in the morning, and I'm dressed in clothes I drown in?"

I glance past him at the East River running alongside the car. With a sudden burst of energy, he accelerates, weaving through the streets until we stop at an all-night convenience store.

"Stay right here. I'll be back. And I'm locking the doors."

He's gone in a flash after his door shuts and the locks click. My curious gaze follows him into the store, catching the top of his head through the glass as he searches the aisles for whatever he wants.

When he returns, he's handing me a bag filled with two ice cream cones, beef jerky, salty peanuts, and a couple of water bottles.

With an amused chuckle, I ask, "What is all this?"

"Brain-numbing food. And now to the place I wanted to show you."

His impromptu actions feel like an unexpected adventure I am up for after being cooped up inside, taking it easy. He doesn't say anything else, is unwilling to give away his surprise, and does not want to ruin it by answering a bunch of questions.

Cozy and content, I sit back and enjoy the ride, albeit my

attention drifts occasionally to his hand, draped so far over the console from where he handed me the bag that his finger grazes my sweatpants. Stop reading into it, I chide internally, forcing myself to pay attention to the scene outside the car, not the one I imagine inside.

With snacks in tow, Gabe drives us to Brooklyn Heights Promenade. The area is quieter at night, and the skyline across the river is a mesmerizing mix of illuminated buildings and shadowy office windows.

"Ah, interesting. Do you know I've never been here before?"

"Brilliant, let's go."

Gabe pulls into a small, nondescript lot near the water. As we step out, the cool night air is sharp compared to my warm seat heat, and I shiver. Always perceptive, he wraps his arm around my shoulder, drawing me into him to share his body heat and setting off many alarm bells supporting that this is more than friends.

"The transfer of body heat is one of the most efficient ways to raise a person's core temperature. The conductive properties of direct contact facilitate the rapid exchange of heat. It's a fundamental principle in treating hypothermia," Gabe suddenly explains, his tone decidedly clinical. He strips the concept of any romantic implications and kills all alarm bells.

"Good to know," I murmur to myself, looking at the dazzling skyline reflected in the choppy black water rippling out from the boats.

He guides us to a secluded bench overlooking the majestic view. The sky is surprisingly light, with low cloud cover capturing the bright skyline and turning it a distinct amber brown with patches of black peering through.

Gabe hands over my ice cream cone and patiently waits while I unwrap it before collecting the wrapper and disposing of it neatly back in the bag. He dips his toward mine when he dispenses of his wrapper.

"Cheers." His smile is perfect as he says it, pulling a big one from me. "Since you are underaged but can still have the same effect."

"Travis let me drink."

It's out before I can stop it. The words cause my smile to fade into the dark as I look away. I don't even know why I said that. It's not as if I want to drink anyway. Growing up with an addict mother is literally the definition of the Scared Straight program. Her problems started with alcohol, and when that wasn't enough, she needed harder stuff. I shake my head as if shaking away the memories that I don't need haunting me now. My brain has already been working overtime. I don't need to add the past as another complication.

Thankfully, Gabe has the grace to let the comment fall away as he eats his cone, having gotten a third of the way through it. The wind picks up, playful and brisk, causing strands of my hair to dance wildly around my face. A few rebellious strands stick to my ice cream cone, collecting a massive glob of it.

"Umm."

I look around for napkins we don't have. Holding the hair away from me, the wind shifts and shoves it across my nose, prompting laughter out of him.

"Screw it."

I drag my hair into my mouth and run it out the other side to clear the ice cream, making him laugh harder. Yet, when I look at him, with his short, coarse hair, he's unaffected.

"Damn wind."

I tuck it behind my ears in a futile attempt to tame it. The wind seems to have its own ideas, whipping it into a frenzy until he gathers the strands and tucks them into the back of my sweatshirt. It's scratchy against my soft back and probably looks ridiculous, but it's slightly working between my ears and the collar.

"It's the simple things, isn't it?" he says, still chuckling and finishing his ice cream. "Like fighting the wind on a chilly night by the river eating ice cream."

"I'm sure they're walking the runways of Milan with this hairstyle," I add, laughing at the absurdity of it. Gabe's eyes twinkle with amusement.

"You always know how to make the best of any situation, Isla."

The laughter between us ebbs into a comfortable silence, filled only by the sounds of the calling boats on the river and the hum of the city across the water. As I continue eating my ice cream, he opens my water bottle and sets it beside me before opening his to take a long drink.

"You know," Gabe starts, breaking the silence, his voice softer now. "I come here on the tough days."

I turn to him, intrigued. "Tough days?"

He nods, gazing out at the skyline.

"Yeah, like when a day at the hospital is particularly brutal, or if I lose a patient."

His admission hangs in the air, raw and vulnerable. I reach out, placing my hand over his.

"I can't even imagine how hard that must be."

He turns his hand under mine, clasping it gently.

"It's part of the job, but it doesn't get easier. Coming here to this spot, it's like hitting a reset button for me." He gestures to the expansive view. "Helps me find some peace, some perspective."

He squeezes my hand, a silent gesture of solidarity, before releasing it while I finish my cone and wash it down with water.

"I know these are tough days for you with tough decisions ahead of you. It's hard dealing with the aftermath." His voice tinges with empathy, understanding the battles ahead if I file charges against Travis. "I wanted to share this with you because, sometimes, you need to find a physical space where you can breathe, where you can let go and put your brain on a shelf."

His eyes meet mine, conveying the depth of sincerity. The vulnerability in his sharing his place and deliberately opening his personal coping space feels like a gift—a way of taking care of me, not just my physical health but my mental health too. I lean into him, my shoulder into his side, until he wraps an arm around me, and I scoot closer.

I don't bother with voicing another thank you. The words come too frequently with all he's done for me. I let my actions speak this time as we sit in silence, the tranquility of his special place washing over me. The peace he keeps doling out is a blessing. "A servant's heart," Aunt Molli once told me when we were working in the church basement, organizing the food pantry before starting on the costumes. Her unpredictable life and the resilience of her human spirit always strike me when I'm dealing with hardships.

"My uncle, the police chief, is married. They have a little girl named Ansley. He once told me all he ever wanted was a girl named Molli. He had loved and lost her. Ten years apart, until one day, she was brought into the station for prostitution and arrested when he was recovering from being shot in the line of duty. I don't know all the details about her. They're pretty tight-lipped. I only know because his best friend, Ricardo, let it slip in front of me before looking for his mom, who was at confession."

"Prostitution? And they're married now?" he murmurs while I continue watching the silhouette of a boat going by, the horn a solo call to the harbor master.

"Yeah, they are. The way he looks at her, after all they have been through, is like a fairytale. Apparently, they were childhood best friends. The three of them grew up together. He did confess that he's loved her his whole life."

Gabe listens intently, his arm tightening around me in a comforting embrace.

"It gives me hope, you know? Makes me believe in second chances, in redemption," I continue, feeling my own situation mirroring Molly's in that I've been through some pretty shitty stuff as well.

His body slacks, his arm around me loosening as our eyes meet, a hint of caution on his face.

"You're not considering going back to him, are you?"

A note of concern threaded through his voice. My response is immediate, my head whipping around so quickly it elicits a sharp pop from my neck.

"Absolutely not. I was meaning me. It gives me hope for myself."

His eyebrows furrow, his hand tightening slightly as a stray hair flies loose from my sweatshirt. I tug the sleeves over my hands, curling the fabric around my fingers to block the chill.

"How so?"

I stare into his dark eyes, illuminated by the park light shining into his face.

"That one day I'll find someone who knows me—all of me, the good and the bad, especially my past and what I've gone through. Find someone who sees beyond my mistakes and wrong choices. Someone like my uncle who doesn't see an arrested prostitute but the girl from his childhood that he loved since he was eight."

The parallel to my current crossroads with Travis is not lost on me.

"I don't want Travis back, but I yearn for someone to look at me the way my uncle does her. And I know people think I'm young and don't know what I want from life. But I do. I've spent years imagining my dream life, counting the days until I'm finally an adult, able to make my own decisions and not suffer the consequences of other decisions. And yet, on most days, I feel like the oldest teenager in the world."

I've never told anyone this. Too private to share with my parents and too deep to share with Lily. Gabe's attention remains fixed on me, the intensity in his brown eyes deepening as he listens. There's a moment charged with unspoken emotion. His hand captures the stray hair, tucking it behind my ear, his knuckles caressing as they depart.

"I believe that such connections exist. That someone can look at you and see not just the sum of your experiences but the entirety of who you are and love you all the more for it."

The previously casual crossing of his legs now becomes a more deliberate movement toward me as his chest expands, almost as if he is positioning himself as the "someone" and sending my brain spinning at the possibilities that he could. Feeling suddenly exposed under the intensity of his gaze, I divert my eyes, the chill of vulnerability causing me to shiver.

"You're cold. Let's head back," he says, blaming the weather for my shaking. "I'd also like to look at your eye before bed."

He stands, removing his body shield blocking the chilly wind for me as he disposes of our trash. I cast a long look at the twinkling lights on the water, committing it to memory as I never want to return here without him.

He returns, enveloping me in a side hug that presses me close to his warmth as we make our way to the car. My arms, previously wrapped around myself, now relax as that body heat he described earlier seeps into me, fending off the cold.

"Gabe, there's hope for you too. To have what you want."

I tilt my head upwards, catching sight of his gentle smile as he looks forward, a peaceful expression on his face.

"I already do."

27

I 'm dragging the next morning, shuffling out to the coffee maker and ignoring the note he stuck on the counter. The night was a tumultuous sea of unrest, with thoughts of Gabe—his unspoken words, his yearning look, wondering if he's my "someone"—being the lighthouse guiding me through the dark waters of Travis's assault surging like rough undercurrents.

The nightmares drag me down into the depths of the ocean, where fear and panic reside. Each brief escape into sleep brought me closer to a calm and peaceful Gabe. Only the haunting images of Travis beating me and intending to rape me jerked me awake in a cold sweat. The dreaming and startling awake cycle continued until dawn crept through the curtains. Surprised I didn't hear Gabe take Anna out like he mentioned he would last night with my interrupted sleep.

As the appliance whirls in the background, I rub my eyes, the injured one still tender and producing a ridiculous amount of crusted sleep over my eyelashes. The bruising is changing colors into something I can hopefully cover with make-up as I'm desperate to return to school and finish my project to make the competition deadline. I plan on returning tomorrow, hoping two days off from school is believable in recovering from food poisoning.

I left my phone on the counter to charge, feeling the distance of leaving it in the kitchen and not in the bedroom somehow equates to distancing myself from my life. It's a ridiculous notion, even if it's helping mentally. With a groan, I muster the courage to retrieve it. Seeing text messages from Lily, Travis, and Uncle Alex on my lock screen.

I ignore the two harder ones and take the easiest first. The *easiest* causes a cynical chuckle to burst from me. Anna pops up over the back of the couch to look at me, wiggling with happiness that I'm awake.

"Good morning, sweet girl," I greet her in my high cartoon voice, leaning over the edge of the counter to see that Gabe has refreshed her bowls again. He is so considerate.

My coffee stops brewing, prompting me to retrieve the rest of the contents to turn it in the same "sugar bomb" Dani always snorts that Uncle Tomlin drinks. The memory makes me smile without pulling too tightly on the healing cut on my lower lip. I take my coffee and phone to the couch. Anna runs over to cuddle with me as I stare out the window and listen to Siri relay my text messages.

> Girl!
>
> You're everywhere.
>
> Have you seen them?

Confusion blankets my woozy brain as I pet Anna, sip my coffee, and watch the city unfold beyond the windows.

> Call me!!!

The fact that she doesn't know where I am at relieves me.

But the oddest part of her messages is that she doesn't know that Travis and I aren't together anymore. I wonder what he's told them. Before moving on to the others, I retrieve my laptop from the coffee table, temporarily squeezing Anna as I lean forward.

Aunt Molli told Uncle Alex that she had seen pictures of me online, and now Lily was referencing them. It didn't occur to me to look them up after talking to my uncle about the potential charges, not while I fretted all day about relaying the information to Gabe.

After a quick search of my name, which has thankfully brought up nothing from the past, there are a dozen results. I click on the first video of me on the red carpet and gasp, my hand covering my mouth as I stare at Travis's stunning creation.

I'm a vision in gold against the velvet backdrop of the night —the lights from countless cameras, like dueling stars, twinkling from both sides of the carpet. My hair, lifted in an elegant updo, is a crown of sophistication, each strand meticulously coaxed into place to frame my face, adding to the allure that holds the attention of every onlooker. The paparazzi clamored over one another to capture the perfect photo for their media outlet.

My mysterious smile draws them in with promises that leave a trail of intrigue. The glimmer of something beyond the immediate spectacle, a depth that speaks of dreams woven into the fabric of my being.

The gold sequins of my dress sparkle against the flashbulbs as they cascade down my form, whispering against my delicate skin as I glance over my shoulder. In an instant, I'm not just an unknown actress working the red carpet.

I'm the embodiment of every tragic romantic tale told under the cover of night, a modern-day muse who captivates not just with her beauty but with the strength and elegance she carries with such effortless poise. As I watch the video again, I

---

can't help but feel that I am witnessing magic, a fleeting glimpse into a story that is hers alone to tell.

Perfection.

What Travis always strived for, demanded of me, and said I was. The woman he turned from innocent into a siren in less than an hour. It was brilliant and completely unsustainable. I was perfect once, at his event, in his play, and will never be again. The drive for perfection is flawed and unobtainable. Leading to the quiet penthouse on Fifth Avenue, where the loneliness stretches for infinity when the love and adoration of his purchased friendship dies off.

After watching it a third time, I sip my coffee, the shock dissipating until I click on the following video of him and me. Once again, taking an observer's point of view.

There he stands, my counterpart, in a tuxedo that speaks of timeless elegance, a sharp contrast to the ethereal vision beside him. His blonde hair, under the luminescence of the spotlight, seems almost haloed, while his blue eyes, precise and piercing, find hers in a connection that transcends the chaos around them.

His hand finds the small of her back, a gesture that appears supportive and endearing. It's as if he's grounding her, reminding her that amidst the whirlwind of fame, they stand together, unshaken. The look they share is one of profound understanding, a testament to the journey that has led them here, to this moment where the world fades away until there is nothing but the two of them.

She sees her reflection in his eyes, not as the world sees her, but as he sees her—fierce, vulnerable, and infinitely cherished. Their shared look carries intimate memories of laughter echoing in quiet rooms and whispered promises in the quiet of dawn. As they gaze into each other's eyes, there's a sense of completeness, a circle closing, the final puzzle piece clicking into place. This is not the beginning of their story, nor is it the end, but an infinite loop of connection and chemistry. It's dazzling and mesmerizing.

This spectacle is a beautifully crafted illusion with its shimmering façade and electrifying exchange between her and her companion. The glamour, as intoxicating as it appears, masks a reality far removed from the authenticity the paparazzi seek.

Their stunning look, suspended in time, speaks not of a genuine connection but of a performance meticulously designed for the public eye. His hand on her back, her smile, the way their eyes lock—all meticulously staged, a dance of appearances on a stage where perception is everything. It hides the brutality of a drunken abuser, willing to attack his lover in a jealous rage and then have the audacity to request her return.

It fuels my resolve to listen to his messages and read his text messages. As his voice echoes on speaker through the apartment, I listen with rage. He pleads for my return, his performance devoid of genuine remorse. His words were a rehearsed script designed to manipulate and coax me back into a role that benefits him most.

He speaks of my success, the audience clamoring for my performance, the limelight we can share, the play that thrives with my presence and flounders with the understudies. She can't replicate my performance of Marcella and cannot speak to the love and anguish Marcella lived and died from. Yet in all that, he offers no proper apology, no acknowledgment of the devastation he's caused.

His promises to never repeat his past actions sound empty without the foundation of accountability. It's a cycle all too familiar, a loop of charm and harm, where the promise of change serves only to reset the stage for the next act of betrayal, having witnessed this prior to him.

Listening to his pleas, my resolve hardens. The contrast between the image he projects and the truth of our situation underscores the importance of looking beyond the surface, of recognizing the signs of manipulation and abuse that were hidden in plain sight, with Gabe the only one seeing the bruises.

His card is hidden away in my backpack, a reminder of discovering that the most glamorous facades can conceal the darkest truths and that the cycle of abuse is a script that needs no audience, only a decisive end.

The end came the second I ran, saved by an angel named Gabriel. After the final pleading message plays, I delete them all and block his number. The act feels empowering as I make my next call—rendering my decision.

"Chief."

When we talk, the familiar sounds of the police station are overtaken by the blaring of rock music, more akin to a bar. I glimpse the clock, noting it's far too early for one to be open.

"Hey, Uncle Alex."

Yesterday's trepidation is replaced with a steely determination, and I am ready to make my decision.

"If this is a bad time, I can call you later."

"Give me a sec."

His voice competes with the loud music. The sheer volume might have blown out my ears if I had not put the call on speaker. Gradually, the music fades, giving way to the gentle chiming of a bell until the faint hum of highway traffic filters through the call.

"I'm outside now."

"Where are you? It sounds like a bar, but it's too early for that."

"Dani's place. It's demo day, and she still likes to do that work herself. She says it keeps her from getting soft."

Humor rings his words, eliciting a smile from me as I relish home's normalcy. I count on the steadiness of how some things never change while my world is completely turned upside down.

"Although, I don't think she'll ever soften up. She ripped Rico a new one the other day over wings. Tomlin had to intercede."

My smile grows into a chuckle. I love that Dani is as unforgivingly brisk and hardheaded as ever. Her overbearing personality and willingness to love fiercely are always a strength to me, something I instantly admire about her.

"So basically, nothing has changed."

"Not with her. But I suspect something has with you."

He detects the lightness in my voice, and it ignites within me a spark of Dani's spirit, kindling a desire to protect those I hold dear, just as she always does.

"I've decided not to press assault charges. I've been wrestling with this decision, turning it over in my mind, and I can't do it. I can't justify sacrificing Gabe after everything he's done to hold Travis accountable for his actions."

I refuse to jeopardize my guardian to vanquish my demon. There is a marked silence on the phone, then a slight rumble in his voice, which I can't determine is disappointment or acknowledgment.

"Isla, I've been giving this a lot of thought since you called yesterday. It's a complex situation, and there are a lot of angles to consider."

I still can't make out what direction he's going in. His inflection is deep and authoritative, but that comes with the job. The line is silent again, and I drink more coffee, waiting for him to continue.

"Not pressing charges carries other ramifications. Yes, it might shield you and your friend from the immediate torrent of legal proceedings—a process that you unfortunately know better than most."

His words flow with deliberate care, each sentence carefully crafted when a sudden nervousness sweeps over me. I don't need his permission not to file charges. I'm an adult. The biggest worry is the threat of disappointment and anger, potentially adding distance to our close relationship.

"There's the matter of accountability. If Travis isn't held to account legally, it could set a precedent, potentially leaving him free to cause harm to others in the future."

The sensitivity with which he broaches whispers to one of the fears occupying my mind and is at the top of the list to file against him.

"I know it's not just about seeking justice for yourself—it's also about protecting others. However, the judicial process can be a double-edged sword, especially for survivors, as you have experienced yourself. And I don't have to remind you that it will force you to relive your trauma in a very public and scrutinized manner."

The nervousness converts to nausea and has me setting down my coffee when my hand trembles.

"Could it . . . could it unseal my records?"

A long, troublesome breath travels through the phone, and I close my eyes as the tears well up.

"In terms of the confidentiality of juvenile records, they are generally well-protected under the law."

He pauses momentarily, his words far too calculating to be good. I pick Anna up and snuggle her closer, needing extra comfort as I try not to vomit.

"However, in certain legal proceedings, if deemed relevant to the case, a court might order the unsealing of these records. This could occur if the information contained within the records is considered necessary for establishing a pattern of behavior, for his defense purposes, or for other reasons that the court deems pertinent to ensuring he receives a fair trial."

His voice softens, a blend of uncle and legal advisor as he continues, "And a good lawyer worth their weight would avoid this strategy. But suppose this perpetrator has a history of abusive behavior, and his legal team has been doling out payout, which we are not privy to. In that case, I'd suspect they'd leave no stone unturned trying to defame your character and request the records be unsealed as part of their defense strategy. If they are high-powered and walk the edge of fairness and ethics, they would likely try to convert this into an opportunistic slander suit. Although if you have pictures, those are damning either way they try to play it."

My eyes open, the fresh tears trailing down my cheek, adding another reason not to pursue charges, ranking right up there with protecting Gabe.

"I-I . . . can't."

I sniff and wipe the tears with the edge of Gabe's sweatshirt that I wore to bed.

"Unsealing my records . . . would mean reliving everything. I've spent years trying to escape the grip of those nightmares, only for them to return that night. I can't subject myself or my family to that ordeal again. The toll it took on them . . . Papa's heart palpitations, and Dad lost all that weight."

My voice breaks at the memory of my parents' suffering. Dani would fly up here just to kill the guy.

"I can't be the reason they endure that pain again, all because I misjudged someone."

"I understand, Isla. It's an incredibly difficult position you're in, and your concerns are valid. The well-being of you and your family and the potential for further traumatization—are significant factors to consider. That must be considered in decisions like these."

I bury my face against Anna, the source that's gotten me through so much. The last three years of my life have been tumultuous with the trial, the nightmares, and the therapy. The lightness of having the family I've always wanted, starting school, and being a typical teenager interspersed with the darkness of trauma, repressed memories, and anxiety.

"Protecting yourself, safeguarding your progress and your

family's peace, is paramount. If the cost of seeking legal recourse is too high in terms of personal and emotional well-being, then focusing on healing and moving forward with your life sounds like the path you need to take. It's about controlling what you can in a situation that's felt out of control since it happened."

I kiss her head, her fur soft against my lips, before lowering her to my lap again when I feel braver.

"It's the only way, Uncle Alex. Right now, only four people know what happened, and that can be contained. If I press charges, the whole world will know, sending everything spiraling out of control. It will unravel the very records Uncle Tomlin's attorneys worked hard to seal away."

"I'm so sorry you're going through this. Nobody should have to endure what you're facing. But remember, you're surrounded by an incredible support system, my family included. You're never on your own. Reaching out to me was the right thing to do. There's nothing I wouldn't do for you, Isla. You're as much a part of my family as my own girls. Just hold onto the fact that you're courageous. You've always been a fighter."

Tears stream back down my face at his kind words of support. He's the same officer who stood watch at the door, facilitating Dani's rule-breaking missions to sneak Anna into the facility for visits—unchanged in his dedication and kindness.

"Thank you for everything. And Uncle Alex? I promise to call my parents and tell them everything. I need more time if you don't mind."

"I understand completely," he responds, his voice as empathetic as it is reassuring. "Take the time you need, Isla. It's important to do this in your own way and in your own time. Just know that when you're ready to talk to your parents, I'm here to support you through that conversation. You're not alone in this, not now, not ever."

Uncle Alex's advice of healing and recovery lingers in my thoughts as I move off the couch to look out the windows as we say our final goodbyes. With my phone in my hand, I gaze at the city, moving forward. The daily lives are uninterrupted by the play featuring beautiful people on a red carpet or the assault that happened afterward. It's a reminder that I need to move on and not let one more abuse define who I am.

You've always been a fighter.

My uncle's words echo back to me. I had never considered these words as I hadn't racked anyone or broken a few guys' noses like Dani had. But maybe in my own quiet way, I am a fighter. Life sure has knocked me down and made me feel worthless and unloved, and I haven't given up on it, not even once.

A ghost of a smile crosses my face as I step into the open living room and practice the defense moves taught me long ago. Perhaps I'll even ask that third-degree black belt to show me more.

"Because I am a fighter."

28

I 'm sprawled on the couch, my fingers aimlessly drawing bodices in my sketchbook. I just assured my instructors of my return to school tomorrow through a flurry of emails. Last night's lasagna was a gut bomb in my stomach, chased by some freshly baked cookies I had delivered. It's making me sleepy as Anna occupies herself with a toy on the floor.

The door unexpectedly opens, and the afternoon sun casts long shadows that emphasize the haggard, haunted look on Gabe's face. His scrubs, usually pristine, cling to him in a wrinkled mess. Without a word, he discards his crossbody bag onto the counter with a thud, his keys clattering against the stone surface, spinning wildly before coming to a rest, echoing the chaos that seems to have followed him home.

His presence last night, while considerate and sustaining, now carries an anger or resentment that has me cautiously watching him. The peaceful and serene day I had is changing with the darkening storm surrounding him, transforming his haven into a place shadowed by the unspoken burdens and possibly today's struggles that started in another building across Manhattan.

"Gabe?"

I keep my voice light and airy, my internal alarm sounding that something is wrong. The lively banter and warmth that usually accompanies him is conspicuously absent today, leaving a silence that speaks volumes. Watching him, a knot forms in my stomach, a tangled mess of concern and help-lessness.

He moves through our shared space with an unsettling vacancy, his steps devoid of their customary purpose and energy. The fridge door opens and closes with a soft click. A beer bottle is now in his grasp, and he tosses the top off and throws it on the countertop with the same velocity as the keys. It careens off the side and falls to the floor.

Without a word, he collapses onto the couch beside me. Then, he places a shoe-clad foot upon the coffee table in a motion that feels almost sacrilegious, disregarding his usual care of the space. It's a small act, but in the context of Gabe's precise nature, it signals a profound disarray within him.

His gaze drifts towards the window, fixating on the world outside with a haunted intensity. It's as if he's looking through the glass and seeing something beyond my grasp that fills him with an unspeakable loss. I sit there, torn between reaching out to bridge the gap his day has created between us and giving him the space to navigate his thoughts alone. It's a fleeting thought as he wouldn't leave me alone to suffer in silence, so I reach out.

"What's wrong, Gabe?"

The urge to comfort him, to somehow lift the weight off his shoulders, is overwhelming, yet I find myself immobilized by the complexity of his sorrow. The man who has been my stead-fast protector and confidant is shrouded in a veil of distress, and I'm unsure how to break through.

"Arseholes. Specifically, aresholes that hit innocent people."

His thick accent coats the words with venom. His haunted gaze against the backdrop of his muted apartment is alarming. The silence stretches between us, filled only by Anna's oblivious play with her squeaky toy. Did Travis track Gabe to the hospital where he works? Did he file a complaint or somehow jeopardize his job?

The knot tights in my stomach, its rope winding up my neck to choke my words of apology.

"Is it . . . Travis? Did he . . ."

I don't finish with the look of contempt and snarky exhalation while his eyes flicker away, taking a long drink.

"He's of no concern, Isla. Trust me when I say he should not bother you again."

The cold calculation in his tone is bothersome enough without the added threat. Yet, the calls and text messages speak to the reality of him bothering me, speaking to the disconnect.

"Then what?" I inch closer, which draws his attention when those dark eyes meet mine. "Did he get you in trouble with the hospital? Is your job in jeopardy because of helping me?"

His expression shifts, easing into a softer, more contemplative look as he gently places his bottle on the glass end table. Then, extending his hand towards me, his movements deliberate and inviting. His eyes convey a silent request for connection.

"You must stop worrying about that, Isla. What's done is done. I wouldn't change how the situation unfolded other than to have insisted you come with me after your performance. Please lay that concern to rest."

If he'd only known how bad that worry had become earlier today, talking to my uncle, my decision of not pursuing charges is firmly cemented in my mind, as is his confidence in not getting in trouble for helping me. I angle closer, slipping my palm against his to provide support or comfort, not knowing which. His thumbs struck across my knuckles like they always do, the only indication of my closer proximity.

"Will you talk to me about it? I want to be there for you as you are for me."

He licks his lips nervously before exhaling deeply. Wrinkles form across his brow as he stares at me for a long time.

"I operated today on a little boy."

Finally, he starts, and even though it's his livelihood, I still marvel at his bravery and commitment to being a brain surgeon to kids.

"No more than five years old. Child abuse."

The revelation sends a shiver down my spine, the room suddenly feeling colder, as if his words have materialized into a chilling mist around us. I let go of his hand to move closer. Curling my legs underneath me, my side presses into the soft back cushion while his arm rests along the top.

"He was brought in with severe injuries," Gabe continues, his voice a mere whisper, yet each word slices through the silence with razor-sharp precision. "Injuries inflicted by his stepfather. The kind of brutality that I've never seen inflicted on a harmless child."

"Oh, Gabe."

My hand covers my mouth, trying to make sense of the unsensible. His hand moves to my back as if needing to touch me to stay grounded, a neutral lifeline in the midst of a stormy day.

"We did everything we could," he says, the burden of his oath and amazing human being weighing heavily. "The surgery was complex, demanding every ounce of skill we possessed. But it's the aftermath, the recovery, the therapy, the cops outside his door, the justice that needs to follow . . . that's where the real battle begins."

The raw pain in his eyes tells of the horrors he's witnessed, the damage he had to repair for the innocent boy he fought to save.

"I'm so sorry."

I reach out to touch his bent leg, barely getting a reaction as I leave my hand on it to comfort him. Gabe's role as a protector of life, often at its most vulnerable, has never seemed more heroic or haunting.

"Seeing that boy, fighting for a life not yet fully lived because of someone's cruelty . . ."

His gaze drifts away, lost to the fading light outside the window. He stares at nothing while trying to make sense of everything.

"First you . . . then him. Fucking aresholes. It's why I do what I do, Isla. To give them a fighting chance. But some days, the weight of it all . . . it's almost too much to bear."

I crawl closer, and his gaze returns long enough to capture my embrace. My knees press into his leg and side as I put my arms around his neck and draw him toward me. The arm loosely at my back tightens, encouraging me closer while he adjusts his position, straightening his knee to make room for me to come closer.

"I don't know how you do it. You're one of the bravest, most kindhearted people I know," I whisper against him, the faint smell of antiseptic and cologne clinging to his skin.

My heart aches for him, the burden he carries, and the silent plea for understanding in his eyes before I hug him. His arm around me tightens just a fraction more.

"Sometimes, I question the truth of it all. In saving him, did I truly do him a favor, or have I condemned him to endure further suffering by denying him peace in death?"

His voice drops to a murmur, each word a brutal torment of uncertainty and the crushing burden of his duties. His question lingers between us, a stark, harrowing insight into his turmoil.

He shifts, his hand falling away, signaling the embrace is over, and I unwind my arms while remaining close.

"When he wakes up, his world is cruel, ripped from his mother, in foster care, in physical and psychological therapy, the list goes on. A life marred by trauma, what then? Have I extended his pain, his struggle, instead of granting an end to his suffering?"

His hand returns to my back, a reflexive gesture of seeking comfort or perhaps offering it, as he grapples with these daunting questions—things I've never entertained in my mind, making my problems pale in comparison.

"And it's not just him, Isla," he continues, the despair deep in those chestnut eyes. "It's every patient, every life I touch. The line between salvation and suffering is so thin. In trying to play angel, am I instead playing fate, deciding who endures and who escapes?"

The enormity of his confession sends a shiver through me, a frosty iciness sliding through my veins as his conflict of playing God. His role as doctor and protector of the innocent comes at a cost unseen to his patients. He is an unsung hero, despondent in the privacy of his home, far away from the superhero he must be to those lives he's saving.

It's a perspective I've never had to consider—the immense burden shouldered by those who stand on the frontline of care, heroes shrouded in the shadows of their doubts and fears. Moved by his openness, I find the courage to share my story with him.

"I'm an abuse survivor."

Hearing my voice articulate my experiences feels foreign. In group therapy, introductions often began this way, yet I remained a silent witness. The turmoil within me was so intense and deeply personal that giving it a voice seemed insurmountable.

The thought of laying my scars bare for others to scrutinize

left me guarded, choosing to confine my story to the understanding of my parents. Sharing, truly sharing, was a boundary
I hadn't crossed until now. His hand stops moving on my back,
pressing against my shirt as his eyes search my face, disbelief
in his.

"I don't talk about it much to anyone. It does not define me,
but it plays a large part in who I am. That's why I'm so mad and
unable to forgive myself for not seeing Travis coming a mile
away."

I shake my head, glancing down at Anna, who's resting on
her toy. Gabe shifts toward me, his knee moving onto the couch
and shrinking my space, forcing me to rest my knees on his.

"Bloody hell. Isla—"

Instinctively, my hand finds his chest, a silent plea commu-
nicated through a single touch.

"Please don't look at me that way. I don't want pity or
sympathy."

"I'm not. I wouldn't."

His eyes widen, his mouth parts, and his reaction is immediate and sincere, dispelling the fear of judgment.

"I'm only going to tell you once, and I won't speak of it
again," I warn, not knowing if I will make it through my long
story. It is too lengthy, too fraught with tragedy and sorrow for
someone my age.

"You don't have to tell me at all. Only if you need to," he
whispers, his other hand seeking mine to anchor me to him or
the here and now as I recant the past.

My lips twist into a frown, trepidation rising as I share my
darkest secrets outside my small circle and subject myself to his
judgment, which could damage our friendship if he views me
in a different light. Yet something in the way Gabe looks, absolutely destroyed by repairing the damage caused by an abuser,
lets me know he'll be sympathetic, especially how caring he's
been through the Travis ordeal.

My hands twist in my lap, playing with my adoption ring as I decide where to start. At the beginning—my real dad. The good times, the ice cream shop, the late nights he'd come in from work thinking I was asleep and kissing me, and the rare moments when I was the center of his attention. Then, the fights, the yelling, the manic fits of my mom screaming and crying until one day, he never came home from work, and I started looking out the window for him.

How it drove mom to drinking, then men, then drugs. I detailed everything from the revolving door of boyfriends until the one she "loved," and I despised—the devil of them all. In the beginning, it was lingering looks and body grazes. Cornering me when mom wasn't in the room or too drunk or high to notice.

Until the night that they argued, hearing the slap from my bedroom, I raced out there to protect her and was beaten myself. That started the cycle of abuse and fear, knowing he had us entirely under his control.

The grueling way his face twisted in joyful glee when the realization settled over him as we both lay bloody and moaning on the floor. I caught a glimpse of his maniacal expression before turning away and burying my face in the floorboards, wishing Dad would come back and save us. He never did.

Throughout, Gabe is even more gutted than before. His hands tighten on me, his fingers nervously toying with my adoption ring as if needing a means to release the rage vibrating through his touch into me.

I don't know when the tears begin to flow, and when I need something to wipe my face, he removes his scrub top for me to use, his undershirt fitting like a second skin. His mouth twists, the discomfort evident as tears brim his eyes when I detail some of the sexual abuse. His jaw pulses, his muscles hardening with rage as his fingers tense.

"There is more, isn't there?"

His question hangs with a hesitancy, a dread of knowing there is and possibly not wanting to hear it. His reluctance is understandable, a protective instinct that flares at the prospect of delving deeper into my darkness. It's hard to listen without being able to rectify it. It's even harder to express the depth of the scars crisscrossing my soul.

"Yes," I whisper, losing myself in the vastness of his brown eyes. His frown deepens.

"Then I shall hear all of it."

The simplicity of his statement and his willingness to bear witness to my story reveal his profound care. He offers a place to voice the unvoiced, to bring into light the shadows that have long shaped my existence, whereas Travis readily agrees to keep the past in the tomb it lies in.

With a shuddering breath, I continue, the catalyst to running away. Needing to escape, or I'd be a prisoner in that house forever when they declined to press charges, and he sneered at me. The time on the road with Rick was more challenging to relay, being fresher and newer, the trial, recanting everything I went through to him, the court, and the jury's pity and sympathy.

At some point, it became too much for both of us, needing a break from the devastation of my past. I don't know if I collapsed into him or if he scooped me up, ending up in his lap, my head on his shoulder sobbing while his chest rapidly rises and falls, letting his own emotions out.

The sanctity of the apartment falls away as our souls join in shared tragedy, him giving his loss as I give mine. An invisible merging of our heartache, pulling it from each other to intertwine in the shared space of our grieving. My clenched chest becomes his, clutching each other as lifelines to avoid drowning in the sorrow of what we've both been through.

His touch is cathartic, his scent soothing, as he clings to me with the same urgency that I cling to him. Both need this connection to deal with his crisis today and mine yesterday. When my sobbing settles, and I pull away to breathe deeply, his hands cup my face, and his thumbs capture my tears to pull them away with the same gentleness in his gaze.

Something changes within me. The yearning in my spirit to be accepted, to share all that I've shared and not be cast aside with a disgusted look teeming at the edge of my being. And here it is, my demons dancing in and out of the shadows haunt me, mixing with his to a far lesser extent and finding a commonality. He's not cowering away from the abuse, trauma, and lasting scars. He's standing as a demon slayer, cutting them down with his fiery blade until they are no more.

His expression is anything but disgusted as his grip cups my sides, clenching to hold me back or draw me closer. The choice is mine. His patience, waiting for me to decide his role in my life, is as valent as slaying the demons lying in charred ashes at my feet.

Travis was the demon paved with roads of gold, collecting tortured souls to act in his will. I see that now. As his namesake, Gabriel is the true angel I had been looking for—quietly waiting and patiently walking beside me until I figured it out.

As I find a semblance of peace, my lips curve into a tender smile. Leaning in, I see the surprise flicker in his eyes just before I brush a gentle kiss against his lips, a gesture as revealing as it is restrained. The initial touch is light, a whisper of contact that speaks volumes, followed by another, each one eroding the last barriers of mere friendship between us.

His hands, previously a comforting presence on my back, pull me closer with a newfound intent, signaling his understanding and acceptance of the shift in our dynamic. Our lips meet again, this time with a shared urgency, a mutual acknowledgment of the feelings quietly simmering beneath the surface.

This kiss is not just seeking comfort but a coordinated longing for what was right in front of me the entire time, waiting to be recognized and embraced. His fingers trail up my spine, resting at the base of my neck, signaling he wants this to go on forever. My head tilts, intending to deepen the kiss, when he suddenly moves away, his thighs tightening under my weight, worry rimming his eyes.

"Isla, forgive me," he breathes out in cautious worry, fearful of the threshold we're teetering on.

Time suspends, each waiting to see if we will tread forward into perilous new territory or retreat to the familiar and known. As my chest rises and falls with desire, acceptance, and under-standing, I cup my neck while his hand falls away. His lack of contact speaks to his uncertainty.

"I took advantage."

He glances away, down toward the floor, with a slight shake to clear away the desire so evident in his face and underneath me. When his gaze returns, it's cloudier and more confused than before.

"You're vulnerable, and I ... "

The remains of his statement hang unfinished, a reflec-tion of his internal conflict. The space between us, filled with the warmth of newfound intimacy, now pulses with the complexity of blurred lines. His concern for my wellbeing and his fear of exploiting me in a vulnerable moment assures me that this is the right choice—one I was too blind to see while chasing a dream that didn't belong to me in the first place.

"It's okay."

I caress his neck, feeling the coarse hairs under my finger-tips as my eyes trace his full lips, still parted as an invitation.

"I initiated this. It was me."

He shifts again, a restlessness that illustrates the uncom-fortableness raging. Bracing myself to move from his lap, his hand on my thigh halts my actions.

"But that doesn't absolve me. The last thing I want is to

become another person who took advantage of your trust, especially in a moment like this."

The intensity of our gaze locks, an electric current running between us, magnifying each word, each breath.

"Gabe, this isn't about taking advantage. It's about . . . me discovering something profound, something real, something that has been right in front of me this entire time. You're the clarity amidst the chaos."

He exhales a sound that seems to vibrate from him into me and the room around us, laying bare his inner conflict.

"You mean more to me than you can imagine. Because of that, I'm paralyzed by the fear of crossing a line that we can never uncross. I'm terrified to hurt you."

My hand finds his in the setting afternoon sun, sending golden light across the walls.

"And I appreciate that. Who's to say you will hurt me or we'll hurt each other? Feeling something for someone, especially now, shouldn't make you or I feel guilty. Maybe this is how it had to happen for me to realize."

His eyes, deep pools of chestnut, lock onto mine with an intensity that has me bracing myself, my hand tightening into a fist on his chest.

"It's not guilt," he corrects softly, yet the tremor in his voice betrays him. "It's the profound sense of responsibility I feel towards you, towards the potential of 'us.' And given everything that's happened, I desperately need to be certain that we're not stepping into something you're not ready for, without doubts, without regrets. Isla, you are barely out of one entanglement, and it is a traumatic one at that. How could I live with myself if you're meant to remain free? To experience the life you intended when you came to this city. How is that fair to you?"

For the first time, I look away. His fears suddenly sound loud and commanding, speaking a truth I hadn't considered. Everything with Travis happened quickly—a breathless whirlwind. Gabe seeing the reality of how things are versus how they should be speaks to his maturity, to the life experiences I have yet to live, and from the sounds of it, what he wants me to live, free and untethered.

"I understand."

The detection is clear in my voice as the gravity of our situation sets in—the weight of his words. This time, I move off his lap, his actions helpful by steadying my waist until I'm further down the couch from him.

"I need you to understand this isn't me pushing you away. Your happiness is paramount to me. All I want is for you to pursue what you're truly passionate about and follow your dreams without reservations or regrets. I'll always be here for you."

"Why does it feel like an ending then?"

Tears brim my lower lids, and I don't care if they fall. My emotions are fraught and all over the place as we try to find some semblance of what we were before the kiss.

His gaze softens, his hand reaching to the empty cushion between us. I glimpse his open palm and return to look at him, not wanting to concede to touching him again.

"Endings aren't always about walking away. Sometimes, they're about taking a step back, giving space so that new beginnings can form. It's not the end of 'us,' Isla, far from it. Just a pause, a moment to breathe, for you to figure out what you truly want, without my feelings factoring into it."

I nod, the tears slipping freely now at his bitter-sweet words. The room feels larger and emptier, and the distance between us is a physical manifestation of the emotional space he's putting between us.

"It's just . . . hard." My voice cracks with rejection and confusion. "To be so close to someone, to feel something and then have to step back."

His hand retracts, curling into a fist on the couch as if strug-gling with this conversation like I am.

"It's not easy for me either—to care for someone and watch them walk their path through hurt and pain caused by others. But I believe in you, in your dreams, and in the incredible journey you have ahead. This isn't goodbye, Isla. You just started your path, and I've been on mine for quite a while. Who's to say they won't converge again when you're truly ready?"

The sincerity in his voice, the promise of a future where our paths might cross once more, is a dagger to my heart and a sliver of hope amidst the heartache—the closing of a chapter to a book barely written.

"Okay."

I bite my lip, trying to hold back the flow of fresh tears while I accept reality. Silence follows as Gabe maintains a steady gaze on me while I look at Anna, who's even settled on the floor. With my mind racing and a general awkwardness forming between us, I stand and collect my sketchbook.

"I think it's time I head home, Gabe. Thank you for everything."

My voice betrays my gratitude as I stand and make my way towards the bed, each step heavier than the last, my efforts to stifle the sobs proving futile.

Suddenly, I feel his embrace envelop me from behind, and before I can fully process the warmth of his touch, he whispers, "Please don't leave. Stay until you are feeling better."

I sniff and straighten my shoulders, knowing I cannot be around him, acting as if things haven't irrevocably changed. Something he knows, or he wouldn't be insisting I stay.

"I'll collect my and Anna's things if we can leave in ten minutes."

29

The assured and brave tone I used in the apartment with Gabe contradicts my sudden panic about leaving his safe apartment to resume a life I desperately escaped from. The closer his vehicle draws to my side of town, the harder I clench the door handle. Sensing my uneasiness, Anna paws at my chest, wanting me to snuggle her and expel some of my anxiety.

"She's restless."

Gabe's low voice cuts through the frosty silence that's occupied the car since we slipped into our seats. Not wanting to divulge that she's trying to calm my freakout, I hum under my breath and continue watching the city go by. The rest of the ride falls back into a tension-filled silence until he pulls up to the curb, and I practically dart out of the car with Anna and my backpack.

Ever the gentleman, he collects the rest of my belongings with his usual care and attention while I wait at the curb. My eyes roaming the evening streets through a new lens. Both wiser and more experienced than when I had that uncomfortable interaction with Lily. How is it possible that I lived another decade in only a few days?

Returning to my old life, the one before Travis's abuse, before I crossed the friendship line, and before Gabe's rejection, feels like a distant memory. The heaviness in my heart is evident in my heavy footsteps leading us to my apartment door. With the quiet slip of the key in the lock, I open the door and gasp.

The space is awash in an array of gifts—flowers in full bloom, a teddy bear with a forlorn smile, and a box of what I assumed to be cupcakes from the half-eaten one sitting on top. We move through the apartment slowly, Gabe follows behind as I set Anna on the floor and gently places my backpack on the table. My gaze roams the room, counting over a dozen possible more gifts placed on every available surface. The collective smell rises to a stunning level that is both divinely fragrant and overwhelming to the point Anna sneezes three times.

"This is a lot," he says, echoing what is running on repeat in my mind as he surveys the room.

"Yeah."

I approach the most elaborate arrangement, an opened note from Travis pleading for reconciliation that has me reading it from afar and not touching it as if it's tainted goods. Other arrangements expressing congratulations or wanting me to call them are signed by people I don't know. The oversized bear has no name, and the sender is shrouded in anonymity.

The realization that these well wishes found their way here into my humble apartment from strangers who have no part in my life and now know where I live makes me worried. As my footsteps sound around the room, Gabe's following closely behind adds to the eeriness, especially when I come across an arrangement from Julian, Travis's good friend.

This gesture sends a shiver down my spine, hinting at a concerted effort by Travis or his circle to reintegrate him into my life. It is as if the facade of fake gaiety from the dinner the night of the assault has crept into my apartment, turning my home into a florist's envy.

I stand frozen, taking in the invasion of my private world. The joy accompanying such gifts is entirely absent, replaced by deep unease. Needing to escape the overwhelming aroma and wanting to take a moment to process what I'm seeing, I move down the hall to my bedroom and click on the light.

Another gasp has me covering my mouth, and Gabe barrels down the hall toward me. The sight is surreal and disturbing. My bedroom has been transformed into the epitome of love bombing. A desperate attempt in grand overtures. An endless sea of red and white "I miss you" balloons hug the ceiling, eclipsing the overhead light.

Hundreds of rose petals blanket the floor and my bed, scattered with romantic intent, and I cast a startling glance at Gabe. His chest presses lightly against my shoulder blade, and my hesitancy to step further into the room blocks his ability to see the entirety of this violation of the personal sanctuary. His eyes, wide with disbelief, meet mine, reflecting the confusion and violation of such an overstep.

"What the . . ." his voice trails off, unable to fully articulate the absurdity and audacity of the scene before us. "I'm assuming you knew nothing of this?"

The dissonance between the supposed affection these tokens are meant to convey and the discomfort they actually inflict is unimaginable. My mouth hangs open in shock.

"You talked to Lily yourself. Did she mention this?"

The realization that she allowed him to come into my bedroom, a place that he's never been, to go to such lengths is not just a violation of my physical space. It's the domineering control over my entire life that had me running away that night.

"No."

I step into the room, still trying to understand what I see.

Gabe follows, his movements cautious as if wary of further unsettling an already fraught atmosphere.

"Isla, I know things between us are . . . not as we would like." His words are as cautious as his movements when his eyes sweep the room again before settling on me. "But you can't stay here, even if we get this all cleaned up."

Anna's sneezes echo down to us after I leave her in the aromatic room. I nervously bit my lips, still unable to wrap my mind around what I'm seeing. Gabe's miles ahead, calculating and analyzing the situation for what it could be—unsafe.

"This is just crazy, right? Like this level of . . . I don't even know what to call it."

Rooted to the floor, I contemplate the man behind these actions. Was he pacing the penthouse, raging, throwing things? Or was he sitting in the playroom with a drink, quietly wondering how it all fell apart and how to get it all back? It's a conundrum I can't get past. Was this an act of desperation for his flurry of unanswered text messages and phone calls? A barge of physical displays of affection in chorus with the barrage of digital ones.

"It's definitely cause for concern made more disturbing with his tendency toward violence." Gabe's being extremely diplomatic for my benefit.

"Particularly towards women," he adds, not shying away from stating the unsettling truth.

In a swift motion, Gabe pulls out his phone, steps back into the doorway, and captures the scene with his camera. He then proceeds to methodically photograph the rest of the apartment. My curiosity is piqued, and I trail behind him, puzzled.

"What are you doing?"

"It's prudent to have a record of all this, regardless of the direction you choose concerning the legal aspects. Consider it additional evidence, much in the vein of what your uncle would advise."

His words trigger a sudden realization—I hadn't shared my decision with him. The decision shaped by my desire to shield myself from the very real possibility of unsealing my juvenile records and to safeguard Gabe's future, his career. These considerations had quietly dictated my choice, yet here was Gabe, unknowingly reinforcing the importance of documentation, of preparation for any eventuality, even if it jeopardized his life.

Actions like this make me question why we are stepping back. Why I need to live life more or chase my dreams further before we can be together? I walk to where he's taking pictures of the signed cards attached to each delivery and touch his arm.

"I-I'm not pursuing charges."

I gaze up at him, those dark eyes settling on mine as those full lips pull together in a silent, unspoken question.

"It could unseal my records. Everything I told you could be presented in court again. And I can't. Gabe, I just can't. . ."

The thought leaves me trembling, and he puts his phone away to pull me into a comforting embrace.

"You won't. We won't. It will stay between us. You have my word," he whispers into my hair, his arms tightening into a ring of protection safer than the apartment that used to be home, now another overrun invasion of Travis.

"I also can't do that to you, Gabe."

"Isla—"

"No, Gabriel."

His full name falls from my lips for the first time, a plea for understanding. He pulls back slightly, though his arms remain a shield around me.

"You say you care about me. Well, I care about you too. I'm not willing to ruin your life either. This stays between the four people who know, and eventually, I'll tell my parents when this is all behind me."

Gabriel's response is a momentary tightening of his

embrace, a physical manifestation of his commitment to my wellbeing and his resolve to face whatever comes next together, as he has said several times before.

"You're sure about this?" His voice is soft, laced with concern and an underlying respect for my decision.

"Yes. It's the only way I can see to protect us both."

He nods, slowly releasing me from the security of his arms to look me squarely in the eyes.

"Do you have your phone?" I nod, and before I can ask, he's saying, "Get it out. I'm going to send you all the pictures I took. Out of the respect and trust you've placed in me, I will delete them from my phone so only you have them."

He communicates it as a command, conveying the seriousness of his intent. I reach for my phone, waiting as he selects the photos and taps my phone to send them to me. Once they are transferred, he deletes them all, keeping his phone at my eye level so I can see his action when it settles on the last picture. One of him and Anna. She's raised to his face, he's smiling, and she has her ears up, looking as sweet as ever. Together, they look adorable, and my chest flutters.

"When did you take this?"

I touch the edge of his phone, gazing at it again, before looking at him for answers. He blushes as if he forgot he had the picture, a soft smile on his lips when he looks from me to it.

"I sent it to my mom. She called me almost immediately to ask if I got a dog. I got myself in trouble having to explain Anna, which led to you. She has a knack for getting the whole story out of me when I try to keep things simple."

His finger taps the side of his phone as if reminded of something uncomfortable before locking it. The fact that he snapped a picture of my dog and then sent it to his mom, telling her about me, does not take a step back and let me chase my dreams. It jumps ahead to the point where I wonder if she'd want to meet me.

"Well, maybe one day I'll get to meet the mom of such a great friend."

I keep my tone and word choice neutral. He's a great guy and friend, and I thought he would be a great boyfriend. His frown flickers momentarily until he inhales deeply and gazes around the room again.

"What do you want to do now? Because I'd really prefer it if you came back with me. Just for a while until we figure out how to deal with all this. Especially if you're planning on going back to school this week."

The heartfelt and genuine suggestion stirs a mix of emotions within me. The idea of returning to his apartment, to that haven of safety and understanding, contrasts the vulnerability I feel in my own space, now tainted by Travis's intrusion.

"I . . . I don't know, Gabe. I felt so sure coming back here, but now, with all this?"

I hesitate. The enormity of cleaning up this mess and disposing of all the love bombing is not only physically taxing but emotionally wearing after an already emotional and somewhat confusing day.

"I know you were," he acknowledges his hand landing on my shoulder in solidarity with what I feel while looking around the place. Anna sneezes again, almost deciding for me.

"But I can't stand the thought of leaving you here alone, not with all this." He gestures around the room at the stuff hanging overhead. "You need a safe space, Isla, and I can provide that. At least for a little while."

His sincerity and the open offer of a sanctuary slowly dismantle the walls of my reluctance.

"And Anna?"

"Anna, too, of course," he chuckles, the sound bringing momentary ease to the tension surrounding us.

"She's part of this package deal, isn't she? My mother has

already asked for more photos—unfortunately, of the both of you."

My laughter rings through the apartment, brief, and cutting, as I mentally run through the list of things I need to do to finish the week at his place.

"Okay."

30

It's stunning. The dress I've spent countless hours designing and crafting is before me, finished and more beautiful than I dared hope. The way the morning light plays off the silver metallic bodysuit, making it glisten and sparkle, is breathtaking against the angelic white fabric that drapes over the form beneath in an elegant cascade.

The delicate silver flowers beaded onto the unrelenting metallic bodysuit bring a delicate element against the post-modern, futuristic design. The flowers sprout from the waist-band, climbing across the bodice. A cluster of the blooms tenderly embraces under the breast line, with a single, blooming stem reaching upward toward a shoulder. The silver beaded pattern is mirrored in the sleeves, with low-lying flowers on one and a longer, reaching bloom on the other, adding a feminine elegance to the sheer white sleeves.

Yards of the poly crepe de chin fabric extends from the delicate neckline and shoulders, wrapping around and flowing behind the dress like white wings. The bunching I struggled with is gone, the dress ending at the bodysuit, allowing the long legs of the potential model to be displayed against the dazzling flow of white. This detail transforms the gown into something more than just an evening gown. It becomes a statement of artistic expression, a symbol of fragile strength and grace.

Standing here, witnessing the realization of my vision, tears fill my eyes as I'm filled with wonder. Who knew how to assemble the bodysuit with the sheer fabric? Who took the liberty of removing the front dress panel and eliminating my bunching problem?

Tears fill my eyes as I stand in awe of the vision brought to life before me. As I approach my design, feeling vaguely familiar and slightly foreign, I discard my belongings on the drafting table. With wonderment and disbelief, my fingertips skim the fine details as if seeing it for the first time, even though this was one of the countless drafts to finally get it right. My touch barely grazes the intricate details of the bodice, which I ruined my fingertips over, and Travis chided me as inferior.

Suddenly, my teacher surges from nowhere, her hands clapping enthusiastically as the room slowly fills with onlookers. I gaze around, confusion settling in. Where are the other students' dress forms? Our eyes connect, and a wave of realization crashes over me. She's beaming, almost unable to contain her excitement.

"Isla, this is phenomenal!" she exclaims, her voice echoing slightly in the now hushed room. "You must have worked to the bone over the weekend to finish it."

"Um, what?"

Oblivious to my confusion, she rattles on, "Imagine my surprise when you said you had food poisoning, and I came in to find this. Well, I can see by the puffiness around your eyes that you must have been vomiting. Poor girl, but look at this vision!"

She notices my bruised eye, still covered in a ton of corrector and concealer, but quickly dismisses it to gush about my creation again. I'm beyond confused at how she thinks I worked all weekend and how the dress came together. It was close but in separate pieces. The bunching and the bodysuit boning were still an issue when Gabe intervened.

Gabe.

He did this. He fixed the bodysuit and assembled it based on my sketchbook, which he stared at intensely like a brain surgeon. He decided to forgo the front panel and elevate the bodysuit to the front of the dress. As realization dawns on me, how? When?

She continues talking, her last sentence drawing me back to reality.

"Your design has been selected as a finalist for your category!"

My heart skips a beat, the words taking a moment to fully register. Finalist? My eyes widen in disbelief, a joy and shock coursing through me.

"My category?"

"Yes. Vision of the Future: Metals and Metallics."

Her eyes sparkle with pride as her fingertips reach for the design and quickly recoil as if not to damage it.

"Your piece embodies the theme perfectly with its futuristic elegance and innovative use of metallics. It's not just a dress, Isla. It's a statement about where fashion is headed."

I'm speechless, my mind racing to comprehend the magnitude of her words. Visions of the Future: Metals and Metallics. It fits so seamlessly, a category that feels like it was made just for my design.

"And," she adds, her voice lowering as if to emphasize the importance of her following words, "We couldn't move your piece to the exhibition hall until you accepted the nomination. It's not just about showcasing your design ahead of the fashion show. It's about celebrating your vision, hard work, and undeniable talent."

The room feels immense and intimate at that moment, every eye on me, waiting for my response. A swell of emotions rises within me—pride, excitement, a touch of disbelief. After everything I've been through this week, this feels like a lifeline, pulling me back to the familiar, what I know now to be my destiny. This dress, a labor of love and a vessel of my creativity has transcended its material form to become a symbol of futuristic fashion while guiding my future in fashion.

"Um, yes. Yes, of course, I accept."

Applause fills the room, a chorus of support and celebration for a journey far from over. The appreciation in this room far outweighs the standing ovation I received on Travis's stage, solidifying where I'm meant to be and whom I'm meant to be with, even if he demands a step back. He doesn't get to dictate our relationship to me. I already had that type of relationship. I won't have it again, even if his intentions are what he thinks is best for me.

Somehow, in all that transpired yesterday, I forgot that I have a choice, a say in the matter like I once did. It isn't over until the fat lady sings, and this fat lady hasn't even stepped on stage yet.

After the initial shock subsides, I carefully move my design into the exhibition hall to join the other finalists. I spend some time evaluating their designs and craftsmanship. The competition is formidable, and winning seems unlikely, but being a finalist is already a victory. I snap multiple photos of my design from various angles, as the overhead lighting turns it into a vision of ethereal beauty, radiating both style and elegance.

With overflowing excitement, I quickly share pictures of my design with my parents and Aunt Molli, eagerly telling them about the entire experience. I also temper their expectations by conveying how the competition is tough and winning might be a long shot. I don't hear back from any, but then again, I don't want to get a back-and-forth started as I only have a few minutes before class begins.

In a burst of generosity and buoyed by my good spirits, I even sent a message to Lily. I let her know that I swung by the apartment earlier to grab a few essentials and casually mention that she's welcome to keep any flowers and gifts that have arrived for me. I add a few emojis to soften the message that she can throw away everything else, and when I get to feeling better, I'd like to go to dinner and talk things over.

She doesn't reply, and I don't expect one. Considering her late performance last night, it's probably too early in the morning. Something I'm curious to read about how everything is going with my understudy and the play, Travis's overly dramatic words echoing in my head. But the overriding need to safeguard my mental health prevails, and I don't.

As I'm about to text Gabe, I opt for a phone call instead. It barely rings twice before he answers.

"Isla, is everything alright?"

His immediate concern for my well-being is both alarming and reassuring. I quickly comfort him, eager to alleviate any worry.

"Yes, better than alright!"

I launch into what happened, happiness lining every word, not leaving a detail out. I describe the electrifying moment of moving my design into the exhibition hall, the awe-inspiring craftsmanship of my fellow finalists, and the surreal feeling of standing among such talented individuals. I will share the few details I know about the upcoming fashion show where the finalists will be awarded scholarship money and send him the pictures I took.

"Brilliant! That's absolutely smashing! I always knew you

were destined for great things. You're going to dazzle them all, no doubt about it."

His words, rich with encouragement and a distinctly British warmth, wrap around me like a cozy blanket. The conversation is about to shift when I confront him about him finishing my design.

"Thank you. I had to call and tell you first. However, imagine my surprise when I get here, and it's not in the same pieces I left it."

"Hmm, sounds like fashion fairies at work," he states with a ring of humor, deflecting responsibility for his actions. His playful remark does little to dampen my curiosity. I press on, seeking a clearer explanation as I lean against the exhibition hall wall.

"Gabe, seriously, how did it come together? I left it in fragments, and now it's perfect."

There's a pause, a moment where I can almost hear him weighing his words.

"Well, I may have had a bit of a hand in it. I couldn't stand seeing your talent not reach its full potential because of everything that happened."

His confession brings mixed emotions. Surprise, gratitude, a touch of annoyance for not asking, and an overwhelming sense of affection.

"You didn't have to do that. I wouldn't have made the competition deadline, but . . ."

Just saying that makes me upset. I wouldn't have made it because of the assault and Travis. Two things keep coming up between him and me, even after I firmly try to put them behind me and move on. His sigh rumbles through the phone, echoing what I already feel.

"You've worked too hard for this to be taken from you."

I frown, gazing down at my shoes, knowing he's right. I worked too hard to have it taken away. Too hard in high school to keep my grades up to get scholarships. Worked too hard at Papa's pet store to make my college applications show I'm well rounded. Far too hard with my audition pieces to get into Parson, to see it all wiped away in one tragic night.

"But how?"

I shake my head, trying to puzzle together the timeline around taking care of me.

"I stayed as late as possible after you left, causing me to nearly miss that phenomenal opening number with the tap shoes. I still love that part and the cigar, which, as a doctor, I'm not enthused you know how to smoke it so well, but after hearing your story, I understand."

His casual chastising about smoking is endearing, even if I don't, though I no longer need that coping mechanism.

"In just one night, you finished it?"

My astonishment is evident as I glance at the time on the clock across the hall and see I need to get to class.

"Well, I'm not exactly proud of this, but I borrowed your badge from your backpack to let myself back in. I worked while you napped, somewhat frantically, I'll admit. I was worried you might wake up needing me, but thankfully, you were still fast asleep when I returned."

Despite the unconventional means, his actions were driven by a heartfelt desire to see me succeed, another gesture of his relentless support.

"I thought you had just come from Travis's with my belongings."

"I had taken a detour, sort to speak."

His admission carries a hint of mischief while clearing up my confusion regarding the timeline.

"And Isla, you had it all there. I just finished a few stitches, nothing you couldn't have worked on if Saturday night hadn't turned out the way it did."

Moved by his efforts and wanting to express my gratitude, I

eagerly suggest, "How about I take you out to dinner tonight? A small celebration for what you've done."

There's a brief pause on his end, followed by an awkward throat clearing.

"That sounds lovely, Isla, but I've got that gala tonight, remember?" His reminder brings a rush of memories back. Amidst the whirlwind of recent events, the gala had completely slipped my mind.

"Oh, right, the gala. I was supposed to go with you," I say, a tinge of disappointment in my voice quickly replaced by understanding. "I'm sorry. I completely forgot with everything going on. Why didn't you remind me?"

"*Love*. I can't ask you to attend, especially after everything that has transpired. However, we could have dinner another night. Perhaps we can celebrate your nomination this weekend."

"Okay, I'm sorry about the gala. But this weekend would work. It'll be my treat, a small token of my appreciation."

He chuckles, and I'm not quite sure why.

"As if I'd ever let you pay, love. Anyway, I must dash. I'll see you at home tonight."

The line drops before I can say goodbye.

Home

He's said it before, but after seeing my own home destroyed by a tacky, makeshift display of affection worthy of Valentine's Day night, I read more into it. Happiness has me floating out of the hall and onto class, with the lingering victory of my beautiful design consuming my thoughts.

The blissful haze remains throughout lunch, and my demanding classes gradually give way to exhaustion. My body's pain is replaced with an achy stiffness, and I've been more active than I was in the last several days of resting and recuperating.

The thought of nothing standing between me and a long,

soothing bubble bath at Gabe's brings a small smile to my face. With this comforting prospect in mind, I hurriedly pack the last of my books into my backpack and sling it over my shoulder.

As I step out into the fading sunlight, I pause momentarily, taking a few deep, cleansing breaths to dispel the fatigue that stubbornly clings to my body. With a slight shake of my head, I start my walk toward the subway, eager for the sanctuary of home.

It changes in a flash, the start of a nightmare, when Travis materializes before me, his presence as shocking as it is sudden. There's no time to react, no space to retreat, as he embraces me. His hands firmly grasp my arms, rooting me to the spot as his grip conveys ownership rather than affection.

"Little one, I've been out of my mind with worry. You haven't returned my calls or texts."

His voice feigning concern that belies the underlying control. Panic surges within me, thick and suffocating, as his words wrap around me like chains. My heart races, pounding against my ribcage as my mind races with possible escape plans. I glance desperately around, my eyes flitting across the faces of passersby, who remain blissfully unaware of the drama unfolding in their midst.

Each second stretches into an eternity, my brain turning over and dismissing different plans at lightning speed. The realization that I am alone, trapped in this interaction with no help from others, sends a shiver down my spine. The hope that someone might notice might intervene dwindles with each passing moment, leaving me to navigate this terrifying encounter alone with my abuser.

"It's okay, though. You've had your few days alone, and now it's time you come back home. There will be no punishments this time."

There's an eerily calmness to him. My fingers clench around the straps of my backpack, anchoring myself as the panic deepens. My breathing becomes difficult. Each inhalation is more labored than the last. His words reveal a delusion so profound it terrifies me.

The idea that my escape from his violence was nothing more than a whimsical outburst in his eyes is a horrifying glimpse into his twisted mindset. His casual mention of "no punishments," as if he's granting me some twisted form of clemency, not only belittles the gravity of his past actions but also unveils the depth of his delusion for which he remains blameless.

This isn't just manipulation. It's his distorted perception of forgiveness. His belief that he can dictate the terms of our relationship, offering absolution as if he's the aggrieved party, is a chilling reminder of the danger he poses. It's a moment that crystallizes the reality of my situation. The man before me is not just an abuser but a deeply disturbed individual who sees his actions as justifiable, even righteous. The road to freedom, I realize, is not just about physical distance but about extricating myself from the web of his delusions.

"Travis," I begin slowly, my voice measured, recalling how I'd carefully address Rick in his drunken, volatile state, aware that any misstep could provoke him. "You hit me and kept hitting me. Intended to rape me."

Being so blitzed that night, I wonder if he remembers the events clearly—Rick never did, and perhaps the same is true with Travis. I attempt to wrench my arms from him, his grip tightening as I step closer.

"You stole my show. Right out from under me."

His voice grows louder, dripping with a self-righteousness that has me trembling. Locked in his vice grip, the pressure is unyielding, a deliberate infliction of pain that signals his desire to dominate and control is unyielding. Agony sears through my arms, a relentless throb that cascades down to my fingertips, stopping the flow of blood and ushering in a relentless onslaught of pins and needles.

"Travis, you're hurting me."

Unfazed by the evident agony etched across my face, his eyes take on a deeper, more sinister shade, reflecting a chilling absence of empathy. The flicker of pleasure that lights up his gaze is haunting, a window to the darkness that lurks beneath the surface. It's as though my pain, the physical manifestation of his control, fuels a twisted gratification within him and a grotesque affirmation of his power and dominance.

"I gave you everything, and that's how you repay me? By taking away what I've worked so hard for?"

He shakes me with a force that renders me powerless, my body flailing helplessly in the tempest of his rage. His justifications spiral into a narrative where he's the victim, a skewed version of events that paints his actions as a response to a betrayal he perceives as monumental.

"You don't understand the pressure I'm under. Everything I did was for us, for our future. Your leaving is not just a betrayal. It's sabotage. But all will be forgiven at home."

The way he frames his aggression as if it were a deserved consequence of my actions reveals a deep-seated belief in his narrative. In his mind, he's not an abuser but a martyr, wronged by the world and now by me. His words are not just a defense but a glimpse into the alarming way he justifies his violence as necessary measures to reclaim what he believes to be rightfully his.

"You gave me a black eye. I can barely hide it with make-up and look at my lip . . . you're justifying yourself by hitting me. I sabotaged you, so you think that it's okay to beat up on me. Now you want me to come home for what? More abuse? So you can finish what you started?"

An icy veil of hatred descends over his features, chilling in intensity, and instantly, my body floods with fear. My stomach knots in dread while the pins and needles of my numb arms intensifies. The transformation is startling as if a shadow has passed over him, turning his expression into something recognizable from my past. From Dale and that last time he assaulted me before I finally confided in a teacher at school about what I was enduring.

"You're not seeing the big picture here. It's about more than just us. It's about what we can be together. But you're too caught up in the now, in your pain, to see that."

Travis steps closer, his face inches from mine while his voice softens in a manipulative mimicry of tenderness. The stark metamorphosis from person to predator evokes a deep-seated panic, leaving me breathless as if the air has been siphoned from around me.

"I know I went too far, little one, but stress does funny things to people. You'll see when you come back with me. We'll put this behind us, and it will be good again."

His plea, laden with false promises and conditional forgiveness, is something I've heard many times before, with my mom believing her boyfriends. The cycle of charm and harm is a living testament to my upbringing. The suggestion that my return could somehow erase the trauma of his abuse is both ludicrous and horrifying. It's clear he views reconciliation as a return to the status quo, where his behavior is unchecked, and my suffering is silenced.

"You need help, Travis, help that I can't give," I find myself saying, words bolstered by a deep-seated resolve I wish my mom had. "What happened between us . . . It can't be undone. You need to take responsibility for your actions, not just for me but for yourself."

In desperation, I lash out against his unyielding hold, channeling every bit of fear and anger into the action. Adrenaline courses through me, catapulting the heel of my shoe onto the top of his foot with as much force as I can muster. A cry of pain escapes him, piercing the air like a sharp note, and for an instant, his grasp weakens. The blood barely has a chance to flow into my arms when he recovers. His expression twists in a grimace of fury and agony, dragging me across the sidewalk to his awaiting car.

As the chilling realization dawns on me that he intends to abduct me, a desperate cry for help tears through the silence that shrouds my fear, raw and piercing. Yet, it dissipates, swallowed by the bustling indifference of the city streets.

"I don't need help. I need you."

Defiance burns in his eyes as he spits the words, each syllable sharp and biting. My body trembles with overwhelming panic, my heart pounding wildly in my chest, and a sloshing sound overtaking my brain. I try to hold back the onslaught of tears, but they burst forth in hot streams down my face, blinding me as we inch closer to the edge of the curb.

"Get in the fucking car, Isla, or I'll release your nudes."

His voice turns into a sinister snarl, hauling me in front of him as a few curious onlookers stop. The physical struggle becomes an emotional turmoil, each step a battle against despair. My breath comes in short, sharp gasps. The naked pictures he took the night of the play after he styled my hair and make-up.

The vicious threat sends silent screams across my mind. In this moment of intense vulnerability, the fight becomes not just for physical freedom but for the preservation of my life and spirit, pushed to the brink by the harrowing ordeal at the thought of ruining me, my family, and everything I'm rebuilding.

"You can't. . . please," I beg through the haze of tears that relentlessly carve paths down my cheeks, a fragment of his face emerges, twisted into a victorious sneer that amplifies my fear.

"I can and will if you don't get in the car."

He propels me with brute force the remaining distance to

his car, my ribs colliding against the vehicle's side with a thud that echoes through my body, stealing the breath from my lungs. In the same motion, he wrenches the passenger door open, the metallic screech of hinges barely registering over the pounding of my heart.

Seconds.

I have mere seconds before I am forcibly removed, ripped away from freedom, and locked up in a luxury prison on the Upper East Side. The threat of the penthouse looms over me like a foreboding fortress, a symbol of the abuse and torment that awaits me within its opulent walls. My mind races with fear and desperation as I am dragged towards my fate, helpless and alone. The horrifying realization paralyzes me, turning my bones to stone—I'm back on that stoop at Mom's house, watching my abuser triumph over me.

His face twists into the smirk of Dale, the haunting day where the gray sky dripped of black crows, an ominous sign. If I get into his car, I'll enter the house of horrors I once escaped. Travis and Dale, their faces dueling between present and past, their intentions mirroring one another.

"Get in the fucking car, Isla!"

His yell runs right through me, attempting to cut me down, chop me up, and send me back to the depths of hell. My breathing becomes erratic, shallow gasps that struggle against the impending doom. The panic of being utterly trapped, ensnared by the machinations of those who claim to want me, is overwhelming. A deep, soul-wrenching sob claws its way up my throat as his hands latch onto my body once more, yanking me off the door as my screams pierce loudly, his wincing evidence of it.

Fight or flight.

Time slows, stretching the second into eternity, my actions suspended in the air. My head bows, and my shoulders hunch as I coil into myself, morphing into an unyielding mass of dead weight. The contracting of my body inward draws him closer, his frame bending over mine to retrieve me from the ground toward which I'm slipping, unwittingly positioning his jaw above the hard crown of my head.

With every fiber of my being flooded with adrenaline, I explode with energy and snap upright. The crown of my head collides with his jaw in a brutal upward thrust, the impact sending a jarring pain through my skull but wreaking havoc on him.

The sound of his jaw snapping is a grotesque symphony to my ears, bone against bone, my skull's unwavering density against the fragile hinges of his jaw that relent under the force. His cry of agony is a vile sound, but in this moment, it's the sound of survival, of refusing to be pulled back into the hell from which I've fought so hard to emerge.

The momentary lapse of his grip, cupping his broken jaw, and the velocity at which I struck sends me reeling backward. The hard collision of my backpack hitting the pavement redistributes the impact into my back, sending shooting pain into my lower extremities. I scream and writhe on the ground. With little time to act, his venomous face is hurtling toward me, distorted with pain and revenge and spewing incoherent threats. Unable to get to my feet, I draw my legs up to my chest, ready to strike back with every ounce of strength left. Travis, intimidating and overbearing, positions himself directly in my path, his stature imposing as he's willing to destroy me here in the streets.

"If you ... if you release those pictures, I-I'll release mine ... and file charges." My voice trembles, laced with fear yet clinging to the hope that reason might prevail. My hands are out in front of me, ready to fend off any blows he's eager to reign down on me. " You'll never be free."

I raise my fists, fingers curled tightly into a fist. My knuckles are white from gripping so hard. His muscles tense as he shifts his weight and readies for an attack. I tighten my core and prepare to dodge or block any blows that come my way.

Undeterred by my logic, he surges forward with ferocity. Transformed beyond recognition from the man I once liked, his eyes have become dark, soulless pits, hovering above a snarl of seething teeth. Instinct overtakes my body. With honed precision, I launch a swift kick to his abdomen, followed by a merciless strike to his groin. His response is immediate and guttural, a primal scream that tears through the air as he doubles over in agony. His hand reaches out in a futile attempt to brace his fall, scraping against the rough texture of the sidewalk, leaving a streak of blood in its wake.

Suddenly, a bystander is beside me, his hand under my arm and pulling me up. His voice is loud and urgent, shouting for someone to call the police. It's a turn of events Travis hadn't anticipated, his eyes shedding the blinding rage to register the reality of our confrontation unfolding on a busy street for all to witness. I quickly pull my arm free from the Good Samaritan, stepping closer to Travis. My voice is a low hiss, meant for his ears alone, laced with a promise of my own.

"Never try to contact me again. Understand? I won't hesitate to get a restraining order and press charges if you dare." I take a step away from him, then add to my threat. "If those photos ever see the light of day, I'll ruin you by making it the biggest fucking media circus you've ever seen."

To solidify my point, I let loose a torrent of sobs, pointing accusingly at him as I unleash a piercing scream. My tears etch new paths over the remnants of past anguish, my display escalating into a full-blown public drama. Onlookers begin to converge, drawn by the commotion. With my head buried in my hands, I feign inconsolable despair, weaving through the crowd as I make my way toward the safety of the school. Some students exit the building, possibly drawn to the commotion outside or the faint sirens wailing against the tall buildings.

Behind the safety of the school's walls, I rush to the closest bathroom, my footsteps pounding against the tile floor as I shove through the door and into the nearest stall. Too urgent to be bothered closing it, I hunch over the porcelain toilet and surrender to the violent upheaval wracking my body. The sterile, echoing sound of the bathroom amplifies the guttural sounds of my distress.

The contents of my stomach eject in a forceful and relentless torrent from the terrifying encounter. My stomach coils tighter and tighter, expanding more and more until the acidic bile burns my throat, the taste metallic on my tongue.

My body trembles uncontrollably, not just from the physical revulsion but from the cascade of emotions flooding out of me. Overwhelming relief that I managed to get away. Disgust and rage at how he sabotaged me and a haunting vulnerability reminiscent of both abusive lifetimes I've worked tirelessly to put past me.

Tears mingle with the sweat on my face, streaking down to blend with the bitter remnants on my lips. Grabbing handfuls of toilet paper, I wipe my face while visions flash behind me. His venomous face, his soulless eyes, the painful grip I couldn't escape, the cold malice in his voice and his threatening stance promising more abuse.

I'm left gasping for breath between stomach spasms. Exhausted and shaking, I rid myself of the tissues in the toilet and flush away the evidence of my ordeal. The aftermath leaves me weak, huddled beside the toilet, a shivering mass of raw nerves and battered emotions. Alone in this sterile bathroom, surrounded by cold tiles, I dig in my backpack for my phone, calling the one person I need the most.

"Help me."

31

The bathroom door bursts open, a sudden explosion as it collides with the wall. The suddenness startles me, sending a jolt of adrenaline coursing through my veins, praying it's my angel and not my devil. His urgent footsteps clack sharply against the tiled floor, the gleam of black dress shoes visible beyond the barrier of the partially open bathroom stall. As my breath catches in my throat, I cling to the fragile thread of anticipation, willing him closer with every beat of my frantic heart.

"Isla!"

His urgent voice slices through the air, his captivating accent never sounding more enchanting. He pushes open the door, his gaze locking onto mine with a cautiously relieved expression in his impeccably tailored tuxedo. He's elegant, the perfectly fitted jacket accentuating his broad shoulders while the crisp white shirt beneath adds a touch of refinement. The black bow tie, expertly knotted, sits neatly against his collar while his trousers tapper flawlessly to those gleaming shoes. Once more, tears fill my eyes as I gaze upon the breathtaking sight of Gabriel.

"Oh, love. Come here," he murmurs softly, his arms opening to receive me.

With swift agility, he moves, his athletic prowess evident as he effortlessly squats to lift me, catching me as I leap into his waiting arms. The scent of his familiar cologne swirls around me. A comfort as I wind my arms around his neck and the tears flow freely down my cheeks. Finding solace in his comforting presence, he carries me out of the restroom and down the hall to the quiet sanctuary of the empty lab.

"I got you." His reassurance rumbles into me, unwilling to let go as he settles onto a stool, carefully balancing me on his lap. "It's alright. I'm here."

As he speaks, I can't help but feel a dam burst and everything that's transpired with Travis pouring out of me. The betrayal of who I thought he was compared to the monster he turned into twice mirrors Dale's vicious intention from all those years ago.

His deceit, knowing what he was, love bombing me into thinking it was all true and faking the start of a future dream life in New York high society. My rage, at myself for falling victim once again to the cycle of abuse and trauma I overcame twice and at him for precipitating it. My disdain for the audacity of playing the victim incensed him for acting as the martyr and gaslighting me into thinking I was at fault.

I cling to Gabe, my rock amidst the swirling storm of emotions. My arms wind tighter around his neck, seeking refuge in the warmth of his solid chest as he rocks us gently back and forth. His murmurs of assurance are a soothing melody in my ears, reminding me that I'm safe.

The relief of knowing he's here, protective and comforting, the fear that had just moments ago gripped me, and the overwhelming adoration I have for him all merge into a single, intense feeling—gratitude.

"Gabriel, thank you."

My arms loosen slightly as his rocking ceases. His hand, large and comforting, remains at the back of my neck, his fingers delicately intertwining with my hair, holding me tightly as if he craves this closeness as much as I do. I focus on the steady rhythm of his pulse beneath my cheek, wondering if he shared in my fears, albeit for different reasons.

"I'm... sorry I scared you."

His arms tighten around me in response, and his breath brushes against my hair as he presses a lingering kiss to my head.

"I was panicked, yes. The thought of you hurt again ..."

He doesn't finish, releasing a shuddering breath. His body acts as a protective shield from the physical altercation I've just been through. I don't know how Dani does it. I never want to experience that again. Not ever.

"But you're safe now, and that's all that matters."

We sit in that quiet lab, wrapped in each other's warm embrace, while the world outside deals with Travis and the aftermath of my disappearance. Inside, Gabe's dealing with my aftermath, and that's enough to worry about right now.

I still need to tell my parents. It was a dreadful thought and something I was prepared to do later this week, but with this happening today, adding more fuel to that fire, I just want to hide away and not deal with any of it. I want to revert to my simple, boring life where I only have to worry about Anna, school, and homework. Possibly Gabe, unless we're still on this step-back thing, he thinks is the right thing to do.

The altercation today only solidified my shifting feelings and the realization that I didn't feel love for Travis. It was lust and intoxication. A fly in the spider's web, drawn to the glistening silk strands, wanting a closer view of the majestic beauty, only to be ensnared in the fateful strings and eaten alive by the predator.

That's what Travis is. What all abusers are—predators.

They prey on the loneliness of a single mom wanting support and means to provide for her and her child. They prey on the innocence of a hopeful child wanting the love her father walked away from. They prey on the destitution of a desperate minor needing food and shelter. They prey on a naïve coming-of-age woman seeking to make a name for herself and escape the past where she wasn't worthy of anyone or anything.

The clarity is crystal clear. The fog of longing and yearning for what I've always wanted greatly deserves lifting to see reality for how it is. Despite the love and support of my large family, there remains an undeniable void—a fundamental need for someone to cherish and be cherished by, romantically and physically.

As Gabe moves beneath me, his hands find my waist, pulling me gently from my introspection and signaling the end of our shared moment.

"Isla?"

I loosen my arms, sliding my hands to rest on his shoulders, when I lean back to gaze upon his handsome face.

"Yes?"

"Can I ask what happened exactly? There are fresh bruises on your arms."

My gaze follows his, and I see the reddening of my fair skin as I look at both of my upper arms.

"Yeah."

I move to get off his lap, the urgent need for closeness and being held having passed, but his hand cups my knee, indicating he'd like me to remain. I can't sit, though. I need to move around as the anxiety begins creeping into my veins and the thought of recanting what happened.

"I need to stand, I . . ."

I shake out my arms, the pins and needles feeling from Travis's grip returning in phantom pain as I take Gabe through everything that happened. As I stand, I pace the small confines of the lab, each step an effort to ground myself. Gabe watches me with concern and quiet anger, the latter not directed at me but at the situation that caused me harm. I take a deep breath, steeling myself to vocalize the fear I felt and the fright of seeing him turn into a monster.

"Travis," I begin, my voice stronger than I feel. "He found me outside of school."

Gabe's jaw clenches at the mention of Travis's name, and his hands roll into fists on his muscular thighs.

"He came out of nowhere, grabbed me, saying I had my space, but I needed to come home, accusing me of ruining everything. His grip was tight," I pause, rubbing my arms as if to soothe the memory of his hold. "And when I tried to pull away, he . . . he got more aggressive."

The words tumble out, tears welling that I try to keep at bay.

"He slammed me against his car, demanding I get in it."

I tremble as I pace. Gabe's on his feet, closing the distance in two swift strides, his hand caressing down my arm in solidarity to comfort me.

"I don't know . . . what happened exactly, but it was like the car door opening triggered me somehow. Taking me back to when the police opened Dale's door, letting that fucker back out. In my mind, it was . . . it was like sitting on that porch again, watching the officers tell him to stay out of trouble and drive away, leaving him with us. Travis's face somehow became Dale's, and I knew . . . fight or flight."

His fingers intertwine with mine, comforting and supportive at the same time.

"I'm so sorry, Isla. You never should have gone through that a second time. I thought my warning was threat enough."

The guilt is not his to own. It belongs to another who will never take responsibility for his actions, evidenced by his skewed reality.

"No, Gabe." I shake my head emphatically that he's not at fault, and I finally realize neither am I. "You've been amazing, saving me that night, risking your career and livelihood for me, and now this? You've been a very dear friend."

His frown is instant as he untangles his fingers from mine to adjust his collar with sudden discomfort. As best as I try not to read into it, I can't help wondering if it's the last word I said that conveys what we are and what he wants us to be.

"He has pictures of me."

Having forgotten about them, I must let Gabe know, as I am unwilling to keep anything from him at this point. I need an ally in my corner, not my Uncle Alex, who is several states away.

"Nudes, artistically done, I guess, and a painting. He threatened to release them somewhere in the middle of the attack. I threatened him back, releasing the abuse pictures, filing charges, and everything I've debated about this week."

The revelation of the naked pictures causes his eyes to bore into mine. His jaw clenches, and he puts his hand on his hips, appearing broader and more intimidating, as if he's holding himself back from attacking Travis.

"Isla—"

"What's done is done. I can't take that back. But I have leverage, Gabe. My evidence is far more damning to him than a few naked pictures of a one-hit wonder, off-Broadway actress."

He takes a deep breath, trying to compose himself. His silence speaks volumes as he processes the gravity of the situation. I can see the wheels turning behind his eyes, the gears churning through all the possibilities.

"I want to murder him."

His accent is thick, the darkness of his voice unrecognizable.

"I understand. But I won't lose you to him. I won't lose me either. I know you think he's not someone to be underestimated, and I agree. I'm making copies of everything and putting them in a safe place in case this happens again."

I walk to him this time, resting my hand on his chest as I gaze up at him.

"But when I threatened him before escaping, I saw real fear in his eyes. He'd lose everything—what he'd built, future projects, his reputation, money, affluence, and maybe even his home on Fifth Avenue. What would I lose? Nothing, and I believe that to be the final straw he finally realized."

Gabe's face softens, his expression lessening from furious to contemplative. He gazes at me, his eyes searching for the truth in what I've said. A small smile tugs at the corner of his lips, acknowledging the reality of the situation.

"You're right," he murmurs, his words vibrating into my hand. "This isn't about him or me. It's about what's best for you. I'm proud of you. You were courageous, standing up to him and fighting him off. I wish I were here to do it for you."

I lean into him, my hand still resting on his chest.

"I appreciate that, but I needed to handle this myself. I didn't know it at the moment, and as terrifying as it was, I think I needed to slay this demon myself—a sacrifice for the one that got away."

"I understand. Sometimes, conquering our demons alone is necessary for healing and closure."

Gabe nods understandingly, his eyes reflecting pride and something else I'm too scared to label. He gently wraps his arm around me, guiding me toward the door.

"What puzzles me is how he knew you were here. Today of all days. You hadn't spoken to Lily, had you?"

I stop, causing him to stop. The thought never occurred to me, but he's right. How did Travis know I returned to school today? I doubt he's sat in front of it every day this week, waiting for a chance. In fact, I only texted Lily about the flowers and stuff, not the pictures I took of my designs and becoming a finalist. I'll leave that for when we're having dinner.

"I don't know."

I stare up at Gabe, completely bewildered.

"No, I texted her to have the flowers, but you know how exhausted I was last night. I went straight to bed when we got home."

His eyebrows raise, questioning and confused.

"It's troubling."

Silence falls between us as we continue walking toward the exit when I realize I have left my backpack in the bathroom. He offers to get it for me, muttering something about not wanting me to return to the traumatic place where he found me in distress. It's a thoughtful gesture, even though it's just the ordinary school bathroom I frequent. I stand in the hallway, studying my new bruises, when Gabe approaches me.

"What is this?"

The constellation necklace Travis gave me is splayed across his hand, the diamonds capturing the school lightning and sending dazzling prisms over the ceiling. I'm stunned into silence as I walk toward him and slowly remove the delicate token of Travis's affection from his palm. The necklace is clasped, perfectly stunning as the first time he gave it to me after he made me fly in the playroom. I lick my lips, my heart thundering as I stare at it.

"Where did this come from?"

Trepidation coats my words as if I'm somehow in trouble for having this. My gaze shifts to the floor, trying to recall how it would be here in Gabe's hand when the last time I saw it was before my punishment or maybe after. I'm not even sure if it was in the nude pictures he took. I can't remember.

"It fell out of your backpack. When I grabbed the handle, it slipped from the pocket on the side."

The backpack dangling from Gabe's hand twists to reveal a

pocket I never used. It's too small to hold anything, but the zipper is ajar with dirt scraps from the concrete where I fell. I study the backpack pocket, my thoughts whirling.

"Isla, what am I missing here? You look very upset."

His voice trembles with worry as he tosses the backpack over his shoulder and removes the necklace from my shaking fingers.

"What does this mean?"

I take a deep breath and close my eyes, trying to push away the memories that flood my mind. I remember the day he gave me the necklace, how his eyes sparkled with joy as I put it on for the first time. But now, seeing it feels like a heavy weight I can't get rid of fast enough.

"Travis gave this to me."

I open my eyes, the concern turning into a flash of hurt on Gabe's face.

"I wasn't keeping it. I don't even know how it got in my backpack." The memories flood back to me now. "He took it off the night of the play. It clashed with my gold gown."

Gabe's been amazing. He's heard all the details of my relationship, stood as my sentinel in these troubled times, and absorbed his feelings to let mine fly free. It's coming at a cost, and I watch the various emotions pass over his face.

"I'm so sorry, Gabe. I had no idea it was in there."

"You wore it Saturday."

His voice is icy cold and detached, making my stomach tighten with dread. His fingers rub the design while he studies it.

"You always wore it."

The hurt in his last sentence propels me closer, reaching out to brush away the glint of diamonds as an invisible chasm forms between us. Desperately, I try to bridge the growing divide, longing to mend what threatens to unravel our bond.

"I'm sorry."

Light as air, but the meaning is a serious plea for understanding. Gabe's expression softens slightly as he meets my gaze, his eyes reflecting his pain.

"Isla," he says quietly, his voice tinged with sadness. "It's not my place to feel this way, but seeing you wear something he gave you. It's difficult."

I swallow hard, his pain settling heavily in my chest, causing it to ache and my stomach to clench harder.

"I understand," I murmur, gently touching his arm. "I promise I'll get rid of it."

"Hold on."

Gabe raises the necklace to examine the back of it closer, then moves down the hall to stand directly under the recessed light. His nimble fingers work the delicate gold backing, separating the clasp holding the largest stone in place to reveal a tiny, nearly invisible black dot.

"What is that?"

As he examines it more, his features contort with a sudden realization.

"Bloody hell."

His voice strains with disbelief. His eyes widen with horror, his gaze fixed on the tiny black dot he's digging out of the back of the necklace. In a sudden movement, he squats, placing it on the ground and smashing it with the heel of his dress shoe. It smashes into dust, the black powder barely noticeable given its tiny size.

"Gabe? What was that?" I repeat, my pulse rising as he jostles the necklace in his hand, looking through the other stones, the biggest one, now loose and unbracketed in his palm.

"It's a GPS tracker," he bites out, the bitterness of his words harsh against the disgust on his face when he levels his gaze with mine. "He's been tracking your whereabouts. That's how he knew you were here."

I gasp, my hand covering my mouth as the realization sets

in. Shock washes over me as I take in his words, my mind reeling with the implications of what he's just discovered. Travis intentionally kept tabs on me all the time. What I mistook for a deeply caring gesture and a lavish gift was disguised as another form of control, an expensive collar with an invisible digital leash tethering me to him.

I step back and hold myself, the hallway growing cold, knowing how far he had gone to ensure I was his. His to control, and his to manipulate. He only took it off me that night, knowing I'd be with him, and there was no need to wear it. And earlier that day, when he "punished me," he demanded to know where I was when he knew all along and manipulated me to get his way. The blowjob, rough and violent, sent me reeling into the rape spiral of Rick and the motel.

Tears spring from the deepest corners of my being at how maniacal and evil he was under the veil of adoration and niceties. It is too abhorrent to comprehend. I turn away, ignoring Gabe calling after me as I walk down the hall, walking away from the costly necklace no more worthy than a dog collar on a wandering pet.

My shoulders shake as I sob quietly into my hands, walking past the lab to who knows where in the safety of the empty school halls. As I pass classroom doors, I'm overwhelmed by the level of deceit. How could I have been so wrong about Travis? The man who promised me the world was nothing more than a vile puppet master, and I was the puppet. He was pulling the strings from behind the scenes as I danced for his pleasure.

Seeking solace, I find myself drawn to the darkened exhibition hall, its empty expanse reflecting the void in my heart. Here, amidst the silence and shadows, I confront the harsh truth of how I could have allowed myself to be so thoroughly deceived after everything I've been through.

"Isla?"

Gabe's voice sounds in the dark, and I move toward the door to click on the lights, causing me to blink against the intrusion. His eyes drift to my creation, the perfect fall of the crepe fabric perpetually flowing, catching, and reflecting the light above it. A flicker of admiration crosses his handsome face, acknowledging the impeccable craftsmanship before his gaze shifts back to mine, carrying a silent compliment that needs no words.

"I can't believe this," I whisper, my voice a rasp as more tears fall. He envelopes me immediately, the strap of my backpack cutting into his shoulder rough against my face as he buries me within him.

"It's extremely unsettling." He kisses the top of my head as I clutch his back, needing his shield of protection even more. "I realized I destroyed more evidence in my fury. Please forgive me."

"I don't care."

In that moment, wrapped in Gabe's embrace within the silent witness of the exhibit hall, everything else fades into the background. The chaos, the fear, and the pain that has marked my life find a quiet corner to rest, even if just for a moment. Gabe's strength and protection envelop me, a reminder that amidst the turmoil, there's a beacon of hope and unwavering support.

His protectiveness isn't just a physical shield—it's emotional, too. It seeps into the cracks of my broken heart, offering repair with the promise of steadfastness and care. Gabriel, my angel in human form, embodies the love and value I've yearned for, the affirmation that despite the scars of my past, I deserve love and am capable of giving it in return.

The idea of stepping back, of exploring the world without him, seems inconsequential now. With its harsh lessons, life has left its marks on me, stripping away the innocence I once held close. But here, in his arms, I find a reason to believe in something more, in a future where the burdens of those lessons don't have to be carried alone.

The concept of needing to experience more of the world or life as a pretext for growth feels hollow compared to what I've already experienced. I'm on my fourth lifetime and thoroughly exhausted by life. It's not about the quantity of experiences but the quality of them, the ability to face life's darkest moments, which I have and still find light in the presence of someone who stands by me, who sees beyond the damage to the worth that remains.

"I don't care about taking a step back," I whisper against the strength of his chest, the vibrations of his heartbeat steady against my cheek before I stir in his arms. "I know what you said about someday we can come together or after I live life, but I don't care about that, Gabe. I'm the oldest eighteen-year-old I know. The life experiences that you say I should get more of, my God, I've had three lifetimes worth. How much more do I need to be with you?"

Gabe's initial surprise at my words gives way to a deep, thoughtful silence. His embrace tightens around me as if to physically underscore his presence.

After a moment, he gently tilts my chin up, encouraging me to meet his gaze. In his eyes, there's an unmistakable depth of emotion—a mixture of admiration, concern, and something more profound, something that resonates with the sincerity of my feelings.

"Isla, I've always admired your strength and outlook on life. You're right. You've lived through more than most people twice your age, certainly more than me. It's not about the number of years in your life, but the life in those years—and you've had more than your fair share of pain, heartache, and devastation."

"Then what is it? What more do you want me to do?"

"When I talked about living life and experiencing more, it wasn't because I doubted your maturity or capacity to do it." He pauses, searching my eyes, ensuring I understand the gravity of his words. "It was out of a desire to protect you, give you space to heal, to find yourself and what you desire. What is owed to you amidst the chaos that has always been thrust upon you."

His hand brushes a strand of hair away from my face, a tender gesture that speaks volumes.

"But standing here with you now, seeing your resilience, hearing in your words the magnitude of your experiences through your voice—I realize that life isn't about waiting for the storm to pass. It's about learning to dance in the rain together. You don't need more experiences to be 'ready' for anything, especially not for me."

His words wash over me, a balm to the years of turmoil and struggle.

"If you're willing to take a chance on me, after everything you've been through, to face whatever comes next together, then I'm here as I have always been. I'm not going anywhere. I want us to build a future where we carry each other's burdens, celebrate each other's joys, and grow together—not apart."

"Definitely together, Gabe."

My words fail to capture the enormity of my feelings, so I let the silence speak as I lean close. The warmth of his breath mingles with mine, an unspoken agreement passing between us. I close my eyes, letting the distance close, and press my lips to his. A gentle yet profound promise of the trust and future we're about to weave together. It's a soft touch, a whisper of lips, that carries the burden of all the trauma we've shared and everything amazing we've yet to discover in each other's arms.

Our lips meet with a gentle pressure, like two puzzle pieces finally fitting together. His soft lips are velvet against mine, his hand gently resting at the base of my neck, familiar and patient. As if allowing me the space to control the kiss, knowing everything I've been through. He groans, his lips parting in welcome invitation as our bodies press into each other. My fingers slip into his hair, pulling him closer to me while his hands hold me tightly.

The kiss is soft and pliable, learning each other in a new way, beyond friends and angels but as lovers and confidants. When my tongue dips into his mouth, seeking his, a dance of give and take ensues, a promise of an equal partnership despite his age outweighing mine and my life experiences outweighing his.

When the kiss comes to a delicate end, he's slow to release me off the balls of my feet. His face is soft and relaxed, and the adoration and care in his gaze are as clear as day.

"Brilliant," I chime in his usual British accent, to which he chuckles, the sound echoing across the hall. His hand moves from my waist to my cheek, cupping it as his thumb wipes away my drying tears.

"Isla, you're not the oldest eighteen-year-old. You're just you—unique, brave, and incredibly deserving of love. My love." His warm chocolate eyes brim with his spoken emotion, and my heart swells. "I've also been wanting to kiss you from the moment you questioned my sexuality in the bookstore."

I burst out in laughter, my echo replacing his from a moment ago. "Maybe you should have. It would have saved us from all this."

His lips touch mine once more, his kiss a promise, a celebration, and a vow before curving into a tender smile, mirroring the laughter and lightness that fills the space between us.

"Perhaps," he agrees, his voice a soft caress. "But you're stronger for it. Through the chaos and the calm, the mess and the magic, my love for you is as extraordinary as you are."

The End

BONUS SCENE #1

M y eyes travel to the wall clock for the umpteenth time as nervousness knots in my stomach. On one of the biggest nights of my life, Gabe is nowhere to be seen backstage as the show's commencement looms. An hour has passed since his text chimed that they were finished sparring and baring showers and getting ready, they'd be right over. Dani threatened an ass-kicking of her own if they were tardy, yet here I am, pacing the floor. The event's cocktail music is nearing the end, soon to give way to the DJ's selections tailored to our creations. The small hand of the clock ticking in sync with my rising heartbeat.

"Can you sit your ass down? You're making me nervous, and I'm already freaking out about strutting down that runway in your masterpiece," Lily snaps, fanning herself with her hands despite her raven hair swept in an elegant updo secured by trailing silver flowers matching the design of the bodysuit. Loose tendrils frame her face to soften her coal-crusted eyes, a homage to what I looked like the day Dani rescued me at the truck stop that fateful day.

Encountering Dani backstage before the event, her gaze

snapped to mine, brimming with a silent question of whether the makeup was some kind of prank. I quickly confirmed it was deliberate, reminding me how far I had come. She let out a huff, commenting I should have warned her before hugging the life out of me, an emotional overreaction on her part for a very memorable day in both our lives.

Lily and her instantly clicked, the former in awe of Dani's brisk and unfiltered personality when she breezed past the teacher's strict backstage restrictions of no visitors. She looked stunning, draped in a gown I had crafted on short notice and shipped to her. The sleek lines of the black poly crepe de chine, with its elegant neckline and translucent long sleeves, hug her generous assets gracefully. Her blonde tresses cascade freely, complementing the ensemble, which was punctuated by the dazzling sparkle of her "damn gumball-sized ring that prevents her from doing any real work" on her ring finger as the only accessory.

"He promised to be here, Lil."

I stop pacing long enough to twist a strand of her hair, falling into her face when she slaps my hand.

"And stop messing with my hair for the umpteenth time. He'll be here."

Her gaze sweeps the room. Her frown directed at my teacher—the one who hates me and scolded Lily earlier for casually sipping a soda, a banned substance in the dressing room containing the array of "masterpieces."

"Besides, they still have to introduce the teachers and faculty here, so that's another wasted fifteen minutes. Is it hot in here, or is it just me?"

She returns to fanning herself before crossing the room to bump another model away from the fan to have it exclusively. The backstage area, crowded with hairstylists, makeup artists, designers, and models crammed into a single space, is growing uncomfortably warm.

I smile, grateful we reconciled after everything that happened with Travis. I never did tell her the truth, which remained sealed between four people at the time. She took my word for it when I assured her Travis was no longer fixated on me, a claim she independently verified upon seeing him publicly parade a new companion shortly after my supposed bout of food poisoning.

We navigated the aftermath of hashing out what her friends had voiced about me, her inaction in my defense, and her remorse over the situation. I shared my apologies for neglecting her and our friendship during my fleeting and tumultuous affair with him, recognizing that my involvement had adverse effects on us both.

In a surprising gesture that mended any remaining tensions, Lily crafted a scrapbook filled with press clippings, photographs, and memorabilia centered on my singular night on stage. Each page chronicled the moments that had briefly catapulted me into the limelight.

Lily told me that he still receives inquiries about my return to the stage, which he deflects by praising me as a special talent that outgrew his platform. He attributes my departure to pursuing grander endeavors—all ostensibly thanks to his "discovering me ." He publicly frames his play as an endeavor to unearth and showcase raw talent, positioning himself as the magnanimous discoverer of artists like me, Isla Frank, whose social media presence has surged in the aftermath.

This narrative, while skewed and a "brilliant sweeping under the rug" per Gabe, unwittingly contributed to my complex feelings toward him and my emerging career. His spin-doctoring a manipulated narrative supporting my genuine talent was surprising and confusing. Lily's scrapbook serves as a heartfelt anchor to the reality of those whirlwind days that I'm thankful to leave behind collecting dust as her book does at the top of my closet.

"There she is!"

Papa's exuberant voice cuts through the bustling room. I turn towards the sound, seeing him pointing in my direction. He then pauses to admire the models and the creations with appreciative "oohs" and "ahs" as he navigates through the crowd. Dad trails behind him, both taking in the chaos around them to make this show happen.

"Is everything okay? Why are you back here?" I question, puzzled since I had already ushered them to their seats during the pre-show cocktail hour.

Eager to arrive early, they had embarked on a photo-taking spree, capturing more shots than a wedding photographer - of us, themselves, and Lily donning my design. Their enthusiastic documentation turned into quite the spectacle, prompting my teacher to intervene and disperse our gathering as the models rehearsed their final runway. Papa's hands skim over my arms until they capture both hands in a reassuring squeeze.

"Yes, everything is just fine except a teensy weensy wrinkle."

His voice slides into a higher register, and his phraseology is the same when something is wrong. Both intend to soften the blow of what he will say next.

"Gabe and Tomlin are running late. Their Uber got into an accident. Now both are fine, but Gabe had to check out the drivers and stay at the scene until the ambulance arrived."

I gasp, untangling my hands from his to cover my mouth with one. Tears, unbidden, start to well in my eyes for reasons I can't quite articulate. Papa draws me into a comforting embrace while Dad rests a reassuring hand on my shoulder.

"He tried to reach you, but when he couldn't, Tomlin called Dani, who in turn told us. Now everything is going to be fine." Dad's calming presence and soothing voice are full of reasoning, with affection in his eyes. "Just a slight delay, okay?"

"Okay," I manage to say, a shaky exhale betraying my attempt at composure. Papa continues to gently rub my back, soothing my nerves. I cling to him as if I'm clinging to the hope that everything will be alright — both for the guys and for the success of my design showcased by Lily. "I just wanted everything to be perfect."

"It will be."

Dad's hand moves to Papa's shoulder, squeezing it affectionately as he pulls away from me, eyes shimmering with emotion.

"Why the tears?"

My heart tugs at the sight. With a dismissive flick of his wrist, he tries to brush off my concern, yet he accepts the handkerchief Dad offers.

"It's nothing, really," he starts, his voice cracking just a bit, betraying the depth of his feelings. He dabs at his eyes, his gaze wandering off in a brief moment of reflection before meeting mine again with an intensity born of raw emotion.

"It's just . . . after everything you've been through. . . ."

He pauses, sighing as he gathers himself while I brush away the tears streaking down my cheeks.

"You're a remarkable young woman."

The full extent of what transpired stayed confined to a tight-knit circle of four until I bared my soul to my parents. I kept postponing telling them until it weighed so heavily on my soul that it made me physically sick. That led to a lengthy and tearful phone call from Brooklyn Heights Promenade, with Gabe offering silent support beside me as I relayed the entire story to them.

They were shocked by the situation, utterly gutted by the abuse, and eager to file charges. When I explained my decision not to pursue them, there was a long silence before loving and supportive words flowed through the phone. They cried, and I cried. Gabe held me the entire time. When they met him in person, Papa hugged him for several long moments, grateful for caring for his precious girls. This appreciation extended into the dinner, particularly as Gabe shared tales of his work, captivating Papa with each story. Meanwhile, Dad's gaze often found me, his eyes reflecting an understanding of my true feelings for Gabe despite my casual reference to him merely as a friend.

Concerned about their reaction to the age gap, I discussed the idea of presenting ourselves merely as friends in front of them with Gabe. This wasn't a significant deviation from our current situation since we were taking things very slowly. Only kissing and heavy petting despite spending most of our free time together.

The matter persisted until the second evening when, with Gabe temporarily called away for work, Papa initiated a conversation about the unmistakable way Gabe looks at me. Dad contributed, pointing out my evident adoration for Gabe in return. The truth unfurled quickly after that, and I openly admitted my feelings for him. Initially, I worried that the substantial age difference might concern them. Yet, following an in-depth interrogation of Gabe regarding his professional life, future ambitions, and plans with me, they came to accept the situation with Gabe's assurances that everything is progressing slowly, allowing me time to heal and recover from everything that has happened. From that point forward, our interactions as a group became effortlessly harmonious, a dynamic Gabe fondly described as "getting along swimmingly."

"Okay, sweetie, we'll go back out there."

Papa, leaning in for another hug, draws me back to the crowded room. Everyone fidgets as the introductions start overhead, signaling the show's beginning.

"You're going to win. You have the best design."

His whispered words rush out before letting go, allowing Dad to embrace me briefly and kiss my cheek. Papa navigates back through the crowd, greeting and conversing with attendees with familiarity as if he's known them for years, a charming sight with Dad amiably trailing behind. I appreciate his vote of confidence, as biased as it is.

"Are you good?" Lily suddenly stands by my side, her hand searching for mine. "I didn't want to interrupt. It seemed like a private moment."

I cup her palm to mine, sending a squeeze through our connection, before adjusting my dress, which is a simple, plain black set-off with minimal makeup. My conservative look ensures that when we join the models on the runway for their final walk, the focus remains on my design, not me.

"They're going to be late."

Not wanting to get into it, my gaze roams the room, taking in the makeup artists packing up and the other designers fretting over their models and making last-minute adjustments. When the event producer calls for the models to line up, Lily squeezes my hand.

"Let's hope I don't fuck up."

I laugh. She's been practicing ever since I asked her to walk for me. It came after the end of our air clearing discussion, my olive branch to restore our relationship.

"You'll be fine. Now go knock them dead."

Despite what she says, her confidence has grown since playing the villain in Travis's play.

With the models lined up against the far wall, the designers gather around the televisions wheeled in to watch the show. When the introduction ends, a hush settles over the room, and the DJ blares the music to kick off the runway show.

My hands wring together, trying to calm the butterflies in my stomach and my heart pounding. I glance between the television and Lily, excitedly fidgeting until it's her turn to sail down the runway. Lily struts out, her movements confident. She clasps the swathes of translucent white crepe in her hands, effortlessly lifting it above her head. I gasp, my hand covering my mouth as others in the room react to her bold move. The fabric cascades elegantly behind her, resembling ethereal wings in graceful flight.

At the end of the runway, Lily's arms sweep downwards, elegantly showcasing the futuristic bodysuit. Its silver floral beading sparkles, catching and refracting the runway's intense lights, creating a dazzling spectacle. The shimmering detail strikingly richly against her dark features adds to the allure. She looks breathtaking.

A lump forms in my throat, and my emotions swell as the designer behind the menswear piece I sent a picture to Gabe all that time ago offers his praise. Tears swiftly carve paths down my cheeks when Lily locks her gaze with the camera, her expression fierce and radiating the poise of the actress she is. Then, with a flare of attitude, she spins, the crepe fabric billowing out behind her like a superhero's cape, capturing the essence of strength and grace in a breathtaking moment.

As the music changes and Lily's runway performance comes to a captivating close, the anticipation backstage is tense. She took it to the next level with her walk. The moment she steps offstage and behind the curtains, I can no longer contain my exhilaration. I dart towards her, emotions surging through me like an unstoppable tide, and wrap her in an embrace to convey every ounce of my gratitude, pride, and relief.

"You were phenomenal."

I'm barely able to articulate the depth of my appreciation for the justice she's done to my design. She pulls away, doing an imaginary hair flip despite her updo preventing it.

"I killed it, didn't I?"

Her smug expression says it all. She knows she did.

"Yeah, you did! That wasn't just a walk. That was a performance of its own!"

I hug her again, tighter this time as I bask in the afterglow of her stellar showcase, united in a moment of pure happiness.

"You bet your ass it was a performance. I channeled you on opening night."

Her comment is gracious but hits with a bitter note for

reasons unknown to her. I step back, smiling at her wanting to burn it down in a stellar way like I burned down his play in a rebellious way.

"It's hot as hell back here. I need water."

I retrieve my bag, grabbing her what she needs while we watch the remainder of the show unfold. It's clear that Lily's presentation sets a high bar—none of the subsequent models carry the same level of boldness or theatrical flair. Amid the procession of talent, the menswear designer approaches, lavishing Lily with praise for her standout walk.

She shifts toward him to engage in a bit of flirtatious conversation as I again battle the butterflies in my stomach. The time is approaching for the designers and models to gather for the final walk, a collective display of creativity and hard work before the judges make their decisions. The atmosphere backstage is a ball of nervous energy as we line up against the wall. I fan my face, trying not to vomit or cry, when Lily takes hold of my hand, muttering for me to follow her lead.

As we stride down the runway, Lily transforms with a dramatic flair. She expertly manipulates the design, making the fabric dance around us as our intertwined hands swing to the beat of the music. The crowd's response is immediate and fervent, their applause swelling an overwhelming display of admiration and support.

Among the sea of faces, Dani stands out, rising to her feet, leading the ovation with an enthusiastic whistle that's both electrifying and out of place. Her actions spark a chain reaction. My parents, Uncle Tomlin and Gabe join in, smiling, crying, and cheering in pure joy. Seeing each person who has been a pillar of support through this journey here ignites a firestorm of emotion.

Tears blur my vision, and my chest squeezes with love and gratitude as the physical manifestation of reaching this point culminates into this triumphant climax.

Ever the showman, Lily raises our hands in the air as victorious, soaking up the applause before guiding us down the runway to stand by the presenters awaiting to award the winners. My teacher explains each category, its significance in fashion, and each student's vision to create their masterpiece in the likeness of the designated theme. Lily practically vibrates next to me, her hand sweating into mine as I'm so nervous I feel sick.

As the teacher begins to call out the first and second-place winners in the other three categories, my heart lurches with every name, a rollercoaster of anxiety and adrenaline mingling in a potent cocktail that courses through my veins as they accept their award and scholarship money.

My palms grow clammy, fingers unwinding from Lily's when I use the excuse of straightening my dress to wipe the sweat from them. My breaths come in short, sharp intakes as if I'm trying to draw in not just air but courage against the fluttering in my chest. Trying to calm down, I search for Gabe. When my eyes fall on him, he looks stunning in his tuxedo. He, alongside my dashing uncle, clad in their elegant evening wear, could easily grace the pages of a Berluti advertisement. Despite the admiring looks he's getting from around him, his attention is focused solely on me. A playful wink breaks across the distance between us, his expression melting into one of tender affection. Our eyes lock in a moment of silent communication, a comforting exchange as I smile at him.

When the category preceding mine is announced, time seems to slow, each second stretching out with the applause for the previous winners echoing around us. My heart beats frantically, I can barely breathe, and the bright lights seem to heat the room. Lily's shoulder bumps mine, and I grab her hand, frantic for someone's comfort, when "Vision of the Future: Metals and Metallics" is announced overhead.

"The first place winner and award of a Parsons scholarship spring semester is . . ."

As the announcer pauses, drawing out the suspense, I close my eyes and brace for the moment that could change everything. Suspended between what was and what could be is the culmination of my journey as my life unfurls in a vivid retrospective.

Cherished ice cream trips with Dad, my mom's descent into substance addiction, harrowing sexual abuse by Dale with the promise of more, the desperation to run away and live on the streets, the fateful night I climbed into Rick's cab, the comfort of Anna, and the salvation found through Dani's intervention.

Uncle Alex's stern support every step of the way, Uncle Tomlin and his legal teams fight for justice, the parents and large family I always longed for, the resilient Aunt Molli and her church pageants, moving to New York, getting into Parsons, my friendship with Lily, the abusive affair with Travis, the one-hit wonder off-Broadway star and the redemption in Gabe's love.

A journey marked by horrific trials, the worst of humanity, and memories I never want to revisit, often wondering how I survived. And the opposite. Blissful days I thought would never end, surrounded by people who showed me love can transcend all and be given openly and freely from the core of their being without seeking anything in return.

Yet, here I stand on the runway, adorned in a creation that bears my name, hand in hand with my best friend, under the watchful eyes of the man who protects me at all costs, and surrounded by a family whose cheers form the soundtrack of my triumphant life. I've transcended my past, crafting a present entirely my own and creating a beautifully unknown future yet to be written—I've already won.

"Isla Frank!"

BONUS SCENE #2

"Just let me win. At least once!"

My voice cracks with frustration, the emotion simmering beneath the surface, ready to erupt. Uncle Tomlin's lessons and Gabe's training should elevate my skills, not make them worse. Yet here I am again, pinned beneath him, every attempt thwarted.

"Is that going to be your defense to your attacker? Just let me win this once."

His taunt is lighthearted yet carries a sharper edge today, underscored by the fresh cut on his cheek—a souvenir from his last spar with Uncle Tomlin before they flew home.

His words are not meant to be taunting, especially not after said cut on his cheek. Fueled by their similar ages, demeanors, and shared interests, the bond between him and my uncle quickly blossomed into a full-blown bromance, catching Dani and me off guard. With their similar fashion tastes, I almost expected them to show up to dinner in matching outfits, something that I said that made my aunt snort her beer. They were more puzzled than amused.

Seeing my family embrace Gabe with such warmth and

immediacy filled me with joy. My parents insisted he come home with me to experience a traditional American Thanksgiving, emphasizing that he should take the holiday off from work for once to spend it with us instead of covering shifts to let others celebrate—a gesture that held special meaning, considering the holiday had previously been just another day for him.

Uncle Tomlin eagerly proposed a visit to his mountain retreat and from there, talk shifted to classic cars, dominating the dinner conversation. It was as if they'd all but adopted Gabe on the spot, making it nearly impossible for me to pull him away. The family's immediate fondness for him was undeniable.

"Are you just going to lie there and let your mind wander, or are you planning to make a move?"

His lighthearted jab tugs me out of my reverie. Truthfully, if I were indulging in daydreams, they wouldn't involve being pinned on a sweaty gym mat but rather a more intimate scenario devoid of clothing. The thought sparks a daring idea, given it's the weekend, my family's away, and he's merely on standby for work today.

"And what's my reward if I decide to fight back?" I ask, infusing my words with a playful, flirtatious edge.

As I bite my lip in anticipation, I catch his gaze drifting to my lips, clearly caught by the gesture. The urge to tear his shirt away is overwhelming, but his firm grip on my wrists leaves me momentarily powerless. His smirk widens, recognizing the challenge in my voice.

"The winner decides their prize."

A hint of mischief dances in his eyes. The game is on, and the stakes suddenly feel exhilaratingly high. With a burst of determination fueled by the promise of a tantalizing reward, which I already have in mind, I muster all the strength I can and shift the balance. Utilizing a technique my uncle taught me, I leverage my position to break free from his hold. For a moment, his grip loosens, surprise flickering across his face at my sudden defiance.

Seizing the opportunity, I manage a swift maneuver, reversing our positions. Now above him, I can't help but revel in the momentary triumph of the tables turning. His surprised expression shifts to admiration, and his smile is an unspoken acknowledgment of my effort.

"Now about that reward . . ." I trail off, leaning closer, the playful tension ebbing into the sexual tension that has plagued us with family around.

With them gone, nothing is holding me back from attacking him. Already straddling him, I lower my chest to rest against his, my lips hovering over his, and I raise a challenging eyebrow.

Gabe's response is a low chuckle, vibrating into me while his earlier confidence mingles with desire. His hands slide over my sweaty shirt, embracing me tightly to the point I can feel his erection pressing into me.

I can feel the heat radiating off his body, and my breath hitches as his hands move up my back, pulling me closer to him. Our chests are pressed together, and I can feel the rapid beating of his heart against mine.

"I guess you've earned the right to name it."

His lips dust against mine, and I can taste the salt from his sweat. The playful sparring has led to something more intimate and inviting that will have to be finished upstairs.

"Well, if you must know, the reward could be quite . . . satisfying."

My voice drops to a huskier tone, promising what's to come. My hands move to either side of his head, fingers splayed out as I kiss him. His tongue dances with mine, soft and exploring, in no hurry to take things further, but I am. I let out a soft moan, my body arching as his fingers trace delicate circles on my skin.

My hips instinctively move against his, seeking more of his touch and igniting a fire within me.

"Gabe, I want you."

My words escape in a low, breathy murmur against his lips as I mirror his actions, my hands tangling into his hair and pulling gently. A deep, primal growl rumbles from his chest, causing a thrill of lust to course through me. As he sits up, leaving me straddling him, his hands move to my backside, firmly cupping it and drawing me closer to him. His throbbing cock presses against me. I grind against him, getting wetter, anticipating what's about to happen.

"Upstairs," he rasps, breaking the kiss for a moment. "We need to take this upstairs. Only if you're ready."

He's never said this before. This is a new side of him, requesting permission for something we've both silently yearned for. Until now, he's been the patient one, setting a pace that respects my readiness and ensuring I'm fully confident in us and in him. His careful approach stems from a deep respect for my past experiences, the abusive hardships he helped me navigate, and a desire not to overstep boundaries that might irreversibly alter our dynamic.

However, when we all dined together after the fashion show, Dani whispered to me that he was a goner—completely head over heels. In a surprising turn, she took his side, cautioning me to handle his heart with care, as it was, unmistakably, already mine.

Since that revelation, I've come to see that his hesitance was not solely for my benefit but held a fraction of self-preservation as well. It was his way of safeguarding his heart until I recognized that he was the one I should have chosen from the start. Hindsight is always twenty-twenty, after all. In the quiet moments, when he's not around, I laugh at myself for ever thinking he was gay—he is far from it. I nod, biting my lower lip as I grind against him once more.

"Yes, definitely upstairs."

I can feel the urgency building inside me, my body screaming for a release that hasn't come with all the masturbating I do each night dreaming of him. I want him, all of him, and I don't care to wait any longer. With my hands leveraged on each shoulder for support, I lift myself from his lap and extend a hand to help him to his feet.

He effortlessly rises without my offer of help, choosing instead to sweep me into his arms and carry me out of the fitness room. The gym is deserted, sparing me any awkwardness as he carries me towards the elevator. This act feels deeply romantic rather than awkward, his heart pounding against my side as I gaze up at him.

"Literally sweeping me off my feet, I could get used to this."

He responds with a series of soft kisses, each one sending a thrill through me until the sound of the elevator arriving breaks the spell. The doors slide open, and he steps in, still holding me close.

"So could I."

The way his desire-filled voice vibrates against my lips makes my heart flutter. He gently nudges me toward the panel, signaling me to choose our floor. When I do, I wrap my arm around his neck, drawing him into an intense make-out session before the short elevator ride ends with another chime.

He ends the kiss before stepping out, carrying me down the hall until he lowers me to my feet to search for the door key in his shorts. With it in hand, he pauses, his dark brown eyes filled with so much affection that I blink at the intensity.

"I've been waiting for this moment," he says softly, breaking the silence without breaking the spell of our connection. His eyes search mine, looking for something—perhaps reassurance. "Tell me if it's too soon or if I'm rushing it. We don't have to, love. We can wait—"

I immediately step toward him, my hands cupping his worried face.

"No, no more waiting. I want you, and not just in the way I mentioned downstairs. I want to be with you in every way that counts."

My declaration leaves little doubt about what I want. My desire is not just for physical closeness but to move us into an official relationship—one that I'll cherish as much as I cherish him. I want to dispel his worries and finally cross the threshold of hesitation and waiting to be a couple.

His hands gently cover mine, drawing them away from his face and kissing each palm. His fingers play with the adoption ring on my right ring finger, a piece I proudly wear daily when Gabe slides it on my finger, mirroring what might happen someday.

"I've been yours since we met, even if I didn't know it then." His chin lowers, searching my eyes as he says it. "I don't need any more time to understand what's right in front of me. You're my person, Isla. There's nothing I want more than to be yours, to move forward from this day as partners."

His words wash over me in a new heat, making love to my ears the way I want him to make love to my body.

"Then make me yours."

His groan pierces the quiet space, an audible expression of his desire and impatience. He unlocks the door with swift, decisive movements, propelling us inside. His key lands with a clatter on the entryway table before his hands find my waist with purpose, lifting me effortlessly.

My response is instinctual. My legs wrap around his waist, drawing him closer, his erection poking harder into me. My hands wrap around his neck, my lips nibbling at his sweaty, salty skin as the urgency builds within me.

Anna's welcoming greeting goes unnoticed by the magnetic pull drawing us together. He strides into the familiar space with a singular intent—his bedroom. His shoe budges the door close with a soft thud, closing off Anna and the outside world to focus on each other this first time.

His lips are pillowy and soft, their fullness enticing as they press against mine in a hungry demand. Our lips move together in a passionate dance, our tongues exploring each other's mouths in a heated frenzy. The minty taste of his toothpaste-laden mouth on me is intoxicating, and I can't get enough.

His fingers wander across my body, tracing the curves and dips of my skin. With each touch, my breath catches in my throat, and I feel a rush of heat between us. Slowly, he moves the fabric of my workout top up and over my head, ending our kiss and revealing the thin straps of my sports bra. As our lips part, his breath is hot against my neck, sending electric currents through me.

"I've envisioned this moment in a hundred different ways."

His eyes close as his head angles toward the ceiling, a shudder running through his body, evidence of his struggle to maintain composure in the face of our intense attraction. My fingers move to tug at the edge of his shirt, desperate to feel his taut skin and rippling muscles. His eyes snap open at the sensation, and he quickly grabs the fabric behind his head to pull it off, exposing his toned chest and defined abdominals beneath.

"And are they as good as this?"

My body aches for him, my hunger for his touch insatiable. I can't even form words as I reach up to pull him closer, our lips crashing together in an urgent kiss. His hand grabs onto my hair, holding me in place as his fingers dig into the fabric of my shorts, threatening to tear them off. With a desperate need, my hands leave his body and frantically help him undress me. Our mouths stay locked together, and I do not want to waste a single moment as I strip off the last remnants of my clothes.

His hands skim over my skin, warm and welcoming, familiarizing himself with every curve until he suddenly breaks the kiss, leaving us both gasping for air. My brain is spun out, conflicted by wanting to savor this moment and needing to rush it along to feel him inside me.

"Without a doubt, this is better in every way."

His eyes are burning pools of lust, scorching me as they travel my body, taking in every inch of my skin. A thrill runs through me as we explore this new dimension where he belongs to me and I to him. Desperate to feel him, my hand eagerly reaches for him just as he kneels, his gaze greedily set on giving me pleasure.

"I've got to taste you, love. I'm going to lick you everywhere."

With little time to respond, his face buries into my pussy, and I gasp. My thighs quiver as he cups my ass, and I moan when a thumb nudges my thigh over his shoulder, ready for the ecstasy that awaits.

"Oh, Gabe."

My head spins as I press my back against the wall, trying to steady myself. Gabe's hot breath tickles my inner thighs as heat surges through me. His large hands grip my hips, pulling me closer to his face as he takes in every inch of me with his tongue. I can feel the pressure building inside me as he expertly swirls and flicks his tongue over my clit.

My fingers tangle in his hair as I moan, unable to control the pleasure coursing through me. His tongue dips in and out of the folds, causing more wetness to spill out of me, driving us both wild. As his hands knead and squeeze my ass, I can't help but arch my back and smother him with my pussy. My moans rise with his groans, both loving what the other is doing while needing more.

"I need you."

Each touch, each breath, each sensual caress of his tongue intensifies my desire to be consumed by him. He ravages me like a man starved for sustenance, but I crave the taste of him on my lips, to devour him the way he devours my core with such reckless abandon and skill. His hunger for me matches my own, creating a primal dance between us as we give in to our carnal urges.

My shoulder blades dig into the wall, helping maintain my balance as my thigh tightens by his ear. His skilled tongue is delicious and unrelenting, alternating between licking my clit and plunging inside my pussy. It's too much and not enough, leaving me to grind into the scruff of his unshaven face.

The sharp prickles add to the sensations, rough against my soft core. His eyes sparkle with dark desire when our gaze connects. Every muscle in my body tightens, my stomach taut as my pelvic bone juts further into his mouth, needing more.

"Ride my face, love."

His words are muffled against my pulsing flesh, my lips contracting, an invitation for his finger or cock, something to penetrate me to bring forth the orgasm teetering on the brink of roaring forward. I lean into the wall, the angle shifting my pussy into his teeth and sending an erotic jolt through me, their hardness an unexpected wall to my engorged clit. This is what I wanted. This connection, this intimacy. This reckless, raw, unfiltered passion. It is not carefully curated, and it is not a game in the playroom, but two people loving each other and wanting to share their love in the most intimate way possible.

His lips lock onto my clit, sucking and licking in a never-ending rhythm. Each gentle pull, each sudden thrust of his tongue, feels like a promise, a hint of everything that's to come. My hips buck, each movement more erratic than the last as the tension within me starts to build.

"Please," I whisper, a delicate plea for more.

He knows what I want. He knows what I need. And in that moment, I surrender to him completely. My eyes close, shutting off the connection we share to focus on the orgasm that's just at bay until his hand lands on my pelvic bone, his fingers spreading me open. My eyes fly open as I gasp at how exposed I am and how deeply vulnerable and intimate this small action is. He nibbles my flesh, and I catch my breath, holding it as I absorb the waves of pleasure surging over me.

My climax builds with a quiet but intense force that threatens to overwhelm me. His skilled touch sends a jolt of pleasure through my body as he slips a finger inside, expertly curling it towards himself. The pressure is divine, causing me to let out shallow pants as I rock into his hand, seeking more of the delicious sensation. His deep groans of appreciation vibrate against my sensitive flesh, intensifying the pleasure and pushing me closer to the edge. With one final surge of ecstasy, I am sent over the brink and into blissful release.

My entire body tenses and convulses against Gabe's skilled mouth and fingers, his name bubbling up from my throat in a long, drawn-out moan. He doesn't stop, continuing to lap up my juices and thrusting his fingers inside me as if he's trying to draw out every last drop of pleasure from my writhing body. My leg gives out from the intensity of my orgasm, but he swiftly catches me with one hand under my knee, the other still resting across his broad shoulder as he stands tall and carries me to the bed. He gently lays me down on my back, positioning himself between my legs and placing soft kisses along my inner thighs. His lower face glistens with my arousal as our eyes lock in an intense, adoration-filled moment.

"I'm the luckiest man in the world," his murmured words tickle my skin as his palm slides up my body to cover my breasts. "I get to do this to you. To be with you."

How he looks at me erases any uncertainty or doubts that he'd accept me after hearing all I have been through. The fact that he knows everything and is still here, giving himself to me in the most emotionally and physically connected way, brings tears to my eyes. I see the future in him—one filled with shared experiences, challenges met together, and the unyielding support that comes from choosing each other every day.

"I feel the same way."

His gaze locks onto mine with an intensity that matches his commitment. He suddenly crawls up my body, a predator on the prowl, until he lowers himself over me, the fabric of his shorts rough against my sensitive core.

"Isla, I know you have your apartment, but I'd love it if you moved in with me. If we could really be together every day, I'd help with Anna, and we could turn the extra bedroom into a studio for you to work on your designs."

His generous offer hangs in the space between us, and a soft smile tugs at the corner of his lips. My heart swells with gratitude and affection, knowing that this man who generously opened his life and home to me has also embraced Anna. The thought of sharing our lives in his cozy apartment, creating a space where we can grow and thrive together, fills me with a sense of peace and contentment that I've been looking for. I raise my hand to his cheek, gently caressing the stubble on his chin.

"Are you sure? It's not too fast?"

I bit my lip, searching his face for an ounce of uncertainty. Any sign that, even though this feels right in every way, it might not be right. It could be us rushing into something that might not last, and that would completely break me.

"I'm going to admit something, and I don't want it to scare you off. I truly don't."

He gently releases my hand only to bring it to his lips, kissing my palm tenderly. Our fingers intertwine, a silent vow of unity, as he positions our joined hands beside my head. His lips capture mine in a deep, meaningful kiss stretching through time.

My heart races against his, anxious about what revelation could scare me away from this remarkable man. It's true. There are parts of his life he hasn't shared, stories untold. But isn't that the essence of growing closer, of falling more profoundly in love—unraveling each other over time?

"Nothing you can say will scare me. You've heard all of my worst. I should probably hear yours."

My words are brave, my voice wavering at the softening of his expression and the love in his eyes. A gentle smile spreads across his face as he takes a deep breath, his eyes searching mine for strength and understanding.

"I'd marry you today if you'd have me."

My mouth parts in astonishment at his candid confession, sending my thoughts into a whirlwind. Marriage has always been on my horizon, a desire to build a family and be the mother mine never was, albeit that's hardly a high standard to surpass. Yet, my life is just starting. Ambitions yet to be fulfilled, experiences to be had, and dreams of headlining my fashion show that I yearn to see realized.

"How? How can you say that? How can you know?"

I'm so taken aback that I doubt his love or conviction for me. Either or both are confusing to me. His smile deepens, and a faraway look overtakes his expression while gazing at me.

"I just do, Isla.

His simple yet profound words are the assurance I needed, the promise of a shared tomorrow. As he holds my gaze, every fear and hesitation melts away, leaving only the undeniable truth of our connection and the endless possibilities that await us.

"I wanted to tell you so you understand—you can rely on me through thick and thin. I'm here for you every step of the way."

His assurance swirls around me, comforting my deep-seated trauma that he won't abandon me or take advantage of me. It grounds me in his steadfast, unconditional, loving presence. Slipping my hand from his grasp, I cradle his face gently, drawing myself up to press our lips together in a tender kiss filled with affection, a silent conveyance of my deep feelings for him.

As the kiss breaks, I whisper, "Yes, I'll move in. And marriage . . . that's a strong maybe."

His laughter, light and filled with joy, resonates in my body as I gaze up at him, and my smile reflects the happiness that bubbles inside me.

"Now, make me yours already."

I wiggle underneath him, the impatience in my voice matching my body. I still need to have him in me as well as around me. His eyes, alight with a spark of desire that matches mine, gaze into mine as he captures my lips again. His hands, tender yet passionate, roam over the curves of my face and neck, stoking my burning fire.

Our tongues dance together in a slow rhythm, conveying our desire and deep connection to become one in the last way possible. As his lips leave mine, they trail down my neck, sending tingles of pleasure across my skin, and I move my hips against him. His hard cock buries into my stomach, the length teasing my mind with fantasies of ecstasy to come.

"Please," I whisper, unable to contain my need for him any longer. "I need you now."

His face lifts, a mischievous grin as his dark orbs glint with excitement.

"Not so fast, love," he says, moving off me to stand at the edge of the bed. "I'm taking my time with you, savoring every each of the woman I love."

I pout playfully, but inside, I know better than to rush this man. It's part of what makes him unique—his patience and willingness to forgo immediate gratification to enjoy and cherish the slow moments. I trust him completely, knowing that it will all be worth it, even if I want him to fuck me fast and furious.

As he slowly undresses, his chin lowers, a hard stare as he

reveals himself to me for the first time. Piece by piece, he slowly sheds the remaining clothing as if adding to the anticipation that has me swirling my clit in excitement. Yet I gasp when he slips out of his underwear, revealing his impressive length and girth. His cock bobs against his stomach proudly, veins pulsing with desire. The sight takes one's breath away, and a flicker of worry mingles with my passion. With his size, we're going to have to go slow.

"Not so fast is right, Gabe. That's a weapon. Do you register it at the door of your hospital before walking in?"

My joke does little to dampen the desire on his face as our eyes greedily feast on each other. I'm sprawled when he placed me, a delicious buffet for his tasting and liking. He, on the other hand, stands tall and proud, naked and beautiful. His body is a testament to his healthy diet, daily runs, and third-degree black belt status. The only mark is the cut on his cheek.

Otherwise, his mahogany skin is flawless, with a sweaty shimmer over the curves and valleys of his muscles. His broad shoulders cut a powerful silhouette. The way the light plays off his chest, highlighting every defined muscle as veins map down his sculpted arms, necessary for the lives he saves every day.

My gaze drifts to his abs, where each muscle of his six-pack seems to pulsate with its own life. The V of his torso, narrowing gracefully to his tight waist and narrow hips where his cock captivates me. His strong legs, I've seen dozens of times, but now flair with power and greatness. I absorb every inch of him.

My heart swells with admiration and profound love, for he is not merely a collection of physical achievements. He embodies everything I've ever wanted and more. His eyes glint with mischief as he crawls over me again. My hands fall away from my body, his body heat radiating into me with a comforting deliciousness.

"Don't worry, I'll always be gentle with you."

His lips dust mine as my hands roam over his body, feeling the muscles on his back flex as he holds his weight off me.

"Well, I hope not always."

I give a playful wink, tilting my hips toward him with a mischievous smile. My wet clit grinds against him, sending sparks of pleasure through my body and encouraging him to where we both want him to be. His deep groan echoes in the room, adding to the intensity of our desire. The warmth of his body against mine fuels the fire within me, and I spread my legs wider.

My roaming hands cup his face, stroking the scruff as we lock eyes. His dark eyes are endless, the brown going on forever as his expression intensifies. His mouth sets into a determined line, his brow furrows in concentration, and his hips tilt away from me.

His enormous cock drags off my stomach, leaving a trail of warmth before pressing firmly against my eager pussy lips. I instinctively slide my knees along the side of his body, using my toes to leverage off his firm thighs as he begins to thrust forward. His bulbous head entering me is even more intense than I could have imagined, and I suck in a startled breath.

"I'll go very slow," he whispers hoarsely, his voice laced with desire and restraint.

He slowly backs out, his fingers gently stroking my swollen lips to distribute my wetness before inching further inside me. Each agonizingly slow movement has me holding my breath and him trembling with restraint, determined to make sure I am comfortable and ready for each inch of him.

My hands fall away when he lowers his lips to mine, kissing me slowly, sensually, and in contrast to his hard cock. His penetration is deliberate and precise, as if he's wanting me to feel every bit of him, and I do. I feel the ridge of his thick cock opening me wider and going deeper. The sensation is overwhelming and deliciously erotic. The intensity is heightened by his chest brushing against mine, his trimmed pubic hair caressing over my smooth skin, and his thigh muscles pressing into my butt. He's in me and over me, just as I had imagined and masturbated to for so many nights. His lips kiss the corner of my mouth, depositing a line of them across my cheek and finishing at my ear.

"You feel amazing. This is . . ."

His words are raspy and rushed, tumbling from his throat while he struggles to control his breath. A guttural groan interrupts his words when he hits my cervix, and he pauses, letting the pleasure wash over him. The journey to this point between us had felt long and short.

Our quick friendship blossomed into a cherished relationship with a slow descent into sexual gratification. Every day spent together, every intimate conversation, every triumph and hardship has led to this. Every touch, every kiss, and every whispered word builds trust, connection, and love between us, leading to the physical culmination of our feelings.

His head tucks into the crook of my neck, his warm breath fanning across my skin as the saltiness of his sweat lingers on my tongue when I kiss his temple. His arm slides under my body, his hand resting on my shoulder blade to pull me down the mattress, impaling me further onto his cock, and we both groan in unison.

My hands return to his body, gripping his shoulder as he begins to pull back, giving me a moment to adjust before thrusting into me again, leaving me breathless. It's painstaking slow, the build-up commendable, and if he weren't so deep, I would have come already. But with his girth and length being what it is, my mind can't figure out what to concentrate on, my orgasm or his size. Both are fighting for dominance in my mind.

"You're so tight, love. I'm trying my hardest not to climax."

His cock fills me completely, stretching me to new heights. I feel the resistance of my walls around him, my body adjusting

GIGI MEIER

to the pleasure of his invasion. Each time he pulls out, my core tightens, and as he pushes back in, I feel the exquisite release of tension.

His effort in holding off is commendable. The desire surging through me wants to come now, and yet I want it never to end. I want to feel this full always both in my pussy, my mind and my heart. He's given everything of himself to me in every way possible, and I want to give him every bit of me in return.

"Like you said, we have forever."

I clutch his shoulders as I drop my feet to the mattress, pushing against it to grind into him, to bring us both what we want. Pleasure. My hands grip his shoulders, nails digging into his skin, urging him to speed up.

"So fuck me already."

His head jolts from my neck, and his surprised expression at hearing my rare vulgar language.

"Il tuo desiderio è un ordine."

He rattles off something I don't understand, but my bluntness works when his resolve wavers and he surrenders to our needs. His thrusts grow more urgent, and his hips move in sync with mine, our bodies merging in one fluid motion. He plunges into me with a newfound intensity. His gaze locked on mine as he takes me higher with each thrust.

Our bodies slap together with a wet, satisfying sound. My breaths come out in gasps, punctuated by soft moans that escape my lips. I can feel the sweat on his forehead, the tension in his muscles, and the animalistic need driving him. My body responds to his, aching for more, craving the raw connection we share. I meet his thrusts, my hips rising to his, my core pulsating around his cock. I can feel my climax building, the need to reach that point of no return becoming almost unbearable.

"Harder," I plead, my voice hoarse with need.

He obeys without hesitation, his thrusts growing harder,

faster. His enormous cock pulls a smaller orgasm out of me on the journey to the big one, just at the edge of everything as my body tightens, my mind thinking of only one thing, How deliciously damaging his cock is plunging in and out of me.

His breaths become ragged, his chest heaving with the force of his exertion. I can see the wild looks in his eyes, the primal hunger that matches my own. He penetrates me deeper, hitting that sweet spot over and over again, sending waves of ecstasy coursing through my body. The tension within me builds. My moans become louder, more desperate, as I lose myself in the sensation of our bodies moving together, perfectly in sync.

Just when I think I can't take any more, the moment arrives. My body tenses for just a heartbeat before releasing tidal waves of pleasure. I cry out, my voice echoing in the room as I surrender to the exquisite pleasure and my nails claw at his back.

He feels my release, his own climax close at hand. With one final powerful thrust, he lets go, growling my name in a possessive claim. He groans, his arms shaking, but he doesn't stop, driven by the same insatiable need that burns within me. Suddenly, I'm flipped, splayed atop of him. The relief on his face is evident as the lines of concentration ebb away. His hands roam my body, dipping into the space where my legs join my hip to push me further down his cock. I moan at the fullness, the depth he's trapped in me, and the feeling of finally becoming one with him.

"Gabriel."

His name is a breathless whisper, not knowing what I need, want, or have to say. Just his sheer intensity and my finally solidifying our relationship, the final barriers of restraint and denial are gone. It's the best I've felt in a very long time. His hand travels to the back of my neck, encouraging me toward him for a kiss, deep and throaty, wanting to suffocate his mouth, the way his monster cock is suffocating the breath in my body. I claim him in the same intense way he claimed me. Fast, feverish, and fierce.

I need this man, all of him. From his caring disposition, his intelligent brain, his amazing body, and the utter way he wrecks me with his cock. My hips rock against his, our combined cum mixing on our legs as I take him deep into my body. His legs widen, moving mine further apart as his fingers trail over my backside to feel where we connect. His groan is absorbed in my mouth, unyielding in my assault to explore every corner while my hands cup his face, intent on holding him in place.

Could I be with Gabe forever?

The question repeats with every thrust of his cock into me and every downward grind into him. Our bodies continue to move in perfect unison, losing ourselves in our raw desires and the primal pleasure that now binds us together. The need to see and watch his face as I ride him is overwhelming, and I break the kiss.

My hands splay across his chest, my ankles tuck over his upper thighs, feeling the clenching of his muscles as he continues to pump into me. With a lingering gaze into his dark eyes filled with love and lust, I push myself up, forcing his cock deeper. His mouth parts, and his eyes roll back. The sheer pleasure in his expression has me burning once more. The thrusting from his hips halts as we both pause, taking in how amazing this feels.

"Isla."

As was his name spoken in a breathless plea a moment ago, mine is a deep rasp, barely holding back from unleashing another robust round of fucking. Despite how sexy he looks and the struggles he's having while his hands now move to my breasts to play with them, I feel empowered, alive, and connected on a level I never thought possible. I own this man, mind, body, and soul. There's nothing he wouldn't do for me.

It's a great responsibility to yield such power, gratification, and love.

As I slowly start my gyrations over his thick, long cock, he mouths, "I love you." I smile, mouth the same, and close my eyes to simply feel him under me and in me, consuming my mind, body, and soul. This man, unlike any other in my life, is the one I need.

Could I be with Gabe forever?

Yes.

Looking for steamy, naughty fun? Turn the page to read *Paolo*, the first book in my Cougars and Cubs Series.

PAOLO: CHAPTER 1
PAOLO AND TAYLOR'S STORY

My fingers dance across the keyboard, basking in the afternoon glow that floods my corner office every Friday. The skyscrapers outside my window stand tall, silent sentinels guarding the bustling financial district below. This view used to fill me with pride, but now it's a constant reminder of the lifestyle that holds me captive.

Golden handcuffs are what they call it. Making too much money to walk away and with too much work to feel accomplished at anything.

The clock on my computer marches toward 5 pm. The echoes of colleagues granting well wishes for a joyous weekend fill the halls as they escape out the door to their family and home lives, leaving the corporate grind behind. It's another weekend, another trio of lonely nights in my high-rise apartment, a routine that's become all too familiar since my divorce a year ago.

The moment I opened that bedroom door and saw them entangled on our bed, my world tipped on its axis. My heart shattered into a million pieces, and the pain was excruciating. In the aftermath, I became a different person. I threw myself into my career with an intensity I had never known before, hoping my success would fill the void the betrayal left behind.

There are days when the questions still haunt me. How did I miss the signs? How could I have been so blind in the first place? The painful days are few and far between, but the loneliness is almost daily.

My phone buzzes, interrupting my thoughts. Glancing at the caller ID, I see it's Chloe, my best friend and colleague. I chuckle because she's probably still in the office too.

"Hey, Chloe."

"Taylor, I just heard Williamson's charging down the hall like a dark storm cloud," she whispers through the receiver. "He's looking for you."

By Williamson, she means Theodore R. Williamson III. Firstborn son and current Chairman of the Board of the expansive investment house that bears the moniker of his grandfather. Rarely is he on this floor. Even more rare is that he's looking for me.

My heart rate spikes as I furrow my brow.

"What for? He never talks to me, not directly, anyhow." He goes through my boss, the Chief Executive Officer, who's a stickler for following the chain of command and never stepping outside of it. When I glance across the glass offices, the CEO is already gone for the day, and his secretary is packing her bags to leave. "I'm buried with the quarterly filing due in two weeks."

Before I can continue complaining to her, Mr. Williamson bursts into my office. His usually impeccable gray hair is in disarray, and his face is a roadmap of bulging veins and angry red splotches.

"Taylor, just the person I wanted to see," he barks with an open collar and his tie hanging askew. "We've got a mess on our hands."

I replace the receiver in its cradle and gesture toward the guest chair on the other side of my desk.

"Please, have a seat."

Mr. Williamson remains standing, slamming a thick folder onto my desk. It hits with a resounding thud, startling me.

"This is Mr. Jacobsen's file, our most lucrative client. He's been with us for over a decade and is threatening to leave."

I blink at the name on the folder. Jacobsen & Associates has been a loyal client for years. They have an extensive real estate holdings company in addition to their oil drilling and mineral rights leases. I can't fathom why they'd want to cut ties now.

"What happened?"

"He's furious about some miscommunication regarding his portfolio. He's been trying to reach Jim all week about some recent trades he took the liberty of making into volatile international stocks, which directly conflicts with Mr. Jacobsen's risk tolerance. And now Jim isn't returning his calls." Mr. Williamson's voice drips with fury.

Fucking Jimothy.

Jimothy is what I call him. It's a disparaging nickname since he doesn't deserve the respect of being called by his proper name, Jim. The man is nearly twenty-five years older than me. He is a narcissistic egomaniac who regularly cheats on his wife with the country club beer cart girls. He broods about the office like he owns the place and treats me as if we are not equals when, in fact, we are. Something I remind my male chauvinistic boss of all the time since he continues to let Jimothy run amuck.

"I'm sorry to hear that, sir."

I'm not. I hope this is the straw that breaks the camel's back in getting him fired since the last three hostile work environment complaints against Jimothy haven't done the trick.

"I knew you would be. Since you're the only one of my senior executives still here, I will need you to get right on it. Familiarize yourself with his portfolio and trades, then be prepared to present your recommendations on Monday on how we save this relationship."

My stomach churns. My inbox is overflowing with emails, and my calendar is a cluster of back-to-back meetings. I don't have the time nor the inclination to handle this just because I'm still here on a Friday afternoon or to save Jimothy's ass yet again.

"Mr. Williamson. With all due respect, I'd love to help. As you know, I'll do anything for the good of the company. However, I have my accounts to handle, and I'm double booked with the quarterly filings due in two weeks. Perhaps another executive . . ." I crane my head to look back to the row of empty glass offices, knowing full well I'm the only one here. "Or perhaps Jim could come in this weekend and work on it. Since he's responsible—"

"Taylor, he's in Mexico on vacation with his wife."

"Oh."

I haven't had a vacation all year, prioritizing work over everything, even my well-being. Now I have to clean up the mess made by this rotten, scheming, and lazy bastard.

"It's settled then." He doesn't look pleased by my objection. That makes two of us. I'm not pleased either. "You'll present first so we can open it up to questions before proceeding with the regular agenda."

I hate Jimothy for this. And right now, I hate Mr. Williamson too. Mostly, I hate my loyalty to this company that goes unacknowledged and unrewarded.

"I'll get right on it and reach out to Mr. Jacobsen." I reach for my phone when his waving hand stops me.

"No need, I already did. Just see what you can find. Then we'll regroup before approaching the client."

He doesn't wait for my reply when he strides out of the office, leaving me alone to grapple with this situation. With an exasperated sigh, I pick up my phone and dial Chloe's number.

She's always the one I turn to when work becomes unbearable, especially since I got her the job here.

She picks up on the first ring. "What happened?"

I lean back in my chair, feeling the weight of the world suddenly on my shoulders.

"You won't believe the mess I'm in right now. Mr. Williamson just dropped this colossal problem on my desk. Jacobsen & Associates is about to jump ship because of some disaster with their portfolio. And guess who's responsible for this disaster?"

"Who?"

"Jimothy."

Chloe lets out an empathetic groan. "Jimothy again? That guy is a menace. I don't know how he keeps getting away with things around here."

I shake my head, my frustration mounting.

"You and me both. I've had it with his antics. The guy must have glossy pictures on someone here because nothing ever happens to him."

As I sift through the mess on my desk, I sigh into the phone.

"I hope this colossal blunder will be the final straw that leads to Jimothy's long-overdue termination from the company. Maybe, just maybe, it's time for him to face the consequences of his actions once and for all."

She grunts in disbelief. "I doubt it. Nothing ever happens to him. Not even when the Head of Human Resources filed a complaint. You know she left because of him."

"I didn't know that," I murmur, flipping open the client folder. "But right now, I must figure out how to salvage this relationship. I am going to have to work late tonight and all weekend to sort through this mess."

"Taylor, you're overworking yourself." Chloe's voice softens with sympathy. "This isn't healthy. When was the last time you went out and had a little fun?"

I can't remember.

"I don't even know, Chloe. It feels like forever. But I can't afford to drop the ball on this."

There's a brief pause on the line before she speaks again.

"I get it. Just promise me you'll take some time for yourself soon. We can plan a weekend getaway or something. Maybe get laid. Oh, wouldn't that be nice? To find two hot guys to wine and dine us, then drill me into the mattress."

I manage a faint smile. I can't remember the last time I had sex either. At least no one since the ex. That's absolutely something that needs to be rectified once I get past these deadlines.

"Yeah, a wild and carefree weekend is long overdue. I'd like that, but after this and after my quarterly filings." I sigh for the third time as if the exhalation will somehow change my reality. "Anyway, I need to order my dinner since security won't let anyone up after 6 pm."

"Okay, call me if you need me."

I put the receiver down, pull the folder closer, and begin poring over the documents.

Fucking Jimothy.

Read the rest of Paolo and Taylor's story in *Paolo*
(The Cougars and Cubs Series, Book 1)

When a weekend fling turns into more . . .

In the heart of the bustling city, Taylor Woods, a seasoned executive, finds herself engrossed in an impromptu work project at an enchanting bakery, and her life takes an unexpected turn. There, she meets Paolo Cavallaro, a younger man whose magnetic charm draws her in. With a boldness that takes her by surprise, Paolo asks her to dinner that very night. Intrigued by the novelty of being pursued by a younger man, Taylor agrees, leading to a passionate one-night stand that neither can forget.

But when Paolo surprises her with a text inviting her for breakfast the next morning, their chemistry ignites a weekend fling that defies age and expectations. As their whirlwind romance unfolds, they find themselves caught in a corporate scandal that forces them into an unexpected partnership. Together, they set out to unmask the corrupt executives responsible for a possible company's downfall, all while navigating the complexities of their age-gap romance, meet-cute beginnings, and the irresistible pull of desire.

Embark on an exhilarating journey of forbidden romance, corporate scheming, and the unwavering strength of their connection. Follow Taylor and Paolo as their paths unexpectedly converge at a quaint bakery, setting the stage for a romance of undeniable chemistry and steamy encounters.

Can their blossoming love withstand the turmoil of the corporate world, or will the pressures of their demanding lives extinguish the flame of their fateful encounter?

Paolo is the first book in The Cougars and Cubs Series and is a connected standalone. It is a steamy, age-gap, forced proximity, multicultural couple, office romance.

ACKNOWLEDGMENTS

To my beautiful Elle, thank you for sitting through far too many brainstorming sessions when I got stuck on her story and had to ask, "Would an eighteen-year-old do this?" on several occasions.

To my handsome Elkan. Thank you for listening to my Isla Frank playlist on Spotify on the long road trips to travel baseball games. It became humorous when, without realizing it, you started singing along to the songs under your breath.

To my sweet sister, Tara. Thank you for encouraging me to keep the cover when it's not a traditional romance genre norm.

To my sweet mother, Judith. Where do I begin? You passed away unexpectedly as I was writing this book. You knew about it beforehand, thought the cover was gripping, and couldn't wait to read it. I miss you so much that my heart clenches, and my stomach hurts. You have been my everything for decades. I am adrift without you. I love you, Mom.

To my brain trust, Erin, Jessica, Kacie, Robyne, and Sally, THANK YOU. Words don't express how much you beautiful ladies mean to me. Your jokes, suggestions, support, encouragement, and friendship are far more than I ever hoped for. Here's to many more books together!

To my ARC team, THANK YOU. You have hung in there with me through this series and the start of my steamy, naughty, fun Cougars and Cubs Series. Thank you for reading, reviewing, posting on social media, and spreading the word about my books. You're a badass group of awesomeness! I can't wait for you to read the new series coming this year!

To my readers. THANK YOU. You loved Dani Winters so much that you wanted a second book, but then you needed to hear Hamilton's story, which led to wanting to know what happened to Isla. If it weren't for you being a voracious reader of this series, her story wouldn't ever have been told. Thank you for bringing her to life and taking me on a journey into her story, which is so heartbreakingly beautiful that it quickly became my favorite. I hope it will become yours too!

ABOUT THE AUTHOR

After retiring from a thirty-year career in corporate America, GiGi Meier is delighted to be writing romance novels about strong female characters and their complicated, swoon-worthy men.

She loves telling stories and figuring out why her characters do what they do. With heartbreaking angst, panty-dropping lust, and enviable love, her stories linger long after you close the book.

When GiGi is not eating over her laptop, she likes to spend time in the pool with her children, walk her furry babies, and film videos for Instagram and YouTube. Whether attending a book club or hosting a game night, she loves connecting with new people and making friends.

www.gigimeier.com

Books by GiGi Meier:

Standalone Book
Coyote
Sammie and Carlos's forced proximity
cartel, kidnapped, Military hero, dark romance

The Cañon Series
Tomlin
The start of Dani and Tomlin's
slow burn, enemies-to-almost-lovers
Tomlin Takahashi Duet #1
The Cañon Series, Book #1

Takahashi
The conclusion of Dani and Tomlin's
friends-to-lovers, happily ever after
Tomlin Takahashi Duet #2
The Cañon Series, Book #2

Hamilton
Hamilton and Molli's second chance,
small town, police officer romance
The Cañon Series, Book #3

Isla
Isla and Gabe's opposites attract,
age gap, forbidden love romance
The Cañon Series, Book #4

The Cougars and Cubs Series
Paolo
Taylor and Paolo's reverse age gap,
forced proximity, office romance

The Cougars and Cubs Series, Book #1

Sebastian
Sebastian and Chloe's reverse age gap
Opposites attract, Christmas romance
The Cougars and Cubs Series, Book #2

Giovanni
Giovanni and Kacie's reverse age gap
Protector, Alpha male romance
The Cougars and Cubs Series, Book #3

Kadus
Kadus and Bex's reverse age gap
Best friend's brother, rockstar romance
The Cougars and Cubs Series, Book #4

IF YOU ENJOYED THIS BOOK

Thank you for reading *Isla,* the fourth book in the Cañon Series.

If you enjoyed it, please consider leaving a review on BookBub, Goodreads, or your favorite retailer to let others know about this age gap, forbidden love, and damsel-in-distress romance.

Reviews are greatly appreciated!

They help independent authors, such as myself, get our books in front of more readers.

Check out my website for deleted or bonus scenes not found in the book.

https://www.gigimeier.com/freebies

HOTLINES FOR HELP

Help for runaway and homeless youth:
- Call 1-800-RUNAWAY (786-2929)
- Visit: National Runaway Safeline
- Live Chat: www.1800runaway.org

National Center for Missing and Exploited Children (NCMEC)
- Hotline: 1-800-843-5678 (1-800-THE-LOST)
- CyberTipline: http://www.missingkids.com/gethelpnow/cybertipline

Childhelp National Child Abuse Hotline
- Call: 1-800-422-4453 (1-800-4-A-CHILD)
- Website: https://www.childhelp.org/

Help for Victims & Survivors of Domestic Violence
- Call 1-800-799-SAFE (1-800-799-7233)
- National Domestic Violence Hotline
- Live Chat: www.thehotline.org

National Resource Center on Domestic Violence

- Call 1 (800) 537-2238

National Indigenous Women's Resource Center
- Call 1 (855) 649-7299

Battered Women's Justice Project Criminal and Civil Justice Center & National Clearinghouse for the Defense of Battered Women
- Call 1 (800) 903-0111

National Health Resource Center on Domestic Violence
- Call 1 (888) 792-2873

National Center on Domestic Violence, Trauma & Mental Health
- Call 1 (312) 726-7020

Resource Center on Domestic Violence: Child Protection and Custody
- Call 1 (800) 527-3223

Asian Pacific Institute on Gender-Based Violence
- Call 1 (415) 568-3315

National Latin@ Network of Healthy Families and Communities
- Call 1 (651) 646-5553

Ujima, Inc.: The National Center on Violence Against Women in the Black Community
- Call 1 (844) 77-UJIMA (844-778-5462)

Expanding Services for Children & Youth Exposed DV Technical Assistance Futures Without Violence Children's Program

- Call 1 (617) 426-8667

National LGBTQ Institute on Intimate Partner Violence
- Call 1 (206) 568-7777

National Suicide Prevention Lifeline
- Call 1-800-273-TALK (1-800-273-8255)
- Website: https://suicidepreventionlifeline.org/

Please be aware that these hotlines are dedicated to offering support and guidance for those impacted by domestic violence, contemplating suicide, or concerned about exploited minors. If you or someone you know is in immediate danger or facing a life-threatening situation, please call your local emergency number or go to the nearest emergency room.

www.ingramcontent.com/pod-product-compliance
Lightning Source LLC
Chambersburg PA
CBHW051938020726
47501CB00001B/172